BEYOND
TIME

E. GASPAR

NOVELAS

F. JORBA

BEYOND
TIME

Classic Tales of Time Unwound

edited by

MIKE ASHLEY

This edition published 2019 by
The British Library
96 Euston Road
London NW1 2DB

Dates attributed to each story relate to first publication.

Cataloguing in Publication Data
A catalogue record for this book is
available from the British Library

ISBN 978 0 7123 5320 5
e-ISBN 978 0 7123 6497 3

Frontispiece illustration by F. Gómez Soler for the front cover of
Novelas by Enrique Gaspar, published in 1887. The device depicted in the
centre of the cover is a time machine from the novel *El anacronópete*;
arguably the first actual time machine in literature.

Front cover image © The Estate of Frederick Siebel, reproduced with the kind
permission of the estate. The illustration originally accompanied Arthur C. Clarke's
time travel story 'A Sound of Thunder' in *Collier's Magazine*, June 28, 1952.

Typeset by Tetragon, London
Printed in England by TJ International Ltd, Padstow, Cornwall

CONTENTS

Time travel has been a staple of science fiction for over a hundred years. It is a useful device for exploring so many possibilities. We can travel into the future and witness the changes in society, or into the past and see what really happened rather than what was recorded. But both these actions create a variety of problems.

If you go into the past, what's to stop you doing something that changes the past and thereby change the present day and all of time hereafter. This gave rise to the "grandfather paradox"—what would happen if you went back in time and killed your grandfather before your mother or father was conceived?

Likewise, if you can travel into the future and return, what's to stop you benefitting from that in knowing the winners of football matches or horse races. You could choose to change anything to your own advantage, and the idea of manipulating the future or the past has become a common theme in science fiction.

But each time you change the past or attempt to change the future you are affecting the natural order of events which gave rise to the theory that every action you or others take may have an alternative and that if your action is changed, it sets up a new time line. Just imagine how many decisions you make every day, and multiply that by everyone alive now plus everyone who ever lived plus all the creatures who have ever lived and those alternative timelines run into billions upon billions upon billions.

So, if time travel was ever achieved it would have to be closely monitored to make sure no one changed anything—but then, how would you know? The timeline you live in is a closed history to you, and if someone changed your past, would you know that, or would you simply believe your life has always been what you've experienced?

It all gets very complicated and that's what makes stories of time travel so fascinating. It isn't just a story that sets an adventure in the past or future, but one that explores the consequences of that journey.

All these ideas and possibilities are explored in this anthology which reprints stories from the classic period of science fiction from the 1890s to the mid-1960s. I have taken one liberty as the first story, "The Clock That Went Backward", dates from 1881, but I include it because it was the first to use the idea of having a machine—in this case a clock—to allow the narrator to travel through time. This, almost a decade before H. G. Wells started to write stories which, following many revisions, ended up as *The Time Machine*. Wells is also included, but with a very different story, about a newspaper from the future that finds its way into the present.

There are stories that take us into the remote future ("Omega") and the remote past ("The Reign of the Reptiles"); stories that look at how we might change the past ("The Branches of Time", "Tenth Time Around"); stories that consider how we might monitor the past and future ("The Book of Worlds") or be trapped in a time loop ("Friday the Nineteenth"). Someone from the past coming to the present is explored in "Manna" whilst "Dial 'O' for Operator" tells of someone from the present trying to help someone desperate in the future. J. B. Priestley provides a sensitive view of what happens if you suddenly find yourself in your own early life whilst Arthur Sellings gradually uncovers the mystery of why two people come to the present from the future. Finally, E. C. Tubb explores the chaos caused when a time traveller is living in a totally different sequence of time to others.

These stories are just a small sample of the wealth of ideas writers have explored in stories about time and time travel. To put them in context and provide a background on the development of the time travel theme I explore the history of time travel below. Feel free to read on, or check out the stories first and come back to the following. All in your own time.

THE PASSAGES OF TIME

Humans have been aware of the passage of time for as long as there have been humans. We experience the passing of day and night, of the seasons and years, and of the passage of the sun, moon and other heavenly bodies across the sky. One definition of time, recorded by the medieval theologian Richard Hooker in the fifth book of his *Of the Laws of Ecclesiastical Polity* (1597), was that it is "the measure of the motion of the heavens".

The prospect that we could somehow turn back the clock or advance it faster than the natural flow of time must have occurred to many people over history. Which of us has not at one time or another wished we could go back and change something we have come to regret, or fast forward to discover the consequence of our actions?

Many ancient religions believed that time moves at a faster rate in heaven than on Earth. In the *Mahabharata*, which dates from perhaps the 8th or 9th century BC, is the story of King Kakudmi who visits the Lord Brahma on his heavenly plane. When Kakudmi returns to Earth he discovers that millennia have passed even though he was with the Brahma for only a short time. This concept passed into our folk tales as "time in faery". For instance, in "Die Elfen" (1811; usually translated as "The Elves"), Ludwig Tieck tells of a young girl who, despite being warned by her parents, wanders into the woods and plays with the elves. Though she spends only a short time there she returns to find years have passed. This time dilation seemed to be the supernatural preserve of the Gods or fairies, but thanks to Albert Einstein it has now been established as part of his theory of relativity. Perhaps the gods of old had faster-than-light travel as one of their abilities!

Fairy tales provided another method of travelling into the future: suspended animation. In Charles Perrault's version of *Sleeping Beauty* (1697), the princess falls asleep for a hundred years before being wakened by the prince. There is the legend of the Seven Sleepers of Ephesus, which dates from the fifth century. It tells of seven Christians during the reign of the Roman emperor Decius who refused to recant their faith and were imprisoned in a cave blocked with boulders. Two hundred years later a farmer opens the cave and finds the Christians still alive, believing they had slept for just a day. The concept was imported into "modern" fiction by Washington Irving in "Rip Van Winkle" (1819) where the eponymous idler wanders into the Catskill mountains, meets men playing nine-pins, drinks some of their liquor and falls asleep. He awakens twenty years later, after the American Revolution, and discovers many changes.

Sleeping into the future became a regular feature of science fiction, whether simply by falling into a deep sleep (which we might now call catatonia) or by some other method. Louis Boussenard had the idea of someone being frozen solid and thawing out millennia later in *Dix mille ans dans un bloc de glace* ("Ten Thousand

Years in a Block of Ice", 1889). In *When the Sleeper Awakes* (1899), H. G. Wells has his hero's sleep induced by drugs.

Whatever the device, sleeping into the future isn't really time travel, because you're still only moving at the same rate as everyone else, and there's no chance of a return trip. It did not stop the idea being used many times in early science fiction as a simple means of having someone of the present become a witness to the future.

The same problem applies to that of the eternal wanderer, a legend which may date back as far as the Biblical Cain who, having killed his brother, is cursed to wander the Earth and never settle. Much the same affliction was placed upon the Jew originally called Joseph who, having taunted Jesus on the way to his crucifixion, is cursed to wander the Earth until the second coming. The Wandering Jew as he became known has featured in many novels and stories since, ranging from *The Monk* (1796) by Matthew Gregory Lewis to *A Canticle for Leibowitz* (1960) by Walter M. Miller, Jr.

Amongst other eternal wanderers the best known must surely be the legend of the *Flying Dutchman*. According to the story, which probably dates back as an oral tale to the mid 17th century, the captain of the ship, Hendrik Vanderdecken, was determined to complete his voyage despite a violent storm, shouting oaths to heaven. As a consequence he was cursed to sail forever. The story has been adapted into many novels, plays and operas, including *The Phantom Ship* (1839) by Frederick Marryat and *The Death Ship* (1888) by W. Clark Russell, but all these tales have a supernatural plot and do not attempt to explain the event scientifically. The same applies to "Peter Rugg; or, The Missing Man" (1824) by William Austin, where Rugg, known for his temper, swears that he and his son will make it back to Boston, in their carriage, despite a thunderstorm. When he arrives, decades have passed, though he believes it is only a short time. He doesn't recognize Boston and continues on his way, forever searching. Rugg is certainly travelling into the future at a different time rate, but as the result of a curse rather than a quirk of science.

The other way that early writers fashioned a trip through time is as a result of a timeslip. It's seldom explained but it's as if a crack has appeared between the present and the past, or future, allowing a sudden shift through time. A famous purportedly true timeslip was that which happened to Charlotte Moberly and Eleanor Jourdain in 1901 and which they wrote about in *An Adventure* (1911). On a visit to the palace and gardens at Versailles they took a wrong turning in the grounds and found themselves in the time of Marie Antoinette. Once they rediscovered their route, they were back in the twentieth century.

Timeslips in fiction date back at least as far as the anonymous "An Anachronism; or, Missing One's Coach" (1838) where a travel-ler hoping to get a coach from Newcastle to Leeds suddenly finds himself in the time of the Venerable Bede and imparts to the renowned monk knowledge of the next thousand years. No expla-nation is given for the time-shift and, following his discussion, the traveller simply finds himself back in his own time. Edgar Allan Poe also wrote a timeslip story in "A Tale of the Ragged Mountains" (1844) where the invalid Bedloe, taking a health walk in the Ragged Mountains in Virginia, finds he is in the midst of battle in India in 1780. Poe leaves uncertainty in the story as to whether Bedloe's trip is an hallucination because of poison from a medical leech, or whether it was some transmigration of souls from an old friend, Oldeb, whom Bedloe had known in Calcutta.

The best known, and certainly most popular timeslip story of the nineteenth century is *A Connecticut Yankee in the Court of King*

Arthur (1889) by Mark Twain. Here, Hank Morgan finds himself in the Middle Ages following a blow to the head. Morgan remains in Arthur's service until the final battle and is then put into a deep sleep by Merlin by which he returns to the present.

A clever variant on the timeslip story appears in *Tourmalin's Time Cheques* (1891) by F. Anstey, the pseudonym of humorist Thomas Guthrie. On a ship returning to England from Australia Tourmalin grows bored but meets a man who claims he can store his wasted time in a bank in exchange for a cheque. At any stage when he needs more time he can withdraw it, just like money. Unfortunately, Tourmalin's cheques get muddled and as a result he finds himself shifting about in time with the inevitable farcical results. Anstey was one of the first to write about the problem of time out of sequence and the inevitable paradoxes, so despite the "it was all a dream" ending, the story itself is great fun.

The timeslip motif is a useful convenience, as nothing needs explaining, and is thus only science fiction by acceptance. There is rarely any scientific explanation involved.

And there were several other time journeys during the nineteenth century which are barely classifiable as science fiction and yet are important in the development of the genre. The most famous is *A Christmas Carol* (1843) by Charles Dickens in which the miserly Ebenezer Scrooge is allowed to see (via three spirits) but not take part in, images of his past, the present and the future that may be. Scrooge discovers he can change his future and thus *A Christmas Carol* is a key text in developing the idea of alternative futures.

Possibly inspired by *A Christmas Carol*, the British historian James A. Froude, writing under the alias 'Zeta', proposed in "The Lieutenant's Daughter" (1847), that if you were able to travel fast enough (he suggests by train) and girdle the Earth at a velocity greater than the Earth's rotation, you would find yourself in yesterday and then the day before and so on. The narrator witnesses history unravel backwards and discovers a key point in a girl's life that eventually led to her suicide. The narrator then witnesses another series of images in which the girl lives a happy life. Although this is hokum, Froude was establishing what later became called the "Jonbar hinge" (of which more later) which are those key episodes in history that, if changed, have a significant effect on the future. Froude may also have been inspired by Edgar Allan Poe whose clever story "Three Sundays in a Week" (1841) shows that if one person travels westerly around the globe and another easterly, both at a thousand miles an hour, when they return, to one of them Sunday was yesterday, to another it will be tomorrow whilst to the third who stayed at home, it is today. Poe was exploring the idea of relativity without realizing it.

So far, all these stories, whilst they explored concepts central to the genre of time travel, were not genuine science fiction of themselves, being either fantasy or philosophical works, merely nudging at the borders of the field. But that was about to change, and in a variety of ways.

The first step was made by the Irish writer Frances Cobbe, writing as 'Merlin Nostradamus'. In *The Age of Science* (1877) she posits the invention of the Prospective Telegraph, a machine capable of trawling the future and bringing back a newspaper. Cobbe gives no details of how the machine functions but states that it is powered by a psychic force, suggesting that this is controlled by the mind. No person travels through time, but the ability to bring something back from the future by the use of a machine teeters into the realms of early science fiction.

Soon after came "The Clock That Went Backward" (1881) by Edward Page Mitchell, which is reprinted here. Mitchell describes an old Dutch clock which normally stands still but when wound the hands rotate backward. It takes two men back three centuries to the Siege of Leyden in 1574 where they discover their role in history. Mitchell does not use any realistic science in explaining how the clock works but hints at a variation of Froude's idea about reversing the Earth's orbit about the Sun. Nevertheless, the story is the first to involve a machine that takes people back through time.

Meanwhile in France in "L'historioscope" (1883), the West Indian Creole French writer Eugène Mouton developed an idea suggested by Camille Flammarion in *Lumen* (1872) that if you were able to travel away from Earth at greater than the speed of light you could look back at the Earth and see past events. Mouton has a scientist construct a powerful telescope that can capture light reflected off the ether in distant space. In effect this is the first time-viewer.

It was a Spanish writer, Enrique Gaspar, who described the first purpose-built time machine in *El Anacronópete* (1887), but his method of travelling back in time is again like that in "The Lieutenant's Daughter", by flying fast around the Earth. The novel was originally written as a comic stage play but was never performed. The story retains the humour in its satirical look at various historical episodes, but is otherwise rather ponderous.

Neither Mouton's nor Gaspar's works were translated into English so it is unlikely that H. G. Wells read them and, in any case, they would not have inspired him. Wells had other ideas which took him several years to develop. His first attempt was an aborted novel, "The Chronic Argonauts" which survives as three episodes in the April, May and June 1888 issues of the *Science Schools Journal*, which Wells himself edited as a student at the Royal College of Science. The story tells of the arrival at a small Welsh village of a stranger who reveals himself to be Dr. Moses Nebogipfel. He moves in to an old ruined house on the outskirts of the village where strange lights and noises cause the villagers to fear him as some kind of warlock. A local clergyman, the Rev. Elijah Cook, befriends Nebogipfel and learns of his time machine. He then accompanies the Doctor on a trip, but apart from hints of visits to the years 4003 and 17,901 we learn nothing of their adventures. Wells was not happy with how the story was developing, fascinating though it was, and dropped it for a few years. The story should not be forgotten, though. It contains a far better description of the time machine, which is called the *Chronic Argo*, than Wells gives in his later, final version:

> It was solid, it cast a shadow, and it upbore two men. There was white metal in it that blazed in the noontide sun like incandescent magnesium, ebony bars that drank in the light, and white parts that gleamed like polished ivory. Yet withal it seemed unreal. The thing was not square as a machine ought to be, but all awry: it was twisted and seemed falling over, hanging in two directions, as those queer crystals called triclinic hang; it seemed like a machine that had been crushed or warped; it was suggestive and not confirmatory, like the machine of a disordered dream.

Wells also provided his theory on time travel which was far in advance of any hitherto. He talks of time, or rather duration, as the fourth dimension, and that humanity had originally only been able to move in two dimensions. The advent of balloons allowed movement into a third dimension, but his invention now allowed travel along a fourth dimension—time.

Wells was fascinated with the future. He openly admitted that he was "impatient with the present" and wanted to "go ahead of Father Time with a scythe of my own." He was also fascinated with evolution and how humans were not the pinnacle of evolution but simply one stage in a continuing process. He had already written a short essay, "A Vision of the Past" (1887) where the narrator has a dream of the distant past and witnesses a lecture given by reptiles on their own place in the world. He also delivered a talk, "The Past and Future of the Human Race", which was not published but which he later revised as "The Man of the Year Million" (1893), where he imagined how humans would continue to evolve, developing large heads to encase their brains but with far smaller bodies—not unlike the Martians he would describe in *The War of the Worlds*.

Wells continued to explore thoughts on the nature and future of mankind in several essays and then in 1894 he wrote a series of seven essays for the *National Observer*, which explored the possibility of time travel, the nature of a time machine and what his traveller might discover in the future. His thoughts were still not fully formed and it was another year before Wells reformulated them in the advance version of *The Time Machine* serialized in the *New Review* from January to May 1895. Although texts were further amended for book publication, and a short section about a possible devolution of humankind deleted, later reprinted as "The Grey Man", this became Wells's final statement. Here he explores in detail how humankind has evolved into two different types of beings, emerging from the class structure, the effete but weak Eloi, and the violent and disgruntled workers, the Morlocks.

It took a long while for writers to come to terms with Wells's achievement. Writers no less skilled or imaginative nevertheless stuck to more traditional forms of temporal travel such as timeslips or dreams. Mary E. Wilkins created a time portal in "The Little Green Door" (1896). Set in the home of her ancestors it allows Letitia to travel back to the time of the early North American settlers. C. J. Cutcliffe Hyne had an unspecified drug take his adventurer back to pre-history in "The Oldest Worship in the World" (1897). Ethel Watts Mumford twisted things around in "When Time Turned" (1901) when, as a result of a nervous shock, a man starts to live backwards. Rudyard Kipling had a most ingenious idea in "Wireless" (1906) and showed his knowledge of Marconi's early experiments. His protagonist believes the wireless receiver may be picking up the voice of John Keats from the previous century. For his first sale, "The Time Reflector" (1905), George Allan England built upon the idea of Camille Flammarion to have a machine, like Mouton's "L'historioscope", that can pick up light reflected from space. Disappointingly in a later story, "The Time Annihilator" (1909), England was still using the idea that if you fly fast enough around the globe you will go back in time. This idea had also been used in the deliberately humorous novel *The Panchronicon* (1904) by Harold Steele Mackaye.

H. G. Wells was still playing with ideas about time. In "The New Accelerator" (1901) a scientist has created a drug that speeds up the human metabolism so that you live at an alarmingly fast rate, meaning the world about you seems to have come to a standstill. The British neurologist, Edward Bousfield, who wrote as Paul Bo'ld, reversed this idea in "The Retardatory Force" (1910), where the force slows down human perception to the point where the world rushes past. In effect the scientist can live ultra-slow, almost like suspended animation, but can still be aware of life progressing, a form of time travel.

These were all experimental stories some more creative than others, but it was down to an American dime novelist to write the next major time-travel adventure. William Wallace Cook was renowned for his ability in creating diverse stories—he later compiled a book showing how to develop plots called, imaginatively, *Plotto* (1928). In *A Round Trip to the Year 2000* (serial, 1903) he uses a variant of the time machine, a time coupé, in which the hero, Lumley, escapes to the future trying to evade police who are hunting him for a crime he did not voluntarily commit. This is no *Back-to-the-Future* DeLorean, though. It is a simple two-seater carriage but instead of wheels it has four globes which spin. The old idea of reversing or speeding up the spin of the Earth to travel through time was proving hard to drop. Cook knows how to write a rousing adventure story against the background of a turbulent future. He includes elements of humour: for example, the year 2000 is full of people from the past who have gone into suspended animation in order to reawaken in what they believed would be a utopia. Lumley has to rescue these people and return them to the past in the coupé.

Cook eventually wrote a sequel, *Castaways of the Year 2000* (serial, 1912–13) but here, as they no longer have access to the coupé, the adventurers return to 2000 via a Time Ball sent from the future. Cook wrote one other unconnected time travel novel, *Marooned in 1492* (serial, 1905) where travel to the past is enabled by the use of drugs made from a seed with the wonderful name *tempus fugitarius*. Cook, more or less forgotten today, was the first author to write not just one, but three time-travel novels.

Time travel continued to fascinate writers who created various ways of experiencing other times. British writer A. E. Ashford postulated the Q-Ray in "The Man Who Went Back" (1913), which is a time viewer, enabling the past to be projected onto a screen. He wrote two other time-ray stories including "Mr. Mauvin's Story" (1917) which projects the past but also allows a prehistoric monster to come through to the present. Alas neither story was strong enough to include here. In "The Runaway Skyscraper" (1919) Murray Leinster has a New York skyscraper too heavy for its foundations and in sinking enters the fourth dimension and travels back in time. *The Heads of Cerberus* (serial, 1919) by Gertrude Bennett writing as Francis Stevens is justifiably acclaimed for its originality, but is barely time travel. A drug alters individuals' vibratory perception and allows them to shift between multiple parallel worlds which are separated by vibrations. The first of these is Philadelphia in the year 2118.

The real future of the time travel story was not simply by having adventures in the past or future, or even in parallel worlds, but in exploring the consequences of travelling through time. In his play *If* (1921), Lord Dunsany considers how the present may be changed by altering one simple thing in the past. In this case a businessman, in possession of a magic crystal, travels back in time to make sure he catches a train that he had originally missed. Needless to say, it sets off a very different chain of events.

The precocious American student, Charles Cloukey, raised all manner of questions in "Paradox" (1929) where he not only reminds us that the Earth moves through space so that in order to travel through time you would also have to keep track of the Earth, but he also raises a chicken-and-egg puzzle. Time travel was discovered in the year 2806, and papers describing the invention are sent back to the present enabling a scientist to invent a time machine, in the form of a sealed cube. He sends a friend into the future who obtains the secret of time travel and returns to his own time placing those details in the scientist's laboratory. "Paradox" and its sequels "Paradox+" and "Anachronism" (both 1930) consider many time anomalies, but the story spends most of its time in the future where Mars and Earth are at war, the end result of which is the destruction of all knowledge about time travel!

Another conundrum is what happens if you meet yourself. Ralph Milne Farley, who enjoyed experimenting with time travel and wrote enough such stories to fill a book, *The Omnibus of Time* (1950), explained in "The Man Who Met Himself" (1935) that there is no paradox at all. A man meets himself (without knowing it) in 1935 and is sent back in a time machine to 1925, lives through those ten years and becomes the man who has the time machine and sends his other self back. Farley argues that there is no paradox because time is still a continuous stream which continues on its way after it has looped over itself for ten years.

Meeting or contacting yourself is a fun gimmick in time travel. In "Sam, This is You" (1955) Murray Leinster has a man contacted by phone by himself twelve days in the future and this sets up a time loop which must be followed for Sam's benefit, though his present-day self has no idea why. Walter Tevis, noted author of *The Man Who Fell to Earth*, used a similar idea in "The Other End of the Line" (1961) where a drunken George Bledsoe manages to phone himself two months in the future. His future self provides much useful financial advice, but two months later when anticipating the call, Bledsoe manages to miss it, with tragic consequences.

Authors delighted in making these time loops increasingly convoluted. The master of them was Robert A. Heinlein in "By His Bootstraps" (1941) and "'—All You Zombies—'" (1959). In the second of these, which has never been bettered, the time loops contrive to have the protagonist end up as both his father and mother!

Meanwhile another theory had been proposed by the British aeronautical pioneer and philosopher J. W. Dunne. He had disciplined himself to record his dreams and was intrigued with how many seemed to come true. He developed his theory of serial time in *An Experiment With Time* (1927), and later books, where he suggested that whilst the brain perceives normal time, which he called t_1, there is a higher dimension of time, t_2, in which our own higher consciousness (a form of transcendental ego) can monitor normal time but is aware of the future. It's as if linear time is a train running one way along a track, but our higher consciousness is hovering above the train and is aware of its present location, where it's going and from whence it came. This theory proved very popular and influenced several writers not least H. G. Wells, who referred to it in "The Queer Story of Brownlow's Newspaper", included here, and J. B. Priestley.

Priestley began experimenting with time in "Doomsday" (1930), better known as "Mr. Strenberry's Tale", which he believed was the first story to feature a man from the future trying to reach the present. His first play, *Dangerous Corner* (1932), is similar to Dunsany's *If*, but instead of a physical shift back in time, Priestley showed what happens if a chance remark is left unsaid. He played a similar trick in *Time and the Conways* (1937) which shows how a series of events unravel and how they might be averted. In *I Have Been Here Before* (1937) a professor has a precognitive dream and visits an inn where his actions change the lives of the others present. His most atmospheric exploration of the theme was in *An Inspector Calls* (1945) where a family are interrogated by an unknown police inspector about the suicide of a young girl whom each member knew in various circumstances. Priestley wrote several more time-travel stories, one of which is included here.

Dunne's theory of time may also have influenced Clare Winger Harris, the first woman contributor to the American science-fiction magazines. In "The Fifth Dimension" (1928), a woman has feelings about future events and takes action, saving her husband from a train crash.

Some of Dunne's views were developed independently by the Scottish-born, American-resident mathematician Eric Temple Bell, who wrote as John Taine. Although *The Time Stream* was not published until late 1931 as a magazine serial, it had been written in a near complete draft as early as 1921. Taine sees time as a constantly flowing stream which loops round upon itself so that the future merges with the past. The events in the time stream are themselves fixed but it is possible to shift along that stream mentally and alter events. Taine thus explores the extent to which predestination can be influenced by free will.

Jack Williamson added more scientific hokum to Dunne's theory in *The Legion of Time* (serial, 1938) where he suggests that at any one moment there are many possible futures one of which becomes more certain as events solidify. Along the way there are critical events that will trigger one future or the other. In this case it rests upon whether a lad, John Barr, picks up a magnet, and thus follows a scientific career, or a pebble. Once time travel was established it was possible for these key moments, now called Jonbar hinges after the boy's name, to be changed, so the past is monitored by the Legion of Time. But that organization is itself prone to time-manipulation, so the flux of time is a constant battlefield between representatives of alternate futures.

The idea of monitoring time, either to produce the best possible future or to avoid dire changes, became a popular theme in science fiction. Isaac Asimov, who enjoyed ringing the changes on time travel, created the organization called Eternity in *The End of Eternity* (1955). This organization exists to safeguard history and to ensure that history follows the path that brings Eternity into existence in the first place. Starting in 1955, Poul Anderson produced a series of stories featuring the Time Patrol, initially collected as *Guardians of Time* (1960), which seeks to protect history but which occasionally faces the dilemma that a change might produce a better future. In *Times Without Number* (1962) John Brunner ingeniously depicted an alternative history where the Spanish Armada was victorious and where the Society of Time is determined to preserve that status quo. H. Beam Piper likewise created the Paratime Police to stop individuals taking advantage of situations in parallel worlds. Although the series began with "He Walked Around the Horses" in 1948, the shorter stories were not collected until 1981 in *Paratime*.

It is self-evident that if time travel to the past is ever achieved it would need to be closely monitored with firm restrictions to avoid any inadvertent changes. The classic story is Ray Bradbury's "A Sound of Thunder" (1952) where hunters are taken back to the time of the dinosaurs to hunt extinct species, but they must remain on a special path. However, one falls off. When they return to the present, they discover a variety of small changes, such as the language being strange and when the errant hunter checks his shoes he finds he had trodden on a butterfly. Such small changes have huge consequences.

Plenty of authors were going out of their way to exploit paradoxes. Killing one's grandfather, or indeed any ancestor, was the most popular. Nathan Schachner had hit this head on in "Ancestral

Voices" (1933) where a time traveller goes back to the fifth century and kills a Hun. When the time machine returns to the present not only has the time traveller vanished but thousands of people of all nationalities. In "The Immortality of Alan Whidden" (1942) Ralph Milne Farley has his character genuinely kill his grandfather and take his place, even fathering the son that became his own father—in other words, Whidden was his own grandfather! F. M. Busby also tackled the paradox in "A Gun for Grandfather" (1957) where he deliberately plans to kill his grandfather to avoid inheriting a faulty gene—until he discovers he was already living in the timeline where his grandfather had been shot.

The other key paradox is that if time travel is possible, how come we don't meet the travellers. Anthony Boucher suggested in "The Barrier" (1942) that there is indeed an impediment to any traveller returning. Lester Del Rey said the same in "Absolutely No Paradox" (1951) where time travel is only one way. In "Unborn Tomorrow" (1959), though, Mack Reynolds shows that we probably do meet time travellers but don't realize it because they only return to large gatherings where they blend in. The young Robert Silverberg put a twist on this by showing how people in the future treat travellers from the past. In "Absolutely Inflexible" (1956) they shoot them off to the Moon.

One of the classic tales of a gathering of time travellers is "Vintage Season" (1946) by C. L. Moore (with a little help from Henry Kuttner) writing as Lawrence O'Donnell. Here a present-day house becomes a desirable rental for people from the future so that they can witness a remarkable meteor strike. The travellers try to blend in but give themselves away.

Moore and Kuttner wrote some of the most enjoyable time-travel stories of the 1940s, mostly under the alias of Lewis

Padgett—"Time Locker", "Endowment Policy", "What You Need"
—and, voted as one of the best of all-time by the Science Fiction
Writers of America, "Mimsy Were the Borogoves" (1943). A scientist from the far future, testing his time machine, sends a box
of gadgets into the past. Unable to retrieve it he tries again, but
once more it fails. In fact the boxes had arrived, one to our present
day and one in Victorian England. Children find the one in the
present day and, as their parents discover, the objects enhance the
children's intelligence and awareness. The other box was found by
a young girl who liked a poem she finds there, which she recites
to her "Uncle Charles". The poem is, of course, "Jabberwocky"
and when the children of the present read the poem they realize
it contains a clue as to how to complete a machine they had been
building from the objects in their box. And with that machine the
children find "the way out."

The idea of items from the future turning up in the present
with dire consequences has appeared in many stories and was
popular in the 1940s. In "The Mechanical Mice" (1941) by Maurice
G. Hugi, it's self-replicating robot mice; in "Film Library" (1946) by
A. E. van Vogt, it's a film; in "Child's Play" (1947) by William Tenn,
it's a human-being assembly kit; in "Tomorrow and Tomorrow"
(1947) by Ray Bradbury, it's a typewriter that starts typing messages from the future; in "The Little Black Bag" (1950) by C. M.
Kornbluth, it's a medical bag; and in "Of Time and Third Avenue"
(1951) by Alfred Bester it's an almanac. Quite often it's a newspaper,
as in H. G. Wells's "The Queer Story of Brownlow's Newspaper"
(1932). In *The Gap in the Curtain* (1932) John Buchan considers a form
of psychic time travel where a group are asked to see if they can
imagine what will be in *The Times* a year hence. The story then
follows their lives to see if their imagined news comes true. In

the film *It Happened Tomorrow* (1944) it's tomorrow's newspaper. Inevitably in all these stories access to items from the future or foreknowledge of events leads to confusion and anomaly.

The Second World War gave rise to various time-travel stories, not least ones where someone plans to kill Hitler. The first was, not surprisingly, by Ralph Milne Farley with "I Killed Hitler" (1941) in which the hero, a distant cousin of the dictator, goes back to when Hitler was a child, but his actions have alarming consequences. The most powerful of these stories, though, must be "My Name is Legion" (1942) by Lester del Rey in which a supposed ally of Hitler uses a time machine to make thousands of copies of the Fuhrer each one slightly older than the first until there is an entire army of Hitlers. At the end of the War, with the detonation of the atomic bomb over Hiroshima, there were several related time-travel stories of which the best known is "The Monster" (1948; also known as "The Brighton Monster") by Gerald Kersh, where the power released by the bomb blasts a victim back in time.

In "Random Quest" (1961) John Wyndham suggests a parallel world where Hitler never came to power and the Second World War never happened. Wyndham was fascinated by time travel and alternate realities. His first published story, "Worlds to Barter" (1931) deals with a future in which the population of a dying far future world comes back in time to occupy the near future and sends all of the current population of the world into the far future. In "Wanderers of Time" (1933) Wyndham imagines a snag in the time-stream, rather like a sink-hole, which captures time travellers from all periods. "The Third Vibrator" (1934) tells of a present-day time traveller who discovers that Atlantis was destroyed by a weapon of mass destruction and warns how the present-day's pursuit of atomic power may have the same consequence. After the War

Wyndham saved his more cosmic work for his novels and his short stories grew more personal. "Pillar to Post" (1951) considers the consequences of an exchange of personalities when the man from the future finds himself in the body of a double-amputee. "Pawley's Peepholes" (1951) has hoards of time-travel tourists upsetting the present. "The Chronoclasm" (1953) is a study of free will: if you suddenly possess knowledge of the future do you just let it happen or try to change things? "Odd" (1959, as "The Man From Yesterday") is a clever little time paradox story while "Stitch in Time" (1961) is a highly personal story of an old lady learning why the man she had once loved had deserted her. Most of these stories were included in two of his story collections, *The Seeds of Time* (1956) and *Consider Her Ways* (1961). The title novella of the latter tells of a woman who suddenly finds herself in a dystopian matriarchal future.

The 1950s was a good decade for British writers. Charles Eric Maine, for example, produced two entertaining time novels. *Timeliner* (1955) sees its chief protagonist thrown into the future, by occupying a series of bodies, and discovering, the further he travels, that there are other "timeliners"—the name for time travellers. When identified they are arrested and tried for, effectively, murdering the body that they inhabit. The novel was developed from a short story, "Highway i" (1953) which highlights the austerity of postwar Britain in that the main character travels into the future via a bicycle. In *Calculated Risk* (1960) Maine has a man and woman from the future escape their apocalyptic times and take over the bodies of two people from the 1950s. It leads to inevitable conflict as the two come to terms with their new bodies and the state of Britain at that time.

That same bleakness of post-war Britain is evident in two stories by Arthur Sellings. In "Time Transfer" (1956) the elderly are

disposed of by being sent forward in time but by how far they have
no idea. In "The Shadow People" (1958), included here, the reverse
is true as elderly people try and escape the future. That bleakness
is also evident in Brian Aldiss's early story "The Failed Men" (1956)
where time travellers from the near future seek to aid mankind in
the distant future which seems on the verge of extinction.

Aldiss's story bears some comparison with Philip K. Dick's
"Meddler" (1954) in that both deal with a future mankind that
seems to have vanished. In Dick's case that's a result of the government meddling in the future through their "time dip". Time travel
stories were suited to Dick's disjointed view of the world and his
novel *Time Out of Joint* (1959) is a good example of how someone
with remarkable predictive qualities is used and misused by the
government. It's not really a time travel story but it does show how
our perception of time can become confused to a disjointed mind.

Like Dick, J. G. Ballard was fascinated with our perception
and awareness of time. His earliest appearance in print was
"Escapement" (1956) where first a husband and then his wife realize that the television is repeating itself and they are caught in a
time loop. In the gimmicky "Now: Zero" (1959) a man discovers
he can predict when someone will die, and having wiped out
most of his work colleagues he turns his ability on the readers. In
"Chronopolis" (1960) we enter a city devoid of time, because all
clocks of any kind have been banned. As a result, the inhabitants
have lost all understanding of the concept of time. Likewise in "The
Garden of Time" (1962) Ballard depicts a garden where, when the
flowers are picked, it seems that time slows down. Its final vision
of the occupants transformed into statues is more suggestive of
humans losing the awareness of time in some form of amnesia or
dementia. These and other early stories show Ballard's fascination

with what became dubbed "inner space" which came into focus in "The Terminal Beach" (1964) whose main protagonist is trying to escape time because of his memories (or delusions) of having bombed people (maybe Hiroshima?) during the War.

Ballard was the herald of the New Wave in British science fiction which crashed on the shores of imaginative literature in the mid-sixties, encouraged by the new editor of *New Worlds*, Michael Moorcock. The first serial that Moorcock published was Ballard's "Equinox" (1964) which formed the first part of *The Crystal World* (1966), a novel we can see as the transition into the New Wave, and it's a novel with time at its core. Ballard describes a virus which turns matter into crystal, but the virus seems to be a form of anti-time (like anti-matter). Time is thus annihilating itself and the whole world is crystallizing.

It may seem ironic that at the same time Ballard was manipulating time to transform British science fiction, that the BBC should launch what has become the epitome of time-travel adventure on television, *Dr. Who*, with its first episode broadcast on 23 November 1963. The first four-part serial, "An Unearthly Child", introduced The Doctor whom we later learn is a time lord who has stolen a time machine, known as the TARDIS ("Time and Relative Dimensions in Space"), which is damaged so that not only does he not know where he will land, but the facility for disguising the machine has malfunctioned so that it always appears as an old-style blue police phone box. That first serial, set in the Stone Age, was uninspiring but was also overshadowed by the assassination of John F. Kennedy that had happened the day before. However, the second serial, "The Daleks", scripted by Terry Nation, caught the nation's imagination and viewing figures doubled. *Dr. Who* has since become part of the fabric of

British TV and might even be seen as the culmination of classic British time-travel fiction.

Time travel stories and novels continue to be popular allowing authors to explore aspects of ourselves and of society. In *Behold the Man* (serial, 1966) Michael Moorcock has his traveller go back to witness the crucifixion of Christ with unexpected results. *Kindred* (1979) by Octavia Butler shows how a present-day African-American woman copes when she slips back and forth to the time of her ancestors who were slaves in pre-Civil War Maryland. The novel is a powerful exploration of the nature of slavery and how it is perceived by a modern woman. In *The Devil's Arithmetic* (1988) by Jane Yolen, intended for young-adult readers, a young Jewish girl, dissatisfied with her religion and stories of the past, finds herself back in 1942 in war-torn Poland where she is sent to a death camp. Connie Willis has written several time-travel novels notably *Blackout* and *All Clear* (2010), really one novel in two halves, which follows the experiences of future historians monitoring the impact of the Blitz on London in 1940 and how they must cope not only with those events but also the criteria regulating time travel. These are just a few examples of where time travel has come of age and is confronting readers with the horrors or perils of the past and challenging us to face them and consider how we would react.

Clearly time-travel is alive and well and performing its task in keeping us not only entertained but educated. I trust the few stories reprinted here from the Golden Age of science fiction, achieve that for you.

MIKE ASHLEY

THE CLOCK THAT WENT BACKWARD

Edward Page Mitchell

Mitchell (1852–1927) was a newspaperman who worked for the New York Sun *for most of his life, serving as editor-in-chief from 1897 to 1927. The majority of his proto-science fiction and weird tales were virtually unknown until the researches of Sam Moskowitz brought them to light and were collected in* The Crystal Man *(1973). Here it was revealed that Mitchell almost certainly wrote the earliest time travel story involving a machine, which is the story that follows, but also early stories featuring matter transmission ("The Man Without a Body", 1877) and a cyborg ("The Ablest Man in the World", 1879). His reputation was thus reassessed as being one of the more significant writers of science fiction between Jules Verne and H. G. Wells.*

A ROW OF LOMBARDY POPLARS STOOD IN FRONT OF MY GREAT-Aunt Gertrude's house, on the bank of the Sheepscot River. In personal appearance my aunt was surprisingly like one of those trees. She had the look of hopeless anaemia that distinguishes them from fuller-blooded sorts. She was tall, severe in outline, and extremely thin. Her habiliments clung to her. I am sure that had the gods found occasion to impose upon her the fate of Daphne she would have taken her place easily and naturally in the dismal row, as melancholy a poplar as the rest.

Some of my earliest recollections are of this venerable relative. Alive and dead she bore an important part in the events I am about to recount: events which I believe to be without parallel in the experience of mankind.

During our periodical visits of duty to Aunt Gertrude in Maine, my cousin Harry and myself were accustomed to speculate much on her age. Was she sixty, or was she six score? We had no precise information; she might have been either. The old lady was surrounded by old-fashioned things. She seemed to live altogether in the past. In her short half-hours of communicativeness over her second cup of tea, or on the piazza where the poplars sent slim shadows directly toward the east, she used to tell us stories of her alleged ancestors. I say alleged, because we never fully believed that she had ancestors.

A genealogy is a stupid thing. Here is Aunt Gertrude's, reduced to its simplest forms:

Her great-great-grandmother (1599–1642) was a woman of
Holland who married a Puritan refugee, and sailed from Leyden to
Plymouth in the ship *Ann* in the year of our Lord 1632. This Pilgrim
mother had a daughter, Aunt Gertrude's great-grandmother
(1640–1718). She came to the Eastern District of Massachusetts
in the early part of the last century, and was carried off by the
Indians in the Penobscot wars. Her daughter (1680–1776) lived to
see these colonies free and independent, and contributed to the
population of the coming republic not less than nineteen stalwart
sons and comely daughters. One of the latter (1735–1802) married
a Wiscasset skipper engaged in the West India trade, with whom
she sailed. She was twice wrecked at sea—once on what is now
Seguin Island and once on San Salvador. It was on San Salvador
that Aunt Gertrude was born.

We got to be very tired of hearing this family history. Perhaps
it was the constant repetition and the merciless persistency with
which the above dates were driven into our young ears that made
us sceptics. As I have said, we took little stock in Aunt Gertrude's
ancestors. They seemed highly improbable. In our private opinion
the great-grandmothers and grandmothers and so forth were pure
myths, and Aunt Gertrude herself was the principal in all the adventures attributed to them, having lasted from century to century
while generations of contemporaries went the way of all flesh.

On the first landing of the square stairway of the mansion loomed
a tall Dutch clock. The case was more than eight feet high, of a dark
red wood, not mahogany, and it was curiously inlaid with silver.
No common piece of furniture was this. About a hundred years
ago there flourished in the town of Brunswick a horologist named
Cary, an industrious and accomplished workman. Few well-to-do
houses on that part of the coast lacked a Cary timepiece. But Aunt

Gertrude's clock had marked the hours and minutes of two full centuries before the Brunswick artisan was born. It was running when William the Taciturn pierced the dikes to relieve Leyden. The name of the maker, Jan Lipperdam, and the date, 1572, were still legible in broad black letters and figures reaching quite across the dial. Cary's masterpieces were plebeian and recent beside this ancient aristocrat. The jolly Dutch moon, made to exhibit the phases over a landscape of windmills and polders, was cunningly painted. A skilled hand had carved the grim ornament at the top, a death's-head transfixed by a two-edged sword. Like all timepieces of the sixteenth century, it had no pendulum. A simple Van Wyck escapement governed the descent of the weights to the bottom of the tall case.

But these weights never moved. Year after year, when Harry and I returned to Maine, we found the hands of the old clock pointing to the quarter past three, as they had pointed when we first saw them. The fat moon hung perpetually in the third quarter, as motionless as the death's-head above. There was a mystery about the silenced movement and the paralysed hands. Aunt Gertrude told us that the works had never performed their functions since a bolt of lightning entered the clock; and she showed us a black hole in the side of the case near the top, with a yawning rift that extended downward for several feet. This explanation failed to satisfy us. It did not account for the sharpness of her refusal when we proposed to bring over the watchmaker from the village, or for her singular agitation once when she found Harry on a stepladder, with a borrowed key in his hand, about to test for himself the clock's suspended vitality.

One August night, after we had grown out of boyhood. I was awakened by a noise in the hallway. I shook my cousin. "Somebody's in the house," I whispered.

We crept out of our room and onto the stairs. A dim light came from below. We held our breath and noiselessly descended to the second landing. Harry clutched my arm. He pointed down over the banisters, at the same time drawing me back into the shadow.

We saw a strange thing.

Aunt Gertrude stood on a chair in front of the old clock, as spectral in her white nightgown and white nightcap as one of the poplars when covered with snow. It chanced that the floor creaked slightly under our feet. She turned with a sudden movement, peering intently into the darkness, and holding a candle high toward us, so that the light was full upon her pale face. She looked many years older than when I bade her good night. For a few minutes she was motionless, except in the trembling arm that held aloft the candle. Then, evidently reassured, she placed the light upon a shelf and turned again to the clock.

We now saw the old lady take a key from behind the face and proceed to wind up the weights. We could hear her breath, quick and short. She rested a hand on either side of the case and held her face close to the dial, as if subjecting it to anxious scrutiny. In this attitude she remained for a long time. We heard her utter a sigh of relief, and she half turned toward us for a moment. I shall never forget the expression of wild joy that transfigured her features then.

The hands of the clock were moving; they were moving backward.

Aunt Gertrude put both arms around the clock and pressed her withered cheek against it. She kissed it repeatedly. She caressed it in a hundred ways, as if it had been a living and beloved thing. She fondled it and talked to it, using words which we could hear but could not understand. The hands continued to move backward.

Then she started back with a sudden cry. The clock had stopped. We saw her tall body swaying for an instant on the chair. She stretched out her arms in a convulsive gesture of terror and despair, wrenched the minute hand to its old place at a quarter past three, and fell heavily to the floor.

II

Aunt Gertrude's will left me her bank and gas stocks, real estate, railroad bonds, and city sevens, and gave Harry the clock. We thought at the time that this was a very unequal division, the more surprising because my cousin had always seemed to be the favourite. Half in seriousness we made a thorough examination of the ancient timepiece, sounding its wooden case for secret drawers, and even probing the not complicated works with a knitting needle to ascertain if our whimsical relative had bestowed there some codicil or other document changing the aspect of affairs. We discovered nothing.

There was testamentary provision for our education at the University of Leyden. We left the military school in which we had learned a little of the theory of war, and a good deal of the art of standing with our noses over our heels, and took ship without delay. The clock went with us. Before many months it was established in a corner of a room in the Breede Straat.

The fabric of Jan Lipperdam's ingenuity, thus restored to its native air, continued to tell the hour of quarter past three with its old fidelity. The author of the clock had been under the sod for nearly three hundred years. The combined skill of his successors in the craft at Leyden could make it go neither forward nor backward.

We readily picked up enough Dutch to make ourselves understood by the townspeople, the professors, and such of our eight
hundred and odd fellow students as came into intercourse. This
language, which looks so hard at first, is only a sort of polar-
ized English. Puzzle over it a little while and it jumps into your
comprehension like one of those simple cryptograms made by
running together all the words of a sentence and then dividing in
the wrong places.

The language acquired and the newness of our surroundings
worn off, we settled into tolerably regular pursuits. Harry devoted
himself with some assiduity to the study of sociology, with especial
reference to the round-faced and not unkind maidens of Leyden.
I went in for the higher metaphysics.

Outside of our respective studies, we had a common ground
of unfailing interest. To our astonishment, we found that not one
in twenty of the faculty or students knew or cared a stiver about
the glorious history of the town, or even about the circumstances
under which the university itself was founded by the Prince of
Orange. In marked contrast with the general indifference was the
enthusiasm of Professor Van Stopp, my chosen guide through the
cloudiness of speculative philosophy.

This distinguished Hegelian was a tobacco-dried little old man,
with a skullcap over features that reminded me strangely of Aunt
Gertrude's. Had he been her own brother the facial resemblance
could not have been closer. I told him so once, when we were
together in the Stadthuis looking at the portrait of the hero of the
siege, the Burgomaster Van der Werf. The professor laughed. "I will
show you what is even a more extraordinary coincidence," said he;
and, leading the way across the hall to the great picture of the siege,
by Wanners, he pointed out the figure of a burgher participating in

the defence. It was true. Van Stopp might have been the burgher's son; the burgher might have been Aunt Gertrude's father.

The professor seemed to be fond of us. We often went to his rooms in an old house in the Rapenburg Straat, one of the few houses remaining that antedate 1574. He would walk with us through the beautiful suburbs of the city, over straight roads lined with poplars that carried us back to the bank of the Sheepscot in our minds. He took us to the top of the ruined Roman tower in the centre of the town, and from the same battlements from which anxious eyes three centuries ago had watched the slow approach of Admiral Boisot's fleet over the submerged polders, he pointed out the great dike of the Landscheiding, which was cut that the oceans might bring Boisot's Zealanders to raise the leaguer and feed the starving. He showed us the headquarters of the Spaniard Valdez at Leyderdorp, and told us how heaven sent a violent northwest wind on the night of the first of October, piling up the water deep where it had been shallow and sweeping the fleet on between Zoeterwoude and Zwieten up to the very walls of the fort at Lammen, the last stronghold of the besiegers and the last obstacle in the way of succour to the famishing inhabitants. Then he showed us where, on the very night before the retreat of the besieging army, a huge breach was made in the wall of Leyden, near the Cow Gate, by the Walloons from Lammen.

"Why!" cried Harry, catching fire from the eloquence of the professor's narrative, "that was the decisive moment of the siege."

The professor said nothing. He stood with his arms folded, looking intently into my cousin's eyes.

"For," continued Harry, "had that point not been watched, or had defence failed and the breach been carried by the night assault from Lammen, the town would have been burned and the people massacred under the eyes of Admiral Boisot and the fleet of relief. Who defended the breach?"

Van Stopp replied very slowly, as if weighing every word:

"History records the explosion of the mine under the city wall on the last night of the siege: it does not tell the story of the defence or give the defender's name. Yet no man that ever lived had a more tremendous charge than fate entrusted to this unknown hero. Was it chance that sent him to meet that unexpected danger? Consider some of the consequences had he failed. The fall of Leyden would have destroyed the last hope of the Prince of Orange and of the free states. The tyranny of Philip would have been reestablished. The birth of religious liberty and of self-government by the people would have been postponed, who knows for how many centuries? Who knows that there would or could have been a republic of the United States of America had there been no United Netherlands? Our University, which has given to the world Grotius, Scaliger, Arminius, and Descartes, was founded upon this hero's successful defence of the breach. We owe to him our presence here today. Nay, you owe to him your very existence. Your ancestors were of Leyden; between their lives and the butchers outside the walls he stood that night."

The little professor towered before us, a giant of enthusiasm and patriotism. Harry's eyes glistened and his cheeks reddened.

"Go home, boys," said Van Stopp, "and thank God that while the burghers of Leyden were straining their gaze toward Zoeterwoude and the fleet, there was one pair of vigilant eyes and one stout heart at the town wall just beyond the Cow Gate!"

III

The rain was splashing against the windows one evening in the autumn of our third year at Leyden, when Professor Van Stopp honoured us with a visit in the Breede Straat. Never had I seen the old gentleman in such spirits. He talked incessantly. The gossip of the town, the news of Europe, science, poetry, philosophy, were in turn touched upon and treated with the same high and good humour. I sought to draw him out on Hegel, with whose chapter on the complexity and interdependency of things I was just then struggling.

"You do not grasp the return of the Itself into Itself through its Otherself?" he said smiling. "Well, you will, sometime."

Harry was silent and preoccupied. His taciturnity gradually affected even the professor. The conversation flagged, and we sat a long while without a word. Now and then there was a flash of lightning succeeded by distant thunder.

"Your clock does not go," suddenly remarked the professor. "Does it ever go?"

"Never since we can remember," I replied. "That is, only once, and then it went backward. It was when Aunt Gertrude—"

Here I caught a warning glance from Harry. I laughed and stammered, "The clock is old and useless. It cannot be made to go."

"Only backward?" said the professor, calmly, and not appearing to notice my embarrassment. "Well, and why should not a clock go backward? Why should not Time itself turn and retrace, its course?"

He seemed to be waiting for an answer. I had none to give.

"I thought you Hegelian enough." he continued, "to admit that every condition includes its own contradiction. Time is a condition, not an essential. Viewed from the Absolute, the sequence by which future follows present and present follows past is purely arbitrary. Yesterday, today, tomorrow; there is no reason in the nature of things why the order should not be tomorrow, today, yesterday."

A sharper peal of thunder interrupted the professor's speculations.

"The day is made by the planet's revolution on its axis from west to east. I fancy you can conceive conditions under which it might turn from east to west, unwinding, as it were, the revolutions of past ages. Is it so much more difficult to imagine Time unwinding itself; Time on the ebb, instead of on the flow; the past unfolding as the future recedes; the centuries countermarching; the course of events proceeding toward the Beginning and not, as now, toward the End?"

"But," I interposed, "we know that as far as we are concerned the—"

"We know!" exclaimed Van Stopp, with growing scorn. "Your intelligence has no wings. You follow in the trail of Compte and his slimy brood of creepers and crawlers. You speak with amazing assurance of your position in the universe. You seem to think that your wretched little individuality has a firm foothold in the Absolute. Yet you go to bed tonight and dream into existence men, women, children, beasts of the past or the future. How do you know that at this moment you yourself, with all your conceit of nineteenth-century thought, are anything more than a creature of a dream of the future, dreamed, let us say, by some philosopher of the sixteenth century? How do you know that you are anything more than a creature of a dream of the past, dreamed by some Hegelian of the twenty-sixth century? How do you know, boy, that you will not vanish into the sixteenth century or 2060 the moment the dreamer awakes?"

There was no replying to this, for it was sound metaphysics. Harry yawned. I got up and went to the window. Professor Van Stopp approached the clock.

"Ah, my children," said he, "there is no fixed progress of human events. Past, present, and future are woven together in one inextricable mesh. Who shall say that this old clock is not right to go backward?"

A crash of thunder shook the house. The storm was over our heads.

When the blinding glare had passed away, Professor Van Stopp was standing upon a chair before the tall timepiece. His face looked more than ever like Aunt Gertrude's. He stood as she had stood in that last quarter of an hour when we saw her wind the clock.

The same thought struck Harry and myself.

"Hold!" we cried, as he began to wind the works. "It may be death if you—"

The professor's sallow features shone with the strange enthusiasm that had transformed Aunt Gerturde's.

"True," he said, "it may be death; but it may be the awakening. Past, present, future; all woven together! The shuttle goes to and fro, forward and back—"

He had wound the clock. The hands were whirling around the dial from right to left with inconceivable rapidity. In this whirl we ourselves seemed to be borne along. Eternities seemed to contract into minutes while lifetimes were thrown off at every tick. Van Stopp, both arms outstretched, was reeling in his chair. The house shook again under a tremendous peal of thunder. At the same instant a ball of fire, leaving a wake of sulphurous vapour and filling

the room with dazzling light, passed over our heads and smote
the clock. Van Stopp was prostrated. The hands ceased to revolve.

IV

The roar of the thunder sounded like heavy cannonading. The
lightning's blaze appeared as the steady light of a conflagration.
With our hands over our eyes, Harry and I rushed into the night.

Under a red sky people were hurrying toward the Stadthuis.
Flames in the direction of the Roman tower told us that the heart
of the town was afire. The faces of those we saw were haggard
and emaciated. From every side we caught disjointed phrases of
complaint or despair. "Horseflesh at ten schillings the pound,"
said one, "and bread at sixteen schillings." "Bread indeed!" an old
woman retorted: "It's eight weeks gone since I have seen a crumb."
"My little grandchild, the lame one, went last night." Do you know
what Gekke Betje, the washerwoman did? She was starving. Her
babe died, and she and her man—"

A louder cannon burst cut short this revelation. We made our
way on toward the citadel of the town, passing a few soldiers here
and there and many burghers with grim faces under their broad-
brimmed felt hats.

"There is bread plenty yonder where the gunpowder is, and
full pardon, too. Valdez shot another amnesty over the walls this
morning."

An excited crowd immediately surrounded the speaker. "But
the fleet!" they cried.

"The fleet is grounded fast on the Greenway polder. Boisot
may turn his one eye seaward for a wind till famine and pestilence

have carried off every mother's son of ye, and his ark will not be a rope's length nearer. Death by plague, death by starvation, death by fire and musketry—that is what the burgomaster offers us in return for glory for himself and kingdom for Orange."

"He asks us," said a sturdy citizen, "to hold out only twenty-four hours longer, and to pray meanwhile for an ocean wind."

"Ah, yes!" sneered the first speaker. "Pray on. There is bread enough locked in Pieter Adriaanszoon van der Werf's cellar. I warrant you that is what gives him so wonderful a stomach for resisting the Most Catholic King."

A young girl, with braided yellow hair, pressed through the crowd and confronted the malcontent. "Good people," said the maiden, "do not listen to him. He is a traitor with a Spanish heart. I am Pieter's daughter. We have no bread. We ate malt cakes and rapeseed like the rest of you till it was gone. Then we stripped the green leaves from the lime trees and willows in our garden and ate them. We have eaten even the thistles and weeds that grew between the stones by the canal. The coward lies."

Nevertheless, the insinuation had its effect. The throng, now become a mob, surged off in the direction of the burgomaster's house. One ruffian raised his hand to strike the girl out of the way. In a wink the cur was under the feet of his fellows, and Harry panting and glowing, stood at the maiden's side, shouting defiance in good English at the backs of the rapidly retreating crowd.

With the utmost frankness she put both her arms around Harry's neck and kissed him.

"Thank you," she said. "You are a hearty lad. My name is Gertruyd van der Werf."

Harry was fumbling in his vocabulary for the proper Dutch phrases, but the girl would not stay for compliments. "They mean

mischief to my father"; and she hurried us through several exceedingly narrow streets into a three-cornered marketplace dominated
by a church with two spires. "There he is," she exclaimed, "on the
steps of St. Pancras."

There was a tumult in the marketplace. The conflagration
raging beyond the church and the voices of the Spanish and
Walloon cannon outside of the walls were less angry than the
roar of this multitude of desperate men clamouring for the bread
that a single word from their leader's lips would bring them.
"Surrender to the King!" they cried, "or we will send your dead
body to Lammen as Leyden's token of submission."

One tall man, taller by half a head than any of the burghers confronting him, and so dark of complexion that we wondered how he
could be the father of Gertruyd, heard the threat in silence. When
the burgomaster spoke, the mob listened in spite of themselves.

"What is it you ask, my friends? That we break our vow and
surrender Leyden to the Spaniards? That is to devote ourselves to
a fate far more horrible than starvation. I have to keep the oath!
Kill me, if you will have it so. I can die only once, whether by your
hands, by the enemy's, or by the hand of God. Let us starve, if we
must, welcoming starvation because it comes before dishonour.
Your menaces do not move me; my life is at your disposal. Here,
take my sword, thrust it into my breast, and divide my flesh among
you to appease your hunger. So long as I remain alive expect no
surrender."

There was silence again while the mob wavered. Then there
were mutterings around us. Above these rang out the clear voice
of the girl whose hand Harry still held—unnecessarily, it seemed
to me.

"Do you not feel the sea wind? It has come at last. To the tower!

And the first man there will see by moonlight the full white sails of the prince's ships."

For several hours I scoured the streets of the town, seeking in vain my cousin and his companion; the sudden movement of the crowd toward the Roman tower had separated us. On every side I saw evidences of the terrible chastisement that had brought this stout-hearted people to the verge of despair. A man with hungry eyes chased a lean rat along the bank of the canal. A young mother, with two dead babes in her arms, sat in a doorway to which they bore the bodies of her husband and father, just killed at the walls. In the middle of a deserted street I passed unburied corpses in a pile twice as high as my head. The pestilence had been there—kinder than the Spaniard, because it held out no treacherous promises while it dealt its blows.

Toward morning the wind increased to a gale. There was no sleep in Leyden, no more talk of surrender, no longer any thought or care about defence. These words were on the lips of everybody I met: "Daylight will bring the fleet!"

Did daylight bring the fleet? History says so, but I was not a witness. I know only that before dawn the gale culminated in a violent thunderstorm, and that at the same time a muffled explosion, heavier than the thunder, shook the town. I was in the crowd that watched from the Roman Mound for the first signs of the approaching relief. The concussion shook hope out of every face. "Their mine has reached the wall!" But where? I pressed forward until I found the burgomaster, who was standing among the rest. "Quick!" I whispered. "It is beyond the Cow Gate, and this side of the Tower of Burgundy." He gave me a searching glance, and then strode away, without making any attempt to quiet the general panic. I followed close at his heels.

It was a tight run of nearly half a mile to the rampart in question. When we reached the Cow Gate this is what we saw:

A great gap, where the wall had been, opening to the swampy fields beyond: in the moat, outside and below, a confusion of upturned faces, belonging to men who struggled like demons to achieve the breach, and who now gained a few feet and now were forced back; on the shattered rampart a handful of soldiers and burghers forming a living wall where masonry had failed; perhaps a double handful of women and girls, serving stones to the defenders and boiling water in buckets, besides pitch and oil and unslaked lime, and some of them quoiting tarred and burning hoops over the necks of the Spaniards in the moat; my cousin Harry leading and directing the men; the burgomaster's daughter Gertruyd encouraging and inspiring the women.

But what attracted my attention more than anything else was the frantic activity of a little figure in black, who, with a huge ladle, was showering molten lead on the heads of the assailing party. As he turned to the bonfire and kettle which supplied him with ammunition, his features came into the full light. I gave a cry of surprise: the ladler of molten lead was Professor Van Stopp.

The burgomaster Van der Werf turned at my sudden exclamation. "Who is that?" I said. "The man at the kettle?"

"That," replied Van der Werf, "is the brother of my wife, the clockmaker Jan Lipperdam."

The affair at the breach was over almost before we had had time to grasp the situation. The Spaniards, who had overthrown the wall of brick and stone, found the living wall impregnable. They could not even maintain their position in the moat; they were driven off into the darkness. Now I felt a sharp pain in my left arm. Some stray missile must have hit me while we watched the fight.

"Who has done this thing?" demanded the burgomaster. "Who is it that has kept watch on today while the rest of us were straining fools' eyes toward tomorrow?"

Gertruyd van der Werf came forward proudly, leading my cousin. "My father," said the girl, "he has saved my life."

"That is much to me," said the burgomaster, "but it is not all. He has saved Leyden and he has saved Holland."

I was becoming dizzy. The faces around me seemed unreal. Why were we here with these people? Why did the thunder and lightning forever continue? Why did the clockmaker, Jan Lipperdam, turn always toward me the face of Professor Van Stopp? "Harry!" I said, "come back to our rooms."

But though he grasped my hand warmly his other hand still held that of the girl, and he did not move. Then nausea overcame me. My head swam, and the breach and its defenders faded from sight.

V

Three days later I sat with one arm bandaged in my accustomed seat in Van Stopp's lecture room. The place beside me was vacant.

"We hear much," said the Hegelian professor, reading from a notebook in his usual dry, hurried tone, "of the influence of the sixteenth century upon the nineteenth. No philosopher, as far as I am aware, has studied the influence of the nineteenth century upon the sixteenth. If cause produces effect, does effect never induce cause? Does the law of heredity, unlike all other laws of this universe of mind and matter, operate in one direction only? Does the descendant owe everything to the ancestor, and the ancestor

nothing to the descendant? Does destiny, which may seize upon
our existence, and for its own purposes bear us far into the future,
never carry us back into the past?"

I went back to my rooms in the Breede Straat, where my only
companion was the silent clock.

THE QUEER STORY OF
BROWNLOW'S NEWSPAPER

H. G. Wells

*As I mentioned in the introduction, H. G. Wells (1866–1946) spent some
years considering how best to develop his idea of time travel which eventually appeared as* The Time Machine *in 1895. The novel became the
focus for his thinking on human evolution and social Darwinism showing
how the way mankind was split between upper and lower classes might
influence how humans would evolve over the next eight hundred millennia. Nothing like it had been written before, and this one book not only
established Wells as a writer to watch, it gave focus to the ever growing
field of what was then called the scientific romance. Wells didn't like the
phrase himself, because science was involved in almost all aspects of life,
but he nevertheless rapidly became associated with the public's fascination for scientific speculation. Over the next few years he produced not
only the novels* The Island of Dr. Moreau *(1896),* The Invisible Man
(1897), The War of the Worlds *(1898),* When the Sleeper Wakes
(1899) and The First Men in the Moon *(1901) but the story collections*
The Stolen Bacillus *(1895),* The Plattner Story and Others *(1897),*
Thirty Strange Stories *(1897) and* Tales of Space and Time *(1900).
No other author, not even Jules Verne, had produced such an outpouring
of scientific speculation in so short a time, which is why Wells is regarded
by many as the Father of Science Fiction. He never lost his fascination for
time and when he encountered the theories of J. W. Dunne he produced
the following story.*

I CALL THIS A QUEER STORY BECAUSE IT IS A STORY WITHOUT an explanation. When I first heard it, in scraps, from Brownlow I found it queer and incredible. But—it refuses to remain incredible. After resisting and then questioning and scrutinizing and falling back before the evidence, after rejecting all his evidence as an elaborate mystification and refusing to hear any more about it, and then being drawn to reconsider it by an irresistible curiosity and so going through it all again, I have been forced to the conclusion that Brownlow, so far as he can tell the truth, has been telling the truth.

But it remains queer truth, queer and exciting to the imagination. The more credible his story becomes the queerer it is. It troubles my mind. I am fevered by it, infected not with germs but with notes of interrogation and unsatisfied curiosity.

Brownlow is, I admit, a cheerful spirit. I have known him to tell lies. But I have never known him do anything so elaborate and sustained as this affair, if it is a mystification, would have to be. He is incapable of anything so elaborate and sustained. He is too lazy and easy-going for anything of the sort.

And he would have laughed. At some stage he would have laughed and given the whole thing away. He has nothing to gain by keeping it up. His honour is not in the case either way. And after all there is his bit of newspaper in evidence—and the scrap of an addressed wrapper...

I realize it will damage this story for many readers that it opens with Brownlow in a state very definitely on the gayer side of sobriety. He was not in a mood for cool and calculated observation, much less for accurate record. He was seeing things in an exhilarated manner. He was disposed to see them and greet them cheerfully and let them slip by out of attention. The limitations of time and space lay lightly upon him.

It was after midnight. He had been dining with friends.

I have inquired what friends—and satisfied myself upon one or two obvious possibilities of that dinner party. They were, he said to me, "just friends. They hadn't anything to do with it."

I don't usually push past an assurance of this sort, but I made an exception in this case. I watched my man and took a chance of repeating the question.

There was nothing out of the ordinary about that dinner party, unless it was the fact that it was an unusually good dinner party. The host was Redpath Baynes, the solicitor, and the dinner was in his house in St. John's Wood. Gifford, of the *Evening Telegraph*, whom I know slightly, was, I found, present, and from him I got all I wanted to know.

There was much bright and discursive talk and Brownlow had been inspired to give an imitation of his aunt Lady Clitherholme reproving an inconsiderate plumber during some rebuilding operations at Clitherholme.

This early memory had been received with considerable merriment—he was always very good about his aunt Lady Clitherholme—and Brownlow had departed obviously elated by this little social success and the general geniality of the occasion.

Had they talked, I asked, about the Future or Einstein or J. W. Dunne or any such high and serious topic at that party? They had not.

Had they discussed the modern newspaper? No.

There had been nobody whom one could call a practical joker at this party, and Brownlow had gone off alone in a taxi. That is what I was most desirous of knowing. He had been duly delivered by his taxi at the main entrance to Sussex Court.

Nothing untoward is to be recorded of his journey in the lift to the fifth floor of Sussex Court. The lift man on duty noted nothing exceptional. I asked if Brownlow said "Good night." The lift man does not remember. "Usually he says Night O," reflected the lift man—manifestly doing his best and with nothing particular to recall. And there the fruits of my inquiries about the condition of Brownlow on this particular evening conclude. The rest of the story comes directly from him.

He went down the long passage with its red carpet, its clear light and its occasional oaken doors, each with its artistic brass number. I have been down that passage with him on several occasions.

It was his custom to enliven that corridor by raising his hat gravely as he passed each entrance, saluting his unknown and invisible neighbours, addressing them softly but distinctly by playful if sometimes slightly indecorous names of his own devising, expressing good wishes or paying them little compliments.

He came at last to his own door, No. 49, and let himself in without serious difficulty. He switched on his hall light. Scattered on the polished oak floor and invading his Chinese carpet were a number of letters and circulars, the evening's mail. His parlormaid-housekeeper, who slept in a room in another part of the building, had been taking her evening out, or these letters would have been gathered up and put on the desk in his bureau. As it was they lay on the floor.

He closed his door behind him or it closed of its own accord; he took off his coat and wrap, placed his hat on the head of the Greek charioteer whose bust adorns his hall, and set himself to pick up his letters.

He was a little annoyed to miss the *Evening Standard*. It is his custom, he says, to subscribe for the afternoon edition of the *Star* to read at teatime and also for the final edition of the *Evening Standard* to turn over the last thing at night, if only on account of Low's cartoon.

He gathered up all these envelopes and packets and took them with him into his little sitting room. There he turned on the electric heater, went to his bedroom to put on soft slippers and replace his smoking jacket by a frogged jacket of llama wool, returned to his sitting room and sat down in his armchair by the reading lamp to examine his correspondence. All these details were routines he had repeated scores of times.

Brownlow's is not a preoccupied mind; it goes out to things. He is one of those buoyant extroverts who open and read all their letters and circulars whenever they can get hold of them. In the daytime his secretary intercepts and deals with most of them, but at night he escapes from her control and does what he pleases—that is to say, he opens everything.

He ripped up various envelopes. There was a formal acknowledgement of a business letter he had dictated the day before, there was a letter from his solicitor asking for some details about a settlement he was making, there was an offer from some unknown gentleman with an aristocratic name to lend him money on his note of hand alone, and there was a notice about a proposed new wing to his club.

"Same old stuff," he sighed. "Same old stuff. What bores they all are!"

He was always hoping, like every man who is proceeding across the plains of middle age, that his correspondence would contain agreeable surprises—and it never did.

Then he picked up the remarkable newspaper.

It was different in appearance from an ordinary newspaper, but not so different as not to be recognizable as a newspaper, and he was surprised, he says, not to have observed it before. It was inclosed in a wrapper of pale green, but it was unstamped; apparently it had been delivered not by the postman but by some other hand.

This wrapper still exists; I have seen it.

He had already torn it off before he noted that he was not the addressee.

For a moment or so he remained looking at this address, which struck him as just a little odd. It was printed in rather unusual type:

EVAN O'HARA MR., SUSSEX COURT 49

"Wrong name," said Mr. Brownlow; "right address. Rummy. Sussex Court 49... Spose he's got *my Evening Standard*... Change no robbery."

He put the torn wrapper with his unanswered letters and opened out the newspaper.

The title of the paper was printed in large, slightly ornamental black-green letters that might have come from a kindred font to that responsible for the address. But, as he read it, it was the *Evening Standard*! Or at least it was the *"Even. Standrd."*

"Silly," said Brownlow. "It's some damn Irish paper. Can't spell—anything—these Irish..."

He had, I think, a passing idea, suggested perhaps by the green wrapper and the green ink, that it was a lottery stunt from Dublin.

Still, if there was anything to read he meant to read it. He surveyed the front page. Across this ran a streamer headline:

WILTON BORING REACHES SEVEN MILES: SUCCES ASSURED

"No," said Brownlow. "It must be oil... Illiterate lot these oil chaps—leave out the s in success."

He leaned back in his chair to take a dispassionate view of any oil-share pushing that might be afoot.

But it wasn't an affair of oil. It was, it began to dawn upon him, something stranger than oil. He found himself surveying a real evening newspaper, which was dealing, so far as he could see at the first onset, with the affairs of another world.

He had for a moment a feeling as though he and his armchair and his little sitting room were afloat in a vast space and then it all seemed to become firm and solid again.

This thing in his hands was plainly and indisputably a printed newspaper. It was a little odd in its letterpress and it didn't feel or rustle like ordinary paper, but newspaper it was.

It was printed in either three or four columns—for the life of him he cannot remember which—and there were column headlines under the page streamer.

It had a sort of art-nouveau affair at the bottom of one column that might be an advertisement—it showed a woman in an impossibly big hat—and in the upper left-hand corner was an unmistakable weather chart of Western Europe, with *coloured* isobars or isotherms or whatever they are and the inscription, "Tomorrow's Weather."

And then he remarked the date. The date was November 10, 1971!

"Steady on," said Brownlow. "Steady on."

He held the paper sideways and then straight again. The date remained November 10, 1971.

He got up in a state of immense perplexity and put the paper down. For a moment he felt a little afraid of it. He rubbed his forehead.

"Haven't been doing a Rip Van Winkle by any chance, Brownlow, my boy?" he said.

He picked up the paper again, walked out into his hall and looked at himself in the hall mirror. He was reassured to see no signs of advancing age, but the expression of mingled consternation and amazement upon his flushed face struck him suddenly as being undignified and unwarrantable.

He laughed at himself, but not uncontrollably. On the console table was a little respectable-looking adjustable calendar bearing witness that the date was November 10, 1931.

"D'you see?" he said, shaking the queer newspaper at it reproachfully. "I ought to have spotted you for a hoax ten minutes ago. 'Moosing trick, to say the least of it. I suppose they've made Low editor for a night and he's had this idea. Eh?"

He felt he had been taken in but that the joke was a good one. And with quite unusual anticipations of entertainment he returned to his armchair. A good idea it was, a paper forty years ahead. Good fun if it was well done. For a time nothing but the sounds of a newspaper being turned over and Brownlow's breathing can have broken the silence of the flat.

Regarded as an imaginative creation, he found the thing almost too well done. Every time he turned a page he expected the sheet to break out into laughter and give the whole thing away.

But it did nothing of the kind. From being a mere quip, it became an immense and amusing, if perhaps a little over-elaborate, lark. And then as a lark it passed from stage to stage of incredibility until as anything but the thing it professed to be it was incredible altogether.

It must have cost far more than an ordinary number. All sorts of colours were used, and suddenly he came upon illustrations that went beyond amazement; they were in the colours of reality.

Never in all his life had he seen such colour printing—and the buildings and scenery and costumes in the pictures were strange. Strange and yet credible. They were colour photographs of actuality forty years from now. He could not believe anything else of them. Doubt could not exist in their presence.

His mind had swung back, away from the stunt-number idea altogether. This paper in his hand would not simply be costly beyond dreaming to produce. At any price it could not be produced. All this present world could not produce such an object as this paper he held in his hand. He was quite capable of realizing that.

He sat turning the sheet over. His sceptical faculties were largely in suspense; the barriers of criticism were down. His mind could now accept the idea that he was reading a newspaper of forty years ahead without further protest of any kind.

It had been addressed to Mr. Evan O'Hara, and it had come to him. Well and good. This Evan O'Hara evidently knew how to get ahead of things…

I doubt if at that time Brownlow found anything very wonderful in the situation.

Yet it was, it continues to be, a very wonderful situation. Only gradually have I been able to build up this picture of Brownlow turning over that miraculous sheet, so that I can believe it myself.

And you will understand how I asked him, to satisfy a devouring curiosity, "What was there in it? What did it have to say?"

What was there in it? In other words, What will the world be doing forty years from now?

That was the stupendous scale of the vision, of which Brownlow was afforded a glimpse. The world forty years from now! I lie awake at nights thinking of all that paper might have revealed to us.

Much it did reveal, but there is hardly a thing it reveals that does not change at once into a constellation of riddles. When first he told me about the thing I was intensely sceptical. I asked him questions in what people call a "nasty" manner.

"I was dreaming, I suppose," he said. "I'm beginning to doubt it all myself."

But then it occurred to me that if he was not allowed to tell and put on record what he had seen, he might become confused about it himself. So we arranged to go down into Surrey for the week-end. There we set ourselves in earnest, first of all to recover everything he could remember about his newspaper and then to form some coherent idea of the world about which it was telling.

The streamer headline across the page about that seven-mile Wilton boring is to my mind one of the most significant items in the story. About that we are fairly clear. It referred, says Brownlow, to a series of attempts to tap the supply of heat beneath the surface of the earth. I asked various questions.

"It was *explained*, y'know," said Brownlow and smiled and held out a hand with twiddling fingers. "It was explained, all right. Old system, they said, was to go down from a few hundred feet to a mile or so and bring up coal and burn it. Go down a bit deeper, and there's no need to bring up and burn anything. Just get heat itself straightaway. Comes up of its own accord—under its own steam. See? Simple…

"They were making a big fuss about it," he added. "It wasn't only the streamer headline; there was a leading article in big type. What was it headed? Ah! 'The Age of Combustion has Ended!'"

Now that is plainly a very big event for mankind, caught in mid-happening, November 10, 1971. And the way in which Brownlow describes it as being handled shows clearly a world much more preoccupied by economic essentials than the world of today, and dealing with them on a larger scale and in a bolder spirit.

That excitement about tapping the central reservoirs of heat, Brownlow was very definite, was not the only symptom of an increase in practical economic interest and intelligence.

There was much more space given to scientific work and to inventions than is down in any contemporary paper. There were diagrams and mathematical symbols, he says, but he did not look into them very closely because he could not get the hang of them.

"Frightfully highbrow, some of it," he said.

A more intelligent world for our grandchildren evidently, and also, as the pictures testified, a healthier and happier world.

"The fashions kept you looking," said Brownlow, going off at a tangent, "all coloured up as they were."

"Were they elaborate?" I asked.

"Anything but," he said.

His description of these costumes is vague. The people depicted in the social illustrations and in the advertisements seemed to have reduced body clothing—I mean things like vests, pants, socks, and so forth—to a minimum. Breast and chest went bare.

There seem to have been tremendously exaggerated wristlets, mostly on the left arm and going as far up as the elbow, provided with gadgets which served the purpose of pockets. Most of these armlets seem to have been very decorative, almost like little shields.

And then usually there was an immense hat, often rolled up and carried in the hand, and long cloaks of the loveliest colours and evidently also of the most beautiful soft material, which either trailed from a sort of gorget or were gathered up and wrapped about the body, or were belted up or thrown over the shoulders.

There were a number of pictures of crowds from various parts of the world. "The people looked fine," said Brownlow. "Prosperous, you know, and upstanding. Some of the women— just lovely."

My mind went off to India. What was happening in India?

Brownlow could not remember anything very much about India.

I found the politician stirring in me. Was there really nothing about India? Was he sure of that? There was certainly nothing that had left any impression in Brownlow's mind.

And Soviet Russia? "Not as Soviet Russia," said Brownlow. All that trouble had ceased to be a matter of daily interest.

"And how was France getting on with Germany?" Brownlow could not recall a mention of either of these two great powers. Nor of the British Empire as such, nor of the U. S. A.

There was no mention of any interchanges, communications, ambassadors, conferences, competitions, comparisons, stresses in which these governments figured, so far as he could remember. He racked his brains. I thought perhaps all that had been going on so entirely like it goes on today—and has been going on for the last

hundred years—that he had run his eyes over the passages in question and that they had left no distinctive impression on his mind.

But he is positive it was not like that. "All that stuff was washed
out," he said.

He is unshaken in his assertion that there were no elections
in progress, no notice of parliament or politicians, no mention
of Geneva or anything about armaments or war. All those main
interests of a contemporary journal seem to have been among the
"washed-out" stuff. It isn't that Brownlow didn't notice them very
much; he is positive they were not there.

Now, to me, this is a very wonderful thing indeed. It means,
I take it, that in only forty years from now the great game of
sovereign states will be over. It looks also as if the parliamentary
game will be over, and as if some quite new method of handling
human affairs will have been adopted. Not a word of patriotism
or nationalism; not a word of party, not an allusion.

But in only forty years! While half the human beings already alive
in the world will still be living! You cannot believe it for a moment.
Nor could I, if it wasn't for two little torn scraps of paper. These,
as I will make clear, leave me in a state of—how can I put it?—
incredulous belief.

It was not only that there was this absence of national politics
from that evening paper, but there was something else still more
fundamental. Business, we both think—finance, that is—was not
in evidence, at least upon anything like contemporary lines.

We are not quite sure of that, but that is our impression. There
was no list of stock-exchange prices for example, no City page and
nothing in its place. That also, it seems, will be washed out forty
years from now.

Is there some tremendous revolutionary smash-up ahead then? Which will put an end to investment and speculation? Is the world going Bolshevik? In the paper, anyhow, there was no sign of or reference to anything of that kind.

Yet against this idea of some stupendous economic revolution we have the fact that here forty years ahead is a familiar London evening paper still tumbling into a private individual's letter box in the most uninterrupted manner. Not much suggestion of a social smash-up there.

Much stronger is the effect of immense changes which have come about bit by bit, day by day and hour by hour, without any sort of revolutionary jolt, as morning or springtime comes to the world.

These futile speculations are irresistible. The reader must forgive me them. Let me return to our story.

There had been a picture of a landslide near Ventimiglia and one of some new chemical works at Salzburg, and there had been a picture of fighting going on near Irkutsk. Of that picture, as I will tell presently, a fading scrap survives.

"Now, that was called"—Brownlow made an effort and snapped his fingers triumphantly—"'Round-up of Brigands by Federal Police."

"What Federal Police?" I asked.

"There you have me," said Brownlow. "The fellows on both sides looked mostly Chinese, but there were one or two taller fellows who might have been Americans or British or Scandinavians."

"What filled a lot of the paper," said Brownlow suddenly, "was gorillas. There was no end of a fuss about gorillas. Not so much as about that boring, but still a lot of fuss. Photographs. A map. A special article and some paragraphs."

★

The paper had in fact announced the death of the last gorilla. Considerable resentment was displayed at the tragedy that had happened in the African gorilla reserve. The gorilla population of the world had been dwindling for many years. In 1931, it had been estimated at 900. When the Federal Board took it over it had shrunken to 300.

"What Federal Board?" I asked.

Brownlow knew no more than I did. When he read the phrase, it had seemed all right somehow. Apparently this board had had too much to do all at once, and insufficient resources. I had the impression at first that it must be some sort of conservation board, improvised under panic conditions, to save the rare creatures of the world threatened with extinction.

The gorillas had not been sufficiently observed and guarded and they had been swept out of existence suddenly by a new and malignant form of influenza. The thing had happened practically before it was remarked. The paper was clamouring for inquiry and drastic changes of reorganization.

This Federal Board, whatever it might be, seemed to be something of very considerable importance in the year 1971. Its name turned up again in an article of afforestation. This interested Brownlow considerably because he has large holdings in lumber companies.

This Federal Board was apparently not only responsible for the maladies of wild gorillas but also for the plantation of trees in—just note these names!—Canada, New York State, Siberia, Algiers and the East Coast of England and it was arraigned for various negligencies in combatting insect pests and various fungoid plant diseases.

*

It jumped all our contemporary boundaries in the most astounding way. Its range was world-wide.

"In spite of the recent additional restrictions put upon the use of big timber in building and furnishing, there is a plain possibility of a shortage of shelter timber and of rainfall in nearly all the threatened regions for 1985 onward. Admittedly the Federal Board has come late to its task; from the beginning its work has been urgency work, but in view of the lucid report prepared by the James Commission, there is little or no excuse for the in-aggressiveness and overconfidence it has displayed."

I am able to quote this particular article, because as a matter of fact it lies before me as I write. It is indeed, as I will explain, all that remains of this remarkable newspaper. The rest has been destroyed and all we can ever know of it now is through Brownlow's sound but not absolutely trustworthy memory.

My mind, as the days pass, hangs on to that Federal Board. Does that phrase mean, as just possibly it may mean, a world federation, a scientific control of all human life only forty years from now? I find that idea staggering.

I have always believed that the world was destined to unify— "Parliament of Mankind and Confederation of the World," as Tennyson put it—but I have always supposed that the process would take centuries.

Let me tell very briefly of the rest of that evening paper. There seemed to be a lot of sport and fashion; much about something called "Spectacle"—with pictures—a lot of illustrated criticism of decorative art and of architecture.

The architecture in the pictures he saw was "towering—kind of magnificent. Great blocks of building. New York, but more so and all run together…" Unfortunately he cannot sketch.

There were sections devoted to something he couldn't under-stand, but which he thinks was "radio program stuff."

All that suggests a sort of advanced human life very much like the life we lead today, possibly rather brighter and better.

But here is something—different.

"The birth rate," said Brownlow, searching his mind, "was seven in the thousand."

I exclaimed. The lowest birth rates in Europe now are sixteen or more per thousand. The Russian birth rate is forty per thousand and falling slowly.

"It was seven," said Brownlow. "Exactly seven. I noticed it. In a paragraph."

But what birth rate? I asked. The British? The European?

"It said the birth rate," said Brownlow. "Just that."

That I think is the most tantalizing item in all this strange glimpse of the world of our grandchildren. A birth rate of seven in the thousand does not mean a fixed world population; it means a population that is being reduced at a very rapid rate—unless the death rate has gone still lower. Quite possibly people will not be dying so much then, but living very much longer.

On that Brownlow could throw no light. The people in the pictures did not look to him an "old lot." There were plenty of children and young or young-looking people about.

"But Brownlow," I said, "wasn't there any crime?"

"Rather," said Brownlow. "They had a big poisoning case on, but it was jolly hard to follow. You know how it is with these crimes. Unless you've read about it from the beginning, it's hard to get the hang of the situation.

"There were several crimes and what newspaper men call

stories—personal stories. What struck me about it was that they seemed to be more sympathetic than our reporters, more concerned with the motives and less with just finding someone out. What you might call psychological, so to speak."

"Was there anything much about books?" I asked him.

"I don't remember anything about books," he said...

And that is all. Except for a few trifling details such as a possible thirteenth month inserted in the year, that is all. It is intolerably tantalizing. That is the substance of Brownlow's account of his newspaper. He read it—as one might read any newspaper. He knew he was reading an evening newspaper of forty years ahead and he sat in front of his fire and was no more perturbed than he would have been if he had been reading an imaginative book about the future.

Suddenly his little clock pinged two.

He got up and yawned. He put that astounding, that miraculous, newspaper down as he was wont to put any old newspaper down; he carried off his correspondence to the desk in his bureau, and with the swift laziness of a very tired man he dropped his clothes about his room anyhow, and went to bed.

But somewhen in the night he woke up feeling thirsty and grey-minded. He lay awake and it came to him that something very strange had occurred to him. His mind went back to the idea that he had been taken in by a very ingenious fabrication. He got up for a drink of water and a liver tabloid, he put his head in cold water and found himself sitting on his bed towelling his hair and doubting whether he had really seen those photographs in the very colours of reality itself, or whether he had imagined them.

Also running through his mind was the thought that the approach of a world timber famine for 1985 was something likely to affect his investments and particularly a trust he was setting up on behalf of an infant in whom he was interested. It might be wise, he thought, to put more into timber.

He went back down the corridor to his sitting room. He sat there in his dressing gown, turning over the marvellous sheets.

He went back to the timber paragraph. He felt he must keep that. I don't know if you will understand how his mind worked—for my own part I can see at once how perfectly irrational and entirely natural it was—but he took this marvellous paper, creased the page in question, tore off this particular article and left the rest. He returned very drowsily to his bedroom, put the scrap of paper on his dressing table, got into bed and dropped off to sleep at once.

When he awoke again it was nine o'clock. His parlormaid housekeeper had just reentered the room.

"You were sleeping so peacefully," she said, "I couldn't bear to wake you. Shall I get you a fresh cup of tea?"

Brownlow did not answer. He was trying to think of something strange that had happened.

She repeated her question.

"No. I'll come and have breakfast in my dressing gown before my bath," he said and she went out of the room.

Then he saw the scrap of paper.

In a moment he was running down the corridor. "I left a newspaper," he said. "I left a newspaper."

She came in response to the commotion he made.

"A newspaper?" she said. "It's been gone this two hours, down the chute, with the dust and things."

Brownlow had a moment of extreme consternation.

"I wanted it *kept!*" he shouted. "I wanted it *kept.*"

"But how was *I* to know you wanted it kept?"

"I must get that newspaper back," said Brownlow. "It's—it's vitally important… If all Sussex Court has to be held up I want that newspaper back."

"I've never known a thing come up that chute again," said his housekeeper, "that's once gone down it. But I'll telephone down, sir, and see what can be done. Most of that stuff goes right into the hot-water furnace, they say…"

It does. The newspaper had gone.

Brownlow came near raving. By a vast effort of self-control he sat down and consumed his cooling breakfast. In the midst of it he got up to recover the scrap of paper from his bedroom, and then found the wrapper addressed to Evan O'Hara among the overnight letters on his bureau. That seemed an almost maddening confirmation. The thing had happened.

Presently after he had breakfasted, he rang me up to aid his baffled mind.

I found him at his bureau with the two bits of paper before him. He did not speak. He made a solemn gesture.

"What is it?" I asked, standing before him.

"Tell me," he said. "Tell me. What are these objects? It's serious. Either—" He left the sentence unfinished.

I picked up the torn wrapper and felt its texture. "Evan O'Hara Mr.," I read.

"Yes. Sussex Court 49. Eh?"

"Right," I agreed and stared at him.

"*That's* not hallucination, eh?"

I shook my head.

"And now this?"

His hand trembled as he held out the cutting. I took it.

"Odd," I said. I stared at the black-green ink, the unfamiliar type, the little novelties in spelling. Then I turned the thing over. On the back was a piece of one of the illustrations; it was, I suppose, about a quarter of the photograph of that "Round-up of Brigands by Federal Police" I have already mentioned.

When I saw it that morning it had not even begun to fade. It represented a mass of broken masonry in a sandy waste with bare-looking mountains in the distance. The cold clear atmosphere, the glare of a cloudless afternoon, was rendered perfectly. In the foreground were four masked men in brown service uniforms, intent on working some little machine on wheels with a tube and a nozzle projecting a jet that went out to the left, where the fragment was torn off. I cannot imagine what the jet was doing. Brownlow says he thinks they were gassing some men in a hut. Never have I seen such realistic colour printing.

"What on earth is this?" I asked.

"It's *that*," said Brownlow. "I'm not mad, am I? It's really *that*."

"But what the devil is it?"

"It's a piece of a newspaper for November 10, 1971."

"You had better explain," I said and sat down, with the scrap of paper in my hand, to hear his story. And with as much elimination of questions and digressions and repetitions as possible, that is the story I have written here.

If it were not for the two little bits of paper, one might dispose of it quite easily. One might say that Brownlow had had a vision, a dream of unparalleled vividness and consistency. Or that he had been hoaxed and his head turned by some elaborate mystification.

Or again one might suppose he had really seen into the future with a sort of exaggeration of those previsions cited by Mr. J. W. Dunne in his remarkable *Experiment with Time*.

But nothing Mr. Dunne has to advance can account for an actual evening paper being slapped through a letter-slit forty years in advance of its date.

The wrapper has not altered in the least since I first saw it. But the scrap of paper with the article about afforestation is dissolving into a fine powder and the fragment of picture at the back of it is fading out; most of the colour has gone and the outlines have lost their sharpness.

Some of the powder I have taken to my friend Ryder at the Royal College, whose work in micro-chemistry is so well known. He says the stuff is not paper at all, properly speaking. It is mostly aluminium fortified by admixture with some artificial resinous substance.

Though I offer no explanation whatever of this affair I think I will venture on one little prophecy. I have an obstinate persuasion that on November 10, 1971, the name of the tenant of 49 Sussex Court will be Mr. Evan O'Hara. There is no tenant of that name now in Sussex Court and I find no evidence in the telephone directory or the London directory that such a person exists anywhere in London. And on that particular evening, forty years ahead, he will not get his usual copy of the *"Even. Standrd"*; instead he will get a copy of the *Evening Standard* of 1931. I have an incurable fancy that this will be so.

There I may be right or wrong, but that Brownlow really got and for two remarkable hours read, a real newspaper forty years ahead of time I am as convinced as I am convinced that my own name is Hubert G. Wells. Can I say anything stronger than that?

OMEGA

Amelia Reynolds Long

Amelia Reynolds Long (1903–1978) was, along with Francis Stevens, Clare Winger Harris, Leslie F. Stone, Lilith Lorraine and Sophie Wenzel Ellis, one of a handful of women who contributed to the pioneer sf pulps in the 1920s and early 1930s. Her father was a railroad engineer which may have sparked her interest in technology, though her real fascination was for weird fiction in the style of Edgar Allan Poe. Her stories were thus full of atmosphere but with enough technical background to stop them being supernatural. She is best remembered, if remembered at all, for her story "The Thought Monster" (1930) in which a psychologist, experimenting with the power of the mind, inadvertently releases a tulpa, or psychic being. It was adapted into the British horror movie Fiend Without a Face *in 1958. The power of the mind also features in the following story which projects an individual's perception through history and into the future.*

Long stopped writing science fiction at the end of the 1930s because it had become too juvenile and shifted to writing crime fiction at which she was quite successful during the 1940s until her preference for the classic mystery was overtaken by hardboiled crime. She spent her final years as a museum curator, surprised that anyone was still interested in her early stories.

I, DOCTOR MICHAEL CLAYBRIDGE, LIVING IN THE YEAR 1926, have listened to a description of the end of the world from the lips of the man who witnessed it; the last man of the human race. That this is possible, or that I am not insane, I cannot ask you to believe: I can only offer you the facts.

For a long time my friend, Prof. Mortimer, had been experimenting with what he termed his theory of mental time; but I had known nothing of the nature of this theory until one day, in response to his request, I visited him at his laboratory. I found him bending over a young medical student, whom he had put into a state of hypnotic trance.

"A test of my theory, Claybridge," he whispered excitedly as I entered. "A moment ago I suggested to Bennet that this was the date of the battle of Waterloo. For him, it accordingly became so; for he described for me—and in French, mind you—a part of the battle at which he was present!"

"Present!" I exclaimed. "You mean that he is a reincarnation of—?"

"No, no," he interrupted impatiently. "You forget—or rather, you do not know—that time is a circle, all of whose parts are coexistent. By hypnotic suggestion, I moved his materiality line until it became tangent with the Waterloo segment of the circle. Whether in physical time the two have ever touched before, is of little matter."

Of course I understood nothing of this; but before I could ask for an explanation, he had turned back to his patient.

"Attila, the Hun, is sweeping down upon Rome with his hordes," he said. "You are with them. Tell me what you see."

For a moment, nothing happened; then before our very eyes, the young man's features seemed to undergo a change. His nose grew beak-shaped, while his forehead acquired a backward slant. His pale face became ruddy, and his eyes changed from brown to grey-green. Suddenly he flung out his arms; and there burst from his lips a torrent of sounds of which Mortimer and I could make nothing except that they bore a strong resemblance to the old Teutonic languages.

Mortimer let this continue for a moment or so before he recalled the boy from his trance. To my surprise, young Bennet was, upon awakening, quite his usual self without any trace of Hun feature. He spoke, however, of a feeling of weariness.

"Now," I said when Mortimer and I were alone, "would you mind telling me what it is all about?"

He smiled. "Time," he began, "is of two kinds; mental and physical. Of these, mental is the real; physical the unreal; or, we might say, the instrument used to measure the real. And its measurement is gauged by intensity, not length."

"You mean—?" I asked, not sure that I followed him correctly.

"That real time is measured by the intensity with which we live it," he answered. "Thus a minute of mental time may, by the standards devised by man, be three hours deep, because we have lived it intensely; while an aeon of mental time may embrace but half a day physically for reverse reasons."

"'A thousand years in Thy sight are but as yesterday when it is past, and as a watch in the night,'" I murmured.

"Exactly," he said, "except that in mental time there is neither past nor future, but only a continuous present. Mental time, as I remarked a while ago, is an infinite circle with materiality a line running tangent to it. The point of tangency interprets it to the physical senses, and so creates what we call physical time. Since a line can be tangent to a circle at only one point, our physical existence is single. If it were possible, as some day it may be, to make the line bisect the circle, we shall lead two existences simultaneously.

"I have proven, as you saw in the case of Bennet just now, that the point of tangency between the time circle and the materiality line can be changed by hypnotic suggestion. An entirely satisfactory experiment, you must admit; and yet," he became suddenly dejected, "as far as the world is concerned, it proves absolutely nothing."

"Why not?" I asked. "Couldn't others witness such a demonstration as well as I?"

"And deem it a very nice proof of reincarnation," he shrugged. "No, Claybridge, it won't do. There is but one proof the world would consider; the transfer of a man's consciousness to the future."

"Cannot that be done?" I queried.

"Yes," he said. "But there is connected with it an element of danger. Mental status has a strong effect upon the physical being, as was witnessed by Bennet's reversion to the Hun type. Had I kept him in the hypnotic state for too long a period, the Teutonic cast of features would not have vanished with his awakening. What changes a projection into the future would bring, I cannot say; and for that reason he is naturally unwilling that I experiment upon him in that direction."

He strode up and down the floor of his laboratory as he talked. His head was slumped forward upon his breast, as if heavy with the weight of thought.

"Then satisfactory proof is impossible?" I asked. "You can never hope to convince the world?"

He stopped with a suddenness that was startling, and his head went up with a jerk. "No!" he cried. "I have not given up! I must have a subject for my experiments, and I shall proceed to find one."

This determined statement did not particularly impress me at the time, nor, for that matter, did the time-theory itself. Both were recalled to me a week or so later, when, in answer to his summons, I again visited Mortimer at the laboratory, and he thrust a newspaper into my hands, pointing to an item among the want ads.

"Wanted—" I read, "A subject for hypnotic experiment. $5.000 for the right man. Apply Pro. Alex Mortimer, Mortimer Laboratories, City."

"Surely," I exclaimed, "you do not expect to receive an answer to that?"

"On the contrary," he smiled, "I have received no less than a dozen answers. From them I chose the one who is most likely to prove the best subject. He will be here in a few minutes to sign the documents absolving me from any responsibility in case of accident. That is why I sent for you."

I could only stare at him.

"Of course," he went on, "I explained to him that there would be a degree of personal risk involved, but he appeared not to care. On the contrary, he seemed almost to welcome it. He—"

A knock at the door interrupted him. In response to his call, one of his assistants looked in.

"Mr. Williams is here, Professor."

"Send him in, Gable." As the assistant disappeared, Mortimer turned back to me. "My prospective subject," he explained. "He is prompt."

A thin, rather undersized man entered the room. My attention was at once drawn to his eyes, which seemed too large for his face.

"Mr. Williams, my friend, Dr. Claybridge," Mortimer introduced us. "The doctor is going to witness these articles we have to sign."

Williams acknowledged the introduction in a voice that sounded infinitely tired.

"Here are the papers," Mortimer said, pushing a few sheets of paper across the table toward him.

Williams merely glanced at them, and picked up a pen.

"Just a minute," Mortimer rang for Gable. The assistant and I witnessed the signature, and affixed our names below it.

"I am ready to begin immediately, if you like," Williams said when Gable had gone.

Mortimer eyed him reflectively for a moment. "First," he said, "there is a question I should like to ask you, Mr. Williams. You need not answer if you feel disinclined. Why are you so eager to undergo an experiment, the outcome of which even I cannot foresee?"

"If I answer that, will my answer be treated as strictly confidential?" asked Williams, casting a sidelong glance in my direction.

"Most certainly," Mortimer replied. "I speak for both myself and Dr. Claybridge." I nodded affirmation.

"Then," said Williams, "I will tell you. I welcome this experiment because, as you pointed out yesterday, there is a possibility of its resulting in my death. No, you did not say so in so many words, Prof. Mortimer, but that is the fear at the back of your mind. And why should I wish to die? Because, gentlemen, I have committed murder."

"What!" We barked out the word together.

Williams smiled wanly at our amazement. "That is rather an unusual statement; isn't it?" he asked in his tired voice. "Whom I murdered does not matter. The police will never find me out, for I was clever about it in order that my sister, to whom your $5,000, Professor, is to be paid, need not suffer from the humiliation of my arrest. But although I can escape the authorities, I cannot escape my own conscience. The knowledge that I have deliberately killed a man, even while he merited death, is becoming too much for me; and since my religion forbids suicide, I have turned to you as a possible way out. I think that is all."

We stared at him in silence. What Mortimer was thinking, I do not know. Most likely he was pondering upon the strange psychology of human conduct. As for me, I could not help wondering in what awful, perhaps pitiable tragedy this little man had been an actor.

Mortimer was the first to speak. When he did so, it was with no reference to what we had just heard. "Since you are ready, Mr. Williams, we will proceed with our initial experiment at once," he said. "I have arranged a special room for it, where there will be no other thought waves nor suggestions to disturb you."

He rose, and was apparently about to lead the way to this room when the telephone rang.

"Hello," he called into the transmitter. "Dr. Claybridge? Yes, he is here. Just a minute." He pushed the instrument towards me.

My hospital was on the wire. After taking the message, I hung up in disgust. "An acute case of appendicitis," I announced. "Of course I'm sorry for the poor devil, but he certainly chose an inopportune time for his attack."

"I will phone you all about the experiment," Mortimer promised as I reached for my hat. "Perhaps you can be present at the next one."

True to his promise, he rang me up that evening.

"I have had wonderful success!" he cried exultantly. "So far, I have experimented only in a small way, but at that my theory has been proven beyond the possibility of doubt. And there was one most interesting feature, Claybridge. Williams told me what would be the nature of my experiment tomorrow afternoon."

"And what will it be?" I asked.

"I am to make his material consciousness tangent with the end of the world," was the astonishing answer.

"Good heavens!" I cried in spite of myself. "Shall you do it?"

"I have no choice in the matter," he replied.

"Mortimer, you fatalist! You—"

"No, no," he protested. "It is not fatalism. Can't you understand that—"

But I interrupted him. "May I be present?" I asked.

"Yes," he answered. "You will be there. Williams saw you."

I had a good mind to deliberately *not* be there, just to put a kink in his precious theory; but my curiosity was too great, and at the appointed time, I was on hand.

"I have already put Williams to sleep," Mortimer said as I came in. "He is in my especially prepared room. Come and I will show him to you."

He led me down a long hall to a door which, I knew had originally given upon a storeroom. Inserting a key in the lock, he turned it, and flung the door open.

In the room beyond, I could see Williams seated in a swivel chair. His eyes were closed and his body relaxed, as in sleep. However, it was not he that awakened my interest, but the room itself. It was windowless, with only a skylight in the ceiling to admit light and air. Aside from the chair in which Williams sat, there was no furniture save an instrument resembling an immense telephone transmitter that a crane arm held about two inches from the hypnotized man's mouth, and a set of ear phones, such as a telephone operator wears, which were attached to his ears. But strangest of all, the walls, floors, and ceiling of the room were lined with a whitish metal.

"White lead," said Mortimer, seeing my eyes upon it; "the substance least conductive of thought waves. I want the subject to be as free as possible from outside thought influences, so that when he talks with me over that telephonic device, which is connected with my laboratory, there can be no danger of his telling me any but his own experiences."

"But the skylight," I pointed out. "It is partially open."

"True," he admitted. "But thought waves, like sound waves, travel upwards and outwards; rarely, if ever, downwards. So, you see, there is little danger from the skylight."

He closed and locked the door, and we went back to the laboratory. In one corner was what looked like a radio loud speaker, while near it was a transmitter similar to the one in the room with Williams.

"I shall speak to Williams through the transmitter," explained Mortimer, "and he shall hear me by means of the ear phones. When he answers into his transmitter, we will hear him through the loud speaker."

He seated himself before the apparatus and spoke: "Williams, do you hear me?"

"I hear you." The reply came promptly, but in the heavy tones of a man talking in his sleep.

"Listen to me. You are living in the last six days of the earth. By 'days,' I do not mean periods of twenty-four hours, but such lengths of time as are meant in the first chapter of the book of Genesis. It is now the first day of the six. Tell me what you see."

After a short interval, the answer came in a strange, high key. While the words were English, they were spoken with a curious intonation that was at first difficult to understand.

"This is the year 46,812," said the voice, "or, in modern time, 43,930 A. I. C. After Interplanetary Communication. It is not well upon the earth. The Polar Ice Cap comes down almost to Newfoundland. Summer lasts but a few weeks, and then its heat is scorching. What in early time was known as the Atlantic Coastal Plain has long ago sunken into the sea. High dykes must be used to keep the water from covering the island of Manhattan, where the world's government is located. A great war has just been concluded. There are many dead to bury."

"You speak of interplanetary communication," said Mortimer. "Is the world, then, in communication with the planets?"

"In the year 2,952," came the answer, "the earth succeeded in getting into communication with Mars. Radio pictures were sent back and forth between the two worlds until they learned each other's languages; then sound communication was established. The Martians had been trying to signal the earth since the beginning of the twentieth century, but were unable to set up a system of communication because of the insufficient scientific advancement of the Earthmen.

"About a thousand years later, a message was received from Venus, which had now advanced to the earth's state of civilization, when Mars was signalled. For nearly five hundred years they had been receiving messages from both the earth and Mars, but had been unable to answer.

"A little over five thousand years later, a series of sounds was received which seemed to come from somewhere beyond Venus. Venus and Mars heard them too; but, like us, were able to make nothing of them. All three worlds broadcasted their radio pictures on the wave length corresponding to that of the mysterious sounds, but received no answer. At last Venus advanced the theory that the sounds had come from Mercury, whose inhabitants, obliged to live upon the side of their world farther from the sun, would be either entirely without sight or with eyes not sufficiently developed to see our pictures.

"Recently something dire has happened to Mars. Our last messages from her told of terrible wars and pestilences, such as we are now having upon earth. Also, her water supply was beginning to give out, due to the fact that she was obliged to use much of it in the manufacture of atmosphere. Suddenly, about fifty years ago, all messages from her ceased; and upon signalling her, we received no answer."

Mortimer covered the transmitter with his hand. "That," he said to me, "can mean only that intelligent life upon Mars had become extinct. The earth, then, can have but a few thousand years yet to go."

For nearly an hour longer he quizzed Williams upon conditions of the year 46,812. All the answers showed that while scientific knowledge had reached an almost incredulous stage of advancement, the race of mankind was in its twilight. Wars had killed off thousands of people, while strange, new diseases found hosts of victims daily in a race whose members were no longer physically constituted to withstand them. Worst of all, the birth rate was rapidly diminishing.

"Listen to me." Mortimer raised his voice as if to impress his invisible subject with what he was about to say. "You are now living in the second day. Tell me what you see."

There was a moment or so of silence; then the voice, keyed even higher than before, spoke again.

"I see humanity in its death-throes," it said. "Only a few scattered tribes remain to roam over the deserted continents. The cattle have begun to sicken and die; and it is unsafe to use them for food. Four thousand years ago, we took to the manufacture of artificial air, as did the Martians before us. But it is hardly worth while, for children are no longer born. We shall be the last of our race."

"Have you received no recent word from Mars?" asked Mortimer.

"None. Two years ago, at her proper season, Mars failed to appear in the heavens. As to what has become of her, we can only conjecture."

There was a horrible suggestiveness about this statement. I shuddered, and noticed that Mortimer did, also.

"The Polar Ice Cap has begun to retreat," resumed the voice. "Now it is winters that are short. Tropical plants have begun to appear in the temperate zones. The lower forms of animal life are becoming more numerous, and have begun to pursue man as man once pursued them. The days of the human race are definitely numbered. We are a band of strangers upon our own world."

"Listen to me," said Mortimer again. "It is now the third day. Describe it."

Followed the usual short interval of silence; then came the voice, fairly brittle with freezing terror.

"Why," it screamed, "do you keep me here; the last living man upon a dying planet? The world is festering with dead things. Let me be dead with them."

"Mortimer," I interrupted, "this is awful! Hasn't your experiment gone far enough?"

He pushed back his chair and rose. "Yes," he said, a bit shakily, I thought. "For the present, at least. Come; I will awaken Williams."

I followed him down the hall, and was close upon his heels, when he flung open the door of the lead-lined room, and stepped inside. Our cries of surprised alarm were simultaneous.

In the chair where we had left him sat Williams; but physically he was a different man. He had shrunken several inches in stature, while his head appeared to have grown larger, with the forehead almost bulbous in aspect. His fingers were extremely long and sensitive, but suggestive of great strength. His frame was thin to emaciation.

"Good Heavens!" I gasped. "What has happened?"

"It is an extreme case of mental influence upon matter," answered Mortimer, bending over the hypnotized man. "You remember how young Bennet's features took on the characteristics of a Hun? A similar thing, but in a much intenser degree, has happened to Williams. He has become a man of the future physically as well as mentally."

"Good Lord!" I cried. "Waken him at once! This is horrible."

"To be frank with you," said Mortimer gravely, "I am afraid to. He has been in this state much longer than I realized. To waken him too suddenly would be dangerous. It might even prove fatal."

For a moment he seemed lost in thought. Then he removed the ear phones from Williams' head, and addressed him. "Sleep," he commanded. "Sleep soundly and naturally. When you have rested sufficiently, you will awaken and be your normal self."

Shortly after this, I left Mortimer, and, although it was my day off duty, went to my hospital. How good my commonplace tonsil cases seemed after the unholy things I had just experienced! I surprised the resident physician almost into a state of coma by putting in the remainder of the day in the hardest work possible in the free clinic; and finally went home, tired in mind and body.

I turned in early for what I deemed a well-earned rest, and fell asleep instantly. The next thing of which I was conscious was the insistent ringing of the telephone bell beside my bed.

"Hello," I cried sleepily, taking down the receiver. "Dr. Claybridge speaking."

"Claybridge, this is Mortimer," came the almost hysterical response. "For God's sake, come over to the laboratory at once!"

"What has happened?" I demanded, instantly wide awake. It would take something unusual to wring such excitement from the unemotional Mortimer.

"It's Williams," he answered. "I can't bring him back. He got awake about an hour ago, and still believes that he is living in the future. Physically, he is the same as he was when last you saw him this afternoon."

"I'll be over at once," I fairly shouted, and slammed the receiver down upon its hook. As I scrambled into my clothes, I glanced at the clock. Two fifteen. In half an hour I could reach the laboratory. What would I find waiting for me?

Mortimer was in the lead room with Williams when I arrived.

"Claybridge," he said, "I need someone else's opinion in this case. Look at him, and tell me what you think."

Williams still occupied the chair in the middle of the room. His eyes were wide open, but it was plain that he saw neither Mortimer nor me. Even when I bent over him and touched him, he gave no sign of being conscious of my presence.

"He looks as if he were suffering from some sort of catalepsy," I said, "yet his temperature and pulse are almost normal. I should say that he is still partially in a state of hypnosis."

"Then it is self-hypnosis," said Mortimer, "for I have entirely withdrawn my influence."

"Perhaps," I suggested lightly, "you have transported him irretrievably into the future."

"That," Mortimer replied, "is precisely what I fear has happened." I stared at him dumbly.

"The only way out," he went on, "is to rehypnotize him, and finish the experiment. At its conclusion, he may return to his natural state."

I could not help thinking that there were certain things which it was forbidden man to know; and that Mortimer, having wantonly blundered into them, was now being made to pay the penalty. I watched him as he worked over poor Williams, straining all his energies to induce a state of hypnotic sleep. At last the glassy eyes before him closed, and his subject slept. With hands that trembled visibly, he adjusted the earphones, and we went back to the laboratory.

"Williams," Mortimer called into his transmitter, "do you hear me?"

"I hear you," replied the odiously familiar voice.

"You are now living in the fourth day. What do you see?"

"I see reptiles; great lizards that walk upon their hind legs, and birds with tiny heads and bats' wings, that build nests in the ruins of the deserted cities."

"Dinosaurs and pterodactyles!" I gasped involuntarily. "A second age of reptiles!"

"The Polar caps have retreated until there is but a small area of ice about each of the poles," continued the voice. "There are no longer any seasons; only a continuous reign of heat. The torrid zone has become uninhabitable even by the reptiles. The sea there boils. Great monsters writhe in their death agonies upon its surface. Even the northern waters are becoming heated.

"All the land is covered with rank vegetation upon which the reptiles feed. The air is fetid with it."

Mortimer interrupted: "Describe the fifth day."

After the customary interval, the voice replied. There was a sticky quality about it that reminded me of the sucking of mud at some object struggling in it.

"The reptiles are gone," it said. "I alone live upon this expiring world. Even the plant life has turned yellow and withered. The volcanoes are in terrific action. The mountains are becoming level, and soon all will be one vast plain. A thick, green slime is gathering upon the face of the waters; so that it is difficult to tell where the land with its rotting vegetation ends and the sea begins. The sky is saffron in colour, like a plate of hot brass. At night a blood red moon swims drunkenly in a black sky.

"Something is happening to gravitation. For a long time I had suspected it. Today I tested it by throwing a stone into the air. I was carried several feet above the ground by the force of my action. It took the stone nearly twenty minutes to return to earth. It fell slowly, *and at an angle!*"

"An angle!" cried Mortimer.

"Yes. It was barely perceptible, but it was there. The earth's movement is slowing. Days and nights have more than doubled in length."

"What is the condition of the atmosphere?"

"A trifle rarefied, but not sufficiently so to make breathing difficult. This seems strange to me."

"That," said Mortimer to me, "is because his body is here in the twentieth century, where there is plenty of air. The air at the stage of the earth's career where his mind is would be too rare to support organic life. Even now the mental influence is so strong that he believes the density of the atmosphere to be decreasing."

"Recently," Williams' voice went on, "the star Vega has taken Polaris' place as centre of the universe. Many of the old stars have disappeared, while new ones have taken their places. I have a suspicion that our solar system is either falling or travelling in a new direction through space."

"Listen to me, Williams." Mortimer's voice sounded dry and cracked, and his forehead was besprinkled with great gouts of sweat. "It is the sixth, the last day. What do you see?"

"I see a barren plain of grey rock. The world is in perpetual twilight because the mists that rise from the sea obscure the sun. Heaps of brown bones dot the plain near the mounds that once were cities. The dykes around Manhattan long ago crumbled away; but there is no longer any need for them even were men here, for the sea is rapidly drying up. The atmosphere is becoming exceedingly rarefied. I can hardly breathe…

"Gravitation is giving out more rapidly. When I stand erect. I sway as though drunk. Last night the curtains of mist parted for a time, and I saw the moon fly off into space.

"Great lightnings play about the earth, but there is no thunder. The silence all around is plummetless. I keep speaking aloud and striking one object against another to relieve the strain on my eardrums…

"Great cracks are beginning to appear in the ground, fro. which smoke and molten lava issue. I have fled to Manhattan in order that the skeletons of the tall buildings may hide them from my sight.

"Small objects have begun to move of their own volition. I am afraid to walk, as each step hurls me off my balance. The heat is awful. I cannot breathe."

There was a short interval, that came as a relief to our tightly screwed nerves. The tension to which the experiment had pitched us was terrific; yet I, for one, could no more have torn myself away than I could have passed into the fourth dimension.

Suddenly the voice cut the air like a knife!

"The buildings!" it shrieked. "They are swaying! They are leaning toward each other! They are crumbling, disintegrating; and the crumbs are flying *outward instead of falling!* Tiny particles are being thrown off by everything around me. Oh, the heat! There is no air!"

Followed a hideous gurgling; then:

"The earth is dissolving beneath my feet! It is the end. Creation is returning to its original atoms! Oh, my God!" There was a sickening scream that rapidly grew fainter with the effect of fading on radio.

"Williams!" shouted Mortimer. "What happened?"

There was no answer.

"Williams! Williams!" Mortimer was on his feet, fairly shrieking into the instrument. "Do you hear me?"

The only response was utter silence.

Mortimer clutched me by the arm, and dragged me with him from the laboratory and down the hall.

"Is—is he dead?" I choked as we ran.

id not answer. His breath was coming in quick,
would have made speech impossible even had

the lead room he stopped and fumbled with his
keys. From beyond we could hear no sound. Twice Mortimer, in
his nervousness and hurry, dropped the key and had to grope for
it; but at last he got it turned in the lock, and flung the door open.

In our haste, we collided with each other as we hurtled into
the room. Then as one man we stopped dead in our tracks. The
room was empty!

"Where—" I began incredulously. "He couldn't have gotten
out! Could he?"

"No," Mortimer answered hoarsely.

We advanced farther into the room, peering into every crack
and corner. From the back of the chair, suspended by their cord,
hung the earphones; while dangling from the chair's seat to the
floor were the tattered and partially charred remains of what
seemed to have been at one time a suit of men's clothing. At sight
of these, Mortimer's face went white. In his eyes was a look of
dawning comprehension and horror.

"What does it mean?" I demanded.

For answer, he pointed a palsied finger.

As I looked, the first beam of morning sunlight slipped through
the skylight above us, and fell obliquely to the floor. In its golden
shaft, directly above the chair where Williams had sat, a myriad
of infinitesimal atoms were dancing.

THE BOOK OF WORLDS

Miles J. Breuer

Miles J. Breuer (1888–1945), who was of Czech descent, was a local physician in Lincoln, Nebraska who had served with the US Medical Corps during the First World War. He was also a researcher, operating his own chemical laboratory, which may have inspired his first story, "The Man Without an Appetite", published in a Czech magazine in 1916. It tells of a scientist who had managed to convert his haemoglobin to function like chlorophyll, so that he had effectively become a plant! Breuer was naturally attracted to the first specialist science-fiction magazine, Amazing Stories, *in 1926, debuting there with "The Man With the Strange Head" in the January 1927 issue. Over the next decade he wrote another thirty stories, including collaborations with Jack Williamson and Clare Winger Harris. Breuer was a true original, fascinated with strange concepts and ideas and keen to share these with others. Most of his early fiction has been assembled in* The Man With the Strange Head *(2008) though curiously it omits the following story which explores all possible worlds.*

T O PSYCHIATRISTS, PROFESSOR COSGRAVE'S CASE IS A STRIK-
ing study in the compensatory psychosis. He perches on the
edge of his bed in a private sanitarium for mental diseases, and
coos and twitters and waves a wreath of twigs in his lips. Whether
he will ever recover his sanity or not is problematical. Whether
anyone else will ever be able to understand and use his hyperstereoscope is also problematical. And whether, if it were figured
out, anyone would ever have the courage to use it, in the face of
what happened to Professor Cosgrave, is still further remote in
the realms of doubt and conjecture.

I have repeated the story for medical men so many times, that
I am beginning to see a sort of logical sequence in things that at
first utterly bewildered me. As Professor Cosgrave's chief assistant,
I was undoubtedly closer to him and knew more about his work
and about the mechanism of his tragic fate, than anyone else.
The physicists who merely went over his apparatus and equations
and did not know the man, did not grasp the significance of what
happened, as did I, who lived and worked with him every day and
many a night.

Yes, the thing begins to look logical to me now, after it has been
on my mind constantly for several months. As no one else has been
able to understand exactly what happened, I ought to do my best
to render a consecutive account of events.

Professor Hemingford Cosgrave was the most highly civilized
man I have ever known. If mankind is in truth becoming more

civilized as time goes on, then it is following in the footsteps of such advanced and refined examples of human progress as was my late superior in the School of Physics. He was a small, delicate-looking man, with classical Greek features; with very little physical strength but with infinite physical endurance. To spend day and night in his laboratory for a week on end seemed to produce no deleterious effects upon him.

When I extol the rare combination of mathematical genius and experimental ability of this man, so well known, I am wasting my breath. But the world does not know so much about his other exquisitely subtle mental sensibilities. He was a poet and an artist; he saw all the beauty of the Cosmos with a wondering eye. And he was as gently sympathetic as a woman. The reports of famine victims suffering in China disturbed him at his experiments. His student-assistants would conspire to guard him against the visits of the old Salvation Army Captain, who more than once lured him away from his desk, with the tale of some woman or child in distress. He was the last man in the world to be permitted to witness the horrors, that he said he saw.

A little over two years ago, he and I were planning together a demonstration for his class in Quadrics. We had considered making models of some of the solids, with whose equations the class was working; but the time and labour involved in this was almost out of question under the circumstances. I suggested that the Mathematics Department of the University of Chicago had all of these models already made. We solved the problem by my going to Chicago and photographing these models with a stereo-scopic camera. The prints of the strangely shaped solids, viewed in a stereoscope, were quite as satisfactory for class purposes as would have been the models.

I had brought the pile of cards to Professor Cosgrave for approval. He had run through three or four of them, and seemed quite pleased. Suddenly he laid them down and stared at me.

"Do you know what just struck me?" he asked in a queer tone. I shook my head.

"You know what I'm working on?" he asked.

"You mean your Expansion Equations—?"

"Popularly called the Fourth Dimension." He smiled at the thought. "And you know what I've begun to suspect about it, especially since the experiment with the gyroscope?"

"Yes, I do—though it's hard for me to grasp that there really might be another dimension. I've always considered the fourth dimension a mathematical abstraction."

"No abstraction."

He said it as one might say, two and two make four.

"Really something here. Do you see the connection now?" He shook the stereoscope at me.

I shook my head. I felt helpless. His mind was always far ahead of mine. He explained:

"This instrument takes a two-dimensional figure on a flat plane and builds it up so that the brain sees it as a three-dimensional solid in space!"

He waited for me to grasp his idea, which I still failed to do. He smiled indulgently.

"*If* the fourth dimension is really a dimension and not a mathematical abstraction—" he smiled confidentially as he emphasized the *if;* "can we not build a hyper-stereoscopic instrument which will build up a three-dimensional model of a fourth-dimensional object into an image perceptible to the brain in its true four-dimensional form?"

I continued to stare blankly from him to the stereoscope and back again.

"As a matter of fact," he continued; "our three-dimensional world is merely a *cross-section* cut by what we know as *space* out of the Cosmos that exists in four or more dimensions. Our three-dimensional world bears the same relation to the true status of affairs as do these flat photographs to the models that you photographed. Surely you can grasp that from our equations?"

"Yes," I assented eagerly, glad to find familiar ground to rest my feet on; "just as the present time is a cross-section of infinity cut by a moving space-sector whose motion is irreversible; it moves in one direction only."

He beamed at me for that. Then in silence he finished looking over the geometrical stereograms and handed them to me.

He spent six months working out his idea on paper. He did not discuss his plans with me very much; but he did give me sections of the problems to work out. For instance he asked me to work out the equations for the projection of a tesseracoid:

$$c_1 w^4 + c_2 x^4 + c_3 y^4 + c_4 z^4 = k^4$$

from eight different directions, each opposing pair of right angles to the other three pairs. Most of the problems he gave me were projection problems; but beyond that I could not grasp the drift of his work.

Then he spent a year in experimental work. As I am a mathematician and not a laboratory man, I had less to do with the actual construction of the hyperstereoscope. But even there I helped. I worked at the refractive indices of crystals that he made in an electric furnace; and I worked out the mathematics of a very ingenious instrument for integrating light rays from two directions into one composite beam.

Apparently the thing was a complex job. Professor Cosgrave spent three weeks in the research laboratory of the Mechanical Engineering Department. He went to Chicago and remained there for a couple of months, leaving as his address the Psychology Department of the Chicago University. One day he announced to me calmly that the hyperstereoscope was finished.

"May I look?" I asked eagerly, expecting to be able to see out into the fourth dimension.

The instrument was pointed out of the window at the campus. It had three telescopes arranged in the form of a triangular parallelepiped. One end of the room was full of apparatus, electron tubes and photoelectric cells, a scanning disk, and tangles of wire strung between boxes and cabinets faced with dials and meters. At a small table there were two oculars to look into. I put my eyes to them.

It made me dizzy. It looked like rolling vapours—dense, heavy vapours, and boiling clouds, rolling and turmoiling swiftly and dizzily. It looked vibrant with heat. Through a rift here and there I got glimpses of a glowing liquid, like the white-hot metal in a foundry coming from the ladle. There were boiling, bubbling lakes of it. I shrank away from the instrument.

"What is it?" I gasped.

"I'm not sure," returned Professor Cosgrave. "Prolonged observation and correlation of observed data will be necessary before we can explain what we see."

He was whirling dials rapidly. I looked again. There were vapours, but they were thin spirals and wisps. Mostly there were bare, smoking rocks. There was a bleak, insufferably dreary stretch of them, extending on into the infinite distance. It looked hot. It was infinitely depressing. I didn't like it.

I stood for a long time behind Professor Cosgrave, as he sat at one little table with his eyes to the oculars of the instrument and twiddled the dials. I was about to turn around and slip out of the room and leave him to play with it alone, when he sat up suddenly. A new idea had struck him.

"Beyond a doubt these places that we see are regions of some sort, not in our 'space' at all, or else infinitely far away. But, in the direction of the fourth dimension they are quite near us. Just as if you are in a window on the top story of a skyscraper office build-ing and a dozen feet away is a man in the window of an adjacent building. To your three-dimensional vision he is quite near you. But to your body, whose motion is confined to two-dimensional surfaces, your friend is a long distance away. To your touch, instead of a dozen feet away he is a quarter of a mile away; that is how far you have to travel before you can reach him.

"Or, if I make a mark at each end of this sheet of paper and then bend the sheet double, from a three-dimensional standpoint the marks are a millimetre apart. But from a two-dimensional standpoint they are thirty centimetres apart.

"This stereoscope *sees across*, in the same way, to some other universe."

He shook his head.

"My analogies are poor. It is a difficult idea to express. But look!"

I went to the eye-pieces. There was water. It was endless. Just water. It swelled and rolled and pulsated. A swing of the telescopes over at the window brought into view some black rocks. Over the rocks was slime. A slime that flowed and rounded itself into worm-like forms. It was hideous. I left the gloating Professor Cosgrave and hurried away.

After that, as my recollection serves, things moved rapidly. I saw him a couple of days later at his stereoscope.

"I have it!" he said elatedly when he saw me. I hastened to look into the instrument.

"No!" he exclaimed, pulling me away. "I mean an analogy. Like points on the leaves of a book. You see?"

I nodded. He continued.

"Points on the adjacent leaves of a book are far apart, considered two-dimensionally. But, with the book closed, and to a three-dimensional perception which can *see across* from one page to another, the two points are very near together. You see?"

I nodded again.

"Now look!"

I saw a dense swamp, among huge trees with broad, rich green leaves. Gigantic saurians stalked about and splashed hugely.

"It is like a story of evolution," I couldn't help remarking.

He nodded in satisfaction and mused on:

"Each of these must be a separate and distinct world. I can go back and forth among them at will. It is not a continuous story. There are steps. Definite jumps. Nothing between. I can see any one of them at any time. Like the leaves of a book!"

I looked again. The professor had not touched the setting and the scene was exactly the same. A huge saurian was devouring some living creature from the water. The water was threshed into a pink foam, and light-red blood was splashed over the green foliage. The professor was talking:

"What we see is worlds or universes arranged side by side in the fourth dimension. Like leaves in a book.

"Heavens! What an encyclopedia!"

"I see," I said slowly, not sure that I really did. "Like serial sections cut in a microtome."

"Comparable. But not really sections. Separate worlds. Three-dimensional worlds like our own. Side by side, each of them one page ahead of the preceding. Three-dimensional leaves in a four-dimensional book."

It was a little difficult to grasp. I thought a while.

"I'd like to have Carver of Purdue see this," I said. "Do you remember his article in the *Scientific Monthly* about your four-space equations? It was almost personal. Ill-becoming to a scientific man. I'd give my shirt to see his face when he sees this. Let's bring him down."

Professor Cosgrave shook his head.

"What object can there be in causing the man any unpleasant feeling? The world holds enough unpleasant situations without our multiplying them. I shall break the news to him pleasantly when the opportunity presents itself."

That was typical of Professor Cosgrave. That is just how considerate and sympathetic he always was. Always he was trying to spare other people unpleasantness or discomfort. The man was wasted on our present-day selfish and discourteous age. He ought to have been born into some future Utopia.

What would he do now? I wondered. There was obviously a vast number of worlds to observe. It would take a lifetime to have a good look at each one of them. Would he spend his time on satisfying his curiosity and turn his back on mathematical physics? He still had numerous important problems ahead of him in the latter field. He was barely started on his career as a mathematical physicist, yet the world was expecting great things of him.

However, for the present there was apparently one phase of the purely observational pursuit for him.

"The 'leaves' in this book seem to be arranged in absolutely orderly succession," he said. "By chance I began at the end where the evolutionary development was lowest. By swinging my visual field through the unknown dimension in one direction, I can see the worlds in succession, each a little further evolved than the preceding. Now, I'm a physicist, and cannot afford to waste much time in gratifying idle curiosity. But, I must spend a few days or weeks in following out this evolutionary series before I turn it over to some biologist. This is too much of a temptation for any kind of a scientific man."

For several days I would come into the room and see him there with his eyes glued to the oculars, too absorbed even to notice my entrance. His attitude was one of tense and motionless concentration. I would steal out again, loath to disturb him. Once I came in and noted that he was trembling violently all over as he gazed into the machine. A couple of days later I found him in the same position, as though he had not moved since I had been there last. His whole body was set and rigid. I was alarmed at the way he looked. I stepped closer; his jaw was set and his breathing was shallow.

I felt concerned about him, and I made a sound to attract his attention. He started suddenly and leaped to his feet, and turned to me a face that was white with horror.

"I've been a student!" he gasped. "A scientific man. I never stopped to realize that men were like that." He sank into a chair, his hands on his knees, his head drooped.

I looked into the stereoscope. This time there were men. An army stood drawn up, with shining helmets and fluttering pennants, extending far into the dim distance. The foreground was red and active; everything was splattered with blood; men were swinging swords. There were rows of captives and men cutting their heads off. I watched only a second before I recoiled, but saw a dozen heads roll on the ground and fountains of blood gush over victims and executioners alike.

"You have no business looking at that!" I exclaimed.

It was incongruous. This delicately organized, unselfish, tender-hearted man to be spending his days gazing at those things.

"It's been that way from the beginning," he whispered, shuddering. "Ever since rudimentary humans appeared in the series ... war, brutality, cruelty, wanton killing of people ..."

But I couldn't keep him away from the thing. He called me to it and explained:

"As far as I can understand this, I am swinging the field of view through an arc in a dimension that extends at right angles to the three known dimensions. At intervals I see a world. In between there is nothing. The swing is accomplished by changing the intensity of the electrical field through crystals of this zirconium compound, which alters their refractivity.

"I am going steadily down my scale toward zero. The worlds are getting further and further advanced in the scale of evolution. I can see it clearly now."

In a moment he was back at the instrument, completely absorbed, and oblivious of me. I was worried about him. I came in daily to watch him, and many a time I came and went without his having been conscious of my presence. There was something wrong about the thing; the intense absorption of a man of his sympathetic type in scenes of inhumanity such as I had seen. One day when I opened the door, he was facing it, waiting for me.

"I am nearly at zero. Look! A world much like ours."

In the lenses I saw the buildings of a city, rather odd, but for all the world suggesting London or Paris; swarming crowds of people, hurrying vehicles. It was quite like our world, but just enough different so that I was sure it was not our world.

Professor Cosgrave was pale and agitated.

"Man's inhumanity to man!" he moaned. "It would drive me distracted, were there not one hope. Just now, in that fair city, I watched a mob drag men and women through the streets and stick their bodies up on poles on a bridge; and blood dripped into the river.

"But, step by step there is more intellect, more material progress. There is hope that man will eventually develop intelligence enough to stop his senseless and cruel fighting, and learn cooperation and altruism. Each of these worlds seems to bring us a little nearer to that."

He called my attention as he turned his dials to zero, and looked into the instrument. He turned to me with a queer smile.

"Look!"

I applied my eye again. There was the campus and athletic field, the gravel drives and the men's dormitory. Through the stereoscope or through the window, I got the same view.

"At zero we see our own 'plane' of the unknown dimension. *Our* page in the book. You see?"

"Now what?" I asked.

"Now negative potential values. Now to see the pages ahead of us in the book. Worlds further evolved than ours. The future! Up to the limits of the inductance of my coils!"

His eyes glowed and his breath came fast.

"The future!" he whispered as he bent over the oculars and carefully turned his dials. "In the future lies man's hope. In intelligence and science!"

Again he sat in motionless absorption. Occasionally he touched a dial or whispered to himself. Finally, as he said not a word for a half an hour, I tiptoed out.

The next day I found him staringly expecting my arrival with wide-open eyes, like a man with exophthalmic goitre.

"I don't know what makes me go on with this!" he gasped. "Men are beasts. Hopeless. They never will be anything else. Twenty airplanes went over a city dropping bombs. Swept it away. It is burning now. In one place I saw through the smoke a small child hemmed in a courtyard by flames. A city as grand as Chicago. A sea of smoke and flame." He sat with his head bowed in his hands.

I didn't know what to say. He seemed utterly crushed; I could not rouse him. Finally I led him out of the room, got him in my car, and took him home. I pondered on how I might get him away from that machine for a while.

But the next day he was back again at the machine. I had classes until four o'clock that afternoon. Then I hurried into the laboratory. I found a changed man.

He was stern and determined. This rather relieved me; for I had been worried about his hopeless depression, and I did not realize what was taking place in the man. It seemed to me then that he had shaken off the depression and had determined to do something about the situation of war and humanity.

"Here is a world thousands of years ahead of ours." he related. "Humanity crowds it densely beyond our conception. Thank God, it is another world somewhere else, and not ours. People have not risen an inch from bestiality in millennia. No—stay away from it; I can't permit you to witness such horrors. Men and women soldiers piled up in mangled, bloody heaps as high as the Capitol Building. Each belch of that machine kills a thousand more—stay away!

"It is not our world. We can still save our world from that. We start today, Harlan, you and I, to prevent such things from happening in our world."

"We've got to stop it!" he said again. But he sat and stared into the instrument.

I was puzzled and not a little alarmed. The sudden, stern determination of the gentle little man fitted him most strangely. I would have thought him play-acting for my benefit, had he not looked most terribly grim. Anyway, I was relieved to see that terrible depression had left him, and that he had got hold of himself. That is what I thought then.

He permitted me to lead him out again, and I took him home. He kept saying with grim determination:

"Not to *our* human race; We *won't* let it happen!"

On the following day I had no classes, and I called for him at his home early in the morning. He had already left. I hurried to his laboratory. He was already there, spinning dials feverishly, and then bending over the lenses. He had an unusual, nervous air about him.

"Destructive rays!" he said to me as I came in, but without looking away from the oculars. "Wither up a thousand people like snowflakes in a chimney-blast. Terrific explosives. Deadly gases. Bombs filled with disease germs. Diabolical inventiveness."

He whirled around and faced me.

"Everything indicates that our world is part of this scheme. It is going the same way. It will be what this is. We must stop it."

★

He stood up in the middle of the room and talked, and I took the opportunity to peer into the lenses. I saw a dead world. Wreckage. Ashes. Explosion holes. Disintegrating bodies. Nowhere a movement. Even vegetable life had withered. There was a pile of bombs ready to fire beside a huge gun and a gunner lay dead beside them.

There was a queer declamatory quality to the speech that Professor Cosgrave was making. He said queer, silly things about Universal Peace. And yet I didn't suspect.

Only the next morning when I came in, it dawned on me. He was perched on a tall stool, with a wreath of twigs in his lips. As I came in, he put the wreath around his neck, and sang in a high key:

"I am the Dove of Peace.
Listen to me: All men are brothers.
There shall be no more war.
I shall spread my wings over the world.
I am the Dove of Peace."

Tears sprang to my eyes as the truth suddenly dawned upon me. I gulped as I hurried to another room to telephone. Poor Professor Cosgrave!

Then, as they led him out, I looked into the lenses. There was a rugged stretch, smooth, gently undulating holes and hummocks as far as the eye could reach, covered with a slimy, disgusting fungus growth. Here and there the fungus covered a ragged shape suggesting the ruined wall of a building. There was no change in this scene during the four days before the machine's batteries ran down (for I did not know how to shut it off). Now, no one knows how to operate it.

Professor Cosgrave knows me. He is always glad to see me at his room at the sanitarium. But he talks to me only about Universal Brotherhood and about my duty to save mankind from strife and bloodshed. And he flaps his arms like wings and coos.

THE BRANCHES OF TIME

David R. Daniels

David R. Daniels (1914–1936) was a young science-fiction fan and promising writer who sold six stories from his first, "Stars" (Astounding, May 1935) to his last "Death Cloud" (Astounding, February 1936). Within two months of the last he was dead of a gunshot wound, reported as suicide but never really resolved. He had that useful enthusiasm for ideas full of a sense-of-wonder and two of his stories explore aspects of time. "The Far Way" (1935) has an individual leap-frogging into the future via another dimension whilst the following story, full of that youthful exuberance and belief that anything is possible, considers how events might be changed to benefit mankind and then explores the consequences.

I MET BELL, JAMES H. BELL, B.S., ON THE CORNER BY WALLER'S Drug Store. It was the first time I had seen him in years, since the summer we graduated, in fact.

"You're looking differently," I told him after we had shaken hands. He did, too. He was much more weatherbeaten than he had been. There was a look about him that a lot of these returned explorers, who really do things, have. "Been off on a Polar trip?"

"Something of the sort," he said noncommittally. "Drop around some time and I may tell you about it. Or better yet, come home to dinner with me and we'll renew our acquaintance. I've got a vintage now that will make the other you praised look sick."

"I'll accept anything before I'll believe that—unless you show me," I bantered. "Because of that statement, I'll accept your invitation. I'm off for the day, anyhow. Wait a minute while I phone my wife."

I was forced to admit that Bell had told the truth after he dug a cobwebbed bottle out of a cupboard and poured a couple of glasses full from it. So I said, "You win, Bell," and drank to his health.

"Where'd you get it?" I asked when I found its taste escaped me.

"You'd be surprised." I noticed a queer look in Bell's eyes.

Since we had been very intimate in the old days, and because of that look, I said, "Bell, there's something on your chest. What is it?" I can usually tell when someone wants to do a little confiding.

He stood a while before replying. "All right. I will tell," he said at last. "I remember you used to read science fiction as avidly as I did."

"That was a long time ago," I replied laughingly, "so don't scare me by telling too much about Mars."

His queer look was more that way than ever. "It's worse than that," he warned.

I searched my memory. "Been dancing among the atoms?"

He shook his head. "Way off."

"I give up then, unless it's time."

"You're right."

"Huh?" I said somewhat louder than was polite. "Come here, Bell."

"Oh, I'm perfectly sane," he assured me. "What's more, I'm sober, which you won't be if you take any more of that bottle on an empty stomach. John, we used to be intimate in the old days, so listen to what I have to tell you. I've given you a warning as to what it's about."

"All right," I agreed. "I probably won't believe it, but I'll listen; and I won't laugh."

"Fine; it's no laughing matter to me."

"Fire away, then."

"I will begin with only a little explanation; you already know the theory of time as a fourth dimension with our egos, or consciousnesses moving along our body extenditures in that dimension—also the other theory that it should be possible to move mundane objects in that dimension.

"I started on that and began experimenting with time machines. The idea behind the thing is not so difficult if one understands tesseracts and the principles of them. But, theory or no theory, it's extremely difficult for a three dimensional essence to construct machinery whose four dimensions can be made to move all at the same *absolute time*. However, I finally managed it, though since

I've been sure I was only lucky. Maybe, though, I was helped somehow.

"Even now I couldn't explain the machine to you; I'd have to let you see it. As for patenting such a device, I don't think the patent office would allow it. Now what are you laughing about?"

"I was only thinking of the rush if they did. Everybody would be sailing off to find past age gold fields; or if that palled, scientists would go back to study prehistoric animals, while dreamers forged ahead to see how their predictions of Utopia were working out. Why, I'm afraid I'd even give up my practice to join in."

"I'd thought about all that, too," Bell said. "It would mess up civilization worse than it is already, though it wouldn't make any difference in the end."

"Before you start giving us time machines, you ought to break the news gently. Kill George Washington, or save Lincoln from being assassinated at the right instant—or something else of the sort," I offered.

"And if I did, we wouldn't be in the same world-line." Bell paused a few moments. "That brings me to what I want to tell you," he went on. "I don't suppose you'll understand; I don't myself. I can't tell it properly. But as far as that goes, neither could that man after a hundred thousand years."

"Been that far?"

"Yes. But to get back to the time machine—finally I built some apparatus which I could move in time when I worked certain levers. At first the thing only had a little power—I could go ahead into the future or back into the past at about double rate. Though this thing was an altogether new invention, one still couldn't do enough with it to ever really get out of his own age. And that was what I wanted to do.

"After a year or so of experimenting, I finally made a traveller more powerful. But you see, it still wasn't strong enough, for I wanted to see the remote past and the far future—and a gasoline engine, for such I was experimenting with, couldn't possibly do that. The distance was too far. It would be like trying to drive to the sun in an automobile. However, after Eckleson solved atomic disintegration, I got an atomic engine; then I could move plenty fast."

"Say," I broke in, "just what's all this you're trying to feed me? Who's Eckleson? And atomic power? If you've got that, it's more than anybody else has done."

Bell looked sheepish. "I made a mistake," he said. "For the second I was mixed up as to when this was. What I meant was that after I'd been working with time machines for a year, I finally found that there's no power today capable of driving one much faster than at the rate of about a year an hour, which is still too slow. But by means of such a machine I was able to go ahead to the year 1987 when a Swede named Eckleson first found how to set free atomic power. I bought one such engine and installed it in my time traveller; and then I was ready to go anywhere. The machine was now able to make over a hundred thousand years a second at top speed, and it would go to the end of the world and back on a few hundred pounds of sand.

"But that was more power, however, than it would take to drive all the ships in existence around and around the world for the next hundred years."

"All very well," I broke in, "but describe your machine to me."

"Oh," said Bell in surprise. "I supposed you'd have an idea of what it would be like. After all the time stories I'd read, I made the thing on the usual lines—enclosed carriage, and all that, and oxygen tanks to supply my own atmosphere in case I ran into a period of noxious gasses.

"Also, after I'd installed the atomic engine, I transferred the whole thing into a twenty-first century flyer. I wanted to penetrate so many ages I knew it wouldn't be safe to stay on the surface of the earth. I might want to stop in some age where I was buried under ground, or in the walls of some great building.

"Speaking of time-travelling, since you want to hear all about it—the sensation is quite like it's been pictured. At first one feels somewhat nauseated and sick in the pit of his stomach—like you feel when an elevator starts down too fast. That's because men's bodies aren't built for too sudden acceleration. But if you apply your power properly, you seem to glide ahead; then it's like flying. After you're moving at even speed, there really isn't much feeling to it—any more than there is to riding in an airplane on even keel. Starting and stopping is nearly always somewhat uncomfortable, and if you're accelerating in time and suddenly fly either upward or downward in three dimensional space, why, it gets you down. Feels like you were being torn apart cell by cell. After I found that out, I always made sure that I was high enough in space before I started moving in time.

"While you're travelling, the sun revolves westward faster and faster, if you are going ahead; if you're going into the past, it moves from west to east. As you gain speed either way, day and night becomes a blur, then the changing colours of seasonal differences, and at very high speeds you move in a grey-white half-light. That's all.

"As I said, I attached an atomic motor in 1987, then I started out to find out what was going to happen.

"It was awful. Cities were springing up everywhere—great towering things like New York on Gargantuan style. There were buildings that covered a square mile of ground and reached two miles high by the year 2050. The world had gone building mad and the people were at nearly the same social status as ever—lots of quarrelling, little governments, and uneducated masses and all that. The countries were always close to fighting among themselves, which would have been like children settling their differences with machine guns and hand grenades.

"I was sure that before long there wouldn't be any world—or rather, any world of mankind, and I was right. There were fleets by that time which could go thousands of miles an hour; there were war horrors which could blow a hundred-mile city off the face of the earth in three seconds.

"Of course, they were always talking about peace, but anyone with half an eye could see that the treaties they were making wouldn't last.

"The end came when the United States and Japan, which by then had spread over nearly all Asia, declared war on each other in 2083. That was the war our philosophers have been prophesying when the East would be arrayed against the West. The whole world joined in. Both sides were about equal—the two Americas, Australia, and Europe had fewer people than the other side, but their men were better educated as a whole and therefore knew how to kill each other better.

"New York, Hongkong, London, Bombay, Melbourne, Berlin, and Rio de Janeiro were destroyed the first day, and that was only a start. They contained over a hundred million people all told. But that many killed didn't make any difference. It went on while the leaders and instigators of the thing stayed back out of sight where they couldn't be touched and where they kept working on the soldiers and keeping them at it until everybody was destroyed."

"Not everyone!" I echoed, horror-stricken.

"Yes, everyone. There's a lot of talk these days about how in the next war the face of man will be destroyed. It will be the truth if that war doesn't come till 2083."

"But you just said it did happen," I contradicted.

"I know. But listen, and you'll see why I say 'if.'

"Right now there is a lot of talk on the subject of wars and it has been said that any great war these days would wipe the race out. However, we aren't far enough advanced, in a mechanical way, to kill everyone. You see, after so much fighting, the horror of the thing strikes everyone and they leave off. Peace is made for that reason.

"By then, they were, though—not that people were any worse then than now, but because of the fact that they could destroy such great quantities of things in so short a time. When a long enough space had passed that the people should be sick of killing each other, there wasn't anyone left to stop it. The carnage died for lack of fuel.

"As I say, it ruined the world. It was because the leaders of the thing had stayed back out of sight until nearly everybody else was dead—though even then they came out of their burrows too soon. If they had been wiped out early in the game, the war might have run itself out, since without leaders there would have to have been a cessation before they all died.

"But that wasn't the way it went. So finally, when the agitators did come out, there was only one fighting man, one soldier left. The war hadn't stayed to the trenches and the air above them; each side had bombed non-combatants, women and children, and everybody, and none could escape. Only the single soldier remained, who was a decent sort though he had destroyed a few cities single-handed. He went into hiding to see what would happen.

"Everybody in South America was dead, in Australia, and in Africa. There were a group of eight or nine who had entrenched themselves in the Rocky Mountains west of Denver; there were the same number in the Alps in Switzerland, and another group in the Indian Himalayas. All told they numbered about two dozen.

"When that fighting man—Lark his name was, I believe—found that out and realized that these people had been the cause of the whole carnage, he gathered a few bombs, took them by surprise, and killed all them off too—first those in America, then Europe, then in Asia.

"And being the only human being left on earth, he did the only thing there was left for him to do—he put a gun to his head and blew his brains out."

"But surely," I said, "a few men and women must have been left somewhere—savages on tropical islands, perhaps, or Eskimos in the far north. It seems that someone would have escaped."

"I hoped so," Bell answered. "In fact I flew almost all over the world to find out. But not a soul was to be seen, and finally I went ahead in time, pausing every now and then till I had reached a million years. There was a sort of civilization of ants by that time. They had built houses and machinery and had learned the use of fire. But to me they didn't seem right. It was all dreary and lonesome with nothing but a tiny realm of ants. Nearly all the large animals had been killed too, you see.

"But I kept on until the year when the moon fell; I don't know how many millions of years that was. I had lost track, but it must have been a hundred or two hundred, I think, at least.

"I kept hoping that men might show up, but they never did, and the ants were too small to evolve very far. Their size wasn't large enough according to earth. They finally built little ships and flyers capable of crossing the oceans, but to do that took them an awfully long time. I don't suppose they ever realized there were other worlds in the sky or tried to reach them.

"I don't know, though. I left when the moon fell. That was a sight to watch! It happened on the night side of the planet. At first it seemed to be growing larger and larger; then there was a roaring in the air like an enormous steam whistle coming closer. Just before it struck I jumped ahead a day in time so the concussion wouldn't hurt me or affect my ship.

"Great cracks had opened in the earth, I found when I looked. The days were made much longer. But the ants went on as ever. A few of them were killed, naturally; but as a race they were too strong in proportion to their weight for the jar to have much effect."

"God," I broke in, overwhelmed for the moment. "If I had found things like that, I would have taken the same way out that last man did!"

"You mean Lark? I came close to it. Watching the horrors of the latter part of the twenty-first century was enough to make anybody sick of his race and of living. But you see, I had the means and the urge to see what came of it. By the time I'd left it all behind about a million years I was thinking of something else.

"It was this way—" Bell stopped, pausing indecisively a moment or two. "Now," he began, "comes the really hard part. But it's beyond me. All I can do is tell it as it occurred.

"As I said, I got to thinking. I had seen it all happen. I had been right there. I knew that I could have an effect on the future because my time machine was powered by an atomic motor, and I moved in common, ordinary space by means of a twenty-first-century flyer. Also, I'd been eating food from animals and plants born long after I should have died a natural death.

"Finally I thought, 'Why couldn't I change it?' And the more I thought of it, the more I came to the conclusion that I could. The only trouble was that I didn't know where to begin.

"I came back to the time of the last war and watched it all carefully. After seeing it two or three times, I picked Lark as the most likely person.

"You see, I'd decided that the two dozen or so leaders who were left when everybody besides Lark had died might be able to remedy things. They were the best educated of the day, and while they were responsible for the thing, they had the best minds.

"I decided to act on the evening Lark had decided he'd blow them up the next day. I went to him right after he'd gone to sleep. You understand, I didn't want to take any chances with him, for I knew he was half insane and I didn't want to die until I saw what came of my decision, anyway.

"I found him sleeping in a ruined building. I didn't try to parley with him or talk him out of it; I shone a light into his face and said, 'Hands up!'

"He awoke with a start. He was so surprised to see a living man that he didn't know what to do, and by the time he realized what was going on, I had snapped two pairs of handcuffs on him—one pair on his wrists and another on his ankles. Then I bundled him into the time-traveller, where, after grunting a few times, he went back to sleep. I believe he was drunk anyway. The solitude was beginning to pall on him and he had to have some outlet.

"With this much accomplished, I went ahead a few days to see what would happen. Sure enough, as I had thought, the two dozen had sense enough to try to fix things up after they had wrecked them. They had all the resources of the world at their fingertips; and what's more, they had the knowledge of how to use those things properly. They didn't try to get together—each group kept a continent to itself and started in.

"It was too slow watching what they did. When I saw that they were headed right, I jumped ahead a hundred years. There were a number of people by that time, comparatively, and all were working toward real civilization. In a thousand years they were ahead of any point their ancestors had ever reached, and there hadn't been any more wars.

"They had all the machines they needed to begin with, so they started in for mental progress and they accomplished it. Utopia didn't come at once, but everybody was at the same social level, and that was all that was needed for them to start pushing out toward the stars."

"But what became of Lark?" I wanted to know.

"He hadn't wakened up even then. I had seen all this, you know, in a few hours, according to my own figuring. I didn't want to keep him with me, so I finally unfastened his handcuffs and dumped him off about five hundred years after I took him on. I still had his welfare in mind, though, so I went ahead ten years to see how he was making out.

"As I said, he was a decent sort. By the time he'd sobered up and found that he hadn't gone crazy, he started out to make himself useful. When I looked him up in ten years, I found him a progressive citizen; in fifty more he died an honoured death. By any measure he was quite an old man by that time, and they remembered him several generations."

★

I had lighted a cigar, but it was cold and forgotten between my teeth by now. The tale was so full of paradoxes that I could make neither head nor tail of it. "But how could it happen like that?" I objected. "You just said a few moments ago that Lark and everybody died before 2200; now you tell how Lark passed out again and was remembered by those who followed him in what must have been 2600 or 2700."

"That's where the difficulty comes in; they had all been dead. You see, *I* changed the world." Bell spoke as nonchalantly as a god in his well modulated, though somewhat jerky speech. "Everybody who has ever lived has changed things somewhat. Think how much Christ did, or Mohammed, or for that matter, Alexander and Caesar. You, too, have, around here. Think how different things would have been if you had died when you were three years old."

When I thought of how the papers howled at what they called my "radical changes" the year I was elected coroner, I was forced to admit that Bell was right. "It's so," I said. "But all this *has* happened; it couldn't be any different."

"So you think," Bell said. "But chew on this: I was in a world of no-humans a hundred million years after the last man died. I saw the moon fall. Everything up to then had happened as I saw it happen; but I went back and changed it, and all history turned out another way."

He chuckled. "Naturally I was all balled up. Here two different histories had unfolded beneath my eyes, and both were real. Now anybody I ask will say the future *can* happen, or *may, or will* happen in numberless ways. But it didn't seem so to me, since I had proven to myself that it would happen one way; then I proceeded to strike it all out, and the first way I had seen wasn't it at all.

"The only answer I could see was that *time itself* must be happening in a higher dimension, and that nothing was so sure that it couldn't be changed—or ever has been so sure. That was the way I theorized it, but still it didn't make sense.

"Nevertheless, people were coming along wonderfully, now that I had stopped Lark's little episode. I thought that if things went on as they should, I could see a really advanced people in a hundred thousand years. I went ahead to see what they could do for me.

"When I stopped my time machine, I found everything beyond my small comprehension. As you know, the only civilizations of men that I had come in contact with were no further advanced than a hundred or a thousand years beyond my time. Naturally, there were things now, a hundred thousand years later, that I couldn't even begin to understand. It was like bringing one of our tree-dwelling ancestors out of the fern forests and showing him our twentieth century civilization.

"Don't ask me to give in details what I saw; I can't. People all lived in the grassy country. There wasn't a sign, usually, of anything Mother Nature herself hadn't provided, yet when those folks wanted a machine or a piece of apparatus, they had it. Maybe they could think such things into existence. Or again, maybe they kept such things somewhere beyond time and brought them out as they chose to. I know they understood dimensions in a way I never will because I haven't sufficient brain power.

"They knew I was coming to see them, and a man was ready to meet me when I materialized. He was taller than I"—Bell stood over six feet—"and he was built like Apollo. His head was like what the gods must have. Honestly, he seemed almost a deity to me. It made me feel proud too, since if it hadn't been for my help, he and his kind never would have existed.

"His face was ultra-human. He looked at me in a benign sort of way, as though he understood everything which ever had been or might ever be.

"'So you have come, James Bell,' was all he said. He didn't speak in English; I'm not sure he even talked, but I understood, nevertheless.

"I was expecting to be greeted as saviour of the race, but when nothing of the sort happened, I wasn't surprised. I don't suppose I'll ever be surprised at anything from now on.

"'Yes, I have come,' I replied.

"'And you wish to understand time?' He came to the point at once.

"'I do,' I said.

"With that he began an explanation, but right away he saw that it wouldn't work. Even though I'd invented the time-traveller, I still didn't have the brains to comprehend what he wanted to tell me. As I've said, I only hit upon the machine by accident.

"The man's massive brow furrowed a little. 'Come,' he said after a moment of thought. 'We shall go back.' With that he led the way to my time-traveller.

"He ran the ship. It was he who knew where we were going, and he understood time much better than I did. My time-traveller accelerated very smoothly in his hands, and he kept going faster until everything was a blur. He left the lever far over for a long time. I knew we were going back almost to the end of the world.

"When we stopped, the sun was a steaming red ball, huge in a cloudy sky. The mountains were all sheer peaks, the tides five times that of the highest today. The forests were only gigantic ferns.

"My companion—I call him that, since I never learned his name— seemed to know what he was doing. He guided the ship over a range of mountains and down into a little bowl-shaped valley almost completely surrounded by mile-high crags. There were a few trees here and a little stream flowing among them between sandy banks. We stopped on the sand right before an egg-shell from which a reptile-thing had just hatched. It was four-legged and scaly and crawled around blinking its eyes. It wasn't all lizard and was one of the most ugly things I had ever seen.

"'Kill it,' the man said and handed me—wonder of wonders—a revolver. Where he got it from is another mystery.

"He had engendered such a feeling of respect in me, I believe, that if he had told me to shoot myself I would have done so. I took the revolver and killed the thing—shot it in the head.

"'Now we will go forward in time,' my companion said.

"Again he accelerated the ship, and we shot ahead a few million years—to about a period analogous with the building of the great pyramid, I think.

"But when we stopped, there weren't any pyramids; there weren't any men. The whole world was inhabited only by reptiles.

"For, you see, I had killed the thing that was a direct ancestor of the first mammal; and it happened that no other animal like it developed after that.

"With one bullet, I killed my companion and myself, killed all men, even all warm-blooded animals, in fact. I killed all such things that would ever live—had ever lived, really, for I'm alive, and you're alive, and right then I was in the company of a man who should normally have lived a hundred thousand years after I died.

"'See what you have done?' he said with a laugh. Then knowing that I was utterly in the dark, he explained. 'But it has all been—this world, your world, the world of the ants, my world. They all exist in the absolute time of the Cosmos, and the possibilities of what have been or what may be are manifold, like tree branches—one moves along one limb and thinks it is the tree; but when he proceeds to another, lo, it is all different.'

"Still, though, its reality was beyond me. True. I could get an inkling of it, but the whole was too wonderful. If I had gone ahead millions of years instead of hundreds of thousands for my explanation, I might have run onto beings capable of making me understand.

"But I hadn't; and though my companion seemed god-like, his brain was only greater than mine by degrees. He understood time and such things in a way I never could, yet there were lots of things in his scheme of the absolute as far beyond him as death is beyond me. There were all sorts of theories around him whose meaning he couldn't grasp. For that matter, however far a creature may develop, whatever he may learn, his knowledge only shows him a multitude of other things to turn his attention to...

"For awhile we explored the world of the reptile races. We went ahead for ages, until the sun was growing cold, in fact. And"—here Bell's voice lowered a note—"in that world the moon never did fall; it just broke into pieces which formed rings around the earth like those around Saturn.

"Before the end there was a race of reptiles nearly as far advanced as the man with me. When there wasn't enough solar heat coming in to make Earth habitable, they migrated to the planets circling some other star, and that was the last we ever saw of them. My companion and I never did show ourselves, however. As with the ant-world, there was something about their civilization which made me homesick. I didn't want to have anything to do with them—nor, for that matter, did the man with me. There are a few ways in which people will never change, I think, not so long as the *genus homo* remain in human form. I'm speaking of *our* world-line now...

"Finally we went back to where the reptile-thing was hatching on the sands in the earth's childhood. There we waited for about a minute, then my time machine appeared in front of us.

"It's a fact! Though the future-man and I were standing together inside the transparent walls of the traveller, he and I and it all appeared in front of ourselves. I saw; it was like looking at the moving picture of one's self, though much weirder.

"My friend gave the other me the revolver. We were too far away to hear what we said, but the actions were all plain. The other me stepped out to shoot our ancestor.

"'Now stop yourself,' the man told me.

"So, as though I were used to doing this every day, I walked over to my other self and said, 'Don't do it this time.' I took the revolver. I suppose the other Bell was too dumfounded to do more than gape as I threw it into the stream. After that my companion and I went off in the time-machine leaving ourselves by our traveller on the sand. I've often wondered what might have happened had we all got into the same machine and left the other one that was still it on the edge of that little stream...

"Now things were as they had been before, since our ancestor lived and thrived. We passed the place where I had kidnapped Lark, and since I did nothing to stop that action, we went on to the era of my companion.

"I was beginning to see something besides black in the ink by now. All I can say, however, is that the world has innumerable dimensions in the Cosmos, and that each one of those dimensions seems very different to us who see only three dimensional cross-cuts of them at a time. *We* and our world are like things seen by some one dimensional being. What, for instance, could such a creature make of an automobile, being able to see no more than a line along its surface. That's how we look at infinity.

"I live, and yet I've seen the world which is this planet peopled by nothing besides races of reptiles, a world into which I couldn't possibly be born. And probably somewhere—in the Cosmos—there is a *me*, a James Bell who never invented a time-machine, but lived a normal twentieth-century life as the other men around him did. However, I know nothing of that, since at present—in absolute time—the ego-which-I-am inhabits the body of the Bell who did travel into time.

"But that there are other Bell-egos, I know. For instance, there was the me I took the revolver from. Both men were Bell, yet in my consciousness there is no memory of that incident when the gun was taken away from me. And as to what that Bell did after that, I have no idea.

"Very probably there is a you, John, who has travelled in time with me, whether you ever do in this consciousness of yourself or not. And as far as that goes, there may have been a planet Earth which fell into the sun ere it cooled, or was stolen by a passing star.

"Well, this absolute theory of time-travelling, which must be the right one, takes away certain of the paradoxes which have baffled imaginative people. Still, you can't really understand it. But there will always be things like that, no matter what we know.

"But if one follows that thought out, he can come to almost any conclusion.

"That's nearly all of the story. After I took my companion back to his age, I returned here. However, I first overshot the mark a hundred years, so I stopped in at a mansion and acquired exactly seven bottles of beverage like you drank tonight. Perhaps the episode has gone down in history as an unsolved wine mystery.

"I returned here because I wanted a space in which to think it all out before I go gazing into infinity again. When I do go back, I believe I shall penetrate into the future until I meet beings who are capable of teaching me the real reasons behind some of my questions. There must be such entities somewhere, if they will let me find them.

"I did have an idea to get together a band of future-men and go back to make past ages more liveable. Terrible things have happened in history, you know.

"But it isn't any use. Think, for instance, of the martyrs and the things they suffered. I could go back and save them those wrongs. And yet all the time, somewhere in absoluteness, they would still have known their unhappiness and their agony, because, in this world-line, those things have happened.

"At the end, it's all unchangeable; it merely unrolls before us."

Bell stopped here; and at that moment, the summons came that dinner was served. I believe that neither of us spoke during the meal.

After we had finished, he asked, "Do you want to see my time-machine?"

I had been thinking it over, and my mind was made up. "No," I told him. "Like you did, I want a space in which to think it all over. As it is, I only have what you told me on the subject, no real proof. If you showed me such a machine, then I would know that part of your story, at least, was fact; and that would be the end of my peace. Or if there is no such machine, it would destroy the wonderful illusion you created."

"But I'm going into the future again," Bell said, "perhaps tonight."

"All right," I returned, "go. Maybe it would be better if you didn't come back to me, for I have a wife and a family and a life here which should be lived. I couldn't ever attend to such mundane things again if I saw happenings such as you relate."

I laughed. "Here I am speaking as though I were sure every word you had spoken were gospel fact. I'm making a fool of myself."

I glanced at my watch. "Well, Bell, I must be going. Thanks for the amusement I received from listening to your little piece of fiction. Let me see you again some time. Drop in and see us all, soon."

"I understand," my friend said as I was putting on my coat. "I believe I shall come back for you."

He was holding open the door for me when he spoke again.

"Yes, I'll be back for you," he said again. "That is, unless I succeed in doing what I hope to. Maybe after that, I won't be able to—or I will see a reason not to. Do you see what I mean?"

"I don't know," I said as the door closed behind me.

THE REIGN OF THE REPTILES

Alan Connell

Alan Connell (1916–2001?) was born in Australia of British parents and was clearly a precocious child, entering and sometimes winning various competitions in newspapers. These included the poem "In 3028" in the Sydney Sun *for 11 November 1928, when he was twelve. After toying with the idea of being a cow-hand, Connell instead bought a typewriter and was soon writing letters to his favourite magazine,* Amazing Stories, *in America, complaining about how difficult it was to find any issues in Sydney. The following story was his first professional sale, published in* Wonder Stories *in 1935. It explored one of Connell's special interests— evolution. The scientific understanding of Darwin's theory of evolution had suffered a setback when the Butler Act came into force in Tennessee in March 1925. It forbid the teaching of the evolution of mankind and of denying the Biblical account of creation. It was under this act that the notorious Scopes Trial took place in July 1925 where John Scopes was found guilty of teaching evolution and fined $100. The author George Allan England was horrified at this and wrote to Hugo Gernsback, the editor of* Amazing Stories, *urging Gernsback to promote and explore evolution in his magazine. Evolution had already featured in science fiction, most notably in H. G. Wells's* The Time Machine *(1895) and Edgar Rice Burroughs also explored it in* The Land That Time Forgot *(1918) which Gernsback reprinted in* Amazing Stories *in 1927. Burroughs proposed that humans had evolved by a process of graduation, with tribesmen moving from one form of evolution to a higher one elsewhere, a* *suggestion that Gernsback noted "taxes our credulity". Edmond Hamilton confronted evolution in "The Man Who Evolved" which Gernsback published in 1931, commenting that "there is no more fascinating subject of speculation" than how humans evolved. Alan Connell decided to bring together the opposing religious and scientific views and suggest a third, more explosive answer in this story.*

During the War Connell worked on aircraft assembly and served briefly as a steward on commercial liners in the early 1950s, before returning to the aircraft business. The Butler Act remained in force until 1967!

K ANE STOOD UP AND STARED AT ME HEATEDLY. "THERE ARE a hundred different things," he said, "that go to prove the theory of man's evolution from lower forms of life. I don't see why you shut your eyes to them and insist that our ancestors were created instantaneously out of nothing."

"I'm satisfied," I said. "I'll stick to religion; you can have science."

"Religion?" said Kane. "In twenty years—"

"Why can't we have them both?" I interrupted him, and quoted:

> "'A Fire Mist and a planet,
> A crystal and a shell,
> A jelly fish and a saurian
> And caves where the cave men dwell;
> Then a sense of law and beauty,
> And a face turned from the clod—
> Some call it Evolution,
> And others call it God.'"*

"Oh, shut up!" said Kane, with customary disrespect for poetry— especially when called upon to support arguments. He got up, went from the room; I heard him tramp down the stairs, slam the front door after him, and I smiled.

Kane Sanders is related to me in some indistinct way, and I first met him when he wrote asking me whether I could give him work. I invited him to come and see me. I liked him then—and

---

* William Herbert Carruth.

have grown to like him even more—and he stayed to look after the business side of my life—which is far from complicated, involving, as it does, a mere disinterested correspondence with the fed-up publishers of my short stories. Fed-up because, through other interests forcing themselves on me, my material has deteriorated from common poorness to something unmentionable.

During my two-year association with Sanders, I discovered only one flaw—and it was of little consequence—in a very pleasant personality; he was too fond of arguments. Since I am a victim of the same fault, and it became habit and tradition to oppose him, things might have been disagreeable if one of us hadn't always been able to see the humour of the thing before it went very far.

On this night I paid little attention to Sanders' departure. He would, I thought, be now walking morosely down the road to the beach; and he would return in his usual high spirits before very long.

I was right on the first score, but wrong on the second.

Some time in the early morning I awoke and remembered that I had not heard Sanders come in. I got up and went along the passage to his room. Just as I opened the door, I heard the click of another door downstairs. I waited, and presently a man came up the stairs. At first I did not recognize him; the clothes were tight on his broad frame, the shoes were laceless; then I saw that it was Sanders.

A stubble of crudely-removed hair grew on his chin and cheeks. I think it was this that struck me as most fantastic at the time— Sanders had left me not many hours before, perfectly shaved; now his face was covered with traces of recently removed black bristle!

There were other incredible things; he was browner than I had ever seen him before; always big-limbed, he was now superhumanly developed; and his hair, I saw when he came closer, was longer than it had ever been before.

He greeted me with a faint smile, took my arm and drew me into his room. When he switched on the light, the half-seen details of his transformation stood out starkly. I had an experience I never hope to have again; I felt the blood running out of my cheeks, felt my face go dead white.

Sanders looked at me with strange eyes. "You remember our arguments about evolution and God?"

I nodded.

"I have an awful kind of suspicion that we were *both* wrong," he said. "Did you know," he went on abruptly, "that there was a time millions of years ago when reptiles ruled land, sea, and air?"

Without waiting for me to answer, he took something from his pocket and unrolled brown paper from it.

Stark in the white light was a black, scaled; five-fingered thing, loathsomely suggestive of the reptilian. It had been severed smoothly at the wrist, and in the bent clutch of the wrinkled fingers was the dim reminiscence of some nameless threat.

Fantastically, too, about each of those members was a blue-jewelled ring!

"Fulu, emissary of Luad," said Sanders, half to himself. "I wonder what he thinks now!"

"Kane!" I said. "What—"

He thrust away the black claw. "Sorry," he said. "Listen and I'll tell you." He hesitated and said fretfully: "These clothes are choking me." Then he took off coat and shirt and sat on the bed with knees drawn up in an odd squatting position; and while I stared dumbly at the leathery brown of his chest, he told me what follows.

CHAPTER II

A Human Guinea-Pig

When he left the house, Sanders wandered down the track to the
road with the idea of walking to Salabec, but dusk fell and he stood
hesitating on the concrete. He heard the sound of a car and saw its
headlights come around the bend. He stepped aside to let it pass, but
it halted, crept slowly forward, and stopped again like a man in doubt.

Presently someone got out and came around to stand between
the headlamps. Sanders felt a man's keen eyes staring at him, and
he turned away, flushed and ill at ease. But a voice stopped him.
"Just a moment—do you mind?"

Sanders said: "Well?" and faced the man. He was short, fragile-
framed, and loosely dressed, and his grey hair was untidy above
a white face. His bright eyes studied Sanders from head to foot,
and sensing the young man's discomfort, he said: "Your pardon. I
was looking for a man."

"Why?" asked Sanders. "Is something wrong with your car?"

"Why—yes! My car—"

"Then I'm sorry," Sanders said. "I can't—"

"I'm sure it's something insignificant," the other interrupted.
"I'd like you to look."

In the face of this point-blank request, Sanders went to the
man's side as the latter lifted the cover from the engine.

"There—I think the trouble's there," said the man, indicating
the ignition. "I'll hold this torch while you look."

Later Sanders was able to see humour in his acting as this man's
mechanic—this man who probably knew more about machinery,
from the simplest system of pulleys to the most complex electrical
apparatus, than anyone else in the world.

For several minutes he fumbled in the yellow light, then straightened. "I can't see anything," he began—and stopped.

There was a peculiar tenseness about the stranger's face, and involuntarily Sanders' eyes went to the back of the car where there were two dim faces. He was conscious of dwelling in a strange atmosphere and his lips formed a question. Then something whipped up from the darkness and smothered his face. He choked and began to fall.

For a time that he could not estimate, a heavy greyness lay about him, then suddenly fell away. For a while he stayed quiet, then opened his eyes. He was lying on the bed of a plainly furnished room. Three men stood over him. One was the man from the car; the second he judged to be a Japanese; the third was a thin, fair youth, whose eyes held something greater than mere genius.

During an unembarrassed silence, the three stared down at him; then the first man said to the other two: "All right. Go and get everything ready. I'll talk to him."

As the two left the room, Sanders made an effort to get up—a vain one, for he was handcuffed to the bed. "Let me up!" he demanded. "What—"

The man held up a hand. "There's not much time to waste. Listen—my companions and I are what you might call experimental scientists. Tonight we were driving to Salabec in search of a man for one of our—experiments. I saw you; I knew you were the type I wanted, so I took you. Do this thing willingly and we'll pay you well, otherwise—"

"You can go and be damned," said Sanders, heaving on the bed.

"I thought you wouldn't. But we'll use you just the same. Now listen even more carefully.

"Juan, the young fellow, is an abnormal. You've heard, I suppose, of mathematical geniuses and people with fantastic memory powers. Juan, too, is frankly a freak intelligence; his brain really belongs hundreds of years in the future. I don't think he has ever read any technical work on higher mathematics, but by sheer power of reasoning, he knows more than all the mathematical giants of the world put together.

"Takashai and I discovered him. We attached ourselves to him because we realized his possibilities and because—to be frank—we want a share in the fame that must inevitably come to him. Juan as yet doesn't worry about making money, so when we began to develop his talents he insisted that our first work of importance be the contriving of an apparatus for transporting objects along time-lines, so that he can confirm certain monstrous theories he has formed from studying palæontological data. Under Juan's supervision, Takashai and I have built that apparatus; already we've tested it on bricks and guinea-pigs—transported them along artificial time-lines to both past and future; and now Juan is impatient to settle his horrible ideas on the origin of Man. He'd go himself, I believe, if his presence were not needed at the apparatus…"

Handcuffed to the bed, reflecting on the oddities of fate that had thrown him among these madmen, Kane Sanders looked straight at the man and said: "You're mad."

His captor bent over him. "I am not mad," he said distinctly. "I ask you, what would a man of the year 100 A. D. think of our present-day science? Wouldn't it be plain magic? And you and I are just the same when confronted with Juan's plans and ideas—for I'm as much a child as you are when Juan speaks. His thought-processes are almost unimaginable…"

The Japanese came into the room. "Everything is ready, Carlyle," he said, "and Juan is impatient."

Carlyle produced a heavily-scented pad and pressed it to Sanders' nostrils, leaving him in an unresisting half-stupor.

"I'm sorry to do this," Carlyle said, "but it's necessary, since I can't convince you that we are only over-zealous scientists."

Sanders was carried into a brilliantly lighted chamber and placed on a metal table. Half-dazed, he looked about him. He felt a shock of doubt. Across the ceiling a giant power cable was slung in drooping loops; in far corners crouched green, polished machines, oddly vital; near at hand, circling him, were bright complexities of copper wire and giant silvered tubes. If the men were mad, Sanders thought, then their madness had followed strange paths...

He felt hands at his waist; a belt was fastened about him. "Water, food, an automatic, and ammunition," Carlyle explained, then went to help Takashai with the machines in the corner. As Juan, silent and aloof, took his place before a keyboard that seemed the vital part of the whole mechanism, Carlyle returned.

"When you next open your eyes," he said, "you will be some-where about the close of the Mesozoic, the great age of the reptiles, some millions of years in the past. But I warn you, don't be afraid. Remember, you are armed—and there is Juan, who will draw you back when he thinks you have had time to examine the conditions."

Juan turned, hesitated, and said doubtfully: "I would like you to notice what life there is."

"Yes," said Carlyle, and he pressed Sanders' hand. "I think I'm insane to force this on you," he went on, "but I can't help myself." He drew back.

The machines in the corners took on a sudden devil-scream; there was strange light through which the room reeled in grotesque colours; the sensation came to Sanders that hundreds of little demons were plucking his body into millions of particles and scattering them far and wide...

CHAPTER III

The Room of Horror

Sanders fell jarringly on one shoulder.

His eyes went swiftly around a vast gloomy room. Through the half-ovals of windows far to his left, white moonlight poured.

He did not know where he was; it did not occur to him that Carlyle's fantastic predictions might be fulfilled, and he wondered where his three captors had gone.

He went to one of the windows, which were glassless, and as he gazed out, the first terrifying doubt came. Below him was a dim expanse of sloping roof, then a period of darkness, then a wall of impregnable thickness that rose sharply, shutting out jungle growth of such unbridled magnificence and gigantic size as he had never imagined could exist. Somehow allied with ferns, but incredibly bigger, they reached their plumes hundreds of feet into the night sky, looming high above the building in which he stood until they seemed to touch the moon. It was a strange moon, big and tinted with green—but its peculiarities were negligible before the chilling terror of the gargantuan forest—chilling despite the warm, tropical breeze that blew in his face.

As he turned from the window, Sanders heard an unnatural screaming emanating from the dark forest, and a roaring and bellowing. He hurried back across the room, blundered into something that rocked unsteadily, and with eyes rapidly becoming accustomed to the half-light, he stared at it. He saw that it

was a glass globe supported on flimsy legs—and in it was a great
wet thing, soft and shapeless, that stirred stupidly. From it came
a nightmarish sucking and squeezing as it heaved itself up and
down...

With a terror that was silent but none the less real, Sanders went
back and forth across the horrid chamber; and each step brought
a new ghastly sight imprisoned in a transparent vessel—luminous
eyes sunk in white membranous bags of skin—eyes that followed
with insensate intentness his every move; things that swam like
butterflies in amber liquid; jelly-like, pulsing things; mutilated
forms floating lifeless in the fluids of their containers. And there
were tables loaded with instruments and shapes he dared not
look at. There was death unspeakable and life madder than the
weirdest dream.

Sunk into one of the walls was a shelf of vessels filled with
strange-smelling chemicals, and as he felt his way along this, he
thought he heard a shuffling sound in other regions of the building, and he groped forward with new speed until he touched what
resembled the bars of a cage. He looked between the bars and at
the sight of the thing that leered at him from within—a swaying,
ape-like creature with pouting lips, sightless eyes, and mutilated
limbs—he involuntarily voiced a hoarse cry.

Almost simultaneously, it seemed to him that the far-away
shuffling took on a quicker and more definite rhythm; and with
an overwhelming instinct to hide, he sank beneath the shadow
of a bench.

For minutes he crouched there, listening to the shuffle and
scrape of the nameless feet as they hastened to their hiding place.
Instinctively he knew that whatever inhuman thing owned this

room of horror was coming to investigate the sounds he had made; and again, in spite of the tropical warmth of the night, he felt cold.

Now the wall farthest from him grew faintly luminous, and soon he made out the outlines of a high, oval-topped doorway, between which, deep in the darkness beyond, a spot of light hopped up and down. Nearer it came, reached the portal, hovered there a moment, and entered the room, shedding a glow of flat white light about it. And now it revealed itself as a transparent sphere filled with some phosphorescent substance; on two sides of its surface were black blurs.

It came closer to Sanders.

He felt the beat of blood at his temples—

The globe was held by a creature like a mythical devil incarnate! Its oily green, needle-fanged head hovered just above the luminous sphere, the hellish red eyes darting from side to side in search of the intruder; and where the shoulders should have been were hunched lumps that made the man think of folded wings. The body and shuffling feet were invisible; the claws appeared in silhouette on the surface of the globe that the monstrosity held before it.

Back and forth like an embodied demon it roamed, thrusting its long, hideous snout suspiciously into corners, pausing to hold its strange lantern beneath benches, and even stopping to peer from the windows as though it suspected someone of having made a hasty exit. But incredibly good fortune was with Sanders, for the devil-thing, though it hesitated near him, eventually passed him by and, satisfied that nothing was amiss, betook itself and its luminary from the chamber and shuffled along the corridor.

Many minutes later Sanders stirred, rose to his feet, and groped to the doorway. In the corridors beyond he soon found himself lost, and in the unrelieved darkness he fumbled and felt as though through a maze, all sense of direction gone. At odd times sounds from other quarters of the building stopped him like an animal at bay, but mostly all was still.

At length, with dying hope and in utter dejection, he sat down with his back to the wall and stared at the dark until his eyes grew heavy.

CHAPTER IV
In the Corridors

He awakened suddenly to daylight and got stiffly to his feet. Before and behind him a corridor reached. It was coloured vividly and grotesquely, and in merging hues which changed so subtly that he could not detect the exact spot of transition.

Sleep had been like a stimulant and clarifier to Kane Sanders. He knew now that all this was neither dream nor imagination—there was no more doubt—Juan's almost magical apparatus had thrown him back across ages of time to a prehistoric past. And recognition of this, without the horror of the night, gave him immeasurable relief and a kind of growing courage to win his way through this new existence. He had brains and strength, and at his hip was a weapon. Behind all that was the everlasting promise that Juan would again bridge the time-gulf and draw him back to reality.

He drank some water and ate a little of the concentrated food at his belt; and before he had finished, he heard a hissing and soughing like the beat of wings. Far along the corridor he saw an approaching shape. Caution uppermost, he ran in the opposite direction until he reached an oblong of curtain cleverly set in the wall. He pushed through it, nor was he too soon, for a moment later a creature soared past him. A little it resembled a gigantic lizard, and the fanged snout, if not the same one, was at least practically identical with the one Sanders had seen in the room of horror. Only now it had lost its supernatural and diabolical aspect, appearing still hideous but only in a reptilian, scaled way. It propelled itself on hissing, leathery wings, and its sinuous body was clad in a blue, silken robe. About its ugly brow was a jewelled diadem; its claws were alight with jewels.

Alive now to the dangers of the main corridors, Sanders made his way along the side passage which the curtain had hidden. He came to another curtained doorway, hesitated, then tentatively parted it.

The room beyond the draping was as fantastically hued as the corridors. From the ceiling, suspended on golden chains, hung a number of canoe-shaped couches, and in each of these sprawled a hideous monster like the flying lizard of the corridor, but these were smaller and evidently females. Their faces were repulsive, with flat, tooth-rimmed snouts and little red eyes, but in their claws they held polished metal plates in which they constantly admired their frightful images. They were garbed in cloths swathed tightly about them and on their smooth skulls were set turbans or headdresses.

Grouped about these monstrosities were smaller, abject creatures of another reptilian species—but these were unclothed and evidently slaves. They held urns from which they sprayed their mistresses with jets of perfume.

Presently one of the monsters in the swinging couches elevated herself and began what seemed like a song—though its compound of garbled hissing and screamings bore no likeness to any music

Sanders had ever heard. At the song's conclusion, the slaves flapped their atrophied wings in applause, and another monster took up the tune. Sanders turned away. And as he did so, his foot caught in the curtain, strained it taut, and released it fluttering.

He stood frozen. There was something ominous—

The singing had stopped!

He parted the curtain and saw that each of the lizard-creatures was staring at him.

As he ran, he heard a shrill shrieking and the flutter of ungainly wings, and intent on escape, he passed back to the main corridor and fled along it. Before long he knew that he was being pursued, and ran even faster amid the clatter of his heavy-soled boots. This last proved his undoing, for one of the flying lizards, attracted by the noise, soared from a side passage and threw itself upon him before he could reach the revolver at his belt. Boney claws dug into his arms and held him immovable until three more monsters arrived.

One, who wore a jewelled circlet about his brow, muttered some shrill words. Sanders stood quiescent, aloof, lips firm. The monster repeated the words, then fastened its crimson eyes on him and gave him his first glimpse of the uncanny power of thought transference possessed by these creatures.

Two questions built gradually up in his mind: "How did you escape? Why did you disobey?"

Sanders did not attempt to answer.

By what seemed like endless mental repetition, another question was forced on him: "To whom do you belong?"

Again Sanders was silent. He watched his questioner dismiss his fellows, then, with both arms tightly held, he was lifted and carried swiftly beneath the clacking wings of his captor, through great lengths of coloured corridor, until they alighted in a room.

It was the room of his ghastly experience of the night before—the room that he was to know as the creative laboratory of the reptile scientists of Luada.

CHAPTER V

The Mystery of the Pit

In the yellow light of day, the room had lost much of its horror, but still there was a breath of unholy mystery in its lizard-like inhabitants as they bent with shining knives over bizarre distortions of human bodies that were stretched on tables before them. Blood trickled from those tables and down into the little gutters that carried it to the brownstained drains in the floor.

On the walls hung parchments inscribed with anatomical cross-sections, some of which suggested vague oddities of inner structures to Sanders...

At the entry of captor and captive, the monsters looked up from their work and stared at Sanders. Again he was aware of the mental question: "Why did you disobey," and then, "To whom do you belong?"

When there was no answer, one of the creatures gave an order. The one who held Sanders gave a garbled reply, then thrust its claws into his clothing and ripped every thread from him, even bending to tear off his shoes. The thing was done so quickly that Sanders' fingers could not reach the revolver before it was torn away with his belt.

As the man's clothing vanished, the reptiles pressed forward with hissing cries. Screeching with fanatical glee, they laid

possessive claws on him, and he caught a jumble of mental communication which they abruptly resorted to.

"A first-class specimen; he must be from my pit."

"No," interposed a second; "You have none as good as this. I
am certain he escaped from my pit."

"He belongs to neither of you," interrupted a third. "I was
working on a particularly good specimen. I feel sure that this is
the one."

Now a monster larger than the rest came forward and took
hold of Sanders. "None of you seems to know whom he belongs
to; therefore he shall go in my pit—where, in any case, he probably belongs."

Sanders was taken down the aisles of tables, past the loathsome
things in the glass vessels, and to a table near the end of the room,
where the lizard scientist opened a metal trap-door in the floor
and dropped him through the opening.

Sanders felt himself fall one or two feet, then he struck a
slide and rushed diagonally through the darkness. A spot of light
appeared ahead, swelled, and he was spilled into hot sunlight. His
prison was a roofless pit walled to a height of twenty feet on four
sides. Behind him, above a slope of lower roof, were the windows
of the laboratory. The far wall held back the gigantic fern forest
that towered green above it to the vivid sky in which burned the
brilliant sun.

Standing back a little, his face turned from the jungle, Sanders
could see the mingling of marble domes and granite turrets
that made up the great city-palace of the reptiles. This pit was
one of many walled squares projecting from the main body of
the palace.

★

Sanders was not the only prisoner. In scattered groups about him were creatures of both sexes and some that were doubtful. Almost without exception they were covered with ape-like hair and all who were not entirely naked wore only meagre strips of cloth. All were human in a disconcerting way, and a few (these were practically hairless and more sanely built) looked comparatively intelligent. Many of the creatures showed the marks of recent wounds, and Sanders could not avoid thinking of the shapes on the tables in the laboratory.

One of the men shouted some words at Sanders; they were oddly like the speech of the reptiles. Sanders did not attempt to answer, but leaned against the wall in a kind of detached wonder. He thought of those three men in the far reaches of Time, of Juan who was to draw him back across the unguessable centuries, and of Juan's quest. There was surely much material about this reptile city, if he could only plumb its significance—this strangely distorted condition where lizard monstrosities dominated a grotesque humanity.

Sanders smiled bitterly. Was it likely that he would ever have an opportunity to present such material to Juan? Wasn't it more logical to suppose that these four walls and the patch of tropic sky would be all he would ever see for the rest of his life?

The day faded into twilight. A number of the smaller reptilian slaves flew overhead erratically and dropped strips of flesh into the pit. Sanders chewed a little, reflecting that he might as well accustom himself to the fare.

That night he slept uneasily on the cold ground, dreaming repeatedly that all was normal again, only to awaken to the hopeless reality.

Sitting in the shade of a wall in the sultry heat of the next morning, to pass the time, he began to fashion a crude loincloth from the furry strips of skin left from the previous night's meal. While he was thus occupied, the man who had addressed him on his advent in the pit squatted before him and again spoke to him, this time at sufficient length to convince Sanders that the tongue was identical with that of the reptiles, though with a minimum of the hissing inflections.

Sanders looked at the heavy-browed squat fellow with a sense of superiority; then he smiled—he himself was more ignorant than a baby in this new world. He made himself open to friendship to Nu-Az, as the man named himself, by a gift of the meat that was dropped in the pit that morning; and the companionship was established which, through the days that followed, gave him an insight of the new language.

When the first glimmerings of coherency were built up, Sanders found he had paved the way to some puzzling questions.

"Who are you?" Nu-Az wanted to know. "You don't belong in this pit."

"I don't understand," Sanders answered. "I don't belong in any pit."

Nu-Az drew back suspiciously, and Sanders realized that he was setting about things in the wrong way. He went on, stumbling over the new tongue taught him, and now he employed subterfuge.

"I can't remember anything. I had a fall and hurt my head. Perhaps if you told me a little, everything would come back."

Nu-Az hesitated, then accepted the story.

"You are in the pit of Lo-Lo, greatest of the evolutionary scientists. You and all of us are the subjects of his experiments. Each of the scientists has a pit like this; and there are many scientists in Luada."

"What is Luada?" Sanders asked.

"Your injury was bad," said Nu-Az. "Luada is the palace and domain of Luad, emperor of the ruling reptiles. I have been told that there are other palaces and other emperors across the great seas and forests, but of these things I am not certain."

"Where do your people live?"

This question puzzled Nu-Az. "These are my people," he said, indicating the beast-creatures about him. "These and those in the other pits."

"But where do the others of your race live?" Sanders pressed— "the people from whom you were captured?"

"There are no others. I was never captured."

"You mean that the reptiles have killed them all?"

"There are no others," Nu-Az repeated patiently. "The reptiles reign everywhere. We of the pits are the only ones of the new race. There are none outside. You and I and the others of the new pits were made by the scientists."

Cold seemed to creep up Sanders' spine; there were vague stirrings of unholy theories in his mind, and he thought of the puzzling, vacant factors in the evolutionary tree built up by men of the twentieth century. A great fear of this ghastly mystery of the past came over him, and he dared not question any further. He looked across the pit at the colossal fern forest, at the shadowy green aisles of its inner depths.

"The jungle would be kinder to us than the reptiles," he said. "You and I could easily escape once we had scaled the wall."

Nu-Az was disturbed. "It is wrong to think of leaving the pits. The scientists have forbidden it. You know that we are to be their new slaves in place of the Zori, who cannot be had in sufficient numbers."

The Zori, thought Sanders, must be those smaller reptiles

who waited on the female Luadans. Evidently there were not enough of them to do all the cloth-spinning and food-gathering that the Luadans required, so there was to be a new race of slaves.

Sanders said: "Yes, it may be wrong to leave the pits—but that's what I'm going to do. Will you come?"

A longing look crept into Nu-Az's eyes. "I will come," he said. "But there is a young girl in the next pit whom I want. She must come with us."

They waited until nightfall, then Nu-Az climbed the wall. Sanders came more slowly, feeling precariously for the little crevices and protuberances; and when he was within reaching distance, Nu-Az leaned down and drew him up. They stood balanced on the top. The dark warmth of the forest stole about them, and they heard the stir of invisible bodies in its far reaches.

Nu-Az was uneasy and hesitant, but Sanders urged him on. They went along the wall a little way, then Nu-Az descended into the darkness of the next pit. Sanders watched. He heard movement, whispering voices, and on the jungle side of the wall there was a vast slithering sound that he could not define.

Nu-Az came back up the wall. At his side was a long-haired, black-browed female who clung to his arm in terror. She wore a strip of stiffening hide, which gave her a certain unconscious superiority over Nu-Az, who wore nothing.

The three crept farther along the wall to where a tangle of thick vines hung within easy reach. "Here we can climb," said Nu-Az. "We can climb to the tops of the trees and there be safe." He thrust the girl, and she grasped the creepers and began to climb agilely, though doubtfully. Nu-Az followed, then Sanders.

CHAPTER VI

The Primeval Jungle

They clambered higher and higher on the rubbery tendrils, and soon Sanders was envying the muscular energy of Nu-Az and the girl, who both climbed tirelessly and without effort. A hundred feet from the ground he had to loop his foot through a creeper and rest, and thereafter he repeated this at every fifty feet.

It was during these rests that he became aware to the full of the creeping, rustling life that seemed to fill this jungle. He saw nothing, but in the sliding and climbing of those invisible entities, he began to sense a greater peril than he had dreamed of. His ascent became faster.

The vines ended in a mat of parasitic upper growth that covered the tree-tops, and here he found Nu-Az and the girl lying on the vegetation with great leaves wrapped around them. He followed their example with the leaves, lay down in a yielding bed of creeper, and slept.

The next day and the ones that followed did not have much significance for Kane Sanders. He was aware that accompanied by Nu-Az and the girl Yzul, he wandered through the upper reaches of that gigantic semi-fern forest, eating peculiar nuts and fruits, drinking from little tree crevices where water gathered; but all this was just like an exotic nightmare—it was too far removed from reality to seriously impress itself upon him.

There were, of course, some things that left a terrific impression. Once he swung down from the upper foliage, climbing in microscopic smallness among the huge leaves and vines, and there below him he saw the ground and on it rolled two horned and armoured beasts in a shrieking death struggle. There was blood, and a hideous roaring, and an earthshaking thunder as the monsters fell over and over each other, crushing the lesser vegetation in a welter of flying green.

Sanders watched, dry-mouthed, until one of the brutes broke away, shook itself, and lumbered out of sight; then he began to climb slowly back to the safety of the upper foliage. He realized now that much of the story of the dawn ages was lost irretrievably to palæontologists of the twentieth century; he had seen many restorations of the prehistoric giants of this era, but none even approached in size the battling creatures he had just witnessed.

When he regained the tangled garden of the tree-tops, he found Yzul in a state of panic and Nu-Az clumsily trying to comfort her. "She says something"—he waved his hands in inadequate descriptive gestures—"chased her."

"Don't worry," said Sanders. "All the monsters are on the ground—this is the only safe part of the jungle."

But he was wrong. That night, as he lay in a natural hammock of leaves and creepers, he awakened suddenly to hear a rustling and sliding; and as he lay there staring at the darkness, an unimaginably huge cylindrical body swayed and heaved across his vision, and two green slant-eyes turned briefly to look at him. Then it was all gone.

The next morning Sanders made himself a rough spear—a tough, six-foot barb that he tore from one of the thorny ferns. He saw too that Yzul and Nu-Az were similarly armed. He no longer felt that the tree-tops were safe.

Towards mid-day he set off to hunt for a yellow berry that was his favourite food. His search took him down to the middle terraces where the berries grew—one of many parasites in this jungle—from crevices in the giant trunks of the ferns. He swung downward with the easy grace of a trapeze artist, slipping down the vines like a spider on a thread. Where the foliage was less tangled, he walked fearlessly across great natural bridges from tree to tree, careless of the green depths below. On one of these bridges he went down on hand and knee to reach down for the yellow berries, and as he crouched there, he felt the great bough vibrate; and looking up he saw the Thing writhing along the aerial path toward him.

It was a snake. But it was two hundred feet in length, and its vast heaving body was six feet thick.

For one instant Sanders stared at the polished coils driving toward him, then he turned and ran. A few dozen paces, a glance back at the sliding monster, and he saw the futility of trying to outpace it. He swerved to the edge of the bough, leaped into space, caught a bunch of creepers and slid down with feverish speed. He looked up. The head of the incredible serpent peered down from the branch above. For a moment, the slanted green eyes watched the escaping prey, then the great spade-shaped head drove downward with the speed of an arrow.

Sanders' feet had touched another bough, but there was a mossy growth on it that gave underfoot and threw him on his face. When he regained his feet, the head was almost upon him and further flight was useless. He had no fear of poisonous venom, for such a monster as this had no need of subsidiary weapons, but one snap of those gigantic jaws would cut his body into two distinct pieces. He snatched his spear from his belt, and as the head rushed upon him, he drove the point into one of the emerald eyes. Then in the brief instant as the monster recoiled, he threw himself from the branch.

For thirty feet he fell, then a matted mass of leaf and creeper caught him and held him. He lay still while a crashing turmoil raged overhead, moving not a muscle until that king of snakes ceased its frenzied lashing and raged away to another region of the forest.

There was quiet again. Sweating from heat and excitement, Sanders resumed his search for food, and when he had eaten, he hurried back to Nu-Az and Yzul and told them that all three must look for a new home.

They moved across the forest-top all the rest of that day and the whole of the next day, putting as much distance as they could between them and the haunts of the giant serpent, though Sanders began to think that flight was useless and had an uneasy conviction that they were surviving in this jungle by luck more than anything else.

Once during their long travels they passed the fringe of the prehistoric wilderness and saw the white breakers and far-reaching blue of an ocean or great lake. For almost an hour, Sanders stood on the limb of a giant tree staring out over the glittering waters as though any moment he expected some weird craft of this forgotten age to hove into the shore; but none came, and soon something of the loneliness of those uncharted waters began to seep into him, and he turned his back on the roaring breakers and hurried back to the companionship of Nu-Az and Yzul. The old bitterness against Juan returned and hope was dying. He felt now that he was doomed to spend the rest of his days in this immemorial world of the past, naked and forever flying from perils whose extent he could not even guess at...

He said to Nu-Az: "In the morning, we'll move on again."

Nu-Az agreed, but this wandering was not what he wanted. With Yzul always at his side, an idea of a place of permanency and stability was developing in him—the desire for a fixed shelter in a fixed locality.

Back across the forest leagues they ranged, dawn after dawn, night after night. Now Yzul began to complain about the restless, aimless roaming. "Stay with me one more day," said Sanders, who hated to part with his companions and found no less abhorrent the thought of settling down to watch their home-making. So they went on through the morning.

In the cool of the afternoon, he swung down to the lower terraces of the trees, and there he found something that froze him into keen-eyed stillness.

Plodding along a newly-beaten trail was a string of about twenty naked human beings, each bearing a woven basket filled with freshly-picked fruit. For an instant Sanders was in doubt, then he guessed that these hairy creatures were from the pits of Luada. And this was soon confirmed, for behind the basket-bearers came two of the ruling reptiles, wings folded, walking on ungainly feet. Each carried a long club, but it was evident that they relied less on force than on the ingrained obedience of their slaves to keep things in order.

From the party's heavily laden state, Sanders deduced that it was on its way back to Luada, so he swung on ahead of them. Presently he glimpsed a patch of granite through the dense green ahead, and his fears were realized. He had wandered right back to the city of the reptiles!

He climbed to the utmost height of the forest, crawled on to a projecting limb of fern, and looked down on the domed roofs of Luada. Even as he watched, a number of the reptile slaves appeared on a high balcony with a great quantity of meat. With pieces of this in their claws they flew over the pits of the scientists, dropping their burdens with piercing cries. It was feeding time.

One of the slaves flew close to Sanders and stared directly at him, so that he drew back and climbed away in search of Nu-Az.

He found him sprawling on a great leaf, basking in the sun, and swung lightly to his side.

"Luada is nearby," he said.

Nu-Az sprang to his feet; Yzul crept to her lord's side.

"We'd better move off again," Sanders counselled. "It wouldn't be safe to stay so close."

"Yes," agreed Nu-Az—then Yzul shrieked and pointed up.

Hovering above and a little behind them were three Luadans!

In a flash Sanders knew that the flying slave had seen him and informed its masters. "Down," he cried. "Down to the lower terraces!"

But it was too late. The reptiles alighted on the huge fern frond. One, robed with grotesque richness and heavily jewelled, stood forward.

"We have found you. But Luad is merciful, and though the penalty for disobedience has always been death, I, Fulu, am charged to tell you that you will not be punished if you return to Luada with me without resistance."

Sanders followed the garbled words with difficulty. "We're not going back."

"You will come," said Fulu, "and for your resistance you will warrant death." He signed to his companions. They darted forward with true reptile swiftness, seized Nu-Az and Yzul, and bore them struggling away in the direction of Luada.

Fulu advanced on Sanders. "Back," said the latter, and he began to retreat.

"Do not try to escape," Fulu commanded. "You are a strange specimen; you exhibit new traits of disobedience for which I cannot find an explanation; and I intend to have you thoroughly examined when I have you back in Luada. Come willingly. I do not want you killed. Look, the other two have been taken and are even now entering Luada—it is foolish for you to resist."

"I'm never going back," said Sanders.

"You shall!" Fulu cried, and sprang with wings and claws extended.

Two things were confusingly synchronized. Sanders saw the crimson-eyed lizard leap toward him; at the same instant he felt a dizziness and the air about him was tinted with blue, crackling sparks. He felt the claw of Fulu fasten about his wrist, then he lost consciousness.

He was lying stretched on a cold table. In his ears was the dying hum of great machinery, the fading of immense power. Bending over him were three faces—and suddenly he remembered and understood.

The faces were those of Carlyle, Juan, and Takashai.

And most concrete reminder of all that had happened—clutched about his arm was the severed claw of Fulu!

"You are back," said Takashai, "and the experiment is a success."

"Yes," Sanders said with a ghost of a smile. "A success."

CHAPTER VII

Man from Reptile

When Sanders finished his story, he thrust his hands into the pockets of his borrowed trousers and slipped his legs back to the floor.

"You don't believe me?" he asked.

I had been staring wide-eyed at him. "Of course," I protested. "Yes, of course. But there's so much—"

"Yes," he interrupted; "there's a lot unexplained—you want to ask questions. Well, go ahead."

I thought over the many things that were puzzling me, then decided to start at the beginning.

"You travelled in time?"

"Yes. Or better, time rates were altered for me. Juan told me something about it, and I'll try to give you what I can remember.

"Time is not a constant. Juan told me about a practical experiment performed about fifteen years ago, which definitely proves this. You may not know it, but the plain sodium atom is a better clock than you can buy in any shop; for, when its electrons are excited, it emits electro-magnetic waves at a frequency of something like 509½ millions of vibrations per second—and this is the same for any sodium atom, no matter what peculiarities of condition and surrounding it is subjected to.

"Now, there's lots of vaporized sodium in the chromosphere of the sun, and spectroscopic analysis of this shows that its atoms vibrate *at a slower rate* than the earth atom. In other words, time—as a measurement of physical change—passes more slowly on the sun.

"That then was Juan's basic principle; time is not a constant. Then he went further to discover what time really is a product of, and the ready solution was that the variation in solar-and earth-time can be accounted for by difference in mass. In other words, in the presence of a gravitational field greater than the earth's, time passes more slowly. Similarly you can conceive of time travelling faster on a midget world."

I said: "I still don't understand how Juan picked you out of a whole vast world of sea and jungle."

"Juan didn't pick me out—that part was practically automatic. You see, I and my clothes were the only foreign elements, the only things that didn't *belong*, at that particular world-point."

"How—" I began.

"Wait. Imagine Juan's laboratory. It is fifteen minutes after my departure into the Mesozoic. Juan is ready to bring about my return. He has calculated—from time and gravitational-potential relationships between earth and sun, and from the power of the gravity field he could create without collapsing space—that my journey to the past would occupy some three hours. But once having dispatched me, he is no longer concerned with that part of my trip. He chooses a point in the world-line—which is the path of a body through both space and time—a point a month in advance of the one he sent me to. Then he creates two more gravitational fields and projects the inner one to that point.

"There it contacted with me, and within its deadening influence, time passed slowly, while outside, as it were, whole centuries of earth-time rolled by, ultimately reaching 1935 and Juan's laboratory. If I had been conscious and watching a clock, it would have been only four hours journey to me."

"Four?" I asked. "Why not three, the same as before?"

"That had Juan puzzled a little. He did suggest that part of the gravitational field must have fastened itself on my clothes somewhere in Luada—thus lessening the power of my field and stretching the trip to four hours. I wonder where those clothes are now? The miniature field may yet land them in the laboratory in a day or two; or, since Juan has relinquished control, they probably finished up in the Ice Age!"

"And to think that the last remnants of that almost unimaginable reptile civilization must have long ago vanished from the earth!" I said.

"Not everything," Sanders reminded me. "Remember the claw of Fulu, who must consider himself lucky that he didn't have his head taken off by the field… Anyhow, that's the wrong way to look at it. It's a queer thing—past, present, and future—all seeming to exist at once, like—like a reel of movie film unrolled along a road. Only by moving along the film do you get the illusion of movement in it and the idea of time. Yet past, present, and future are all there at once, though the people in the film have to follow the path set out for them. If only those people could free themselves from the film—though of course they're only images—they'd have the whole panorama of Time open for their inspection. I think it was something like that with me."

"There's something else," I said. "Those reptiles were intelligent—like human beings."

"Like human beings," Sanders repeated, as though the words held some secret meaning. "Yes; Juan thinks that the civilization of Luada was Nature's last try at giving the reptiles the sceptre of world supremacy. One of the prime essentials of survival is tribe-making, and that's why the ants may one day rule this planet. But when the Luadans started to play about in their laboratories, they undid all Nature's plans and unconsciously brought about their own downfall."

"It's terrific," I said, "just to think of it."

Sanders shook his head. "Just one of the many strange epochs that must lie hidden in Earth's history."

"By the way," I asked, "did you discover where Nu-Az and Yzul and those others *did* come from?"

Sanders sprang up angrily. "My God! Have you missed the whole meaning—the whole truth of the thing? Don't you remember Nu-Az's words: 'and we were made by the Luadans.'? Now do you understand? *The human race was created in the Luadan laboratories!*"

"That's pure madness," I said, controlling myself with difficulty at the grotesque statement. "I'll believe everything else. But that—never."

Sanders sat down and stared sombrely at the wall. "Why not? The human race—the apes—and Heaven knows what else! The Luadans and their laboratory explain a lot of things—I can see them meddling, meddling, everlastingly meddling with life—sending out those puzzling blind alleys and false shoots in the evolutionary tree—starting those dim legends of serpents who ruled—of the great Na-gas..."

"It's insane," I said. "If I were to believe you, then I couldn't have a little lizard cross my path without wanting to shut my eyes and run. Besides, your evolutionists and palæontologists state that Man appeared long after the last of the reptiles."

"No," said Sanders. "There was never any definiteness of time. And I was on the last fringe of the Mesozoic where all was changed." He was talking half to himself. "Man and Apes both from the reptiles—Darwin and others knew this, but the bridging of the gap between reptile and mammal seemed insurmountable. The Luadans hold the key."

"They couldn't create life," I said in an effort to make him see reason.

"Why? Life is only a chemical curiosity. And anyhow, that isn't the solution as Juan sees it. The scientists of Luada experimented *with germ-cells from their own bodies*—a warped and planned ectogenesis—and man and his evolution were started. So you see, Juan isn't so far from the common theory of Man's descent from the reptiles. He's just filled in the main link."

"I refuse to believe," I said. "It's too fantastic—it's revolting. You were misled."

"I hope to God I was—though it all fits in with what Juan had anticipated before the experiment."

"That reminds me," I said suddenly. "Those men—you must know where they are. I'll call police headquarters and have them taken for—"

"No," Sanders said, smiling wanly at my excitement, "you won't do anything like that. You see, I've made arrangements. Tomorrow I'm going back to the fern-jungle and Luada—to learn the truth once and for all."

And even as he promised me that night, so he went; and as I write the conclusion to this, my mind toys with Sanders' incredible theories. Reptiles—man—and next the insects.

And who knows what non-protoplasmic cycles of malevolent monstrosities shambled in the primal ooze and vapour of a coalescing Earth, aeons before Nature even thought of the reptiles? And who can even guess at what anthropomorphic shapes will straddle the deathless night of this planet when our sun is an ember and reptile, man, and insect are all a forgotten dream?

Sometimes, in moments of religious doubt, I envy Sanders, for it is in his power to know these things—from beginning to end, one and all, indisputably.

FRIDAY THE NINETEENTH

Elizabeth Sanxay Holding

Elizabeth Sanxay (1889–1955), who took on the surname Holding when she married British diplomat George Holding in 1913, came from an upper-middle class New York family and might well have lived happily as a society hostess. But she wanted to write, producing scores of stories for the major magazines from 1920 onward, as well as several romance novels. By 1927 she had shifted to crime and suspense fiction publishing eighteen novels from Miasma *(1929) to* Widow's Mite *(1953). She was one of Raymond Chandler's favourite writers: "she's the top suspense writer of them all," he wrote. Occasionally Holding liked to experiment with fantasy and borderline science fiction. Her children's book,* Miss Kelly *(1947) is about a talking cat. She also wrote three stories published in* The Magazine of Fantasy and Science Fiction *of which this is the first. The magazine's editor, Anthony Boucher, later wrote, at the time of Holding's death, that her stories of psychological suspense were "so far ahead of their times in delicacy and depth that she may almost be said to have created the modern murder novel." Much of that is evident in the following story of an ever increasingly frustrating time loop.*

W HEN BOYCE CAME DOWNSTAIRS, THE TABLE IN THE breakfast nook was set, and Lilian was moving about, quickly and crossly, in the kitchen. He had once thought her pretty, a neat, small, dark-haired woman, but he no longer liked to look at her, or to think about her. Her quickness had no grace in it; she bustles, he thought, that's the word for it, slamming things around, always cross, always with a grievance.

If she knew about Molly…! he thought. It was almost funny that, with all her accusations, her suspicions, she never suspected the one thing that mattered. She had accused him of 'flirting' with the dreary blonde next door, of 'carrying on' with his secretary. Yet she could see him and Molly together, here, in her own house, and feel no uneasiness. I asked Molly and Ted over this evening, she would say, or, why don't you call up Ted and see if they'd like us to come over?

He sat down on the bench beside the table, and he hated it; everything red and white—red and white checked curtains at the kitchen windows, the cabinet drawers full of little knives, spoons, all with red handles, even the can-opener, the egg-beater. Her life was made up of things like that. There had to be a blue shower-curtain in the bathroom, and a blue bath mat; she was always looking for blue soap. And worst of all was her closet; her dresses all in green cellophane bags, her jaunty hats in green cellophane, her high-heeled shoes in the pockets of a green ruffled bag.

He was sick of this little house, of the smug suburban street and the people who lived on it; he hated his job. He was sick of everything but Molly.

And what did that amount to, after all? He and Molly had never had more than a few minutes alone together; while Ted was in the kitchen mixing drinks; while Lilian was at the telephone in the hall. Then, in their little moment, their hands would meet, in a desperate clasp; they would kiss, without a word. They had never had time for words; Lilian would come back, with a full report of her conversation with a neighbour; Ted would come in with drinks on a tray, always whistling.

All through the war, Ted had been the most important figure in his life. Time and absence had made Lilian grow fainter in his mind; all his past life had become a little shadowy; only Ted was the friend dearer than a brother, the indispensable comrade. Now he was an enemy, like Lilian, to be outwitted; the sight of his ruddy face, the sound of his fluty whistle were odious.

"You've *got* to trim the hedge when you get home tonight, Donald," said Lilian, taking away his empty cereal bowl and setting down a plate of eggs and bacon before him.

"Not compulsory," he said.

"It is!" she said. "It's the only ragged, nasty-looking hedge on the street."

"Terrible," said Boyce.

"Well, it is," she said. "And if you haven't any self-respect, Donald Boyce, I have. If you won't trim that hedge, I'll *pay* someone to do it."

"I'm not interested in the hedge," said Boyce. "Or the street."

"I know that," said Lilian. "You're just too superior. Every other man on this street has a better job than you have, and *they* can trim their hedges, and do lots of little things—"

"For God's sake," said Boyce, "let's not start this again. I pay the rent—and everything else. But it's *your* house. You run it to suit yourself. You love it."

"What else have I got left?" she asked.

Sitting in the smoker, Boyce held up a newspaper so that nobody should talk to him, ask him to play gin rummy, bother him. The quarrel had made him feel sick; one of the worst quarrels they had had; he wanted to forget it, and to think about Molly. God! he said to himself. When you think what life could be like—and what it actually is ... If Molly and I could go away together...

He had never thought anything like that before. He had never seen her, never heard of her until six months ago when Ted had come to tell him about his marriage. And, because Ted was not an enemy then, but his friend, he had moved heaven and earth to get Ted a house on the same street. I want you and Molly to meet, Ted had said.

At Grand Central, Boyce took a taxi downtown to the office. If Lilian knew it, he thought, she'd never stop talking about my 'extravagance'. All right! What she doesn't know won't hurt her. And she's never going to know about my last two raises. Damned if I'm going to spend all the best years of my life in that office, just for Lilian's benefit.

He was thirty-eight now, the same age as Lilian, but anyone would think she was older, she with her sulky mouth, her quick, graceless bustling. He was tall, limber, fair-haired and grey-eyed, with a look of boyish good-humour. Even now, shaken by that quarrel, he was good-humoured and friendly to the others in the office.

He was popular here; he got along well with everyone; he had been like that in the army. Lilian likes to quarrel, he thought.

Every one of these wretched women she gets in to do a day's work now and then does something that makes her angry. The last one washed the bath mat in something that faded it, so that it doesn't match the shower curtain, and that's a tragedy. That's her life.

What else have I got left?

Let her find something else. Let her be something else. He turned to his work, routine work which he could handle without effort; it was dull enough, but it soothed him.

"Someone on the telephone for you, Mr. Boyce," said the secretary he shared with three other men.

He picked up the telephone without interest, and for a moment he did not believe what he heard.

"Not—you?" he said.

"Yes," she said. "It's Molly. I just wondered if you could get off a little early, and we could have a cup of tea?"

"Yes," he said. "Where?" He had to be careful; there were a dozen people who could hear every word.

"I'll meet you in the lobby of your building, shall I? At four?"

"Yes," he said, again.

He could not believe this; he could not understand it. They had never tried to meet alone; never mentioned it, and, in all his wretched longing for her, Boyce had never seriously made any sort of plan for meeting her. They had never even had a talk together; there had been nothing but those hand-clasps, those kisses, hurried and dangerous and silent.

He went at once to the head of his department.

"Will it be all right if I leave a bit early, Mr. Robinson?" he asked. "There's something my wife wants me to look after."

Why did I say that? he thought. But it didn't matter.

★

He was down in the lobby at ten minutes to four, and he was filled with a curious anger. If she's going to say we mustn't see each other any more, he thought, I won't listen. If she's going to start talking about Lilian, about Ted being my friend, I won't listen, that's all. Nobody's obliged to live a life like mine. It's hell. Everybody has a right to try to get out of hell, if he can.

There was, he thought, something hellish and insane about the activity in the lobby, the clacking of heels on the tiled floor, the people, all hurrying, silent, preoccupied, getting in and out of elevators, going up, going down, all in a hurry. A boy in a hurry with six bottles of a popular soft drink; a girl in a hurry with a sheaf of papers; a stout man with his straw hat pushed to the back of his head, in a hurry to go up, a thin woman in pince-nez coming down in a hurry.

He stood where he could watch the entrance, and people came in and out, one after another. Why didn't anyone know anyone else? Why didn't anyone say hello, or smile? And why didn't Molly come?

It was five minutes past four. She's not coming, he thought. He *knew* that. He was so sure of it that he was not going to wait. She's changed her mind, he thought. It's too much of a risk. She can't take it. He was so sure that he went to the newsstand and bought an evening newspaper; he went out of the building, and she was there, her black-gloved hand on the revolving door.

"You're late," he said.

"Only a minute," she said. "Where can we go?"

"There's a rather nice little place near here where we can get a drink," he said. "Unless you insist on tea …"

"I don't care," she said.

They set off along the narrow downtown street, crowded with these hurrying people, jaded in the fierce midsummer heat. He glanced at her sidelong, and his anger increased. She was a tall girl, broad-shouldered and, lean, in a dark-green dress and a wide hat that looked countrified here. She walked so easily; she alone was cool and easy.

She's not pretty, he thought. Her face with high cheekbones had a gaunt look, a hungry look; her mouth was too big. Not pretty; not a girl, either. She's as old as Lilian, and she's divorced and remarried. She's no girl.

"Here we are," he said, and took her arm, to steer her into a tavern. It was dim in here, with a sour smell; two big electric fans spun with a hollow roar, like wind in a tunnel. They went to the back of the room and sat down in a booth, facing each other.

"Oh, beer, thanks," she said.

He ordered a rye for himself and lit cigarettes for both of them.

"I've got a job!" she said.

"That's nice," said Boyce.

"It's such a *funny* little job," she went on. "It's with a woman radio-writer. She wants me to come in three days a week and stay in her apartment in the Seventies, to take telephone calls and open the mail and do a little typing. So that she can stay out at her country place."

The bar was blankly and strangely silent; even the bartender was gone; only the fans were spinning, sending against his face a thin stream of musty air. He sat looking down at the table; then he glanced up at Molly, and her dark eyes were brilliant in her thin face.

"You're going to be alone in this apartment?" he asked.

"Yes," she said. "From nine to five. Starting tomorrow."

Their eyes met steadily.

"Shall I come tomorrow?" he asked.

"Yes," she said...

She had to leave at five.

"I told Ted I'd meet him on the five-forty train," she said.

"I don't want you to go," Boyce said.

"I don't want to go, either. It's been so wonderful," she said, "this little time alone together. I love this funny little bar; I've loved every moment here. I wish today would never end."

She rose and stood, pulling on her gloves; he rose too, and suddenly she came to his side; she put her black-gloved hands on his temples and kissed him, hungrily and desperately; he held her close to him, so that he could feel her heart beating.

"I *must* go, Donald!" she said. "Till tomorrow!"

"Till tomorrow," he said.

"*Will* you trim the hedge, Donald?" Lilian asked, as she opened the door.

"All right," he said.

The morning's quarrel would never be mentioned; that was how it was with them now. In the early days of their marriage, he had always been able to end her quick-tempered little outbursts with a kiss, a smile, a joke. But he was tired of that; tired of her instant remorse. Let her nag; let her sulk. He put on an old jacket, and taking up the pruning shears, he went out of the house into the last of the afternoon sun.

"Hello, Boyce!" said the man next door, trundling his lawn-mower. "No rest for the weary, eh?"

After tomorrow I can stand all this, Boyce thought. Because then he would have his secret life, his own life with Molly. The shears made a sharp biting sound; the lawn-mower rattled; two radios were playing nearby, music on one of them; on the other a woman's voice, monstrously sweet and false, was talking on and on. I'll be so damn glad when this day is over, Boyce thought.

Lilian talked, while they ate dinner. She was angry and hurt and sulky, but she could not help talking. She had to tell him what she had said to the gas company; what the milkman had told her about those people who don't pay their bills. Boyce was polite, in a bleak aloofness. Oh, did you? Oh, really?

"I've got to go in to the office tomorrow," he said.

"On *Saturday*?"

"On Saturday. But there's no need for you to get up. I'll stop in Grand Central and get a bite."

But he knew she would get up; her alarm clock waked him in the morning. He had bought an alarm clock for himself, to keep in his own room, so that she should not come in to wake him, grasping him by the shoulder, speaking sharply. Donald! *Donald!* Now, *don't* go to sleep again!

He lay in bed until he heard Lilian go down the stairs, and he tried to think about Molly. But he could not, and he could not feel anything except a desperate impatience to get away, out of this house.

Lilian had his breakfast on the table when he came downstairs.

"Another hot day," she said. "And the paper says hot tomorrow."

He hated her to look at the newspaper before he had read it. I'll order another one for you, he had said. No, she had said. It would just be a waste of money. *I* don't have time to sit down and read newspapers. Only once in a while I like to glance at it.

She had opened the newspaper and turned over a page. He folded it back, and frowned a little. Senate Committee Calls McGivney. They printed that yesterday, he thought, and this one too. Hotel Cashier Foils Hold-up. He glanced at the weather report.

Continued warm and sunny. Highest temperature in upper 80's. Tomorrow and Sunday—

"This is Friday's paper!" he said, angrily.

"But it *is* Friday, Donald," said Lilian.

He looked at her for a moment and then turned away.

"It is Friday," she said again.

He did not want Lilian to drive him to the station. "I'll walk," he told her. "It'll do me good."

"But you'll miss your train, Donald."

"All right. I'll get the next one," he said.

It made no difference what train he got this morning; he was not going to see Molly until noon. He was leaving early only because he wanted to get away from that house. He set off down the street, walking fast, too fast for this hot weather, to get away from Lilian. Fool...! he thought. She doesn't even know what day of the week it is.

"Hi-ya!" called a cheerful voice, and Matthews, his next-door neighbour, slowed down his car. "Hop in, and we'll give you a lift to the station, Boyce."

"You're going in to town today?" Boyce asked, as he got into the sedan with Matthews and his wife.

"What?" said Matthews. "Well, why not?"

"You don't often go in on Saturdays, do you?" asked Boyce.

"But this isn't Saturday, man!" said Matthews. "It's Friday."

Boyce felt his throat contract; his mouth was dry. Take it easy! he told himself. You and Molly made a mistake, that's all. A mistake about what day of the week it was. That happens, now and then. Nothing unusual. Nothing to be upset about. I'm glad I found out in time, though; otherwise I shouldn't have shown up at the office today.

Only this was not the day he was going to see Molly. There was all this day to go through, with his wearisome job; dinner with Lilian, another evening, another night, like a desert to be crossed. Molly will have realized our mistake by this time, he thought. She'll take it for granted that I'll come tomorrow instead of today.

He sat down at his desk, and his routine work seemed to him like yesterday's; he went out to lunch with the same fellow-worker.

"Well, Friday's fish day," Haley said. "I think I'll have a try at this codfish."

"You said that yesterday," said Boyce.

"I certainly didn't say that yesterday was Friday," said Haley, a little offended.

"No, no," Boyce said, quickly.

It seemed to him that he had never felt such hot weather; he felt sick from it, and stupid. He went back to his desk, back to those papers that were like yesterday's papers, and his hands were unsteady.

"There's someone on the telephone for you, Mr. Boyce," said his secretary.

"It's—you?" he said.

"Yes," Molly said. "Donald, could you get off a little early—?"

"Yes," he said.

"I'll meet you in the lobby of your building at four," she said.

He went at once to Robinson.

"Will it be all right if I leave a little early, Mr. Robinson?" he asked. And then, because he thought Robinson was looking at him in an odd way: "There's something my wife wants me to look after," he said.

He was in the lobby at ten minutes to four, but this time he was not restless or troubled: He knew she would come.

"Wasn't that a queer mistake?" she said, as soon as she came. "For both of us to be so sure that yesterday—"

"Let's go and get a drink," said Boyce. "I could do with one."

It was dim in the tavern, and very quiet; only the big fans spinning, sending a stream of musty air against his face.

"It's such a *funny* little job," she said. "It's with a woman radio writer—"

"Yes," he said. "You told me yesterday."

They were silent for a moment.

"How was your day, Donald?" she asked.

Like yesterday, he thought. But, with a great effort, he answered in his usual debonair way.

"This new office boy we have…" he said. "I sent him up to the eleventh floor with a claim—"

He stopped short, because of the look on her face.

"But I told you that yesterday," he said.

"Yes," she said. "You did."

She rose and stood before him, pulling on her black gloves.

"Until tomorrow, Donald!"

"Until tomorrow!" he said.

I'm not going to say anything to Lilian about going in to the office tomorrow, he thought. I'll simply set my alarm, and get out of the house without waking her.

But her alarm clock waked him; when he went downstairs, she had his breakfast ready.

"Another hot day," she said. "And the paper says hot—"

"Shut up!" he said.

"Donald!" she cried.

"Sorry," he said. "Hot weather nerves. I'm sorry." He waited for a moment. "Hand me the newspaper, will you please, Lilian?"

When he saw it, he grew blind for a moment; he could not draw a breath for a moment. The date line was Friday the nineteenth.

He was waiting for her in the lobby at ten minutes to four, and he did not even notice the passing of time until she came.

"Donald," she said, "what's *happened*?"

"I don't know," he said.

"It's hard to see how we could both have made such a mistake—about the days of the week," she said. "I mean—"

"Let's go and get a drink," he said. "I could do with one."

It seemed to him that the tavern was darker than before; the air stirred by the fans was sickeningly tepid; he and Molly were alone; even the bartender was gone.

"It's such an *idiotic* mistake!" she said, and laughed.

"Don't do that!" he said.

"What d'you mean, Donald?" she asked.

He did not tell her how he hated her laugh, harsh, loud, ringing in his ears.

"But tomorrow we'll forget all this," she said, laying her hand over his. "Won't we, darling?"

The touch of her hand in its black glove made him wince.

"I've got to go now," she said. "I promised to meet Ted on the five-forty."

"Yes," Boyce said. "Yes. You'd better go."

And, he thought, if only she would never come back.

★

She looked haggard and ill when she came into the lobby the next day a little after four.

"I don't understand this," she said. "It *can't* still be Friday."

"Let's go and get a drink," said Boyce. "I could—"

"For God's sake, don't say that again!" she said. "I'm sick of it."

"We'll go somewhere else this time," he said, and he took her to another bar nearby. But there was a sign on the door. Closed For Repairs.

"I know another place," he said.

"I haven't time," Molly said. "I promised to meet Ted on the five-forty."

"So I've heard," said Boyce.

They went back to the tavern.

"Let's sit at another table," said Molly.

They sat down at a table nearer the door, but the heat there was intolerable; the air from the fans did not reach them.

"Let's try the next table," Molly said.

"It's no use," said Boyce, and led the way to the table where they had first sat.

"*Why* is it no use?" she demanded. "Do you mean you think it's got to go on like this?"

"What do you think, yourself?" he asked.

Their eyes met, in a long look of wonder and fear.

"For God's sake, haven't you any ideas?" she asked. "Aren't you going to do anything? This is—simply hell."

"Yes," he said. "I think you're right."

They met the next day, because he had something to say to her.

"I don't pretend to understand this," he said. "I don't know what's happened to us. Nobody else seems to notice anything wrong. It keeps on being Friday the nineteenth ... But I thought of this. Perhaps if we don't see each other again, we can get out of this."

"Let's try it!" she said eagerly. "Let's shake hands on it."

He took her black-gloved hand with a shiver of aversion.

"We promise never to see each other again," she said, and he repeated it.

She took a sip of her beer, and she gave her harsh little laugh.

"Our wonderful love didn't last very long, did it?" she said.

"It never began," said Boyce.

"None of that!" she said, angrily. "You were crazy for me. You'd have done anything to get me."

"Oh, no," he said. "I never even thought of doing anything for you. Except a little lying, to Lilian and Ted."

"Keep quiet!" she said.

"Or you for me," he said. "We weren't going to give up anything for each other. We were just going to take, all we could get."

She rose. "I'm going," she said. "I've got to meet Ted on—"

She stopped abruptly, and turned away, leaving him at the table.

If only it works ... he thought. Oh, God, if only this is the end! And he thought that it might be; hope was rising in him. If we don't see each other again, he thought, it *has* to stop. Maybe even making up our minds never to see each other again will stop it. Maybe tomorrow ... Oh, God, if only tomorrow will be Saturday...

He went home, more tired than he had ever been in his life, yet he slept poorly, restless in the hot dark. If this thing is over now, he thought, I'm going to make some plans. I'm going to start saving my money, so that I can get away. I'm—tired. If tomorrow is Saturday, I'll take it easy, all Saturday and Sunday.

But if it isn't Saturday ... I've got to be prepared for that. It may take a little time to stop this thing. Only I'm so damn tired...

The sound of Lilian's alarm clock waked him, and he got up at once; he went downstairs, barefoot, in his pyjamas, to bring in the newspaper. His hands were trembling as he held it up, his eyes did not focus. But he thought he saw an S, bold and black.

"Donald!" called Lilian from the head of the stairs. "Why ever did you go rushing down—?"

"Come here," he said. "Come here and tell me..."

The newspaper rattled in his shaking hands.

"What's—the date?" he asked her.

"But, Donald—" she said, looking up into his face.

"What's the date, I say?" he shouted.

"But it's Friday, the nineteenth, of course," she said. "Donald, aren't you well?"

"No," he said. "It's just the heat. Let me alone."

I've got to have patience, he thought. As long as we've stopped seeing each other, this thing will have to end. If not today, then tomorrow. As long as I don't see her.

Lilian drove him to the station.

"Bye-bye, Donald," she said, as he got out of the car.

"Bye-bye," he said, with a twitch of a smile, and started along the platform.

"Hello, Sarge!" called Ted's voice.

There was no escape from this. Boyce had to go all the way in to New York with Ted; he had to listen to Ted talking about Molly.

"This job she wants to take..." Ted said. "I wish she wouldn't do it. She went through hell, in her first marriage, you know. I want her to take it easy now, poor girl."

"I see!" Boyce said.

"Maybe Lilian could talk to her," said Ted. "Lilian's a regular little homebody; maybe she could persuade Molly it's better to stay home."

"Maybe she could," said Boyce.

"Lucky break for us, that the two girls get on so well together," said Ted. "Sometimes a marriage will pretty well break up a friendship between two men, if the wives don't hit it off."

Shut up, you fool! Boyce was crying in his heart. Shut up, and let me alone.

"Well, be seeing you!" said Ted, when they reached Grand Central.

"So long!" said Boyce.

His work was the work he had done yesterday; he made the same minor mistake he had made yesterday. He had lunch with the same man.

"There's someone on the telephone for you, Mr. Boyce," said his secretary.

It can't be Molly, he thought. She wouldn't do that.

"Donald," she said, "I've got to see you."

"Well, you won't see me."

"I've *got* to! Donald, I've found a way out for us."

"I don't give a damn. I won't see you."

"Donald, it's our only chance."

"All right," he said, after a moment, and hung up the telephone.

He realized that he had been speaking loudly and violently, yet no one had noticed. If Robinson will only notice, he thought. If Robinson would say, What? You want to get off early again? This won't do, Boyce.

"Certainly, Boyce," said Robinson.

★

He was surprised to see how ugly she was, pale, gaunt, moistening her lips with the tip of her tongue. As they walked to the tavern, he thought of names for her. Hyena, he thought, and that pleased him best.

They sat down at the table together.

"All right," he said. "Let's hear your idea."

She did not answer.

"Come on!" he said. "Let's hear it."

"Donald," she said, "I—can't remember."

"What d'you mean?"

"There was something … something I had to tell you. But I can't remember."

"Damn you!" he said. "You mean you got me here for nothing?"

"There was something," she said, in tears. "I know there was. But I can't remember."

"You've spoilt everything," he said.

"I?" she said. "You're trying to blame *me* for this? It's *your* fault. That first time we met, in your house, the way you looked at me…"

"I hope to God I never have to look at you again," he said.

She rose, and began pulling on her black gloves.

"Now I've made up my mind," she said. "Now I know what I'm going to do. I'm going to tell Ted what you've done to me. I'll tell him how you've been making love to me, how you planned to come to that apartment. He'll forgive me, but he'll *kill* you."

Their eyes met again, in a complete understanding. She wanted Ted to kill him. And Boyce would have been utterly happy to see her dead here, on the floor, this instant.

He stayed on in the booth after she had gone, because he was so tired. But after a while the noise of the electric fans began to worry him, and he rose. Again, as this morning, his eyes did not focus; the bar seemed filled with smoke. When he went out into the street, the sunshine was smoky; the crowded street seemed completely empty. No people, no traffic, not a sound. I hate her, he thought. I hate her so much that I can't see, can't hear.

He saw the truck, though, towering above him; he heard a monstrous confusion of sound, roaring, thundering, little squeaks and yelps. He went spinning high up into the air and then he came down with a thud so hard, he thought, that he broke through the street into a black, wet stairway, and he fell down it, thudding on every step, heavy, yet soft as a rag.

He could hear Lilian's voice, almost in his ear.

"Donald! Donald, darling!"

Her voice, he thought, was too insistent. But she was trying to call him back from the place where he was lying, and it was a very lonely place; he thought that he would be glad to go back with her. It would be good, he thought, to sit in the kitchen with the red and white checked cloth. Lying here was very lonely and Lilian, at the very least, had long been his companion. She was holding his hand now, and he was willing that she should keep on doing that.

In a way, he felt very comfortable. He was lying, he thought, on a cloud, and if he chose, he could move his hand a little and send the cloud floating off, away from Lilian. But he had also the choice of remaining here; it was clear to him that he lay in the most delicate balance.

Let Lilian hold my hand, he thought. I'll go back with her. I won't mind trimming the hedge. No, he thought, I'll like it. He could recall the sharp sound of the shears in the late summer afternoon; he could remember the feel of the grass under his feet;

he could remember some sweet fragrance, a flower, perhaps, or the blossoms of a fruit tree.

Now he heard a loudspeaker calling Dr. Dawson Dr. Dawson Dr. Dawson; he could hear Lilian sobbing; he heard some sort of jingling table go by along the corridor. He liked to hear these sounds; he wanted to come back; he wanted to put on his shoes and walk out of here. Poor Lilian ... he thought. He had been gone away from her for a very long time; he had left her alone, but he thought he could get back, find her young and pretty as she had once been, always a little cross because she felt herself not pretty enough.

There was another sound, though; a sweet and delicate little bell. It was growing clearer and louder. A fire alarm? he thought. The other sounds were very dim now; Dr. Dawson Dr. Dawson, oh, Donald, darling, come now, Mrs. Boyce, nurse ... But the bell grew louder and louder, ringing in his ears.

"There's someone on the telephone for you, Mr. Boyce," said his secretary.

That's Friday the nineteenth, he thought. I wish this day would never end, Molly had said. And it never had. If he went back there would be nothing else.

He sighed, and let his hand drop from Lilian's careful clasp. He moved his fingers a little, to push off the cloud on which he was stretched; he lay stiff and quiet under the sheet and floated away.

Dr. Dawson Dr. Dawson. The telephone bell was ringing, and Molly was waiting. But he was not coming back.

LOOK AFTER THE STRANGE GIRL

J. B. Priestley

John Boynton Priestley (1894–1984) scarcely needs an introduction, renowned as a playwright, novelist, essayist, critic and broadcaster. Not everyone associates him with science fiction or fantasy. He first met success with his novel about the fortunes of a travelling concert troupe, The Good Companions *(1929) which won him the James Tait Black Memorial Prize. Both this and* Angel Pavement *(1930), following the troubles of a small London firm, could not be further from the realms of the bizarre. But, as discussed in the introduction, he soon became fascinated with the serial-universe theory of J. W. Dunne. With his play* Dangerous Corner *(1932) Priestley began to speculate on the consequences of actions through time. He also explored the strange and unusual in several short stories, later collected as* The Other Place *(1953), which includes the following.*

T HERE WAS A GLASSED-IN PASSAGE THAT RAN FROM THE FAR end of the smoke-room to the big conservatory; it was probably a favourite sitting-out place at dances, and the basket chairs might have been left over there from some recent dance. Mark chose a chair, sagging and rather lop-sided, that was nearer the smoke-room than it was to the conservatory, so that he could still see the group round the piano. He could hear behind the singing and the piano the steady *chug-chug-chug*, from somewhere not far away, of the primitive electric light plant that Lord Broxwood had been boasting about at dinner. The voltage must be low and the bulbs could not be more than fifteen watt; they did not give much light but had a golden glow that was rather attractive. In the smoke-room, however, not far from the piano, there were also two large oil lamps. It was this lighting, low-toned, mellow and a trifle theatrical, Mark concluded, that brought the only suggestion of unreality to the scene.

He was smoking a very fat Egyptian cigarette and not enjoying it, but then there had been no sign of any Virginian cigarettes anywhere and he had not felt like tackling any of the cigars he had been offered after dinner. He was still feeling some bodily discomfort. It was some years since he had last worn white tie and tails, and of course these evening clothes were not his; and the collar was appallingly high. No wonder some of the older men looked apoplectic.

All the younger men and the girls were clustered round the piano, played with energy and not without skill by the monocled

Captain Waterhouse; and now they were beginning in chorus 'Tell Me, Pretty Maiden' from *Florodora*, which Mark had heard on an old gramophone record. "Now tell me, Pretty Maiden," roared the men, beefy and bold in their black-and-white, "are there any more at home like you?" And the girls, giggling a little and sounding very innocent with their wavering soprano, replied: "There are a few, Kind Sir, and better girls you never knew." With their hair piled so high, with such generous offerings of pink arms, white shoulders, plump soft bosoms, these girls seemed both larger and sillier than any girls he had known before. They aroused in him a vaguely lustful and predatory feeling, as if he were a schoolboy again and they were so many giant chocolate cakes. They made him understand all those winking references to 'girls' and 'curly-curls' in the old music-hall songs. He was now looking at the prettiest of all earth's extinct creatures. "Then take a little walk with me, and then we shall see," sang the men, having some difficulty with the rather subtle modulations of the tune, but loud and rich with masculine libido. They made him feel desiccated, about a thousand years old.

He dug the heels of his dress pumps, which did not fit him too well, deep into the coconut matting. First, just after it had happened, he had merely felt bewildered. Then for the next two or three hours, before and during dinner, he had felt frightened—of the fantastic situation he was in, and of any social complications it might produce, ending inevitably with questions that would have been an appalling embarrassment. (Thank God he had landed among this casual upper class, still so certain of themselves!) But now—and it was this and not fear that had driven him out of the smoke-room—he was possessed by a sense of loneliness that reached out and darkened to a feeling of utter desolation. The professional social historian in him was completely defeated; and even if he had had a notebook he could not have made a single note. All that the indomitable observer who never quite fails us could remark was that distance in time was apparently harder to bear than distance in space. Here he was, not two hundred feet away from his study and bedroom, but back in his own time he would have felt less desolate, he was certain, if he had suddenly found himself wandering on South Cape, Tasmania, half the globe away from home. Was home, then, more in time than in space? Yesterday he would have said No, he told himself, but now he was not sure. Odd how the young high spirits of the group round the piano, the sight of their flushed faces, the laughter breaking through the straggling chorus, widened and deepened his desolation.

But here was company; further need for care. For the elderly lady, plump and mottled, who had sat opposite to him at dinner came waddling in from the smoke-room, and sank with relief into the chair next to his. "I don't think we were introduced," she began. "They're always so casual here, especially when the youngsters have filled up the house. I'm Mrs. Buller—Lord Broxwood's sister—and, let me see, you're Ronald's friend, aren't you?"

This was rather tricky. "Well—yes—in a way."

"I'm abominably curious—my family are always teasing me about it—so don't mind. But wasn't there something about a bathing accident—Mr.-er-?"

"Denbow—Mark Denbow." What would she think, how would she behave, if he told her he had finished taking his evening seminar—yes, here in this house—at seven o'clock, had then hurried across to the lake for a quick dip before supper, and had dived—into all this? He gave her what he hoped was a friendly but apologetic smile. "Yes, I was bathing in the lake, and somehow lost conscious-ness—probably hit something when I dived in. And then your nephew—Ronald—fished me out."

"How fortunate!" Although she was so plump and smiling and comfortable, her eyes, with no more colour in them than a February sea, were cold. "One of his Oxford friends, I imagine, Mr. Denbow."

"I was at Oxford," said Mark, "but not with Ronald. As a matter of fact, we hadn't met before." One glance at her told him he could not leave it there. "I happened to be staying in this neighbour-hood and—er—thought I'd bathe in the lake. And after I'd got into difficulties and Ronald pulled me out," he continued, gaining confidence, "I was rather exhausted and he very kindly insisted on my spending the night here."

"That's so like Ronald," she said, smiling. "So brilliant too—even when he was a little boy he was quite shockingly clever. We all feel he has a great future."

And now what would happen if he gave Mrs. Buller a hard look, tapped her on her broad silken knee, and told her Ronald's future? For the memorial tablet in the chapel declared that Ronald had been (or would be) killed at Neuve Chapelle in 1915. But while he was making some vague agreeing noise by way of reply, Mrs. Buller found another topic.

"It's rather odd," she began, "but my niece Muriel followed her brother's example—so that there are two of you—"

"Two of us?" This really startled him.

"Oh—I don't mean this girl was bathing too. You probably haven't seen her because she didn't come down to dinner, not having anything decent to wear—mislaid her luggage apparently. Ann—something, I didn't catch her name. Indeed, I only caught

a quick glimpse of the girl herself—a curious little creature. I
gathered she'd been abroad—France, I believe—and arrived here,
thinking it was some other house. And she'd walked from the station and been out in that dreadful thunderstorm, so Muriel, who's
always sweet and kind, wouldn't let her go—"

"Was there a thunderstorm?" asked Mark innocently.

Mrs. Buller stared at him. "Where can you have been? The one
that started just before six o'clock—"

"Oh—yes, of course," he cried. "How stupid of me! I ought
to have remembered." But what he ought to have remembered
was that Mrs. Buller's weather, before seven-fifteen tonight, was
not his weather, belonging to a very different set of depressions
and anti-cyclones.

"Ah—here's Dorothy—my daughter," cried Mrs. Buller, with
maternal satisfaction. "Well, darling—are you tired of making a
noise in there?"

Dorothy was a rather large, pretty girl in pink, all curves and
down and delicate perspiration. She perched on the creaking arm
of her mother's chair. "It's so jolly hot in there, Mummie," she said,
smiling vaguely at Mark above her mother's head. "And I'm hoarse
trying to sing. I hope they'll stop soon—and dance or something."

During the next few minutes, while the three of them talked
and said nothing, Mark kept looking at Dorothy's eyes. They were
bluer and altogether finer than her mother's, but what fascinated
Mark was that they had a peculiar slanting set to them, and he
remembered having noticed similar eyes in some elderly woman,
quite recently. Nothing changes less about us, he knew, than the
setting, the characteristic shape, of our eyes. And now he remembered whose eyes were set like these—they belonged to a member
of the family here—old Lady Purzley. Were pink, smiling Dorothy

and that grim old survivor, Lady Purzley, who had questioned him so ruthlessly about the school, the same person? He decided, as the hair on his neck felt queer, that they were.

Mrs. Buller thought she would try the card room, and gave Dorothy permission to show Mark the conservatory. It was almost big enough for Kew, and full of that rich tropical smell which arises from so much growth and yet seems to have more death in it than life. He had never seen it before; it must have been taken down or allowed to fall into decay just before or during World War Two. Among that cascading greenery, and the smell of warm damp earth, and in the dim undersea light of the place, Dorothy looked like some giant pink blossom that had set itself adrift. Yet somewhere along time's Scenic Railway, just before it dipped into the darkness, she would be Lady Purzley, gnarled in tweed, staring at him mistrustfully, opening thin and bitter lips to put insulting questions to him, before taking a not too unfriendly farewell of him and all the works of his kind. What was it she had said? "I suppose there's some point in all this adult education we're compelled to pay for, although the results are not very obvious. But I remember this house when it was full of young and hopeful life—brave young men who had manners, pretty girls who had charm—" And hearing Dorothy chattering on, he could now discover the likeness in the two voices. In his desolation he felt the need of some physical contact in this other time into which he had been thrust; so he put a hand under Dorothy's rounded elbow, presumably to guide her, then let it slide along her forearm until their hands met and, perhaps because she intuitively perceived his mood and need, their fingers intertwined, and he felt her moist warm palm against his. He laughed, although he had no idea why he should.

"Why are you laughing?" she asked.

"I really couldn't tell you. Do you know anybody called Purzley?"

"Yes, I know a young man called Purzley—Geoffrey Purzley. He rather likes me but I don't like him much. Do you know him?"

"No," said Mark, smiling, "I hardly know anybody. Except you."

"You don't really know me," she told him, with the sudden huge solemnity of girlhood. They had stopped and were half-facing one another, in what might have been a jungle path.

He laughed again, and this time not without amusement. "In a way I know you better than you know yourself." He hesitated, wondering if he was making a fool of himself. "I can tell your fortune."

"Can you?" She was all credulity and eagerness. "How do you do it?"

"Just by looking at you. Want me to try?"

"Yes, of course. Go on, please."

After a longish stare, which he tried to make rather sinister: "You'll marry Purzley, who'll do something important and be given a title. You'll have three or four children, who will also do very well. You'll live to a ripe old age and become a most formidable old lady, striding around in old tweeds and thick shoes."

She gave an uncertain little laugh. "That's absurd. You don't know really, do you?"

He nodded. "In your case—yes, I do."

"Well, you might. Do you remember when we were all in the drawing-room, after dinner, and you talked for a minute or two to my cousin Maud and me? Well, when you left us, Maud and I were talking about you. Shall I tell you what we said? You might be flattered—or you might be furious—I don't know. But I'll risk it. Well, we agreed that there was something frightening about you. Maud said it was your eyes. I said I thought it was your manner—"

"Rude?"

"No, not really, though some people might think so. Odd—abrupt. As if you weren't English—and you are, aren't you?"

"Miss Buller, I'm very very English," he told her, with immense mock gravity.

"Now you're making fun of me. Shall we go back and see what the others are doing?"

"Yes—this time. But I warn you, it can be dangerous."

"I don't understand. What can be dangerous?"

"Going back and seeing what the others are doing." And as he followed her, at a sauntering pace, he began trying to work it out. Here, floating before him, all pink and downy, was young Dorothy Buller who in fifty years would be the old Lady Purzley who came to see what he and the others were up to with this house. Now if, when he got back (and he still refused to consider any alternative), he asked Lady Purzley if she remembered having her fortune told in this conservatory, when she was a girl, what would she reply? But wait a minute. He, Mark Denbow, couldn't possibly be part of Lady Purzley's youth, because he wasn't born then. Yet here he was with Dorothy, who undoubtedly *was* Lady Purzley round about the age of twenty. And then, trying to work it out, he was off again, just as he had been before dinner when Ronald Farspeare had left him to dress, and he had begun losing himself in a maze of time orders and dimensions. Whether he was now existing in a time quite different from that of ordinary world history, was moving in some unknown dimension where all possibilities might be realized, one sombre fact remained, that outside the immediate sense of bewilderment, like a vast dark space empty of stars, was a feeling of utter desolation, ultimate heartbreak.

The group around the piano was dispersing, but the energetic
Captain Waterhouse, with the monocle still screwed into his fiery
countenance, had not deserted his instrument. He began playing
waltzes, dreamily at first and then, in response to several cries of
encouragement, with the rhythmical emphasis of a dance pianist.
Dorothy melted into the arms of a bulky young man called Archie,
and was whirled away. All the ripe, soft girls, like giant peaches
and plums, were soon twirling in the arms of their beefy, scarlet-
faced young men. Mark loitered near the piano, seeing it all as a
tiny lighted dream against the immeasurable dark.

"Now don't tell me you can't waltz," cried Maud, the middle
one of the three daughters of the house. She had arrived with a
footman who had brought a tray of drinks. She held up her arms
invitingly, and after hesitating a moment, for it was some time
since he had done any waltzing, Mark took hold of her and off
they went. She was a dark, high-coloured girl, blazing with some
mysterious inner excitement, passionate love or secret dreams of
glory. All Mark knew about her, from the family memorial in the
chapel, was that she died—or would die—in 1923, after a long illness bravely borne following upon her nursing service in Serbia.
And it was not easy to dance well with a glowing creature who
would soon be a long illness bravely borne and then three lines
cut in marble on a chapel wall.

"I believe you hate dancing," she told him.

"Am I so bad?" He had to make an effort to find the right tone.

"Oh—no, not at all, rather good in fact. You keep good time,
which most of the others don't. It's just the look on your face—in
your eyes."

Pom-POM-tee-iddle-om-tiddle-om, went Captain Waterhouse,
now happily launched into the *Valse Bleu*. Whirling and twirling

and whirling the rest of them went, like the times-beyond-time, the unknown dimensions, the planets and stars.

"I've heard about my eyes already—from Dorothy Buller." And he smiled into the fiery darkness of Maud's eyes.

"Now that was jolly unfair of Dorothy," cried Maud. "I ought to have warned her—she always tells everything. But there *is* something odd and disturbing about your eyes, Mr. Denbow. Ronald never explained properly—he never does. Were you nearly drowned?"

"I'm not sure," he replied carefully. "Perhaps I was."

"That would explain it if you were," she said gravely. "As if you'd seen something we hadn't seen."

"Oh—I have—I have—I have—" he whirled her round and round, faster and faster—"lots—and lots—and lots—of things—that I couldn't—begin—to tell—you about—"

"Oh!" she cried, out of breath, "I—love this—don't you—?"

Captain Waterhouse decided that he must have a drink, while the dancers waited rather uncertainly for the music to begin again. It was then Mark noticed the girl who was standing near the door. She was an odd figure, and he knew at once that she had not been at the dinner table and that this was probably her first appearance downstairs this evening. She looked thin and ill; her dress hung badly; and there appeared to be something wrong with her hair.

"That girl over there," said Mark, "is she the one Mrs. Buller mentioned to me—Ann something—who came to the wrong house?"

"I suppose so," said Maud. "Poor darling—she does look peculiar, doesn't she? It's all rather confusing. My sister Muriel knows all about it, I don't. She's English but she's just come from France—and thought she'd been invited to stay here by some people she'd met in Paris. We think it must have been the Ferrers over at Winbone Manor—they're always going to Paris—and I believe Muriel has sent a message to them about her. Came to the wrong house, mislaid her luggage, was half-drowned in the thunderstorm—poor girl! She wouldn't come down to dinner, had a tray upstairs, but I suppose she found it too boring staying out of sight. Though I think in her place I'd have stayed upstairs. She does look all lost and strayed, doesn't she? I wish you'd go and ask her if she'd like something to drink, and generally look after her. Will you?"

"As the other lost and strayed type," said Mark, "it's the least I can do."

"That's another thing Dorothy and I noticed," said Maud, smiling over her shoulder. "You talk in an odd way—not like anybody else we know."

As he approached her, the strange girl gave him one quick look and then never looked at him again. "Oh—well—thank you, yes I will," she cried, in what seemed almost a parody of the high girlish voices there. "Just a little lemon squash, I suppose—or something equally innocent. Shall I come with you—and see what there is?" When they reached the drinks, she said, without looking at him: "What are you going to have? And what's your name, please?"

"Mark Denbow. And you're Ann—something—aren't you?"

"I'm Ann—" and then she broke off abruptly, as if she had changed her mind about telling him her surname.

"And I am going to have some whisky," he said firmly.

The footman poured out a lemon squash for Ann while Mark helped himself to the largest whisky-and-soda he ever remembered having. This was neither greed nor desperation; the glasses were so large that they made a giant helping inevitable. It was very good whisky too. But not many of the other men were drinking it, he noticed; they were asking for brandy-and-soda. All the girls were sipping soft drinks.

"I don't like this lemon squash," cried Ann suddenly, her voice higher than ever. "Mr. Denbow, would you think me terribly wicked if I asked you to get me a whisky?"

"No." He could never see her face properly. But he saw what was wrong with her hair, which had been padded out with false hair that was not quite the same colour.

"Well, all the rest of 'em would." She giggled. "So you'd better pretend it's for yourself. Look—I'll hold your glass—and you take back this lemon stuff."

The whisky he brought her was not much smaller than the one he had given himself. "We'll go in a corner with these," she announced, and led the way. They sat on an old leather settee. There was not much light. "Nobody'll bother about us here. Or do you want somebody to bother about you?"

"No, I don't."

"Are you the one who was rescued from the lake? Yes? Well, we're a pair then. Look—they're going to dance again. Wouldn't you like to go whizzing round again with one of those jolly fat girls?"

"I'd rather stay here," said Mark. "What about you?"

"Never, never, never." She took a good long drink, and cried: "Lord—that's strong. No, no dancing for me. I can't bear any of this. Not just because I look like a freak among all these great frilly bosomy girls. It's like a sort of children's party with everybody three times the right size. I hate it."

She had stopped talking in that ridiculous high girlish voice. She turned and looked at him, so that even in that bad light he was able at last to see her face properly. And now she didn't look thin, ill, rather grotesque, she looked beautiful. For several moments, in silence, they stared at each other.

It was then that he found the first crack in this other time. As he stared at her, wondering at her beauty, everything but her face changed. They were somewhere else and—what was more important—in his own time, as he knew at once when he saw behind her the bookshelves of the school library. Just beyond her cheekbone were the green volumes of the cheap reprint of the *Cambridge Modern History*; so that he knew exactly where they were. And without looking round he knew too that Dorothy and Maud and Archie and Ronald and Captain Waterhouse and the footman and the piano and the lighted smoke-room had vanished.

She gave a sharp exclamation. Then they were back in the old smoke-room, and Captain Waterhouse was playing a polka, and the beefy black-and-white men were taking hold of the plump pastel girls.

Her hand fastened on to his, and her sharp little nails were pressing into his palm. "Don't ask me why I'm doing this," she muttered, white-faced. "Just let me do it, there's a good kind man. I can't explain. And if I did, you wouldn't believe me."

"Yes, I would. Because I can explain too."

"No, you can't," she said crossly. "And don't start being clever and showing off. Just be a comfort—or leave me alone."

He grinned at her, and then indicated the prancing girls, billowing in their full skirts. "*They* wouldn't talk to me like that. And you shouldn't."

"Right both times," she said gloomily. She had wonderful dark hazel eyes; and the delicate yet strong moulding of her face, with its wide cheekbones and hollows beneath, was a joy. "They wouldn't

talk like that—and I oughtn't to. You were kind too. I apologize."
She jumped up. "But I can't stand any more of this. I'm going."

She was running out of the room while he was still pushing
himself out of the deep settee. It was no use running after her.
These people were fairly free-and-easy but they might be annoyed
if they saw the two interlopers running round the house. Perching
himself on the end of the settee, he watched the dancers. They
were there all right, solidly there, with nothing shadowy about
them, all real people; but if they had been dolls performing a polka
he could not have felt further removed from them. And now the
feeling of desolation returned. It had left him, he realized now,
while he had been with the girl Ann.

Just as he had decided to go and find her, if she were still somewhere downstairs, the dancing stopped and the next moment
Ronald and Dorothy Buller were barring his way.

"It's no use, Denbow," said Ronald, smiling, "she won't stop
talking about you."

"I only said you told fortunes," said Dorothy. "And Ronnie's
dying to have his told, but won't admit it."

"If Denbow will tell my fortune, I'll be delighted," cried Ronald.
"What about it, old man?" Of all the young men there, he was the
most dazzling: golden-haired, pink-skinned, and with the bright
blue eyes of a happy baby. He made the girls, for all their opulence,
look dim and dowdy. Looking at him, Mark wondered if those
stupid battles of the First World War, like that of Neuve Chapelle
which would blot Ronald from this earth, had not destroyed for
ever this vivid and even gorgeous masculine type. Although some
Americans, in their own way, resembled it.

"Who's he going to marry?" cried Dorothy, while Mark still
hesitated. "I'll bet you know, or think you do, just as you did with

me—though of course you're all wrong about Geoffrey Purzley. Too absurd. But please—go on, tell him. Marriage first."

"You girls and your marriages," said Ronald, fingering his golden moustache. But he looked expectantly at Mark.

"I don't know," said Mark unhappily. "I believe you will marry—but I don't know who it is. Sorry!"

"Are you feeling all right, Denbow?" asked Ronald.

"No, you're not, are you?" said Dorothy, anxious now. She was staring hard at him, with a flicker almost of fear in her eyes.

"I feel—a bit peculiar," said Mark carefully. But he knew in fact that something odd was happening. It was as if the years were coming between him and them like a sort of thickening of the air, in which all colour was draining away and shapes losing their sharp edge. Their voices were still clear enough, but they seemed to be coming from further away.

"Better turn in, old man," Ronald was saying. "Like me to give you a hand? Or I can ask one of the servants to show you up to your room."

"No, thank you," said Mark. "I think I'm finding it rather hot in here. I'll take a turn outside. Excuse me."

As he slowly crossed the room, he heard the piano again behind him, starting another waltz, but its tinkle was far away, like that of a piano heard distantly in the night. He turned at the door, for a last look at the dancers, suddenly convinced that he would never see them again. There was no colour at all in the scene now. They were shadows waltzing, to the tiny ghost of a tune...

He made his way along a corridor to the large front hall, and there he saw the old butler preparing to bolt the great doors. "Just a minute," he cried, hurrying forward. "I want to go out."

The old man never looked up but reached down towards another bolt. Probably he was deaf.

"No, hold it," cried Mark, now nearly at his elbow.

But the last bolts went home. The butler slowly straightened himself and then turned a complete blank face to Mark, who was not more than two feet away from him. And Mark realized that the man could neither see nor hear him. So far as this butler was concerned, he no longer existed—or rather had not come into existence. Yet the hall to Mark was still the hall of a night in 1902, had not yet turned itself back again into the hall he knew so well.

He stayed there a few minutes after the butler had gone, wondering what to do. One thing he felt fairly certain about, that this evening of 1902, into which he had dived so inexplicably, would not last much longer for him. Already he himself had ceased to be a visible presence in the scene, and at any moment now, he felt, it might disappear from his sight and hearing, as it had done when he had suddenly seen Ann, for a few seconds, against the background of the school library. When he had seen her, in fact, in his own time, not in this other time. And did this mean that she was in his own time? He had already guessed she was, just after she had demanded some whisky and had talked as if she had made this time-jump too. He began wondering if she too were now invisible to these people of fifty years ago. He decided to go in search of her.

He found her in the large drawing-room, sitting stiffly at the edge of a group of the older people. Although she was taking no part in the talk, he was certain that the others were clearly aware of her and that she was still part of the scene. He was equally certain that nobody there was aware of him, not even Ann. But unlike the others, who never gave a glance in his direction when he arrived near them, Ann knew that something had happened. As he came near he saw a look of bewilderment cross her face. But he knew she had not actually seen him.

All the older and important guests seemed to be there: a politician, some general, a wealthy industrialist, a bleached old gnome of a banker; and Lord Broxwood himself, massive and purple, was with them, a sort of chairman. They were important and weighty men, and spoke of important and weighty affairs—the state of the country, of Europe, of the world, and the future of the country, of Europe, of the world. They were men of experience, they were experts in one field or another; so they made pontifical announcements, and without hesitation, un-shadowed by any doubt, they produced their solemn prophecies, to the accompaniment of approving grunts and nods. Until Ann jumped up, fiery-eyed and rather shrill, and made her speech.

"I know this seems horribly rude and that you'll all be furious," she cried, "but I can't help it. Please listen for once—and stop being so grand and thinking you know everything. I've listened to you, haven't I? All about what's going to happen here in England, and what France will do to Italy and Russia to Germany and all that—"

"Really, Miss—er—" Lord Broxwood began, turning a deeper shade of purple with annoyance. "I don't think—"

But Ann could not be stopped. "I know, I know. Who am I—and all that. But please—please—listen for once. I shan't take long. But I must warn you that you're all talking nonsense. It may weigh a ton but it's all just rubbish, bilge and rot. I know roughly what's going to happen during these next fifty years—never mind how, but I do—and I can assure you that it's all quite different from what you think. Nothing you've said is going to come true. Honestly it isn't. You're all miles and miles out. So you just might as well stop thinking you know it all, because you haven't a clue. Not one of you—not a clue. It's pathetic. And I'll never believe people like you again. Well, I *am* shutting up."

This final remark was addressed to Lord Broxwood, who at the risk of giving himself a fit of apoplexy was now lumbering forward, apparently ready to shut her up by force. Before he could reach her, Ann had turned and, finding herself facing an open french window, had bolted into the night. Mark hurried after her, followed her across the lawn, and finally caught up with her inside the old summer house. She was crying.

"Leave me alone," she mumbled, hearing him but not looking up. "I know I was damned rude—but you don't understand."

"Yes, I do," said Mark. "I'm just the one who does."

There was very little light in there but it was not quite dark. She looked up, though it was probably his voice she recognized. "Oh—it's you again." She sounded much relieved. Indeed, he felt hopefully, she sounded almost delighted.

"You can see me now?" he asked.

"Not very well of course, but I can see that it's you. Why?"

"You couldn't see me in that drawing-room."

"Were you there?"

"Yes. But nobody knew."

"I felt that somebody came in," she said, rather eagerly. "But I'll admit I didn't really see you. You heard me, then?"

"You said just what I wanted to say." Mark was enthusiastic. "But I doubt if I'd have had the guts to say it."

She came closer, stared through the dark into his face, put out a hand and pressed it into the lapel of his coat, as if to make sure he was solid and real. "You're not one of them—are you? I wondered before, when you got me the whisky. But then I thought there couldn't be two of us. Oh—you've changed your suit."

"Why—no—I—" But then he felt the familiar soft collar round his neck, and one quick movement of a hand told him he was wearing his tweed coat and corduroy trousers.

"And I've changed my clothes—thank God!" she cried. "And look! Isn't the light from that drawing-room different?"

It was the usual light that came from the main recreation room any night the students were using it. Before he knew what to say to her, they were crossing the lawn towards the uncurtained french windows. Above the confused sounds of voices and a subdued samba on the gramophone, they could hear the clatter of table-tennis balls.

"Do you have tournaments?" asked Ann in an easy offhand way.

"Yes," he told her. "They're probably playing in one tonight."

Then he drew in his breath sharply, noisily. How could she be standing there with him, looking through the window at the students, and asking a question in that tone, as if she had already asked scores of questions and he was showing her round the school? As if she had never been back fifty years? As if neither of them had been back?

"What's the matter, Mr. Denbow?" she enquired innocently. "Are you cold? Shall we go in—back to the library?"

"Why yes—I think we might as well." He heard himself saying this, remotely from all the questions buzzing in his mind.

Not wishing to disturb the students, they walked round to the side door and along the back corridor towards the library. He said nothing, not knowing what to say, still trying to understand what had happened. She was walking half a pace ahead of him, so that he could look at her without appearing ill-mannered. A mop of soft dark hair; a figure, now trimly clothed, as delicate and strong as her face; yes, a beautiful girl, typical of the best of our time. But what about that other time? Didn't she know she had been there?

They had the corridor to themselves. Within a few feet of the library door, she stopped and turned on him. "Mr. Denbow, I like what you're doing here," she began, with a touch of severity, "though I thought I wouldn't. And I'm ready to like you. But I feel you resent me—and I think that's terribly unfair. I'm not my grandmother, you know."

"I'm sorry if I've behaved as if I thought you were your grandmother," said Mark, without a clue to what they were talking about. "And I've never met anybody I felt less like resenting. But let's talk about this in the library."

"In front of my grandmother? Surely that wouldn't be a good idea. That's why I stopped here."

"Oh—your grandmother's in the library—is she?" Mark stared at her blankly.

"Well, that's where we left her," said Ann impatiently. Then she looked at him curiously. "You don't look very good. Perhaps that little accident in the lake was worse than you thought—"

"Just a minute," said Mark earnestly, going closer and lowering his voice. "Please tell me something. Have I been showing you round this place—?"

"But of course—for the last hour. Then we went out for some air, and then you said you'd better take an aspirin and I said I'd wait for you in the old summer house—you remember?"

"This is terribly important." And he found himself gripping her just below each shoulder. "Tell me, please, what happened to you while you waited in the summer house. It doesn't matter how absurd it seems—please tell me."

"Well—I had a confused sort of day-dream—I'm a dreamy type though I may not look it. By the way, you're hurting my arms—but go on, if it helps. No—no apologies. I can see this is serious for you. You see, on the way here—perhaps you don't remember, but my grandmother and I are staying with some people called Ferrers at Winbone Manor, and I wanted to drive over, so she came with me—well, on the way here she was telling me how she used to stay here as a girl—she was the niece of the Lord Broxwood who owned it then. So I began imagining what it would be like here in those days—oh!" And she stared at him, as if she had suddenly remembered something.

"Ann," he whispered desperately, "I'm going to take a chance and say this now. Don't think I'm mad. I'm not. But I tell you I spent most of this evening there—in 1902, it was. And you were the strange girl who'd turned up in some queer way, just as I'd been rescued from the lake—by the son of the house, a chap called Ronald. Then I saw how beautiful you were—yes, the most beautiful girl I'd ever known. And I knew you didn't belong to that time but to this. There were just the two of us in a different world that didn't understand. And I've never been really in love before, and I know this is it—and that whatever happens you'll always be the beautiful strange girl who turns out not to be strange but really the other one in a different world that couldn't understand. That's how it'll always be, whatever happens. Do I sound quite mad?"

"Yes," said Ann. "But I like it. Though of course there's a lot more you'll have to tell me."

The library door opened. "Don't stand there looking moon-struck," cried a sharp old voice. "Either come in or go somewhere else."

He felt he ought to have known at once that this grandmother would be Lady Purzley—once Dorothy Buller, bosomy and downy in pink.

"If you two were talking about adult education out there," said Lady Purzley, after examining their looks critically, "then I no longer understand anything."

"Yes, you do, darling," cried Ann, stiff glowing away. "But it was a kind of adult education."

"I must say," said the old lady, turning to Mark, "you're a more enterprising young man than I thought you were."

"I'm far more enterprising than I thought I was," said Mark, smiling at her. "By the way, Lady Purzley, when you stayed here as a girl, did a strange young man ever tell your fortune in the conservatory?"

"Now why should you ask me that, Mr. Denbow?"

"I just wondered."

"Because," Lady Purzley continued slowly, "I dozed a little after you two left me, and dreamt I was back here as a girl, before I was even engaged to Geoffrey Purzley, and somebody told me I would marry him. But whether that really happened once or I merely dreamt it, I can't remember. It's often difficult to tell, you know. Things can be very complicated."

"So I've suspected," said Mark.

MANNA

Peter Phillips

Peter Phillips (1920–2012) was a British writer and journalist who is (or should be) best remembered for "Dreams Are Sacred" (1948), one of the earliest sf stories about entering the mental landscape of another person, and a major influence on later works about virtual reality. Phillips had served in the Army during the Second World War but was invalided out due to asthma. He became a journalist but also tried to succeed for some years as a freelance writer, which proved difficult, as he was meticulous and spent too long polishing the finished product. After his death his family produced a limited edition volume of his short fiction, Manna (2016) of which this is the title story.

T AKE BEST-QUALITY SYNTHETIC PROTEIN. BAKE IT UP, BREAK it up, steam it, steep it in sucrose, ferment it, add nut oil, piquant spices from the Indies, fruit juices, new flavors from the laboratory, homogenize it, hydrolize it, soak it in brine; pump in glutamic acid, balanced proportions of A, B1, B2, C, D, traces of calcium, copper and iron salts, an unadvertised drop of benzedrine; dehydrate, peptonize, irradiate, reheat in malt vapour under pressure compress, cut into mouth-sized chunks, pack in liquor from an earlier stage of the process—

Miracle Meal.

Everything the Body Needs to Sustain Life and Bounding Vitality, in the Most DEEE LISHUSSS *Food Ever Devised. It will Invigorate You, Build Muscle, Brain, Nerve. Better than the Banquets of Imperial Rome, Renaissance Italy, Eighteenth Century France—All in One Can. The Most Heavenly Taste Thrills You Have Ever Experienced. Gourmets' Dream and Housewives' Delight. You Can Live on It. Eat It for Breakfast, Lunch, Dinner. You'll Never Get Tired Of* MIRACLE MEAL.

Ad cuts of Zeus contemptuously tossing a bowl of ambrosia over the edge of Mount Olympus and making a goggle-eyed grab for a can of Miracle Meal.

Studio fake-ups of Lucretia Borgia dropping a phial of poison and crying piously: "It Would Be a Sin to Spoil Miracle Meal."

Posters and night-signs of Joe Doe—or Bill Smith, or Henri Brun, or Hans Schmitt or Wei Lung—balancing precariously on a pyramided pile of empty M.M. cans, eyes closed, mouth pursed in slightly inane ecstasy as he finishes the last mouthful of his hundred-thousandth can.

You could live on it, certainly.

The publicity co-ordinator of the Miracle Meal Corporation chose the victim himself—a young man named Arthur Adelaide from Greenwich Village.

For a year, under the closest medical supervision and observation, Arthur ate nothing but Miracle Meal.

From this Miracle Meal Marathon, as it was tagged by video-print newssheets, he emerged smiling, twice the weight—publicity omitted to mention that he'd been half starved to begin with—he'd been trying to live off pure art and was a bad artist—perfectly fit, and ten thousand dollars richer.

He was also given a commercial-art job with M.M., designing new labels for the cans.

His abrupt death at the end of an eighty-storey drop from his office window a week or two later received little attention.

It would be unreasonable to blame the cumulative effect of M.M., for Arthur was probably a little unbalanced to begin with, whereas M.M. was Perfectly Balanced—a Kitchen in a Can.

Maybe you could get tired of it. But not very quickly. The flavor was the secret. It was delicious yet strangely and tantalizingly indefinable. It seemed to react progressively on the taste buds so that the tastes subtly changed with each mouthful.

One moment it might be *omelette aux fines herbes*, the next, turkey and cranberry, then buckwheat and maple. You'd be through the can before you could make up your mind. So you'd buy another.

Even the can was an improvement on the usual plastic self-heater —shape of a small, shallow pie dish, with a pre-impressed crystalline fracture in the plastic lid.

Press the inset button on the preheating unit at one side, and when the food was good and hot, a secondary chemical reaction in the unit released a fierce little plunger just inside the perimeter fracture. Slight steam pressure finished the job. The lid flipped off.

Come and get it. You eat right out of the can it comes in. Keep your fingers out, Johnny. Don't you see the hygiplast spoon in its moisture- and heat-repellent wrapper fixed under the lid?

The Reverend Malachi Pennyhorse did not eat Miracle Meal. Nor was he impressed when Mr. Stephen Samson, Site Adviser to the Corporation, spoke in large dollar signs of the indirect benefits a factory would bring to the district.

"Why here? You already have one factory in England. Why not extend it?"

"It's our policy, Reverend—"

"Not 'Reverend,' young man. Call me Vicar. Or Mr. Pennyhorse. Or merely Pennyhorse—Go on."

"It's our policy, sir, to keep our factories comparatively small, site them in the countryside for the health of employees, and modify the buildings to harmonize with the prevailing architecture of the district. There is no interference with local amenities. All transport of employees, raw materials, finished product is by silent copter."

Samson laid a triphoto on the vicar's desk. "What would you say that was?"

Mr. Pennyhorse adjusted his pince-nez, looked closely. "Byzantine. Very fine. Around 500 A.D."

"And this—"

"Moorish. Quite typical. Fifteenth century."

Samson said: "They're our factories at Istanbul and Tunis respectively. At Allahabad, India, we had to put up big notices saying: 'This is not a temple or place of worship,' because natives kept wandering in and offering up prayers to the processing machines."

Mr. Pennyhorse glanced up quickly. Samson kept his face straight, added: "The report may have been exaggerated, but—you get the idea?"

The vicar said: "I do. What shape do you intend your factory to take in this village?"

"That's why I came to you. The rural district council suggested that you might advise us."

"My inclination, of course, is to advise you to go away and not return."

The vicar looked out of his study window at the sleepy, sun-washed village street, gables of the ancient Corn Exchange, paved marketplace, lichened spire of his own time-kissed church; and, beyond, rolling Wiltshire pastures cradling the peaceful community.

The vicar sighed: "We've held out here so long—I hoped we would remain inviolate in my time, at least. However, I suppose we must consider ourselves fortunate that your corporation has some respect for tradition and the feelings of the… uh… 'natives.'"

He pulled out a drawer in his desk. "It might help you to understand those feelings if I show you a passage from the very full diary of my predecessor here, who died fifty years ago at the age of ninety-five—we're a long-lived tribe, we clergy. It's an entry he made one hundred years ago—sitting at this very desk."

Stephen Samson took the opened volume.

The century-old handwriting was as readable as typescript.

"May 3, 1943. Long, interesting discussion with young American soldier, one of those who are billeted in the village. They term themselves G.I.'s. Told me countryside near his home in Pennsylvania not unlike our Wiltshire downs. Showed him round church. Said he was leaving soon, and added: 'I love this place. Nothing like my home town in looks, but the atmosphere's the same—old, and kind of comfortable. And I guess if I came back here a hundred years from now, it wouldn't have changed one bit.' An engaging young man. I trust he is right."

Samson looked up. Mr. Pennyhorse said: "That young man may have been one of your ancestors."

Samson gently replaced the old diary on the desk. "He wasn't. My family's Ohioan. But I see what you mean, and respect it. That's why I want you to help us. You will?"

"Do you fish?" asked the vicar, suddenly and irrelevantly. "Yes, sir. Very fond of the sport."

"Thought so. You're the type. That's why I like you. Take a look at these flies. Seen anything like them? Make 'em myself. One of the finest trout streams in the country just outside the village. Help you? Of course I will."

"Presumption," said Brother James. He eased himself through a graystone wall by twisting his subexistential plane slightly, and leaned reflectively against a moonbeam that slanted through the branches of an oak.

A second habited and cowled figure materialized beside him. "Perhaps so. But it does my age-wearied heart a strange good to see those familiar walls again casting their shadows over the field."

"A mockery, Brother Gregory. A mere shell that simulates the outlines of our beloved Priory. Think you that even the stones are of that good, grey granite that we built with? Nay! As this cursed simulacrum was a-building, I warped two hands into the solid, laid hold of a mossy block, and by the saints, 'twas of such inconsequential weight I might have hurled it skyward with a finger. And within, is there aught which we may recognize? No chapel, no cloisters, no refectory only long, geometrical rooms. And what devilries and unholy rites may not be centred about those strange mechanisms with which the rooms are filled?"

At the tirade, Brother Gregory sighed and thrust back his cowl to let the gracious moonbeams play on his tonsured head. "For an Untranslated One of some thousand years' standing," he said, "you exhibit a mulish ignorance, Brother James. You would deny men all advancement. I remember well your curses when first we saw horse-less carriages and flying machines."

"Idols!" James snapped. "Men worship them. Therefore are they evil."

"You are so good, Brother James," Gregory said, with the heaviest sarcasm. "So good, it is my constant wonderment that you have had to wait so long for Translation Upwards. Do you think that Dom Pennyhorse, the present incumbent of Selcor—a worthy man, with reverence for the past—would permit evil rites within his parish? You are a befuddled old anachronism, brother."

"That," said James, "is quite beyond sufferance. For you to speak thus of Translation, when it was your own self-indulgent pursuit of carnal pleasures that caused us to be bound here through the centuries!"

Brother Gregory said coldly: "It was not I who inveigled the daughter of Ronald the Wry-Neck into the kitchen garden, thus exposing the weak flesh of a brother to grievous temptation."

There was silence for a while, save for the whisper of a midnight breeze through the branches of the oak, and the muted call of a nightbird from the far woods.

Gregory extended a tentative hand and lightly touched the sleeve of James's habit. "The argument might proceed for yet another century and bring us no nearer Translation. Besides, it is not such unbearable penance, my brother. Were we not both lovers of the earth, of this fair countryside?"

James shrugged. Another silence. Then he fingered his gaunt white cheeks. "What shall we do, Brother Gregory? Shall we—appear to them?"

Gregory said: "I doubt whether common warp manifestation would be efficacious. As dusk fell tonight, I overheard a conversation between Dom Pennyhorse and a tall, young-featured man who has been concerned in the building of this simulacrum. The latter spoke in one of the dialects of the Americas; and it was mentioned that several of the men who will superintend the working of the machines within will also be from the United States—for a time at least. It is not prudent to haunt Americans in the normal fashion. Their attitude toward such matters is notoriously—unseemly."

"We could polter," suggested Brother James.

Gregory replaced his cowl. "Let us review the possibilities, then," he said, "remembering that our subetheric energy is limited."

They walked slowly together over the meadow toward the resuscitated grey walls of the Selcor Priory. Blades of grass, positively charged by their passage, sprang suddenly upright, relaxed slowly into limpness as the charge leaked away.

They halted at the walls to adjust their planes of incidence and degree of tenuity, and passed inside.

The new Miracle Meal machines had had their first test run. The bearings on the dehydrator pumps were still warm as two black figures, who seemed to carry with them an air of vast and wistful loneliness, paced silently between rows of upright cylinders which shone dully in moonlight diffused through narrow windows.

"Here," said Gregory, the taller of the two, softly, "did we once walk the cloisters in evening meditation."

Brother James's broad features showed signs of unease. He felt more than mere nostalgia.

"Power—what are they using? Something upsets my bones. I am queasy, as when a thunderstorm is about to break. Yet there is no static."

Gregory stopped, looked at his hand. There was a faint blue aura at his fingertips. "Slight neutron escape," he said. "They have a small thorium-into-233 pile somewhere. It needs better shielding."

"You speak riddles."

Gregory said, with a little impatience: "You have the entire science section of the village library at your disposal at nightfall for the effort of a trifling polter, yet for centuries you have read nothing but the *Lives of the Saints*. So, of course, I speak riddles—to you. You are even content to remain in ignorance of the basic principles of your own structure and functioning, doing everything by traditional thought-rote and rule of thumb. But I am not so content; and of my knowledge, I can assure you that the radiation will not harm you unless you warp to solid and sit atop the pile when it is in full operation." Gregory smiled. "And then, dear brother, you would doubtless be so uncomfortable that you would dewarp before any harm could be done beyond the loss of a little energy that would be replaced in time. Let us proceed."

They went through three departments before Brother Gregory divined the integrated purpose of the vats, driers, conveyor tubes, belts and containers.

"The end product, I'm sure, is a food of sorts," he said, "and by some quirk of fate, it is stored in approximately the position that was once occupied by our kitchen store—if my sense of orientation has not been bemused by these strange internal surroundings."

The test run of the assembly had produced a few score cans of Miracle food. They were stacked on metal shelves which would tilt and gravity-feed them into the shaft leading up to the crating machine. Crated, they would go from there to the copter-loading bay on the roof.

Brother James reached out to pick up a loose can. His hand went through it twice.

"Polt, you dolt!" said Brother Gregory. "Or are you trying to be miserly with your confounded energy? Here, let me do it."

The telekineticized can sprang into his solid hands. He turned it about, slightly increasing his infrared receptivity to read the label, since the storeroom was in darkness.

"Miracle Meal. Press Here."

He pressed, pressed again, and was closely examining the can when, after thirty seconds, the lid flipped off, narrowly missing his chin.

Born, and living, in more enlightened times, Brother Gregory's inquiring mind and insatiable appetite for facts would have made him a research worker. He did not drop the can. His hands were quite steady. He chuckled. He said: "Ingenious, very ingenious. See —the food is hot."

He warped his nose and back palate into solid and delicately inhaled vapours. His eyes widened. He frowned, inhaled again. A beatific smile spread over his thin face.

"Brother James—warp your nose!"

The injunction, in other circumstances, might have been considered both impolite and unnecessary. Brother James was no beauty, and his big, blunt, snoutlike nose, which had been a flaring red in life, was the least prepossessing of his features.

But he warped it, and sniffed.

M.M. Sales Leaflet Number 14: It Will Sell By Its Smell Alone.

Gregory said hesitantly: "Do you think, Brother James, that we might—"

James licked his lips, from side to side, slowly. "It would surely take a day's accumulation of energy to hold digestive and alimentary in solid for a sufficient period. But—"

"Don't be a miser," said Gregory. "There's a spoon beneath the lid. Get a can for yourself. And don't bother with digestive. Teeth, palate and throat are sufficient. It would not digest in any case. It remains virtually unchanged. But going down—ah, bliss!" It went down. Two cans.

"Do you remember, brother," said James, in a weak, reminiscing voice, "what joy it was to eat and be strengthened? And now to eat is to be weakened."

Brother Gregory's voice was faint but happy. "Had there been food of this character available before our First Translation, I doubt whether other desires of the flesh would have appealed to me. But what was our daily fare set on the refectory table: peas; lentils; cabbage soup; hard, tasteless cheese. Year after year—ugh!"

"Health-giving foods," murmured Brother James, striving to be righteous even in his exhaustion. "Remember when we bribed the kitchener to get extra portions? Good trenchermen, we. Had we not died of the plague before our Priory became rich and powerful, then, by the Faith, our present bodies would be of greater girth."

"Forms, not bodies," said Gregory, insisting even in *his* exhaustion on scientific exactitudes. "Variable fields, consisting of open lattices of energy foci resolvable into charged particles—and thus solid matter—when they absorb energy beyond a certain stage. In other words, my dear ignorant brother, when we polt. The foci themselves —or rather the spaces between them—act as a limited-capacity storage battery for the slow accretion of this energy from cosmic sources, which may be controlled and concentrated in the foci by certain thought patterns."

Talking was an increasing effort in his energy-low state.

"When we polt," he went on slowly, "we take up heat, air cools, live people get cold shivers; de-polt, give up heat, live people get clammy, cold-hot feeling; set up 'lectrostatic field, live peoples' hair stan's on end"—his voice was trailing into deep, blurred inaudibility, like a mechanical phonograph running down, but James wasn't listening anyway—"an' then when we get Translated Up'ards by the Power That Is, all the energy goes back where it came from an' we jus' become thought. Thassall. Thought. Thought, thought, thought, thought—"

The phonograph ran down, stopped. There was silence in the transit storeroom of the Selcor Priory Factory branch of the Miracle Meal Corporation.

For a while.

Then—

"THOUGHT!"

The shout brought Brother James from his uneasy, uncontrolled repose at the nadir of an energy balance.

"What is it?" he grumbled. "I'm too weak to listen to any of your theorizing."

"Theorizing! I have it!"

"Conserve your energies, brother, else will you be too weak even to twist yourself from this place."

Both monks had permitted their forms to relax into a corner of the storeroom, supine, replete in disrepletion.

Brother Gregory sat up with an effort.

"Listen, you attenuated conserve of very nothingness, I have a way to thwart, bemuse, mystify and irritate these crass philistines—and nothing so simple that a psychic investigator could put a thumb on us. What are we, Brother James?"

It was a rhetorical question, and Brother James had barely formulated his brief reply—"Ghosts"—before Brother Gregory, energized in a way beyond his own understanding by his own enthusiasm, went on: "Fields, in effect. Mere lines of force, in our unpolted state. What happens if we whirl? A star whirls. It has mass, rate of angular rotation, degree of compactness—therefore, gravity. Why? Because it has a field to start with. But we are our own fields. We need neither mass nor an excessive rate of rotation to achieve the same effect. Last week I grounded a high-flying wood pigeon by whirling. It shot down to me through the air, and I'd have been buffeted by its pinions had I not stood aside. It hit the ground—not too heavily, by the grace of St. Barbara—recovered and flew away."

The great nose of Brother James glowed pinkly for a moment. "You fuddle and further weaken me by your prating. Get to your point, if you have such. And explain how we may do anything in our present unenergized state, beyond removing ourselves to a nexus point for recuperation."

Brother Gregory warped his own nose into solid in order to scratch its tip. He felt the need of this reversion to a life habit, which had once aided him in marshalling his thoughts.

"You think only of personal energy," he said scornfully. "We don't need that, to whirl. It is an accumulative process, yet we gain nothing, lose nothing. Matter is not the only thing we can warp. If you will only listen, you woof of unregenerate and forgotten flesh, I will try to explain without mathematics."

He talked.

After a while, Brother James's puzzled frown gave way to a faint smile. "Perhaps I understand," he said.

"Then forgive me for implying you were a moron," said Gregory. "Stand up, Brother James."

Calls on transatlantic tight-beam cost heavy. Anson Dewberry, Miracle Meal Overseas Division head, pointed this out to Mr. Stephen Samson three times during their conversation.

"Listen," said Samson at last, desperately, "I'll take no more delegation of authority. In my contract, it says I'm site adviser. That means I'm architect and negotiator, not detective or scientist or oculist. I offered to stay on here to supervise building because I happen to like the place. I like the pubs. I like the people. I like the fishing. But it wasn't in my contract. And I'm now standing on that contract. Building is finished to schedule, plant installed—your tech men, incidentally, jetted out of here without waiting to catch snags after the first runoff—and now I'm through. The machines are running, the cans are coming off—and if the copters don't collect, that's for you and the London office to bat your brains out over. And the Lord forgive that mess of terminal prepositions," he added in a lower voice. Samson was a purist in the matter of grammar.

Anson Dewberry jerked his chair nearer the scanner in his New York office. His pink, round face loomed in Samson's screen like that of an avenging cherub.

"Don't you have no gendarmes around that place?" Mr. Dewberry was no purist, in moments of stress. "Get guards on, hire some militia, check employees. Ten thousand cans of M.M. don't just evaporate."

"They do," Samson replied sadly. "Maybe it's the climate. And for the seventh time, I tell you I've done all that. I've had men packed so tightly around the place that even an orphan neutron couldn't get by. This morning I had two men from Scotland Yard gumming around. They looked at the machines, followed the assembly through to the transit storeroom, examined the electrolocks and mauled their toe-caps trying to boot a dent in the door. Then the top one—that is, the one who only looked half asleep—said, 'Mr. Samson, sir, do you think it's… uh… possible… that… uh… this machine of yours… uh… goes into reverse when your… uh… backs are turned and… uh… sucks the cans back again?'"

Grating noises that might have been an incipient death rattle slid over the tight-beam from New York.

Samson nodded, a smirk of mock sympathy on his tanned, humour-wrinkled young face.

The noises ended with a gulp. The image of Dewberry thrust up a hesitant forefinger in interrogation. "Hey! Maybe there's something to that, at that—would it be possible?"

Samson groaned a little. "I wouldn't really know or overmuch care. But I have doubts. Meantime—"

"Right." Dewberry receded on the screen. "I'll jet a man over tonight. The best. From Research. Full powers. Hand over to him. Take some of your vacation. Design some more blamed mosques or tabernacles. Go fishing."

"A sensible suggestion," Samson said. "Just what I was about to do. It's a glorious afternoon here, sun a little misted, grass green, stream flowing cool and deep, fish lazing in the pools where the willow shadows fall—"

The screen blanked. Dewberry was no purist, and no poet either. Samson made a school-kid face. He switched off the fluor lamps that supplemented the illumination from a narrow window in the supervisor's office which, after studying the ground plan of the original Selcor Priory, he had sited in the space that was occupied centuries before by the business sanctum of the Prior—got up from his desk and walked through a Norman archway into the sunlight.

He breathed the meadow-sweet air deeply, with appreciation.

The Reverend Malachi Pennyhorse was squatting with loose-jointed ease against the wall. Two fishing rods in brown canvas covers lay across his lap. He was studying one of the trout flies nicked into the band of his ancient hat. His balding, brown pate was bared to the sun. He looked up.

"What fortune, my dear Stephen?"

"I convinced him at last. He's jetting a man over tonight. He told me to go fishing."

"Injunction unnecessary, I should imagine. Let's go. We shan't touch a trout with the sky as clear as this, but I have some float tackle for lazier sport." They set off across a field. "Are you running the plant today?"

Samson nodded his head toward a faint hum. "Quarter speed. That will give one copterload for the seventeen-hundred-hours collection, and leave enough over to go in the transit store for the night and provide Dewberry's man with some data. Or rather, lack of it."

"Where do you think it's going?"

"I've given up guessing."

Mr. Pennyhorse paused astride a stile and looked back at the grey bulk of the Priory. "I could guess who's responsible," he said, and chuckled.

"Uh? Who?"

Mr. Pennyhorse shook his head. "Leave that to your investigator." A few moments later he murmured as if to himself: "What a haunt! Ingenious devils."

But when Stephen Samson looked at him inquiringly, he added: "But I can't guess where your cans have been put."

And he would say nothing more on the subject.

Who would deny that the pure of heart are often simple-minded? (The obverse of the proposition need not be argued.) And that cause-effect relations are sometimes divined more readily by the intuition of simpletons than the logic of scholars?

Brother Simon Simplex—Simple Simon to later legends— looked openmouthed at the array of strange objects on the stone shelves of the kitchen storeroom. He was not surprised—his mouth was always open, even in sleep.

He took down one of the objects and examined it with mild curiosity. He shook it, turned it round, thrust a forefinger into a small depression. Something gave slightly, but there was no other aperture. He replaced it on the shelf.

When his fellow kitchener returned, he would ask him the purpose of the objects—if he could remember to do so. Simon's memory was poor. Each time the rota brought him onto kitchen duty for a week, he had to be instructed afresh in the business of serving meals in the refectory: platter so, napkin thus, spoon here, finger bowls half filled, three water pitchers, one before the Prior, one in the centre, one at the foot of the table—"and when you serve, tread softly and do not breathe down the necks of the brothers."

Even now could he hear the slight scrape of benches on stone as the monks, with bowed heads, freshly washed hands in the sleeves of their habits, filed slowly into the refectory and took their seats at the long oak table. And still his fellow kitchener had not returned from the errand. Food was prepared—dared he begin to serve alone?

It was a great problem for Simon, brother in the small House of Selcor, otherwise Selcor Priory, poor cell relation to the rich monastery of the Cluniac Order at Battle, in the year 1139 A.D.

Steam pressure in the triggered can of Miracle Meal did its work. The lid flipped. The aroma issued.

Simon's mouth nearly shut as he sniffed.

The calm and unquestioning acceptance of the impossible is another concomitant of simplicity and purity of heart. To the good and simple Simon the rising of the sun each morning and the singing of birds were recurrent miracles. Compared with these, a laboratory miracle of the year 2143 A.D. was as nothing.

Here was a new style of platter, filled with hot food, ready to serve. Wiser minds than his had undoubtedly arranged matters. His fellow kitchener, knowing the task was thus simplified, had left him to serve alone.

He had merely to remove the covers from these platters and carry them into the refectory. To remove the covers—cause—effect—the intuition of a simple mind.

Simon carried fourteen of the platters to the kitchen table, pressed buttons and waited.

He was gravely tempted to sample the food himself, but all-inclusive Benedictine rules forbade kitcheners to eat until their brothers had been served.

He carried a loaded tray into the refectory where the monks sat in patient silence except for the one voice of the Reader who stood at a raised lectern and intoned from the *Lives of the Saints*.

Pride that he had been thought fit to carry out the duty alone made Simon less clumsy than usual. He served the Prior, Dom Holland, first, almost deftly; then the other brothers, in two trips to the kitchen.

A spicy, rich, titillating fragrance filled the refectory. The intoning of the *Lives of the Saints* faltered for a moment as the mouth of the Reader filled with saliva, then he grimly continued.

At Dom Holland's signal, the monks ate.

The Prior spooned the last drops of gravy into his mouth. He sat back. A murmur arose. He raised a hand. The monks became quiet. The Reader closed his book.

Dom Holland was a man of faith; but he did not accept miracles or even the smallest departures from routine existence without questioning. He had sternly debated with himself whether he should question the new platters and the new food before or after eating. The aroma decided him. He ate first.

Now he got up, beckoned to a senior monk to follow him, and paced with unhurried calmness to the kitchen.

Simon had succumbed. He was halfway through his second tin. He stood up, licking his fingers.

"Whence comes this food, my son?" asked Dom Holland, in sonorous Latin.

Simon's mouth opened wider. His knowledge of the tongue was confined to prayers.

Impatiently the Prior repeated the question in the English dialect of the district.

Simon pointed, and led them to the storeroom.

"I looked, and it was here," he said simply. The words were t6 become famed.

His fellow kitchener was sought—he was found dozing in a warm corner of the kitchen garden—and questioned. He shook his head. The provisioner rather reluctantly disclaimed credit.

Dom Holland thought deeply, then gave instructions for a general assembly. The plastic "platters" and the hygiplast spoons were carefully examined. There were murmurs of wonderment at the workmanship. The discussion lasted two hours.

Simon's only contribution was to repeat with pathetic insistence: "I looked and it was there."

He realized dimly that he had become a person of some importance.

His face became a mask of puzzlement when the Prior summed up:

"Our simple but blessed brother, Simon Simplex, it seems to me, has become an instrument or vessel of some thaumaturgical manifestation. It would be wise, however, to await further demonstration before the matter is referred to higher authorities."

The storeroom was sealed and two monks were deputed as night guards.

Even with the possibility of a miracle on his hands, Dom Holland was not prepared to abrogate the Benedictine rule of only one main meal a day. The storeroom wasn't opened until early afternoon of the following day.

It was opened by Simon, in the presence of the Prior, a scribe, the provisioner, and two senior monks.

Released, a pile of Miracle Meal cans toppled forward like a crumbling cliff, slithering and clattering in noisy profusion around Simon's legs, sliding over the floor of the kitchen.

Simon didn't move. He was either too surprised or cunningly aware of the effectiveness of the scene. He stood calf-deep in cans, pointed at the jumbled stack inside the storeroom, sloping up nearly to the stone roof, and said his little piece:

"I look, and it is here."

"Kneel, my sons," said Dom Holland gravely, and knelt. Manna.

And at a time when the Priory was hard pressed to maintain even its own low standard of subsistence, without helping the scores of dispossessed refugees encamped in wattle shacks near its protecting walls.

The countryside was scourged by a combination of civil and foreign war. Stephen of Normandy against Matilda of Anjou for the British throne. Neither could control his own followers. When the Flemish mercenaries of King Stephen were not chasing Queen Matilda's Angevins back over the borders of Wiltshire, they were plundering the lands and possessions of nominal supporters of Stephen. The Angevins and the barons who supported Matilda's cause quite impartially did the same, then pillaged each other's property, castle against castle, baron against baron.

It was anarchy and free-for-all—but nothing for the ignored serfs, bondmen, villeins and general peasantry, who fled from stricken homes and roamed the countryside in bands of starving thousands. Some built shacks in the inviolate shadow of churches and monasteries.

Selcor Priory had its quota of barefoot, raggedy men, women and children—twelfth-century displaced persons.

They were a headache to the Prior, kindly Dom Holland—until Simple Simon's Miracle.

There were seventy recipients of the first hand-out of Miracle Meal cans from the small door in the Priory's walled kitchen garden.

The next day there were three hundred, and the day after that, four thousand. Good news doesn't need radio to get around fast.

Fourteen monks worked eight-hour shifts for twenty-four hours, hauling stocks from the capacious storeroom, pressing buttons, handing out steaming platters to orderly lines of refugees.

Two monks, shifting the last few cans from the store, were suddenly buried almost to their necks by the arrival of a fresh consignment, which piled up out of thin air.

Providence, it seemed, did not depend solely upon the intervention of Simon Simplex. The Priory itself and all its inhabitants were evidently blessed.

The Abbot of Battle, Dom Holland's superior, a man of great girth and great learning, visited the Priory. He confirmed the miracle—by studying the label on the can.

After several hours' work in the Prior's office, he announced to Dom Holland:

"The script presented the greatest difficulty. It is an extreme simplification of letter-forms at present in use by Anglo-Saxon scholars. The pertinent text is a corruption—if I may be pardoned the use of such a term in the circumstances—of the Latin '*miraculum*' compounded with the word '*maél*' from our own barbarous tongue so, clearly, Miracle Meal!"

Dom Holland murmured his awe of this learning.

The Abbot added, half to himself: "Although why the nature of the manifestation should be thus advertised in repetitive engraving, when it is self-evident—" He shrugged. "The ways of Providence are passing strange."

Brother Gregory, reclining in the starlight near his favourite oak, said: "My only regret is that we cannot see the effect of our gift—the theoretical impact of a modern product—usually a weapon—on past ages is a well-tried topic of discussion and speculation among historians, scientists, economists and writers of fantasy."

Brother James, hunched in vague adumbration on a wall behind, said: "You are none of those things, else might you explain why it is that, if these cans have reached the period for which, according to your abstruse calculations, they were destined—an age in which we were both alive—we cannot remember such an event, or why it is not recorded in histories of the period."

"It was a time of anarchy, dear brother. Many records were destroyed. And as for our memories—well, great paradoxes of time are involved. One might as profitably ask how many angels may dance on the point of a pin. Now if you should wish to know how many atoms might be accommodated in a like position—"

Brother Gregory was adroit at changing the subject. He didn't wish to speculate aloud until he'd figured out all the paradox possibilities. He'd already discarded an infinity of time-streams as intellectually unsatisfying, and was toying with the concept of recurrent worlds.

"Dom Pennyhorse has guessed that it is our doing."

"What's that?"

Brother James repeated the information smugly.

Gregory said slowly: "Well, he is not—unsympathetic—to us." "Assuredly, brother, we have naught to fear from him, nor from the pleasant young man with whom he goes fishing. But this young nan was today in consultation with his superior, and an investigator's being sent from America."

"Psychic investigator, eh? Phooey. We'll tie him in knots," said Gregory complacently.

"I assume," said Brother James, with a touch of self-righteousness, "that these vulgar colloquialisms to which you sometimes have recourse are another result of your nocturnal reading. They offend my ear. 'Phooey,' indeed. No, this investigator is one with whom you will undoubtedly find an affinity. I gather that he is from a laboratory—a scientist of sorts."

Brother Gregory sat up and rubbed his tonsure thoughtfully. 'That," he admitted, "is different." There was a curious mixture of alarm and eagerness in his voice. "There are means of detecting the field we employ."

An elementary electroscope was one of the means. An ionization indicator and a thermometer were others. They were all bolted firmly on a bench just inside the storeroom. Wires led from them under the door to a jury-rigged panel outside.

Sandy-haired Sidney Meredith of M.M. Research sat in front of the panel on a folding stool, watching dials with intense blue eyes, chin propped in hands.

Guards had been cleared from the factory. He was alone, on the advice of Mr. Pennyhorse, who had told him: "If, as I suspect, it's the work of two of my... uh... flock... two very ancient parishioners... they are more likely to play their tricks in the absence of a crowd."

"I get it," Meredith had said. "Should be interesting."

It was.

He poured coffee from a thermos without taking his eyes from the panel. The thermometer reading was dropping slowly. Ionization was rising. From inside the store came the faint rasp of moving objects.

Meredith smiled, sighted a thumb-size camera, recorded the panel readings. "This," he said softly, "will make a top feature in the *Journal*: 'The most intensive psychic and poltergeist phenomena ever recorded. M.M.'s top tech trouble-shooter spikes spooks.'"

There was a faint snap beyond the door. Dials swooped back to zero. Meredith quit smiling and daydreaming.

"Hey—play fair!" he called.

The whisper of a laugh answered him, and a soft, hollow whine, as of a wind cycloning into outer space.

He grabbed the door, pulled. It resisted. It was like trying to break a vacuum. He knelt, lit a cigarette, held it near the bottom of the nearly flush-fitting door. A thin streamer of smoke curled down and was drawn swiftly through the barely perceptible crack.

The soft whine continued for a few seconds, began to die away.

Meredith yanked at the door again. It gave, to a slight ingush of air. He thrust his foot in the opening, said calmly into the empty blackness: "When you fellers have quite finished—I'm coming in. Don't go away. Let's talk."

He slipped inside, closed the door, stood silent for a moment. He sniffed. Ozone. His scalp prickled. He scratched his head, felt the hairs standing upright. And it was cold.

He said: "Right. No point in playing dumb or covering up, boys." He felt curiously ashamed of the platitudes as he uttered them. "I must apologize for breaking in," he added—and meant it. "But this has got to finish. And if you're not willing to—co-operate—I think I know now how to finish it."

Another whisper of a laugh. And two words, faint, gently mocking: "Do you?"

Meredith strained his eyes against the darkness. He saw only the nerve patterns in his own eyes. He shrugged.

"If you won't play—" He switched on a blaze of fluor lamps. The long steel shelves were empty. There was only one can of Miracle Meal left in the store.

He felt it before he saw it. It dropped on his head, clattered to the plastocrete floor. When he'd retrieved his breath, he kicked it savagely to the far end of the store and turned to his instruments.

The main input lead had been pulled away. The terminal had been loosened first.

He undamped a wide-angle infrared camera, waited impatiently for the developrinter to act, pulled out the print.

And laughed. It wasn't a good line caricature of himself, but it was recognizable, chiefly by the shock of unruly hair.

The lines were slightly blurred, as though written by a needle-point of light directly on the film. There was a jumble of writing over and under it.

"Old English, I suppose," he murmured. He looked closer. The writing above the caricature was a de Sitter version of the Riemann-Christoffel tensor, followed in crabbed but readable modern English by the words: "Why reverse the sign? Do we act like anti-particles?"

Underneath the drawing was an energy tensor and a comment: "You will notice that magnetic momenta contribute a negative density and pressure."

A string of symbols followed, ending with an equals sign and a query mark. And another comment: "You'll need to take time out to balance this one."

Meredith read the symbols, then sat down heavily on the edge of the instrument bench and groaned. Time out. But Time was already out, and there was neither matter nor radiation in a de Sitter universe.

Unless...

He pulled out a notebook, started to scribble.

An hour later Mr. Pennyhorse and Stephen Samson came in.

Mr. Pennyhorse said: "My dear young fellow, we were quite concerned. We thought—"

He stopped. Meredith's blue eyes were slightly out of focus. There were beads of sweat on his brow despite the coolness of the storeroom. Leaves from his notebook and cigarette stubs littered the floor around his feet.

He jumped like a pricked frog when the vicar gently tapped his shoulder, and uttered a vehement cuss-word that startled even the broad-minded cleric.

Samson tutted.

Meredith muttered: "Sorry, sir. But I think I nearly had it."

"What, my son?"

Meredith looked like a ruffle-haired schoolboy. His eyes came back into focus. "A crossword puzzle clue," he said. "Set by a spook with a super-I.Q. Two quite irreconcilable systems of mathematics lumped together, the signs in an extended energy tensor reversed, merry hell played with a temporal factor—and yet it was beginning to make sense."

He smiled wryly. "A ghost who unscrews terminals before he breaks connections and who can make my brain boil is a ghost worth meeting."

Mr. Pennyhorse eased his pince-nez. "Uh... yes. Now, don't you think it's time you came to bed? It's four A.M. My housekeeper has made up a comfortable place on the divan in the sitting room." He took Meredith's arm and steered him from the store.

As they walked across the dewy meadows toward the vicarage, with the first pale streaks of dawn showing in the sky, Samson said: "How about the cans?"

"Time," replied Meredith vaguely, "will tell."

"And the guards?"

"Pay them off. Send them away. Keep the plant rolling. Fill the transit store tonight. And I want a freighter copter to take me to London University this afternoon."

Back in the transit store, the discarded leaves from Meredith's notebook fluttered gently upward in the still air and disappeared.

Brother James said: "He is alone again."

They looked down on the sandy head of Sidney Meredith from the vantage point of a dehydrating tower.

"So I perceive. And I fear this may be our last... uh... consignment to our erstwhile brothers," said Gregory thoughtfully.

"Why?"

"You will see. In giving him the clue to what we were doing, I gave him the clue to what we are, essentially."

They drifted down toward the transit store.

"After you, Brother James," said Brother Gregory with excessive politeness.

James adjusted his plane of incidence, started through the wall, and—

Shot backward with a voiceless scream of agony.

Brother Gregory laughed. "I'm sorry. But that's why it will be our last consignment. Heterodyning is painful. He is a very intelligent fellow. The next time, he will take care to screen both his ultra-short generator and controls so that I cannot touch them."

Brother James recovered. "You... you use me as a confounded guinea pig! By the saints, you appear to have more sympathy with the man than with me!"

"Not more sympathy, my beloved brother, but certainly much more in common," Brother Gregory replied frankly. "Wait." He drifted behind Meredith's back and poltered the tip of one finger to flick a lightly soldered wire from a terminal behind a switch. Meredith felt his scalp tingle. A pilot light on his panel blinked out.

Meredith got up from his stool, stretched lazily, grinned into the empty air. He said aloud: "Right. Help yourselves. But I warn you—once you're in, you don't come out until you agree to talk. I have a duplicate set and a built-in circuit-tester. The only way you can spike them is by busting tubes. And I've a hunch you wouldn't do that."

"No," James muttered. "You wouldn't. Let us go."

"No," Gregory answered. "Inside quickly—and whirl. Afterward I shall speak with him. He is a youth of acute sensibilities and gentleness, whose word is his bond."

Gregory urged his fellow monk to the wall. They passed within.

Meredith heard nothing, until a faint whine began in the store. He waited until it died away, then knocked on the door. It seemed, crazily, the correct thing to do.

He went into the darkness. "You there?"

A low and pleasant voice, directionless: "Yes. Why didn't you switch on your duplicate generator?"

Meredith breathed deep. "I didn't think it would be necessary. I feel we understand each other. My name is Sidney Meredith." "Mine is Gregory of Ramsbury."

"And your—friend?"

"James Brasenose. I may say that he disapproves highly of this conversation."

"I can understand that. It is unusual. But then, you're a very unusual... um—"

"'Ghost' is the common term, Mr. Meredith. Rather inadequate, I think, for supranormal phenomena which are, nevertheless, subject to known laws. Most Untranslated spirits remain quite ignorant of their own powers before final Translation. It was only by intensive reading and thought that I determined the principles and potentialities of my construction."

"Anti-particles?"

"According to de Sitter," said Brother Gregory, "that is what we should be. But we are not mere mathematical expressions. I prefer the term 'energy foci.' From a perusal of the notes you left behind yesterday morning—and, of course, from your use of ultra-short waves tonight—it seems you struck the correct train of deduction immediately. Incidentally, where did you obtain the apparatus at such short notice?"

"London University."

Brother Gregory sighed. "I should like to visit their laboratories.

But we are bound to this area by a form of moral compulsion that I cannot define or overcome. Only vicariously, through the achievements of others, may I experience the thrill of research."

"You don't do so badly," Meredith said. He was mildly surprised that he felt quite so sane and at ease, except for the darkness.

"Would you mind if we had a light?"

"I must be semipolted—or warped—to speak with you. It's not a pleasant sight—floating lungs, larynx, palate, tongue and lips. I'd feel uncomfortable for you. We might appear for you later, if you wish."

"Right. But keep talking. Give me the how and the why. I want this for my professional journal."

"Will you see that the issue containing your paper is placed in the local library?"

"Surely," Meredith said. "Two copies."

"Brother James is not interested. Brother James, will you kindly stop whispering nonsense and remove yourself to a nexus point for a while? I intend to converse with Mr. Meredith. Thank you."

The voice of Brother Gregory came nearer, took on a slightly professorial tone. "Any massive and rotating body assumes the qualities of magnetism—or rather, gravitic, one-way flux—by virtue of its rotation, and the two quantities of magnetic momentum and angular momentum are always proportional to one another, as you doubtless know."

Meredith smiled inwardly. A lecture on elementary physics from a ghost. Well—maybe not so elementary. He remembered the figures that he'd sweated over. But he could almost envisage the voice of Brother Gregory emanating from a black-gowned instructor in front of a classroom board.

"Take a star," the voice continued. "Say 78 Virginis—from whose flaming promontories the effect was first deduced a hundred years ago—and put her against a counter-whirling star of similar mass. What happens? Energy warp, of the kind we use every time we polt. But something else happens—did you infer it from my incomplete expression?"

Meredith grinned. He said: "Yes. Temporal warp."

"Oh." There was a trace of disappointment in the voice.

Meredith added quickly: "But it certainly gave me a headache figuring it out."

Gregory was evidently mollified by the admission. "Solids through time," he went on. "Some weeks ago, calculating that my inherent field was as great in certain respects as that of 78 Virginis, I whirled against a longitudinal line, and forced a stone back a few days—the nearest I could get to laboratory confirmation. Knowing there would be a logical extension of the effect if I whirled against a field as strong as my own, I persuaded Brother James to cooperate with me and you know the result."

"How far back?"

"According to my mathematics, the twelfth century, at a time when we were—alive. I would appreciate your views on the paradoxes involved."

Meredith said: "Certainly. Let's go over your math together first. If it fits in with what I've already figured, perhaps I'll have a suggestion to make. You appreciate, of course, that I can't let you have any more cans?"

"Quite. I must congratulate your company on manufacturing a most delicious comestible. If you will hand me the roll of infrared film from your camera, I can make my calculations visible to you on the emulsion in the darkness. Thank you. It is a pity," Gregory murmured, "that we could not see with our own eyes what disposal they made of your product in the days of our Priory."

When, on the morning of a certain bright summer day in 1139, the daily consignment of Miracle Meal failed to arrive at Selcor Priory, thousands of disappointed refugees went hungry.

The Prior, Dom Holland—who, fortunately for his sanity or at least his peace of mind, was not in a position to separate cause from effect—attributed the failure of supply to the lamentable departure from grace and moral standards of two of the monks.

By disgracing themselves in the kitchen garden with a female refugee, he said, they had obviously rendered the Priory unfit to receive any further miraculous bounty.

The abject monks, Brother Gregory and Brother James, were severely chastised and warned in drastic theological terms that it would probably be many centuries before they had sufficiently expiated their sins to attain blessedness.

On the morning of another bright summer day, the Reverend Malachi Pennyhorse and Stephen Samson were waiting for Sidney Meredith in the vicar's comfortable study.

Meredith came in, sank into a century-old leather easy chair, stretched his shoes, damp with dew from the meadow grass, toward the flames. He accepted a glass of whisky gratefully, sipped it.

He said: "The cans are there. And from now on, they stay in the transit store until the copters collect."

There was an odd note of regret in his voice.

Samson said: "Fine. Now maybe you'll tell us what happened yesterday."

Mr. Pennyhorse said: "You... uh... liked my parishioners, then?"

Meredith combined a smile and a sigh. "I surely did. That Brother Gregory had the most intense and dispassionate intellectual curiosity of anyone I ever met. He nearly grounded me on some aspects of energy mathematics. I could have used him in my department. He'd have made a great research man. Brother James wasn't a bad old guy, either. They appeared for me—"

"How did you get rid of them?" Samson interrupted.

"They got rid of themselves. Gregory told me how, by whirling against each other with gravitic fields cutting, they drew the cans into a vortex of negated time that threw them way back to the twelfth century. After we'd been through his math, I suggested they whirl together."

"What—and throw the cans ahead?"

"No. Themselves, in a sense, since they precipitated a future, hoped-for state. Gregory had an idea what would happen. So did I. He'd only discovered the effect recently. Curiosity got the better of him. He had to try it out straight away. They whirled together. The fields reinforced, instead of negated. Enough in-going energy was generated to whoop their own charges well above capacity and equilibrium. They just—went. As Gregory would put it—they were Translated."

"Upwards, I trust," said Mr. Pennyhorse gently.

"Amen to that," said Samson.

Upwards—

Pure thought, unbound, Earth-rid, roaming free amid the wild bright stars—

Thought to Thought, over galactic vastnesses, wordless, yet swift and clear, before egos faded—

"Why didn't I think of this before? We might have Translated ourselves centuries ago."

"But then we would never have tasted Miracle Meal."

"That is a consideration," agreed the Thought that had been Brother Gregory.

"Remember our third can?" came the Thought that had been Brother James.

But there was no reply. Something of far greater urgency and interest than memories of Miracle Meal had occurred to the Thought that had been Brother Gregory.

With eager curiosity, it was spiralling down into the heart of a star to observe the integration of helium at first hand.

TENTH TIME AROUND

J. T. McIntosh

J. T. McIntosh was the best known pen name of Scottish writer James Murdoch Macgregor (1925–2008), who was a mainstay of the science-fiction magazines from his first sale, "The Curfew Tolls" in 1950 to his last "The World of God" (1979). Thereafter he ceased writing, chiefly because his key markets dried up. His most important work was One in Three Hundred *(1954) which considers in stages how people are chosen to leave Earth in advance of the planet's destruction from solar flares and how those will then survive, if at all, on Mars. Other novels of note include* The Million Cities *(1963) portraying a frightening overpopulated Earth and* Time for a Change *(1967) where Earth is visited by time-travelling aliens. Surprisingly none of McIntosh's short stories, of which he wrote close on a hundred, were reissued in collections and yet these were often amongst his best works. In this story, so typical of its period in describing sexual attitudes, McIntosh asks just what do you have to do to win another's love.*

H AVING SAID GOODBYE TO THE LAST OF HIS FRIENDS, GENE Player took a cab to the Second Chance building; as far as his particular friends went, he was now dead. They'd never see him again—not in this universe.

He would see them again, of course...

The taxi-driver stared at his tip. "Maybe I should keep my big mouth shut," he said, "but I couldn't sleep nights. This is five thousand dollars, Bud."

For answer Gene pointed at the Second Chance building.

"Oh," said the cabbie. "I get it. All the same, ain't you got anybody to leave it to?"

"No," said Gene.

He'd given money to such of his friends as he thought needed it and would be better off with it. He'd left some to charity. The rest was to go to Belinda—even if she was Mrs. Harry Scott.

He paid no attention to the big display ads in the lobbies of the vast Second Chance building. He'd seen them before, in nine similar but slightly different universes. He paid still less to the hesitant, worried, uncertain people who were looking at the displays, biting their nails, taking a step back and two forward, or vice versa.

It was a big decision, the first time. If you were at all successful in life at forty, fifty, sixty, the glorious thought of being young again, strong, healthy and probably in love, was considerably tempered by the consideration that you'd be pushed around again, that you'd have to get up at seven and work hard all day for less than a

tenth of what you made now, that you'd have to go through this
or that operation again, that you'd have to see your father and
mother die again...

Besides, there was no guarantee that you'd be successful the
second time. Weakened by success, you might not work as hard.
Or you might make a mistake you'd avoided before.

You could do better with your life, or you could do worse.

It was the failures in life who wanted a second chance, and they
were about eighty-five per cent likely to achieve the same failure.
Not many of them got the opportunity—failures didn't have the
money for a flashback.

Merely because he happened to see a visiphone booth vacant
and open, Gene suddenly thought of calling Belinda. It was a
purely spontaneous idea—he hadn't said goodby to her and hadn't
intended to.

However, before he had consciously made up his mind he was
in the booth and dialling Belinda's number.

Her face faded in on the screen and assumed surprise. "Why,
Gene," she said. "You promised—"

"I'm at the Second Chance building," he said. "I'm going back
to 1975."

Her eyes softened. She didn't say anything.

In her thirties, Belinda Scott was lovelier than she had been in
her twenties, because she was that type of woman. She had always
been magnificent, but her magnificence sat more gracefully on her
maturity than on her youth.

"You won't be seeing me again," Gene said. "But I'll be seeing
you."

There was affection in her eyes, but not love. Never love.

"Gene," she said quietly, "can't you just accept the fact that for me it must always be Harry?"

"Suppose Harry were dead? Suppose I killed him?"

She shook her head, smiling. "You wouldn't do that, Gene."

"No," he said heavily. "I wouldn't do that."

"Good luck, Gene," she said, and her warm smile faded as he cut the connection.

He left the booth and made his way upstairs. He knew exactly where to go. Pethick's secretary was a different one this time. He wondered what had happened to the honey-blonde, wondered what she was doing instead of being Pethick's secretary.

Pethick was always the same. He didn't know Gene; that didn't matter.

Pethick was a little round duck of a man, an egg over a balloon over two sad little overworked legs. He came forward with his hand outstretched.

"Mr. Player?" he said. "It's a pleasure to meet you. I've read all your books."

The first time Gene had been flattered, had talked about his novels and found out that Pethick really had read them all. Since that time, he had not bothered.

"Frankly, Mr. Player," Pethick said, "though I'm glad as a director of Second Chance Incorporated that you're considering flashback, I'm sorry as a reader."

"Thank you," said Gene automatically. Even sincere things sounded pretty thin the ninth time around. "But I'm not considering it. I've already considered. I'm going."

"There are certain things I have to tell you—"

"I know them. I've done it before."

"Oh." Pethick was interested. "Have you met me in other universes?"

"Always."

"Always? How often—"

"Nine times. This is the tenth."

Pethick looked startled. "And you come back here every time? You must have a very good reason—"

"I have."

"Mr. Player, if you're trying to change something and have failed eight or nine times, there must be a strong possibility that you're up against a buttressed situation, what we call an immutable. In that case—"

"I know about that. It's my worry."

"Of course, but—"

"I want to go back to June 3, 1975."

"That's the very first day we can reach," said Pethick, struck by the coincidence. "And it's only this week we've been allowed to extend flashback as far as that."

"I know. That's why I'm here."

"You've waited till 1986 to be able to go back to 1975?"

"Yes."

Pethick was quite excited over all this. Gene Player was his most interesting client for a long time.

"Does it always work exactly as planned?" he asked. "Do you always land exactly—"

"Eleven-twenty, Tuesday, June 3, 1975. It's always raining and I always get soaked. I wasn't wearing a raincoat that day."

"Perhaps we could make it a little later in the day, say—"

"Please, Mr. Pethick. I don't want to be rude, but I've already been through something very like this conversation nine times already."

"Of course, Mr. Player."

"Then could we cut the cackle and get to business?"

Pethick was hurt, as usual.

Few things changed as little from universe to universe as Pethick did. From the moment of flashback you were doing, thinking, saying different things and creating a new world. That didn't matter to the one you'd just left; it went on happily without you. The one you'd entered, or re-entered, was another matter. Within days you could have been the cause of some remarkable changes.

There were, however, a few things, some big, some small, some important, some unimportant, which didn't change. Which couldn't be changed.

The immutables.

They didn't bother with a medical; this body was going to be as good as dead within seconds anyway.

It wasn't time-travel, exactly. Nothing travelled except consciousness and memory. Which was why nobody could ever take any money.

Your consciousness and memory were put back into the you of another universe, at any time between June 3, 1975, when the whole business started, and the current date. In Gene's case that was February 9, 1986.

Naturally there wouldn't be any point in this unless you knew about it. Gene would know exactly what he knew as of February 9, 1986, plus what he had known on June 3, 1975. It would be quite a jolt for the 1975 Gene Player, but Gene knew he could take it.

Gene paid no attention to the technical side; this was an old story.

Pethick had been flabbergasted when he produced a check for $191,732, the exact fee with all dues and extras and tax. That never changed either.

They warned him that it was just about to happen, and he nodded. He knew he was exasperating everybody by being so casual about it all...

He was in a city street, running for shelter in a sudden shower.

The brain and body belonged to a Gene Player who was twenty-six, not thirty-seven, and though he tried to take over with his 1986 mind, the shock was so great that he stumbled and fell headlong.

By the time he'd picked himself up, he was already soaked, and shelter no longer mattered so much. People huddling in doorways stared at him curiously.

It wouldn't occur to any of them what had happened, because though some of them must have heard about flashback, due to operate from that day, hardly anybody believed it yet.

The rain stopped abruptly, very much to Gene's surprise. His arrival couldn't possibly have any immediate effect on the weather. He glanced at his watch and saw it was eleven-forty-one. Twenty-one minutes later than usual.

If Pethick had to fiddle with his time of arrival, he might have made it five minutes later, after the rain was off.

The sun blazed and the streets steamed. The hordes emerged from the doorways and clacked along the sidewalks.

The 1975 Gene was marvelling incredulously, but as usual it was the 1986 Gene who was really in control. Within an hour or two they'd have merged completely.

People were always the same, but fashion was always a momentary surprise. It seemed impossible that the Twentieth Century could include a phase of super-modesty, yet here it was, right at its peak. In 1975, city councils were stopping theatres from showing movies more than two years old, because of the shocking depravity of feminine dress before 1973. Girls of twenty were hotly denying that at seventeen they had worn shorts and frequently had left their shoulders bare.

It was a brief, curious phase and would last, Gene remembered, just six more months before fashion started to swing towards the salaciousness of the early eighties and the comparatively innocent nudity of the middle eighties, if the swing went as far as it had done in run six.

Drab colours went with the repressive clothes, naturally— dark blues and browns, greys, blacks, bottle-greens. Nobody, but nobody, wore red.

Gene shook off his surprise. He knew all about 1975 and its superficial drabness. It was a shock merely as it is a shock to see an old photograph.

He knew what to do.

First he went to the bank and cleared the account. With what he had had in his pockets, he now had three hundred forty-seven dollars and seventy-one cents. Not much, but enough. There was a little more to come. He was about to be fired.

He didn't go to see Mr. Kynock of Wheatie Puffets. And when he entered the Motet Advertising offices at twelve-ten, Mr. Carswell was waiting, fuming.

"Player, Kynock just called," said Carswell. "It seems you didn't go to see him."

"No," said Gene laconically.

"Why not?"

"I had more important things to do."

Carswell boiled over. "Player," he said furiously, "you're fired."

"Thank you," said George gratefully. That was even shorter than usual.

When he had collected his things—and his pay-check—Carswell was waiting in the outer office. He had cooled down considerably. "Perhaps I was a little hasty, Player," he said. "I've no doubt you have an explanation. We don't really want to lose you. You have a certain touch with advertising copy—"

"Thank you," said Gene again, automatically, sidestepped him and walked out.

If you wanted them, they didn't want you. And vice versa. Gene was philosophizing about this as he hit the sidewalk again, and felt the blast of the midday heat.

The first time, and to a lesser extent the second time, he had wanted to keep his job. He had pleaded with Carswell, who had been adamant. Subsequently Gene had wanted nothing more than to be fired—and Carswell had pleaded with him.

Perhaps there was a pointer there to the way he should act with Belinda. He thought about that over lunch.

No point in trying to see her now. She'd already met Harry Scott—he could never get to her before that vitally important point in her life, and his.

Harry Scott was a friend of Gene's, and first time round Gene had met Belinda only after they were married. Subsequently Gene had arranged not strictly chance meetings in all sorts of circumstances and places. Going to Canada, where Belinda was now, was a complete flop. Belinda's aunt was with her, the aunt always took an instant dislike to Gene, and the results were disastrous.

No, Gene had found a strange, improbable, dangerous and apparently wildly coincidental way of meeting Belinda the day she returned from Canada in a few weeks' time, and since it had worked effectively several times already there seemed no reason why it shouldn't work again. There was never anything wrong *then*. It was later that Belinda was so much in love with Harry that there was no shifting her.

This time he'd have to make better use of that first meeting. If he failed then, there was never any chance later.

Meantime, he had work to do. He needed money, like everybody else. It was so hot, however, that he was reluctant to go to his tiny, stuffy room and get busy. He lingered in the park after lunch, as he had never done before—and right away the sequence of events began to change.

His apartment, if you could call it that, overlooked the park. He could be hard at work in five minutes. He knew he ought to get started, but for a few moments he sat in the sun, gathering his strength for the long, concentrated effort he would have to make.

And he saw the blonde.

She should be in a sweater and shorts instead of that hideous ankle-length grey skirt and black bodice. Funny her being alone. Even in 1975 a girl like that ought to pick up men like flies.

Having his whole course so completely preordained, knowing exactly what was going to happen, he was somehow freer, more reckless, less self-conscious than he would otherwise have been. He stopped beside her.

"You didn't drop your handkerchief," he said.

She pretended he didn't exist. Now that he was close to her, he saw she was very young, probably still in her teens. She was also even more pretty than he had thought.

"Why didn't you drop your handkerchief?" he pursued.

"I couldn't," she said rather nervously. "I haven't got one."

"You mean if you had one, you'd certainly have dropped it?"

"I don't mean anything of the kind!" she retorted hotly. "Now if you'll please—"

"Thank you," he said. "I will." He sat down beside her.

Though flustered, she couldn't help very nearly smiling. Promising, he decided. Funny how the fact that there was only one woman in the world for you made things go so much more smoothly with other women. Perhaps it was like the Motet Advertising job. You could get anything at all, provided you didn't want it.

"You would be pretty," he told her.

That got her. She turned a cute little nose to him. "If what?"

"If you wore something feminine."

She turned the cute little nose in the air.

"My name is Gene Player and I'm a writer," he said.

No answer.

He didn't really care, and he had work to do anyway. He got up.

"I'm Doreen Barrett," she said quickly.

He sat down again.

This didn't count, of course. Belinda was the only woman who mattered. He'd been in love with her for ninety-nine years—11 x 9.

At the same time he was beginning to be fatalistic. If the same thing happened with Belinda as always did happen with Belinda, there was no harm in having somebody like Doreen Barrett as a second string.

When in the early evening he got to work, he tore into it to make up for lost time.

He rolled a sheet of paper into the ancient machine, banged out *"One Face for Heaven,* a novel by Gene Player," and proceeded to rush through pages at an average rate of one every ten minutes.

When he stopped at 3 a.m. he had finished sixty pages, about 15,000 words.

If anything, *One Face for Heaven* was better every time he wrote it. The dross dropped out; only the really good sections were written word for word. Every time it was stronger, surer. The curious thing was that it always sold almost exactly the same number of copies, despite the minor changes, each time which in total should have been considerable.

Originally he had written *One Face for Heaven* some years after this, after many months of indifferent success. The first time he had committed it to paper in 1975 he had done so with misgivings, knowing that a book which was a tremendous success could easily be a flop ten years before or ten years after. Particularly a book like *One Face for Heaven*, the sexy passages of which might kill the novel stone dead in the censorious mid-seventies.

However, he needn't have worried. In the mid-seventies, as in the Victorian age, public morality was balanced by private immorality. Everybody would censure *One Face for Heaven*, but everybody would read it.

The next day he wrote another 15,000 words before staggering out to see Doreen in the park again. She wasn't there, despite her promise. The hell with her. He went back and wrote another 10,000.

Early next morning, haggard and unshaved, he dug in again. At lunchtime he suddenly noticed how hot and tired and limp he was. He was soaked in sweat.

Without shaving, washing or changing his clothes, he went out in the park again, merely for fresh air.

And Doreen was there waiting for him, pouring out apologies for not being there the day before after promising she would be...

She had been so eager to explain that she hadn't looked at him properly, but she soon noticed the state he was in. "Why … what's the matter?" she said. "You look as if you'd been through hell."

"I have," said Gene. "Because you weren't here yesterday."

She was very young. "Do you really care as much as that, Gene? I didn't know…" But she was also intelligent. "You're ribbing me," she said indignantly. "It was nothing to do with me."

He grinned at her. She was sweet.

"What have you really been doing?" she asked.

"Writing a book. I've done 40,000 words since I saw you."

"Is it worth working so hard on it?"

"Oh yes. It's a best-seller."

"How do you know?"

"Call it Faith."

She was puzzled, but impressed. She was no more than eighteen, and Gene was beginning to wish he had never spoken to her. She had obviously stayed fresh and frank and innocent because she had never been in love and had had no trouble in dealing with men whom she didn't love. But already she was falling in love with Gene, and that was a new complication.

He had never lost Belinda because some other girl was in love with him, but there had to be a first time for everything.

Of course, if he fared with Belinda as he always had, Doreen needn't break her heart. Once he had duly lost Belinda he'd be prepared to turn without much enthusiasm to some other girl, who might as well be Doreen.

But this time he wasn't going to lose Belinda, and that was why this wasn't fair to Doreen.

Belinda's love for Harry Scott couldn't be an immutable. Gene refused even to consider the possibility.

Immutables … nobody knew quite what they were or what caused them. They were things which just had to happen, however they happened.

There was the atomic explosion in Pittsburg in 1981. After it had happened, a technician was sent back a few days to fix it. It had happened in one universe and couldn't be avoided there. But in all other universes it could.

It was not surprising that the technician who volunteered to go was a man whose wife and family had been killed in the explosion.

He saved his wife and family, but the explosion still happened. It happened in all the universes Gene knew, and he was something of an expert on universes. Though the effects of the disaster could be limited, and were, it nevertheless happened—always.

There was a lesser immutable that Gene happened to know about.

First time round he'd been at a heavyweight title fight in which Frank Bolsey knocked out Fats Homeier in the seventh. Second time round he didn't bother to go, since he knew what would happen.

On that occasion Bolsey beat Homeier on points over fifteen rounds.

Gene didn't think much about this at the time, but was sufficiently interested to have a ringside seat the third time round. That time Homeier battered Bolsey all round the ring until the ninth round, when suddenly Bolsey won on a knock-out—his first real punch.

Gene had found since then that this fight, which was quite obviously not fixed, must be another of these strange immutables. Anything could happen in it. Homeier could be an obvious winner nine tenths of the way or Bolsey could ride easily through it—but whatever happened, Bolsey had to win.

Knowing all this, Gene stubbornly refused to believe that there was anything immutable about Belinda's love for Harry Scott.

This time the immutable was going to be mutated.

And that was why he felt guilty about Doreen.

By the next time he saw Doreen he had finished well over a hundred thousand words.

She worked in an office which closed for two hours at lunchtime, and as she merely pecked for fifteen minutes or so, this left her a lot of time to spend in the park.

By now there wasn't the slightest doubt of it—she was in love with him. Being a well-brought-up girl, she wouldn't invite him to invite her to do something more than just see her in the park for an hour or so each day, but she did all that a well-brought-up girl could do to make herself as attractive as possible to him. In 1975, when clothes weren't allowed to play their part, this wasn't much. She might have a figure like Aphrodite, or like Aphrodite's grandmother, for all that Gene knew.

In any case, he was a dedicated man. Apart from washing and shaving before going out to meet Doreen, eating and sleeping when he remembered, he was spending twenty-four hours a day at his typewriter. He had to—publishers take their time about handing over money for a novel, and also Gene wanted the book off his hands before Belinda got back from Canada.

He preferred doing it that way. Normally a novelist has to take time off to revise and think, or he may find himself having to throw away big chunks of what he has written. But Gene knew his story, characters, everything. He also knew that *One Face for Heaven* was better than ever this time, which helped.

Ignoring Doreen's wistful hints, he went back to work. When

it was quite late, he was so near completing the book that he decided to go straight on, and around 7 a.m. he banged THE END, and thankfully flopped in bed.

When he opened his gummy eyes Doreen was bending over him. He saw with acute surprise that even with dresses the way they were, a pretty girl of eighteen bending over far enough could be quite sensational.

He didn't sit up. "How did you get up here?" he said indistinctly. "Did you have to shoot Mrs. Schukelmacher?"

"Your landlady? I saw her go out. Gene, this place is filthy. You've been living like a pig."

"I know," he sighed. He sat up, wincing; Doreen wasn't bending over him any more. His throat was raw from too much smoking, his head ached, and he had a whale of a hangover, which was unfair as he had drunk nothing alcoholic since 1986.

Doreen threw open the window to let out the blue-grey fog in the room. The temperature must have been close to a hundred, the air was used up, and it was no wonder Gene had a tongue four sizes too big and a skull six sizes too small.

"I came when I didn't see you in the park," Doreen said. "I was afraid you…"

She turned away quickly and started picking things up.

Gene got to his feet, swaying. He remembered something. "This is Saturday," he said.

"Yes."

"You don't work at all today."

"No."

"You usually go home for the weekends."

She didn't reply. She kept her face turned away from him.

★

It was too late to retreat. She had said she'd see him in the park as usual, and he saw now that she had remained in town specially to do so. He hadn't realized that the day before, being too soaked in *One Face for Heaven* to notice anything.

He knew that if he said he had work to do, she'd go away meekly, disappointed and hurt but bravely concealing it. Trying hard to think rationally, he decided it would be a lot better if she did.

Yet if he sent her away he'd feel a heel. If he sent her away he'd *be* a heel. Also a fool.

"Doreen," he said, "let's leave this place exactly as it is, go out in the country, swim, laze in the sun, maybe dance in the evening." The thought of swimming made him shudder, but he knew it would make a new man of him. That would be all to the good, too, for the one he was was shot.

Doreen's eyes were shining. "Wonderful, Gene, but—what about your book?"

He picked up the pile of sheets and started to knock them into a neat oblong. "Finished," he said thankfully. "I ought to check it over, cut out anachronisms, but what the hell. They'll like it as it is, and all that can be done afterwards."

He started clumsily wrapping the fat pile of quarto paper in brown paper.

"Let me do that," said Doreen quickly.

"With pleasure."

While she did so he had a quick shower and put on his lightest clothes. He didn't eat anything, merely washed out his mouth. When he was good and hungry he'd eat.

They left the gloomy rooming-house and he mailed the

typescript. Then, recklessly, he hired an old car and drove Doreen to the apartment she shared with another girl.

Before she went in, she hesitated. "Were you serious about swimming, Gene?" she asked.

"Sure, why?"

"Oh, nothing." But still she hesitated.

"What's the matter? Can't you swim?"

"Yes, but … my costume isn't … it's old, and…"

He got it. "I promise not to be shocked," he said kindly.

She wasn't sure how to take that, and went slowly up the steps while he waited in the car.

They drove far enough for Gene to become ravenous and then stopped at a drive-in for lunch. They picked up a packed lunch while they were there, and drove on until they found an uncommercialized lake.

It was so uncommercialized that in getting to it the car got stuck and had to be left blocking the alleged road. Nobody was at the lake when they walked the rest of the way; and nobody could get there later with the car blocking the road.

When Doreen emerged reluctantly from the bushes in a white two-piece swimsuit which might have fitted her at fifteen but was pleasingly inadequate now, Gene's mind reeled. For all of a couple of seconds he forgot Belinda.

The fact that he hadn't previously seen even her arms or ankles, let alone the gorgeous rest of her, made the impact nearly fatal. However, he rallied.

"Honey," he said weakly, "get into the water before I lose control of myself."

She gulped and said recklessly: "I don't think I'd run screaming if you did, Gene."

Gene Player fought a short but violent battle with himself. He was careful not to look at Doreen as he did so, because if he had, there would have been no battle.

She was in love for the first time, and like everybody in love for the first time, she was ready to throw everything out of the window. If it weren't for Belinda...

He won his battle. "Let's swim," he said.

Afterwards, when they lay in the sun, he told Doreen about his flashback. He didn't think it necessary to tell her he'd done it nine times.

She wasn't incredulous. She'd heard about it.

"It really works?" she said. "You've come back from the year 1986?"

"Not exactly. I've never really left 1975. It's just that I know what happened in the next eleven years in another universe—not this one."

Her eyes searched his, puzzled. She was wondering what this had to do with her, what effect it had on her relations with Gene.

He told her about the novel, that he knew it would be an enormous success.

"Why don't you just bet on horses?" she asked. "Or on the market? Or—"

"There's going to be a big legal case about that very soon," he said. "A big betting firm is going to sue Second Chance Incorporated and half a dozen people who have won big bets, claiming that flashback makes their business impossible. There's no way of telling, you see, whether a man has made a flashback or not, short of hypnosis and truth drugs. The ruling is going to be that whenever anybody makes a lot of money fast by betting or investments or insurance or any other form of legal gambling, he may be asked to submit to hypnosis or truth-drug questioning. If he's made a flashback, his gains are forfeit."

Doreen was interested. "Suppose instead of making the investment himself, he sells the information?"

"You've got a brain too," said Gene admiringly. "Yes, that's going to be tried too. And it won't work either, because whoever *is* questioned will reveal where he got the information, if any, and it'll be tracked down that way. No, flashback doesn't mean easy money. My book's different. I really did write it."

"Suppose somebody else stole your book? I mean, made a flashback, wrote it down and sold it as his own?"

"He'd have to carry it all in his head—and that's not easy for anybody but the author."

Doreen went on talking animatedly about the ramifications of flashback, and Gene realized with mixed feelings that he'd been all too successful in diverting her. An hour before she'd have given herself to him. Now she was talking as if he were an interesting item in *Readers Digest*.

As far as he was concerned she hadn't changed. She was still in her white two-piece, and he was fully aware of her breathtaking physical presence.

He forced his attention back abruptly to his reason for telling her about the flashback.

"Doreen," he said, "I must have had a reason. You know that."

At once that puzzled, doubtful look returned to her eyes.

"I can't tell you about it," he said. "Not yet. Doreen, can you wait a few days—a week or two?"

"And then?" she breathed.

"I don't know." He felt a heel again. What he was saying was: *Will you hang around so that I can condescend to notice you if another girl turns me down?*

"I'm not to see you during that time?"

"Well … suppose we keep on just meeting in the park?"

She was radiant again. Anything so long as he did not cut her out of his life.

He jumped up. It was cooler now, wearing on towards evening. "Let's go somewhere and dance."

"Just one thing, Gene," she said. "Last time—did you and I meet?"

"No," he said.

She whispered something which he didn't hear, and she wouldn't repeat it when he asked her to.

This time the publishers offered an advance of $5,000, which was a mild surprise. Previously it had been only $3,500.

As before, there was a lot dickering about serialization and it came to nothing. Also two film companies heard about *One Face for Heaven*, demanded copies, and made ridiculously small offers which were turned down.

Five thousand was quite enough for Gene's immediate needs. He knew the book would really make money in about six months' time.

One Sunday in July he met Doreen as usual in the park. He had tried to get her to go home that weekend, but she had said no, she had things to do in town anyway. Gene wondered if it was the last time he'd be seeing her.

Afterwards, timing his movements carefully, he drove his recently acquired 1969 Buick—not the same one he had had before, but that shouldn't matter—to a certain boulevard and turned in to park.

He cursed.

A cab was dropping a fare precisely where Gene wanted to put the Buick. However, the passenger, an elderly woman, was paying off the driver, and in a few seconds he would move off.

Unfortunately he didn't. The cabbie, a slow, lean-jawed man with iron-grey hair, sat back, took an apple from his pocket and proceeded to bite into it reflectively.

Gene was getting desperate. The taxi would undoubtedly move within a few minutes, but a glance at Gene's watch showed him there weren't many minutes to spare. If the driver took his time over eating that apple, it would be too late.

He had to be shifted.

Gene thought wildly of ramming him. That wouldn't do; there would be an argument.

He thought of jumping in the cab and getting the driver to start out somewhere. Then Gene could suddenly remember something and jump out. Or he could get the driver to go round the block.

But there wasn't time.

Gene leaped out of the Buick and ran to the cab.

"Will you deliver a message?" he said breathlessly. "It's urgent."

The grey-haired driver removed the apple reluctantly from his mouth and was about to say something. But Gene's wallet was under his nose, open.

"Sure," he said. "Where and what?"

"Miss Doreen Barrett," Gene said. While he gave the address he tried to think up a message— any message. Finally he said weakly: "Tell her I'll call at eight tonight. Hurry, will you?"

The cabbie made no secret of the fact that he thought there was something decidedly nuts about all this, but Gene's ten-dollar bill was real. He took it, put the car in gear, and moved off.

Almost as soon as the wheels of the cab began to turn, Gene was back in the Buick and putting it where the taxi had been. He looked at the trees lining the boulevard and saw he wasn't in exactly the right spot. He started to back out, then saw the salmon-pink Cadillac in the distance, coming fast.

Gene nearly exploded when he saw the elderly taxi-driver at his elbow, bending towards him.

"Did you say seven or eight?" he asked.

"Eight!" Gene almost screamed, and the taxi-driver turned to go back to his cab, twenty yards away. Then he paused and looked round. His eyes widened, and Gene heard a squeal of brakes and a scream of tires.

Gene's head banged sickeningly against the side window as the salmon-pink Cadillac smashed into the rear of the Buick and slewed it sidewise. Sick, dizzy, less than half conscious, he slumped over the wheel.

Vaguely he was aware he'd hit his head a lot harder than usual.

Seconds later the far door of the Buick was opened, someone who smelled nice slid along the seat, and abruptly his head was on a soft breast and a gentle hand was probing his head. He tried to look up.

She was as wonderful as ever. Glorious black hair; the softest, kindest eyes he had ever seen; a face so lovely that he caught his breath as he always did; and a figure that proclaimed its perfection even through the long blue dress which swathed it.

"Lady, dames like you should take a cab," a voice was saying. "If I'd stayed where I was you'd of hit me!"

Irritation brushed away some of Gene's daze. All the other times Belinda and he had had this moment to themselves.

"I'm all right," he said.

"I'm terribly sorry," Belinda was saying. "There was a patch of oil—"

"Bud, if you want a witness," said the other voice, the voice Gene wished would go away, "I'm your man. Dames like this one—"

"I'm all right," Gene insisted. "Go and deliver that message."

"You're badly shaken," Belinda said. "My house is right here. Could you walk if I helped you?"

That was the last he remembered for a while. He had a vague idea the taxi-driver conquered his indignation sufficiently to help Belinda get him inside. Gene was thinking dazedly: *This is new. This never happened before.*

Previously she had driven him home. He'd never been taken into the house.

When he opened his eyes again he was lying on a sofa and Belinda was bathing his head with cold water. Apparently she had got rid of the taxi-driver.

"Lie still," she said. "I'll send for a doctor in a minute."

He didn't want a doctor. He wanted Belinda to go on caring for him.

"Don't bother," he said. "I'll be all right soon."

"I guess you will," she said, sponging his head gently, "but we'd better make sure."

"I'm allergic to doctors. And you're doing a wonderful job."

She smiled, that wonderful warm smile.

"All right," she said. "I won't excite the patient. Now I'll have to go out and move the car. You stay where you are and don't worry about anything. The accident was entirely my fault and I'll have your car fixed right away."

Gene felt dizzy again after she had gone. He had certainly had a much harder knock on the head than usual. That must have been because in his haste he hadn't put the Buick in exactly the right place.

He marvelled at the way tiny differences created a whole new series of events. Already, only minutes after meeting Belinda for the first time, he was on a completely new track. He was in her house. This was better, much better.

Belinda was back. "Don't move," she said. She sat on the sofa in front of him, looked at the side of his head and a worried expression came into her eyes. "It's bleeding again," she said. "Sure you don't want me to send for a doctor?"

"Quite sure," said Gene. "I'll be all right in a minute. My name's Gene Player, by the way."

"I'm Belinda Morton. Player ... I wonder if I know a friend of yours. Do you know Harry Scott?"

"Yes," said Gene.

"He's talked about you," said Belinda. "He's a great friend of mine. As a matter of fact…"

She jumped up. "I must bathe your head again," she said. And in a moment she was back with a sponge and cold water.

"I can't say how sorry I am about this," she said. "I braked too hard, skidded on a patch of oil, and—"

"Don't keep apologizing," said Gene. "I'm beginning to be very glad it happened."

She laughed deliciously. Belinda was no Doreen. She was poised, assured.

"That's the nicest compliment I ever had," she said. "And you managed to say it as if you meant it."

"I did mean it. It wouldn't be a compliment if I didn't. Let me apologize for a change. I'm afraid there's some of my blood on your dress."

She smiled. "As if that mattered."

Gene realized then that he'd had a vague hope that when he met her, buttressed by Doreen's love, he'd find he didn't really care about Belinda after all, and could return happily to Doreen. It was no good. He was in love with Belinda all over again.

Once again, through the superficial things they were saying, he felt her warmth and kindness and sincerity, and he ached for her as always.

"Why are you allergic to doctors?" she asked.

"If you must have the truth, I'm not really. I'm just afraid he'd find out I was malingering and then I'd have no excuse to lie here and look at you."

Belinda laughed again. There was some surprise in her laugh. Gene sounded as if he meant these things he was saying. But he *couldn't* mean them. She'd never seen him before in her life.

"You sound to me like a very accomplished wolf," she observed.

He sighed. "I guess if I said I'd fallen in love with you at first sight I'd merely confirm your opinion?"

"You certainly would."

"Then I'd better not say it."

She was frowning now. "Don't do it, Mr. Player," she said.

"Don't do what?"

"Don't say so earnestly things you don't mean. I'm old-fashioned. I like truth. I like to believe I know the truth when I hear it. It bothers me to hear anybody lying so convincingly."

"Isn't there a simpler explanation?"

"What?"

"That I am telling the truth. That I am in love with you—Belinda."

She was at a loss, a rare occurrence. She remembered the blood on her dress and seized on it as an excuse to do something. "Excuse me while I change my dress," she said. "Don't move."

"Do you really think I would?"

With a last quizzical glance, she was gone.

Gene knew he was gambling wildly. He might be throwing away an excellent chance; on the other hand, everything else had failed...

The telephone on the table beside him buzzed. He picked it up.

"Belinda?" said a voice he knew well.

"No—guess who," he retorted.

There was a surprised pause. "Gene Player," said Harry's voice. "I didn't know you knew Belinda." He didn't sound pleased.

"Well, I do," said Gene.

"Is she back? I guess she must be or you wouldn't be there. Can I speak to her?"

"Not just at the moment. Shall I ask her to call you back, Harry?"

"Maybe it doesn't matter." The tone was faintly huffy. "If she's forgotten she was supposed to be meeting me—"

"Oh, was she? I didn't know about that. She hasn't said anything about it to me."

"She wouldn't." And this time Harry's tone was decidedly huffy. "Well, never mind. Be seeing you."

Gene's heart was pounding again. A real turning point! The way it had gone before was that Belinda had caused a minor accident, met Gene, taken him home, and gone on to meet Harry. Harry had been affectionate after her long stay in Canada, and Gene hadn't yet registered on Belinda's life. By the time Gene had seen her again five days later, it was too late.

Gene wondered what to say when she came back. Not mention the call? But later Harry would say he had called and spoken to Gene.

He had no more time to think, for Belinda was back, in a flowered-silk negligée. For a couple of seconds Gene gaped at her. She just wasn't the sort of girl to entertain strangers in a negligée.

"Did I hear the phone?" she said.

So that was it. She'd heard the phone and slipped on a wrap.

"Yes—Harry Scott," Gene said. "He said something about it didn't matter."

"Oh."

"Harry isn't a rival, is he?" Gene demanded.

She stared at him, then laughed helplessly. "I never met anybody like you. You lie on my sofa bleeding and making violent love to me five minutes after I smash your car and knock a hole in your head."

"Sit down and smooth my fevered brow," said Gene.

She did so. Her wrap fell open and she didn't seem to mind. Not that she was anything like indecent underneath—she wore a slip which would have been a respectable dress in any other year but 1975. Nevertheless, she wasn't exactly discouraging him.

"Is he?" Gene asked.

"Is who what?"

"Is Harry a rival?"

She laughed again. "Not exactly. He's just a friend. And if he didn't really care whether we went out today or not, probably not as close a friend as I thought."

She didn't seem to care about that, either.

And Gene knew that he'd won.

Not over weeks, months, years, as he'd expected. Not with a tremendous effort. Not by brilliant planning, passionate love-making, tender love letters.

Simply by hitting his head a little harder and telling Belinda honestly that he loved her, before Harry had a chance to tell her the same thing.

He hadn't won Belinda yet, but he'd won the chance to win Belinda. Something he'd never had before.

He wasn't up against an immutable.

But now there was something to clear up, before it became important. "Look, Belinda," he said. "I took that call from Harry just now. I don't want ... you said you didn't like people who lied. I don't want you ever to think I lied. He only said it didn't matter after I gave him the idea that I was in love with you myself. That wasn't a lie."

She was staring steadily at him. "No," she said. "I don't think it was."

He sat up. The room swam as he did so, but then he caught Belinda's shoulders and was all right. Direct action had taken him a long way already. It didn't seem that it would let him down now.

He kissed her.

As he did so the doorbell rang.

They could have ignored it, but Gene drew back involuntarily, thinking of Harry, and by the time he realized it couldn't be Harry, because Harry hadn't had time to be at the door even if he phoned from the nearest callbox, it was too late.

Belinda got up and went out.

Five seconds later a whirlwind burst in. It was female and it was crying. It threw itself across Gene' legs, crying now with relief, because he was not badly hurt.

It was, naturally, Doreen.

"I got your message," she said. "The man who brought it said you'd been hurt. Oh, Gene, I hope nothing like that ever happens to me again. I know what we agreed. But I can't help it, I love you."

Over her blonde head Gene saw Belinda come back into the room. She was surprised, a little hurt. Only very slightly hurt, because she couldn't possibly be in love with him yet.

Gene knew he could still have Belinda. A few kind words to Doreen, to show that she had never been anything important to him, and she would control herself with an enormous effort and go. He could tell Belinda the truth about Doreen, and she would believe him, because it would be the truth.

His gaze met Belinda's over Doreen's golden head, and he saw Belinda halt suddenly and stare. She was staring at his eyes, and her own were softening.

Only then did he realize his own eyes were full of tears, and why.

He couldn't do it. He had lost Belinda again. He still loved her, would always love her. But he loved Doreen too, and knew it had to be she, not Belinda.

Belinda wouldn't believe what he wanted to tell her about Doreen, because it wouldn't be the truth.

He *was* up against an immutable.

He folded Doreen in his arms. "And you know what?" he said to her. "I love you. Always. Forever." He raised his eyes again to Belinda, who was still looking tender and puzzled. "And that's final," he added.

THE SHADOW PEOPLE

Arthur Sellings

Arthur Sellings was the writing alias of book- and art-dealer Arthur Gordon Ley (1921–1968) who cruelly died of a heart attack aged 47 just as he was establishing himself as a writer. He had started selling short stories to the magazines in 1953, some of which were collected in Time Transfer *(1956) and* The Long Eureka *(1968), but from 1962 on he turned to novels, starting with* Telepath *(1962), published in Britain as* The Silent Speakers *(1963). Both this and his next novel,* The Uncensored Man *(1964) showed Sellings's ability for developing character-driven rather than idea-driven plots, and his emphasis on character is evident in the following story from 1956. Sellings's last novel* Junk Day *(1970) was an especially bleak story of survival in a post-holocaust London. It contrasts with the intrigue of* The Power of X *(1968) which considers how the invention of matter transmitters raises problems of who or what is genuine.*

T HEY CAME TO OUR HOUSE ONE EVENING IN OCTOBER. I opened the front door to their ring. It was a dark, squally night; the lighting in our street isn't all it could be, and I hadn't got around to fixing a porch lamp; so that the way they looked to me then was no different from the way any ordinary couple would have looked—as dim shadows against the darkness.

"You ... let rooms?" said the man. His voice was quiet, precise.

"We do have one room to let," I told him. "Come inside, won't you?"

It was then, when they stepped into the hall, that I felt the oddness of them. It wasn't just the shy way they entered. Nor the fact that they were both dressed in clothes so new, I noticed, they still had store creases in them. Perhaps it was the way they stood there. Perhaps there's a set of attitudes we all unconsciously choose from, so that if somebody doesn't it looks stranger than such a little detail should.

I met their eyes, and was abruptly conscious that I must be staring. "If—if you'll just come this way," I said, and led them to the living-room to meet Kay, my wife. I realized now that the oddest thing about them was their faces. Not the shape of them, but the colour. Both were dead white—white with a hint of underlying grey, so that the lights and shadows alike were blurred, giving them a strangely negative expression.

But Kay seemed not to notice. "People for the room," I told her. "Mr. and—"

"Mr. and Mrs. Smith," the man filled in for me.

Kay, who is much more practical with people than I am, gave me a meaningful look. To the couple she said, in a hard-boiled manner that was slightly out of character, "The room is two guineas a week, in advance."

The couple nodded, and Kay showed them upstairs. I followed behind.

Well, the couple's reaction to the room was strange, too. They went from one piece of furniture to another, poking here, lifting a cover there. Over one piece, an old leather armchair, the woman lingered with something like wonder. I began to feel uneasy.

"Of course," I said, "this is only provisional. It's the first time we've let a room. Things being as they are, we thought—" I felt Kay glaring at me and finished, "Well, if there's anything else you need, just let me—"

"There's no linen, of course," said Kay.

"No … linen?" said the woman. It seemed to trouble her.

"We've got spare linen," I said quickly. "Haven't we, dear?"

"Linen," said Kay firmly, "would be five shillings a week extra."

The couple looked at each other with something like relief. The man drew out a bundle of notes. "We'd like to move in right away if we may."

"You may," Kay told him, taking the money. "What about your baggage?"

"Baggage?" the man said. He exchanged glances with the woman again. "Is that—necessary?"

I had to turn away at the sight of Kay's face. She must have recovered quickly, for I heard her saying, "Why no, it's not necessary, but—" The hardboiled manner faltered. "Oh—you mean it's coming on?"

"Ah, yes—it's coming on." Mr. Smith sounded grateful.

"You're from out of town then?" I said.

"Yes—we're from out of town."

I didn't pursue it. If Mr. Smith wanted to be as uncommunicative as that, that was his business. Or so I thought then.

Kay got them the linen and we went downstairs. Back in the living-room, Kay leaned against the door—and drooped.

"Oh, Paul, have I done the wrong thing, letting the room to them?"

I roared. "There's my big tough landlady! Hard as nails and—" I stopped. "Why, darling, what's wrong? Surely not that Mr-and-Mrs-Smith business? Perhaps their name really is Smith."

Kay jerked her head crossly. "Of course not. It's just that—" She broke off.

"Just what?" I said. I wasn't going to be drawn. Perhaps she could put a finger on it.

"Well, didn't you notice?" …

I gave in. "All right—" I ticked off on my fingers. "So they haven't got any baggage. So they're both wearing brand-new clothes. So they speak English with the funniest kind of accent because there's no accent there at all. So they look as if they've lived under a stone for years. So—"

I stopped, waiting for Kay to add to the list.

But she evidently couldn't. "But they're so *strange*," she said. "Oh, Paul, they might be crooks, spies, anything."

I sighed heavily. "So crooks, spies, make themselves look as odd as they can? Just so people can play cops and robbers" But the worried look didn't leave her face. I took her in my arms. "Look, Kay, I'm sorry enough people don't like my paintings for us to buy a new house. I'm sorry you're going to have a baby—no, you know I don't mean that—I mean I'm sorry we have to let rooms to meet the expense. But if you say the word, I'll take their money straight back up there and tell them to leave."

I was being more than somewhat crafty, I realized. But Kay smiled wanly. "It's all right, I'm just being silly. I'll get used to having strangers about the house."

"That's my girl. Hey! I've got it. They're D.P.'s from Europe. They've been cooped up in some camp, that's why they look so pale. They've been learning English for years because all that time they've been dreaming about getting here. And now the dream's come true. The new clothes were given to them when they arrived, by some charity. They say their name's Smith—well, because the real one is Sashamako-lovitch, and—"

Kay was laughing now. "All right, all right. So I'm a silly idiot. Don't rub it in."

The next morning I went into town to make a round of the junkshops for frames. Kay seemed to have recovered her usual placidness. Neither of us mentioned the new tenants.

But in town I heard something that sent me scurrying back home.

I must have been breathless when I got back. I burst into the living-room and Kay looked at me as if I was crazy. I told her what I'd heard:

"Last night a couple walked into Mendl's, the pawnbrokers, and sold him a diamond for several hundred pounds. Mendl took the diamond home to show his wife—and lost it. The couple sound like our Mr. and Mrs. Smith."

Kay looked at me in puzzlement. "You mean—they're wanted for questioning?"

"No, nothing like that. Old Mendl is pretty sore at himself, but the diamond wasn't stolen. Somewhere between the shop and his home it disappeared from his pocket. He can't explain it—losing a diamond isn't exactly a habit of his. But—"

"Then what's all the fuss about? Who's being silly now? Look." She took my arm and steered me to the window. The Smiths were in the big untidy back garden. The man seemed to be examining the plants. The woman was gathering a bunch of chrysanthemums.

"So?" I said.

"They're all right, Paul," Kay said. "A few minutes ago there was a timid knock on the door. It was Mrs. Smith, wanting to know if she could buy some flowers out of the garden. Imagine! When I told her she could have a bunch free if she wanted, she didn't seem to catch on. She said something about she thought it was the system."

"Your hard-headed landlady act last night might have had something to do with that," I said. "But—this business about the diamond. Ordinary people don't have diamonds worth several hundreds. Shouldn't I at least ask them a few questions about themselves? Surely that's only a landlord's right?"

Kay surprised me by flaring up. "Diamonds! There was only *one*, wasn't there? Perhaps they *are* D.P.'s. Perhaps the diamond was all they had left. Refugees put their money into something small and negotiable like that. I've read about it."

"But all the same—"

"Oh, Paul, you'll make me mad in a minute! You're always talking about individualism and people being free to live their own lives. You claim it for yourself. Now you want to deny it to somebody else."

I was beginning to get annoyed now. "Well, at least other people can see what my standpoint is."

"But you've got a standpoint because you've got roots. These people haven't. Wherever they've come from, it's obvious that they're unsettled yet. It's also obvious they don't want to be reminded about their previous life. So leave them alone."

Kay's brown eyes looked straight into mine, then she turned to look out of the window again. She plainly felt strongly about the matter. I wondered if there might be something more to it—whether she might be concealing a fear that she didn't want to voice. Was she, with the baby coming, instinctively shutting out any perplexity? Or simply that, with that dream unfolding within her, nothing else was important enough to worry over for long?

I followed her gaze. The Smiths were coming in from the garden now. The chill October sun slanting down at their faces made them look even more pale—immaterial even. It was as if the light of day somehow went *round* them without striking any response. The only colour was in the woman's face, reflected from the bronze and gold flowers she held to her breast. But even they could strike no life in lips as grey as ash.

For the first time I felt the *sadness* of them, an aura of loss that seemed to cling to them. As they passed out of sight the straggling garden seemed to grow more bright, as if a shadow had passed over and lifted ...

Many times in the weeks that followed I told myself that I was being irrational. Mr. and Mrs. Smith were model tenants; quiet, unobtrusive, making no demands. With sales of pictures continuing at their usual unsensational rate, I should have been grateful for the money they brought down every Friday. But something rankled.

Kay's rebuke about intolerance hadn't helped. Hell, a man's got to know what he's being tolerant *of.* So I tried to find excuses to get closer to them. Like calling to ask if they'd like me to fix up the big cupboard on the landing as a kitchenette. Or whether they wouldn't like the dressing table painted.

But they met me each time with polite evasions. Oh, it was very good of me and they were grateful to be offered but no, it was all right, really. I was getting to the point once of *insisting* that I rigged up some lighting points, but Kay came on the scene and gave me a queer look. I covered up and retreated.

I don't know whether Kay guessed what was going on. If she did, she didn't mention it. Perhaps she realized by now that I was obeying a male impulse to do the worrying for her. Which was slightly comical, because she seemed not to be worrying one bit—as if what she had told me that first morning had been the truth of her attitude. But still I tried.

I even told myself that I was being moved by a worthier impulse than mere curiosity; that it would be a good thing for the Smiths if I managed to bring them out, to convince them that their barrier of reserve wasn't really necessary. Just how hypocritical can a person get!

Anyway, whenever I got the chance, I'd throw out a line. Like, "I suppose this is a whole lot different from where you come from?" All I got from that one was a polite smile and a non-commital shrug.

Neither of them got a job—although once, when I was in their room on some excuse or other, I noticed papers open at the Jobs Vacant pages, and somebody had been busy with a pencil. I managed to get in a query to Mr. Smith about the work he did.

He hesitated for a moment then, with a faint smile, said, "I'm a mnemonic integrator."

"Really?" I said, annoyed at being brushed off with double-talk.

It must have shown, for he added, "That is, I was. But there aren't any openings here for that."

I felt like asking where exactly it was that he used to practice mnemonic integration, but one glance at that blank face of his stopped me. I had a feeling that he had an answer all ready in the same kind of uncommunicative English.

So my efforts got me nowhere. All I learned was what was obvious. That they seldom went out. That they lived pretty meagerly. Their only extravagance was flowers. They seemed to love flowers; they always had some in their room.

And then, a week or so before Christmas, a break came in the barrier. I was going out to my studio. It had originally been an old-fashioned conservatory, but the changes I'd made had cut it off from the house, so that I had to go round by way of the garden.

It was snowing hard, had been all the day and night before, so that my footsteps must have been muffled to silence. Anyway, Mrs. Smith didn't notice my approach. She was standing there in the snow, her head tilted back.

My first thought—of her craziness in standing there, coatless as she was—was pushed to one side as I took in the expression on her face. It wasn't a simple one, nor was my reaction to it.

For on her face was all the ecstatic wonder of a child watching snow; watching and dreaming of the wonders that snow is to children—Mother Carey's chickens being plucked, or flowers from some faery region fluttering down. There was, too, a look of unutterable sadness, of pure hopeless longing.

What made my reaction really complicated was the realization that this woman was *beautiful*. I wondered how it was that I hadn't noticed before—and knew why. Because I hadn't looked closely enough at the faces of either of them, or when I had, had looked them straight in the eye—the two ways I suppose most people treat somebody whose face is odd or mutilated. Another reason was that I hadn't seen it before in such a light as this.

For under the double illumination, the yellowish light filtering down from the whirling sky and the white glare thrown up from the snow, her features gained life at last. The delicate lines of her nose, of the arch of her brows, were thrown into relief. Snow frosted her silver-blonde hair. I knew then what I had to do. *Had* to; it isn't often as urgent as that.

I stepped forward, feeling clumsy as a bear beside such delicacy. She started as she saw me. Her eyes jerked back from the sky. The expression vanished abruptly, as if some inner guardian had snatched it away.

"I'm sorry to intrude," I blurted. "But I'd ... like to paint you." She seemed not to know what to say.

"The way you were standing there," I said. "The look on your face. It's something I must get onto canvas."

She seemed almost frightened.

"I can remember the look," I said. "I'd only want you to pose for the likeness, the memory. In my studio the light will fall the same way." I took her by the arm when she still didn't answer. "*Please*. I must do it. I'll pay you a fee for the sitting. I can't afford a lot, but—"

I wasn't sure whether that last part was the right thing to say. But it seemed to have an effect.

"I'd—I'd have to talk it over with my husband," she said.

"All right. But make it quick, will you? In case the light changes. I'll be in my studio there, waiting."

★

I didn't have to wait long. Five minutes later a timid knock came on the door.

I worked quickly, excitedly, in tempera, a medium I rarely used, but one that I felt instinctively was right for this. Under my brush the colours spread thin and clear and luminous.

I was too busy to talk much, or to worry at all about the enigma of the Smiths. I was painting, wrestling with appearances now, not reasons. And I felt that I was creating something important. For three days I worked in a blaze of energy, and when it was finished, I knew I was right. I'm usually too self-critical for that to be a common feeling—but I felt it now.

I stood back from it. "Look," I said to its subject.

She came forward shyly. I watched her face as she looked at it. And suddenly the face on the canvas seemed to be looking into a mirror, for that same indescribable expression came back into it.

"It's lovely," she breathed at last. "It—"

I was signing it now. I looked up as I heard her take in her breath.

"*Davy?*" she said. "But——your name is Nash, isn't it?"

"Davy's my brush-name," I explained. "There's already been one Paul Nash, so to avoid confusion I—"

But she seemed not to be listening. Her pale eyes widened. Her hand flew to her face and something between a sob and a cry broke from her lips. Then she turned and rushed out of the studio.

I stood there, gaping at the open door, at the snowflakes whirling in. All my puzzlement about her and her husband came flooding back. What had made her act like that? And why had my name seemed so important?

I went after her, determined to find out. To find out that—and more. I was in the reckless mood I'm always in after finishing something worthwhile. As if I've just justified myself to the gods for whatever talent I've been given.

An excited conversation was going on behind their door. It stopped abruptly as I knocked and went in.

The Smiths were standing together in the middle of the room. Now that I was here I didn't know how to begin.

It was the woman who said, finally, "I'm sorry I burst out like that." Her voice was calm now.

"But *why*?" I said. "What did I do?"

They looked at each other. The man said quietly, "You painted a fine picture."

I looked at him blankly. "But you haven't seen it."

"Ah, but I have." I must have looked stupid, for he added, "Sit down. I'll explain. Firstly, I should mention that I've noticed your curiosity. It's only natural, though I'm rather disappointed that we couldn't fit in without rousing it."

"But what's this got to do with the picture?" I said, cursing myself the next moment for interrupting.

"Only that that was a climax, something that threw our position into relief. Although we're neither of us well acquainted with the arts—our world is highly specialized—we have both seen your picture before. You see, we come from a future time."

"*What!*"

Mr. Smith smiled. "It was just as much a shock to us to learn that my wife is the subject of a painting that in our time hangs in a museum. *Study by Snowlight*, I believe you will call it."

I knew then that he was speaking the truth. That was the title I'd already thought of giving it—and I hadn't mentioned it to anybody. No other explanation of his knowing could be less fantastic.

★

"That was something we weren't prepared for," he went on. "We tried to learn up everything. I don't think we made a bad job of it. But fitting-in isn't just a matter of passing muster. It's a matter of surviving too. That's why I agreed to my wife sitting for you—the money was important. We tried to get jobs, but—"he shrugged—"people probably sensed our oddness. Anyway, there wasn't much we could have handled. Our nerves are finer, for one thing."

I was beginning to recover. "But surely you've got special skills—skills that we haven't got at all?"

"Indeed. That's the crux of it. You have skills—pardon my putting it like this—that a caveman hasn't. Would that make it easier for you to survive in *his* world? Could you out-hunt him? Out-fight him with his own weapons?"

"With *his* weapons, no. But if I took a rifle—"

"But say you couldn't? I told you that ours is a highly-specialized world. Could a man of your time, no matter how expert at using a rifle, *build* one—with no tools, and with the raw materials still in the ground?" He spread his hands. "Similarly with us. We could bring nothing. Time travel requires not only enormous energy but purposiveness, an act of will, on the part of the thing transmitted. Any material object that one takes along, and one can take little, stays only a short time—then drifts off into some limbo of space-time."

An obvious question came into my mind. How then had they got money? But the answer to that one came on its heels—*the diamond*. But I didn't mention it. Old Mendl could stand the loss. They would have had to resort to some such deception. I didn't blame them, and I didn't want to embarrass them.

But I had to ask other questions. I had to get this crazy situation straight. "From what year did you come?"

"From 2149."

That shook me. "But your comparing our level with a cave-man's, I thought—"

"That we had come from some remoter future? No, the rate of change has accelerated enormously. It had started even before this time, hadn't it?"

I stumbled over the next question I wanted to ask him. The reason for their sadness, their strange pallor. "But—are you typical of your time? I mean—"

He smiled sadly. "You mean in the way we look? We *were* typical. But not as you see us. You see, the—the complete creature can't get across. In a way we are little more than shadows. Oh, we're solid enough. We see the visible world and can act upon it. But there's a—a dilution, of impact, of sensibility, of—" He broke off, as if explaining the measure of that loss was beyond him—or beyond my understanding.

"But when you return you'll revert to normal?" I said.

He looked at me for a long moment. "There is no return." He exhaled sharply. "But now that I have told you this we must go."

"Go? But where?"

"I don't know. Somewhere to try again, to settle in if we can without—" he smiled sadly—"without rousing curiosity." The sudden remorse I felt then must have showed, for he waved a pale hand. "You mustn't blame yourself. It was only natural. And we may have learned from it."

"You can forget you ever told me," I said quickly. "I'll tell nobody else. I'm too grateful for what you've given me—the picture, I mean—to let you go. And I won't ask you any more questions, I swear."

"That isn't the only reason we must go," he said. "There are too many reminders here, in this house, of what we have left behind us."

"How do you mean?"

"You and your wife are young. You have love and—and its promise."

I stared at him as something of the measure of their sacrifice dawned upon me. Now I understood their near-reverence for flowers—because they were *alive*, however humbly, in a way these two could never be again. Or was it that in cut flowers, severed from their source to wither, they saw some cruel but companionable symbol of themselves? I didn't pursue that one. I was more closely involved; I knew now just what I had painted into that picture—and it made me feel guilty.

I was conscious that the woman had started to pack.

"*No!*" I protested wildly. "We'll work something out. We'll—"

The man was shaking his head slowly. It wasn't that which brought me up short, but the realization that there was still one question I hadn't asked—the question I had wanted the answer to from the beginning. Now, after what he had told me, I *had* to ask it.

"But *why?*" I said. "If it meant such sacrifice?"

"You said you would ask no more questions," he said. "But, because you need an answer, I will tell you. We … were wanted by the police."

"You're lying," I told him.

He shrugged. "I told you our world was highly-specialized. Lying was not my speciality. Can't you see why we cannot stay? Because, however kind you are, your curiosity would never be satisfied."

"But it would be," I said urgently. "I just have to understand, that's all. Then everything will be all right. You can stay on here. I'll find work for you. You'll see you're being too complicated about it."

"Will I?" he said. "Very well, I'll tell you. But you won't thank me. We came—to avoid the end of the world."

I suddenly felt like bursting out laughing. I managed to restrain it, but said, "Hell! so what's that? People have wondered it's held together as long as it has. It's a *relief* to know it's still got nearly another two hundred years."

The woman had finished packing. All their possessions were in one pitiful small case that she held in her hand. She was standing by the man's side now. Neither of them answered me.

I answered myself. It was true, wasn't it? After all, I lived my life—painted and loved and begot children—because I had to. For today, not tomorrow. It was gratifying to know that posterity was going to be pleased with at least one of my activities. So why should I mind knowing that posterity finished at 2149 sharp?

Then, looking into their eyes, I knew. That there was a difference between fearing something and knowing it, And between knowing it and being reminded of it every day. It would be like a condemned man having the executioner, masked and gloved, as a lodger in his cell. Not that these gentle people were executioners—but they might as well have been.

They must have read it clearly enough in my face, for they turned and left the room. I made no move to stop them. I heard their footsteps descending the stairs, then the front door closing behind them with a sound like the shutting of a tomb.

THIRTY-SEVEN TIMES

E. C. Tubb

E. C. ("Ted") Tubb (1919–2010) was one of Britain's most prolific writers. In a career spanning close on sixty years he produced over 130 novels and 230 stories. The majority were science fiction, but he also wrote westerns, historical adventure and even a Foreign Legion novel. He used many pseudonyms and his first three books, Saturn Patrol *(1951),* Planetfall *(1951) and* Argentis *(1952) appeared as by King Lang, Gill Hunt and Brian Shaw respectively. He is probably best remembered as the author of the 33-volume series about Earl Dumarest's search to find his home planet, Earth, that began with* The Winds of Gath *in 1967. Tubb's novels and stories are full of gritty realism. They go out of their way to reflect how difficult life can be, and how determined we must be to cope. The following story first appeared in 1957 under his alias Alan Guthrie.*

THE FUNERAL WAS MUCH THE SAME AS ANY OTHER FUNERAL. The day just an ordinary spring day. The cemetery was patterned after ten thousand other similar resting places and the casket which held the mortal remains of Professor Gregor Wantage just an expensive box of polished wood. To Sam Howard it seemed all wrong. There should have been terrible storms and portentous happening, earthquakes and reeling stars, sickness and bleak despair. Instead of which the world continued on its even way while Gregor made his final onslaught against the unknown.

Sam mentioned it to Armsworth on the way home.

"It depends on the point of view," said Jeff indifferently. Now that the professor was dead he had his own, personal worries.

"To you, Gregor was father, mother, employer and friend. To others he was just another man, to me just the boss. When he managed to get himself killed he did more than prove his pet experiment a flop, he eliminated my only visible means of support."

It was bitter, cynical and true. No one had felt about the old man as Sam had. He changed the subject.

"There'll be money," he said. "The patents were all made out to the firm and Gregor had made a will. Things will go on much the same as before." He swallowed. "As much as they could ever be," he whispered, "without Gregor."

"Sure." Jeff felt uncomfortable in the presence of grief. He produced cigarettes, lit them, passed one to Sam and sat back, smoking and staring through the windows of the cab. "You certain about that?" he said. "About things carrying on just the same?"

"Pretty certain." Sam felt the warm sunshine on the back of his hand, thought of a polished box in cold, damp ground, shivered and filled his lungs with smoke. "Gregor told me once that the Institute was self-supporting. The income from the battery, the solar cell and the other things he invented will be sufficient to keep us in business."

"With you in charge?"

"I wouldn't know about that."

"Not much doubt, is there?" Jeff flicked ash from his cigarette, "With you and the old man so close it's obvious." He sighed with relief. "Well, it suits me. I liked the work and I liked the job and don't fancy going back into normal, industrial research." He looked at Sam.

"When will we know?"

"Tomorrow morning, the lawyer's going to read the will then." Sam leaned forward. "How about dropping me off? I'll see you at the Institute tomorrow morning about ten. Suit you?"

"To the ground." Jeff stared through the windows, feeling more cheerful now that his future seemed assured. "Where shall I drop you, at the Institute?"

"No, here will do."

Jeff nodded and gave instructions to the driver. The cab swung from the main stream of traffic and came to a smooth halt at the kerb. Sam dismounted, slammed the door and stood watching as the vehicle drove away. He sighed, dropped the cigarette, trod on it and turned to see Gregor Wantage walking down the street.

*   *   *

Sam arrived early at the Institute the next morning. Since Gregor's death the place had been closed and he let himself into the building, passed through the main offices, the laboratories and workshops and stepped into the inner sanctum. Slowly he closed the door behind him, letting his eyes wander over the appointments of the office, Gregor hadn't used it much, he had been more interested in his private experiments than office routine, but it was luxurious and contained framed portrait of the professor taken when he had won the Nobel Prize.

It was a good likeness. The artist had given full justice to the high forehead, the thick, white, sweeping hair, the firm line of the jaw and the shrewd but kindly blue eyes. Even the small, crescent-shaped scar beneath the right eye had been depicted, the scar resulting from a laboratory accident. Sam didn't remember the accident, it had happened just before Gregor had sought him out and made him his assistant. It was a minor disfigurement and one easily overlooked or forgotten but it was there and it was unmistakable. Sam stared at it with mounting relief.

The man in the street had not been Gregor Wantage.

Not that he could have been, of course, Gregor Wantage was dead and buried. But the man had had the same hair, the same eyes; the same face. He had walked the same and looked the same and Sam had felt sick as he chased after him. He had spoken and the man had stared blankly at him with no trace of mutual recognition. Sam had felt like a fool, had muttered apologies and hurried away. And yet...

It had taken the evidence of the scar to reassure him.

Jeff arrived closely followed by the lawyer and Sam turned his mind to business.

"Has everything been settled?"

"As far as possible." The lawyer waited until they had taken seats, produced papers from his briefcase and cleared his throat.

"The terms of the will are explicit and, as there are no surviving relatives and as the professor was without wife or family there should be no disputes."

He paused and Sam restrained an impulse to tell him to get on with it.

"The monies from all patents both held by the professor and the Institute will be devoted to the advancement of pure science as conducted by the Institute at the time of the professor's death. You, Mr. Howard, will be in fall charge with Mr. Armsworth as your chief assistant. Both positions are permanent and subject only to the jurisdiction of the Board of Trustees as appointed by the professor. The remainder of the staff will be subject to your authority." He folded the papers, tucked them away and smiled at the two men.

"The legal details will be sent to you in due course. Are there any questions."

"Is that all?" Sam lit a cigarette, conscious of the painted eyes of the portrait following his every move.

"Aside from several minor bequests, yes."

About the money," said Jeff. He shrugged at the lawyer's expression. "Let's be practical about this. Saying that the Institute must continue as usual is all very well, but only if the money is there to permit it. Was the old man well-off when he died?"

"He left a great deal of money," said the lawyer. "A very great deal."

"From the inventions?" Sam looked puzzled. "I know that we are getting royalties from them, will they be sufficient?"

"In themselves, no," confessed the lawyer. "But the professor owned an immense private fortune and there are certain investments." He obviously wasn't going into details. "There will be ample funds have no fear as to that."

"Good." Jeff grinned as he rose to his feet. "Then what are we waiting for? Let's send for the rest of the staff and get back to work." He looked defensive. "Well, it's what the old man would have wanted isn't it?"

"Yes," admitted Sam. "Get to work on it, Jeff, and commence work where we left off." He followed the lawyer from the office, not speaking until they had emerged in the street below. "Was there anything else?"

"How do you mean, Mr. Howard?"

"Those private bequests, was there one for me?"

"No." The lawyer was sharp. "Were you expecting a legacy?"

"No." Sam bit his lip. "No, of course not." He turned and re-entered the building.

*   *   *

A month passed and the work of the Institute settled into routine, Jeff came into the inner office one afternoon, his hands full of papers and a crease between his eyes.

"I've been checking up on the old man's pet experiment," he said "He seemed to be working with neutrinos, using filed equations and a theory of his own." He shook his head. "Think it's worth following up?"

"I don't know." Sam stared thoughtfully at the portrait on the wall, "Gregor spent five years to my knowledge working on his experiment and the only concrete result was his death." He leaned back in his chair. "I've been checking the figures and more money was spent on that project than any other. Just what Gregor hoped to accomplish only he knew, on that subject he was the most secretive man I ever saw."

"He was a strange one all right." Jeff helped himself to a chair. "A brilliant man, no argument about that, but strange. Remember how he used to shut himself up in his private lab for hours at a time?"

"I remember."

"Odd too, the way he selected his staff." Jeff looked thoughtful. "How did you two meet up, Sam?"

"He sent for me," said Sam shortly. "Why, I never learned. He seemed to know quite a bit about my background too, must have had me checked before contacting me." He dismissed the subject. "How are the investigations into the gravity fields progressing?"

"Slow," said Jeff. "Slow but sure. Negative results so far but that's to be expected." He stared thoughtfully at the portrait. "You know, Sam," he said suddenly. "It's just struck me. Did you notice how fast the old man was ageing just before his death?"

"No, was he?"

"I'd say he was. Seemed to be getting older all of a sudden." Jeff shrugged. "Nothing in that though, lots of men seem to be hale and hearty one day and almost senile the next. When old age comes it sometimes hits all at once." He glanced at his papers. "So you don't think we should continue the old man's experiments?"

"There doesn't seem to be any point in doing so," said Sam. "We don't know just what he was after, he left no notes or legible papers, and the equipment was so badly damaged in the explosion that it doesn't tell us much." He toyed with a pencil. "Better forget it and concentrate on other lines of research."

"As you wish." Jeff obviously didn't care one way or the other. He and Gregor had never been close so there was no inclination to carry on with the old man's work from sentimental motives.

Such motives would apply to Sam but, if he didn't want to make the investigation, that was up to him.

After further small talk Jeff returned to his bench and Sam sat alone.

He didn't mind being alone, he was used to it. Before Gregor had taken him up he had followed his own path and could do so again. The difference now was that, instead of being a subordinate, he was the boss. Sam smiled up at the portrait as if sharing a secret with the painted image then, selecting papers from the pile before him, buried himself in work.

The afternoon drew towards evening, the staff went home and Jeff looked in to see if Sam was finished for the day.

"Coming?"

"No, I want to finish this work." Sam glanced at his watch. "You'd better get off, your wife will be expecting you."

"Mary expects me when she sees me." Jeff hesitated. "I could phone that I'll be late if you want me to stay and help."

"I can manage, thanks all the same. See you in the morning."

Jeff shrugged and left. Sam reached for more papers and began to work out the research programme for the coming week. The work was engrossing and he lost all account of time. He lifted his head in annoyance as the door opened, thinking that Jeff had returned.

"Hello, Sam."

It wasn't Jeff. It was Gregor Wantage.

Shock affects people in different ways. For one terrible moment Sam thought that his heart had stopped and then, with a gasping sigh, he dragged air into his lungs and felt the cold sweat of fear ooze from his body.

"Hello, Sam," repeated Gregor. He smiled, crossed the room and took a chair. The wood creaked a little as he sat down. "Busy?"

He looked just the same, even to the scar beneath his eye. In the light from the tall windows his hair shone with a soft whiteness and his eyes were as shrewd and as kind as ever. Sam looked at him, then at the portrait, then back to his visitor. His tongue seemed to have become glued to the roof of his mouth.

"How is everything going?" Gregor seemed perfectly at ease. "Did you concentrate on the non-ferrous force fields I told you about?"

"Told me about?" Sam wet his lips. Gregor had never mentioned any such thing.

"Yes. Easbach has some good ideas on that field, you'd better contact him and get him under contract before someone else snaps him up." Gregor frowned across the desk. "What's the matter?"

"You…" Sam fought to control himself. "You're dead."

"No I'm not." Gregor held out his hand. "I'm real enough. Feel."

"No!" For some reason Sam couldn't bring himself to touch the hand Gregor extended towards him. "You're dead I tell you! Dead!"

Gregor vanished.

*   *   *

The cemetery was the same as he remembered it, the same tended plots, the shrubbery, the irreverent birds chirping as they settled for the night. It was late, the last lingering light fading from the sky and, in the growing dusk the new-laid turf covering the mortal remains of Gregor Wantage showed against the deeper, richer surrounding green. Sam shivered, knowing himself to be a fool for having come all this way and yet feeling a faint relief at the sight of the undisturbed grave.

Gregor was dead. Gregor was screwed in his coffin and buried eight feet deep. Gregor simply couldn't be walking around alive and well. And yet he was.

Gravel made gritty noises beneath his shoes as Sam hurried from the cemetery. A cab answered his hail and dropped him at a bar. Brandy warmed him and more brandy dispelled some of the depression. Hallucination brought on by overwork. The hypnotic effect of the life-sized portrait and the associations of the familiar office. A trick of the brain and that was all. Sam drank his brandy and felt relief as he thought about it. And yet...

Mary answered the phone, her voice heavy with sleep.

"Yes?"

"Is Jeff there?"

"Who is it?"

"Sam. Sam Howard." He chewed his lip as faint noises came from the receiver, wondering if he were doing the right thing. Jeff's voice, hard and strong, came just as he was about to hang up.

"Sam?"

"That's right. Sorry to have woken you, Jeff, but there's something I want to know." Sam paused, conscious that he was speaking too fast. "Would it be possible for Gregor to still be alive?"

"What!" Jeff snorted. "Is this your idea of a joke?"

"No, Jeff, I'm serious. Could he?"

"Not a chance." Jeff's voice altered. "Why, have you been seeing things?"

"Yes, no, that is I think so." Sam dabbed at his forehead, knowing that he had said too much not to say more. "I thought I saw him in the street," he said carefully. "It was only a glimpse but it gave me a turn and set me wondering. Could there have been a mistake?"

"No." Jeff was very positive. "You didn't see him after the explosion, he was a mess. And there's no way he could have got out of the coffin either. Even if he had you wouldn't have recognized him, not the shape he was in when they screwed him down."

"I see," said Sam. "Thanks."

Jeff hung up and looked thoughtfully at his wife.

"That was Sam," he said. "My boss, he's been seeing ghosts."

"He sounded drunk to me," said Mary. She was a woman with little imagination and she didn't like being woken up.

"He'd been drinking but he wasn't drunk." Jeff lit a cigarette and squinted through the smoke. "Sounded as if he'd just had a terrific shock. Now why would he feel shocked at seeing a man who was everything to him?"

"Gregor? But he's dead isn't he?"

"Sure, but so is your mother. If you thought you'd seen her you'd be shocked, yes, but not in the same way. Certainly you wouldn't go out and try to get drunk afterwards." He blew a thoughtful smoke ring. "I don't like Sam," he said. "And I wasn't too fond of Gregor. I don't like men who act as if they own another body and soul and I don't like a man to be so possessed."

"Sam and Gregor?"

"Yes. I'd have respected Sam more if he'd shown enough guts to tell the old man to go to hell."

"Would you have done?"

"I did," said Jeff. "Twice." He smiled at her expression. "Sorry dear, but there it is. Job or no job a man's got to remember that he's a man, not a doormat." He stubbed out the cigarette. "Anyway, I lost nothing by it so you needn't worry." He yawned. "What the hell? Let's go back to bed."

Halfway across town Sam finished his brandy and made his way home. He was a little unsteady on his feet but still far from being drunk. He sobered as he found the door to the apartment unlocked He became more than sober as he saw who was waiting for him.

"Hello, Sam."

Gregor Wantage smiled from the comfort of a chair.

*   *   *

It was time travel, of course, Sam should have guessed it all along, The mysterious experiments, the strange reappearances of a man dead and buried, it all made perfect logical sense.

"I stumbled on it a long time ago," said Gregor. He gestured with his pipe, he always smoked a pipe. "More by luck than judgement I will admit. My first trips were short, a matter of a few years only, but they showed the way."

Sam sat and listened to the man who, according to Jeff, had been his father, mother, employer and friend. Had been? Was rather, it was difficult to think of a person in the past tense when he sat firm and very solid in the bright lighting of an apartment.

And Jeff, like all the other members of the Institute, was just about as wrong as he could be. Sam hated Gregor, had done for years because he was the better man and had made Sam feel like dirt. He had stuck with the professor from weakness and hope of a legacy and had paid for his weakness over and over again. He had been glad when the old man had died. It had meant a final release from the sarcasm, the barely hidden contempt, the constant needling and false display of affection. Now it appeared that his relief was premature. Gregor was still alive.

"It requires energy, of course," continued the professor. "Fortunately most of that energy is reclaimed when the object pushed forward in time returns to its own era. You can understand the analogy of a rubber band, Sam? I, in effect, am at one end of a piece of rubber which stretches from the present into the future or, as you would put it, from the present into the past. My past. When the propulsion effect, to coin a phrase, weakens, then I will be snatched back to my laboratory in the Institute."

"I see." Sam nodded, the scientist in him overcoming his detestation of the professor. "That accounts for what happened before. We were talking and suddenly you vanished."

"Indeed?" Gregor tamped the tobacco in his pipe. "When was this?"

"A few hours ago, at the Institute, surely you remember?"

"I don't remember," said Gregor casually. "Probably because it has yet to happen."

"Yet to happen?" Sam was baffled. "But it has happened. I saw it."

"Your past, my future," said Gregor calmly. "To you it has already happened, to me it has yet to happen." Abruptly he changed the subject. "Have you commenced working on the machine yet?"

"No."

"Why not?" Gregor's tone held the familiar iron of command. "I distinctly remember ordering you to commence work on the project. Why have you not done so?"

"You ordered no such thing!" Sam controlled the rising of his voice. "How could you? This is only the second time we've met, the third if you count the time in the street, and you haven't explained or ordered anything."

"In the street?" Gregor frowned then smiled. "Of course, I remember now. It was during one of my early trips and was before

I sent for you." Sam inwardly cringed at the tone of off-hand arrogance he had come to detest.

"But you haven't ordered anything."

"Haven't I?" Gregor became thoughtful. "No, perhaps I haven't. At least I have but you wouldn't know about it yet." He shrugged. "It's due to the variability of the temporal projector. The time jumps are not predictable to a certain degree of accuracy. To me this is the thirty-seventh time we have met, to you the third. Later the ratios will adjust themselves."

"Will they?" Sam felt that he was living in a nightmare. For the sake of something to do he rose, poured two drinks and offered one to the professor. "Scotch?"

"Don't be a fool! You know perfectly well that anything I take in this age will remain behind when I return to my own time. That is why I have to memorize all the data and particulars you collect for me." Gregor gave his deep laugh. "Will keep for me. I keep forgetting that all this is new to you. We have had some amusing conversations at cross-purposes. You should keep a diary and record so that you can keep me up to date." He corrected himself again. "You will keep such a record."

"Will I?" Sam felt his hands beginning to quiver.

"Naturally. If you did then you must." Gregor's voice deepened. "I want no nonsense about this, Sam. You will do exactly what I order at all times and without question."

"Like hell I will!" Something, it may have been the knowledge that, despite appearances, this man was dead and buried gave Sam the strength and confidence he had lacked for years. "Don't count on it, Gregor. I'm a free agent now and don't you forget it. I've eaten dirt for long enough and don't intend to eat more. We're finished, understand! Finished!"

Gregor wasn't annoyed. Instead he was gentle, the gentleness of the cat with a mouse. He sat, calm and solid, his face wreathed in the smoke from his pipe. "Forgotten something, Sam?"

"No."

"I think you have." Gregor was still gentle. "You are in charge of the Institute at this moment only because I wished it that way. You were probably surprised that I left you no legacy but that was deliberate." Gregor knocked out his pipe, heedless of the hot ash ruining the carpet. "You are weak, Sam, I've known it for years. You depend on me for everything you have. If you go against me then I shall throw you back into the gutter where you belong."

"You can't." Sam forced himself to remain calm. "You're dead and buried and you can't touch me. I'm free, understand!" Free of you at last!"

"You talk like a fool," said Gregor dispassionately. "You can't help that, of course, but I wish that you would try. Hasn't it occurred to you that I'm telling you what you will do, not what you may do? Time travel is a peculiar thing, Sam, it appears paradoxical but it isn't. For example, those inventions I perfected. I didn't really invent them at all. I learned the details in the future and learned too that I had invented them. So, when I returned, I did."

"You can't take away that money," said Sam. "Nor my job at the Institute."

"My fortune also," continued Gregor, he ignored the interruption. "Naturally I was able to learn the winners of various races, stock market valuations, things like that, so I gambled and won. Again no paradox because I had already gambled and won. I merely did what I had to do." He leaned forward. "The same as you will have to do, Sam, and for the same reason. You will do what you have to do because it will be what you have already done."

"I'm a free agent," repeated Sam. He seemed to find comfort in the words. "I can walk out of here now and there's nothing you can do to stop me."

"You won't because you didn't." Gregor glanced at his watch. "And there is another good reason why you will do exactly as I order. You are what you are at this moment because of my will. Refuse to obey me and I will alter that will. You will be ruined. No comfortable apartment, no job at the Institute, nothing." Gregor smiled and relaxed a little. "You wouldn't like that to happen, would you, Sam?"

"You swine!" Sam felt the quick sickness of fear as he imagined Gregor carrying out his threat. He was capable of it too and, for him it would be easy. He had merely to alter his will so that, when he died, Sam would be left with nothing.

But if he had done that then Sam wouldn't have what he now had. So Gregor hadn't altered his will after all. But if Gregor was alive, and he was, then there could be no security against him not doing it. Sam felt his head swim as he tried to resolve the paradox. Gregor wouldn't because he hadn't. He hadn't because he couldn't. He couldn't because...?

Because he was dead and buried and, in law, it is impossible to murder a corpse.

"You'd like to kill me, wouldn't you, Sam?" Gregor rose and stared mockingly at the other man. "But you won't, you know. If you had then I'd know it." He sneered. "Anyway, you haven't the guts or courage to even try it."

"You think not?" Sam rose to his feet, the drink still in his hand. He was breathing hard. "You know too damn much," he said nastily. "Maybe I could tell you a few things. Like the exact hour and date of your death, for example. Shall I?"

"Some other time," said Gregor coolly. "This visit is about to terminate." His face darkened. "But I shall remember this, Sam. Believe me, I shall remember."

"Then remember this too!" Sam felt his right hand move almost of its own volition and the spirit in the glass shot towards Gregor's eyes. He yelled in rage, staggering as he clawed at his face and, as he moved backwards, his foot caught on a chair, and he toppled heavily towards the floor.

He never reached it. There was a rush of displaced air and, aside from Sam, the apartment was empty. Gregor had gone back to his own time and place. Sam knew just what would happen when he arrived.

Gregor had been falling when he left and would still be falling when he arrived. He would reach out to save himself and grab at the high-voltage equipment in his laboratory. Jeff had already described what he would look like when they found him.

So there was no paradox, none at all; Gregor was dead and would stay dead and Sam had no need to fear him ever again. He poured himself a drink and sat down, smiling into the glass. "To freedom!" he toasted then, with the glass almost to his lips, paused. He had just remembered something. Gregor had said that this was the thirty-seventh time they had met. To Sam it was the third. There were still thirty-four visits to come.

Dully Sam wondered just how long he would be haunted by the man he had indirectly murdered.

DIAL "O" FOR OPERATOR

Robert Presslie

Robert Presslie (1920–2000) was by profession a pharmacist, managing a chain of outlets, but he was also a talented writer, one of those who contributed to the science-fiction magazines during the 1950s and 1960s but was virtually unknown beyond. As a consequence he has been all but forgotten, but the following story shows his talent for atmosphere and effect. Like E. C. Tubb his stories tend towards gritty realism rather than starry-eyed romance. His first appearance was with "Trespassers Will be Prosecuted" (1955), a frightening vignette about creating human life. He wrote nothing at novel length, though he did have a serial novella, "The Creep" (1956), which explores the difference between the morals of humans and aliens. Presslie observes how humans as individuals are usually easy to deal with, but humans en masse are dangerous. The following story appeared in 1958 when telephone boxes were a common sight in towns and, of course, long before smartphones.

I N GOVERNMENT DEPARTMENTS, HIGH AND HUMBLE, THERE IS an edict which states that it is permissible to put the central heating apparatus into use as from the first day of October. This edict is nearly always misconstrued. The usual interpretation is that the heating *must* be put into operation on the specified date. In a telephone exchange this can lead to a high degree of discomfort, particularly for the night staff who must work when the windows are closed and the shutters are drawn against the darkness outside.

The life of a night operator is fit only for vegetables. From ten in the evening until eight next morning there is nothing to do but wait for the occasional call which the dialling system cannot handle. Yet in spite of its mind-stupefying properties the job is much sought after by students working their way through university. It is the regulars, men like Charley Groom, who tend to be moronic.

Charley is a type. Half the night staff are part-time workers such as students. Half the remainder are physically disabled men of average mental calibre. Charley is a representative of the rest. He can read, write and count as well as the next man. But his social and cultural interests are nil. His life centres on the exchange. The night staff comprises his entire sphere of acquaintance.

He sat at the switchboard with no coat, his shirt sleeves bunched by frayed elastics. When the female day staff clocked out at ten, the men were allowed to shuck their coats. Charley cursed the muggy heat and wished he could strip off his shirt too. And he could have. There was no law against it. But nobody ever did it so Charley was uncomfortable and fretted because of it.

A light came alive on the switchboard. Automatically he reached for the ticket pad, scribbled in the number below the light and entered the time: Eleven-fifteen. His left hand plugged a jack into the hole corresponding to the light, he pressed forward the speaking key and asked morosely if he could help the caller.

He scowled when the only sound he heard was a deep shuddering wheeze. Kids, he thought. Damfool kids crawling home late after their first night on the beer. You could always count on at least one smart pup to play the fool about this time. He reversed the speaking key. In the backward position it made the calling phone ring. A jarring earful should teach the budding comedian.

The wheeze stopped. In its place, after a brief click of throat-catching, there came a sob. Then a voice. "Please!" it said.

"Please what?" Charley mumbled irritably. "Run away, sonny. I've got better things to do than—"

"Don't go away!" the voice begged. It seemed to have slightly more control to it. "Please, please don't go away!" Charley's scowl became a frown. It was a woman speaking. Women did not usually play the fool.

"Do you want a number?" he asked.

"No! No!"

"What do you want, then? Police? Ambulance?"

"Yes, anybody. I don't know—"

Make up your mind, Charley thought. Then he found a little sympathy. "If you'll just get hold of yourself and tell me what the trouble is, I'll put you through to somebody."

"No, don't go away!"

"I won't."

"You said you were putting me through—"

"If it makes you feel any better I'll keep the line open until you get whoever you need. Now, what do you want?"

The woman started to cry softly. Charley was married. He knew it was best to let her have a minute of two of tears. Dogs and children vomit in distress. Women cry.

"I can't get out of the phone booth," she said. "I daren't go out. It's still there."

"What is?"

"I don't know. It came out of the water, I think. It must have. It was dripping wet. I ran. It chased me. I came in here. Dialled O. Couldn't think what else to do."

The information was too much and too muddled for Charley to absorb as quickly as she gave it. He was silent so long that the woman said, "Hello!" in a shrill voice of fear.

"Just a minute," Charley said. He added, "Don't worry, I'm not going to leave you."

He looked along the switchboard at the four other operators, decided they could not help much and buzzed for the supervisor. Sloane came through from the staff room with a cup of coffee in his hand. He was annoyed at being called in.

"A woman," Charley explained. "In a call box. Says somebody or something chased her into it."

Sloane checked the time. "Eleven-thirty," he said. "Where is she?"

"Dockside somewhere, I think. She mentioned water."

"She should know better than to be alone down there at this time of night. Get the police. No—let me talk to her first." He picked up a set of phones.

Each number is repeated on the switchboard every twelve feet. Sloane slung a jack into the Call-box hole in the next section.

"Supervisor speaking," he said. "Do you wish the police?"

"Anybody. I told the other man. There's a black thing outside the booth. It's waiting for me to come out. For God's sake send somebody to—"

"Black thing?" said Sloane. "What exactly do you mean? Are you quite sure it isn't a dog? Describe it."

"I can't see. It's too dark."

Sloane looked disgusted. "If you can't see it, how do you know it is still there?"

"I know it is. I tried pushing against the door. It wouldn't move. The … whatever it is must be lying against it."

Sloane still thought it was a dog. He said, "I'll get in touch with the police. Don't you move. They'll be along shortly and get rid of—they'll see you safely home."

He tugged out the jack and nodded to Charley to take over while he consulted the directory. He found the address of the call box and rang through to police headquarters.

"Exchange supervisor," he introduced himself. "There seems to be some trouble at one of our booths. Corner of Coldwater Lane. That's right. No, I don't think so. Some hysterical female. Yes, ring me back. Got to make a report, you know. Yes, always something isn't there?"

He asked Charley, "Is she still there?"

"Weeping again. Quiet like."

"Probably drunk. You know what she is, of course? That's the only kind you get down at the docks at night."

Charley turned sharply to face the switchboard. He put his lips close to the mouthpiece to exclude external noise. "I missed that," he said. "Tell me again."

"The thing," the woman repeated, her voice high as an E string. "It hasn't gone. I saw it. I lit a cigarette. It was there. It comes more than half way up the side of the booth. All black and shiny. No shape to it."

Charley wanted to ask if she was what Sloane had said. But he stuck to more relevant matters. "The police will be along in a minute," he told the woman. "You'll be all right."

She screamed. Short, sharp, staccato. Cut off suddenly as if she had stopped breathing.

"Are you there?" Charley asked. Sloane strode down to the next position, picked up the number with a jack and switched in to hear what had made Charley sound so agitated.

The woman gibbered. Meaningless words drifted across the phone line. Sounds without sense, yet their tone was unmistakable in its prayerful pleading. Then she asked for God a dozen times and finished the garbled stream of words by saying, "Sorry."

Sloane said, "What is it?"

"The door. It was pressing against the door."

"They open out," Charley said to the Supervisor. "Nobody could push them inwards."

She heard. "That's all you know," she said. "The whole booth seemed to move. It has stopped now. I struck a match. It stopped pushing when I struck a match. Why don't the police come? You said they would."

"They have been notified," Sloane used his official voice. He pulled the jack and inserted it in the police number.

"They left immediately," the station sergeant told him. "Should be back any minute."

"Get the inspector to ring me."

A new light came alive on the board. Sloane cleared the station line and picked it up. It was the inspector ringing from downtown. He said the booth was empty and there was nothing outside it. Not even a damp patch.

"Wait," Sloane asked. He called to Charley. "What's that number?"

"One, four, seven, eleven."

It checked. Sloane leaned to the left, got the directory between two fingers and pulled it towards him. The page was still open. Opposite 14711 he read Coldwater Lane. He put an auxiliary jack into the number hole and pressed the listening key. The woman was still telling Charley about the door. Sloane opened the two keys under his hand at once and quickly closed them again.

"Hear that?" he asked the police inspector. "That's her. She's in the booth at the corner of Coldwater Lane. She's still there, as you can hear."

The inspector snapped at him. "And just where do you think this patrol car is?"

The exchange began to fill up. Every extra body seemed to add to the heat.

Since there are few manual calls after eleven, most of the night staff passed the time by pricing up daytime charge sheets for trunk calls. Only three or four are actually on the switchboard at any time, unless there happens to be an emergency in which case the tickets are dropped and the board fully manned. Nobody had left the board since Charley first picked up the call yet somehow the others had sensed excitement and had started drifting in.

Sloane elbowed his way through them to the central island which was an internal switchboard. He called the duty engineer.

"Crossed line," he told him. "We've got an urgent coming through on 14711 but it must be originating somewhere else. Of course, I'm sure. The police have been to 14711. All right, and hurry it up. We don't know what this is but it sounds bad. Yes, we'll maintain contact with the caller."

"Don't lose that line," he barked to Charley. "Rubens will be across pretty quick. Keep her talking. Ask her where she is."

"I thought of that. She won't calm down long enough to tell me. Just keeps on about the thing at the door."

He had not closed the key in case she thought he had cut her off. She heard what he said to Sloane. "Listen," she whispered, "If you think I'm the kind that gets the heebies at nothing, think again. I've been down here every night for the past two years and nothing has ever happened to me before. Nothing I didn't want to happen. But I'm finished with it now. I'll never come here again."

"Where?" Charley got in. "You'll never go where again?"

Upwards of a dozen pairs of ears strained for her answer. Phone jacks had picked up her number all round the board and the operators were listening with speaking keys closed. All they heard was another demented scream, a clatter as the phone rattled on the coin box, a scuffle, another clatter as she picked up the phone again, fumbling it.

"It's trying to come in!" she screeched.

"Take it easy, ducks," Charley begged. "Nothing can push that door in. And if it was anything with hands it could have pulled it open before now."

Sloane came across and hissed in his uncovered ear. "What the hell are you trying to do? Send her up the wall? Anything with hands! Now she'll imagine she's being hunted by flaming monsters!"

"It *was* trying to get in," the woman insisted. "Through the crack where the door shuts. Don't ask me how I knew. I just felt it was coming in, struck a match to see low down and there it was. A bit of it, anyhow. Oozing through the crack like mud. It sucked back when I struck the match."

Any ideas about it being a dog or similar large animal went right out of Sloane's head. He told the woman, "It must be scared of light. So long as you have matches you have a weapon, something to keep it scared off. Don't waste them. D'you hear me? Don't waste your matches unnecessarily."

Her wail, "But it's so dark outside!" was pathetic.

"So it's dark," Sloane said, keeping his voice hard. "Do what I said. Strike a light if there seems to be anything happening. Otherwise save them. We'll get help to you as soon as possible. We sent the police to the booth corresponding to the number we have coming up on the board but the line is crossed. If you can tell us where you are calling from it will help a lot."

She told him: "I'm in the booth at the corner of Coldwater Lane!"

Rubens the engineer arrived, disappeared into the maze of wires behind the switchboard and came out again to confirm the woman's story.

"Nothing wrong with the selectors or relays," he said. "That's one, four seven, eleven calling. Nothing else but."

Sloane acted promptly. He got through to police headquarters again, asked for the inspector, told him the emergency was still on but gave him no details and asked him to come over to the exchange. He told Rubens to stand by in case he was needed again.

Charley looked wistfully at the clock. Twelve midnight. He should be having a half-hour break now, time for a cigarette and a cup of tea. He wiped the sweat off the back of his neck and wondered how much longer it would be before he got away from the board. The tea he didn't care about. The cigarette he could have used.

The way coincidences sometimes happen! Sloane tapped his shoulder and said, "You may smoke if you want to, Groom. I'll make up your time later on but I don't want you to leave the board right now. You're the one she knows. It will be better if you stay on the line."

Charley nodded miserably. His cigarettes were outside in his locker.

The inspector arrived in a filthy mood. He too should have been off duty. He had been in the station when Sloane's first call came in and he had intended the police car to drop him at his house after attending to the call. But when he learned that both he and the woman had apparently been using the same booth he decided to stay with the case. There could be recriminations later if he didn't.

"Hazel," he introduced himself. "What's all this nonsense about? I was in that booth. There was nobody else there."

"We're trying to work it out," Sloane hedged.

"Is the woman still on the line?"

"The operator is keeping her talking. She must have mistaken her whereabouts. Groom is doing his best to find where she went wrong."

Hazel grunted. "Give me a phone. I'll talk to her."

"I wouldn't," Sloane advised. "She has got accustomed to Groom. Every time anyone else speaks she panics. Thinks we're cutting her off."

The inspector *humphed* and went across to Charley's position. "Has she told you anything yet?" he snapped.

It had been in Charley's mind to cadge a cigarette. One look at Hazel's face made him forget it. He said, "She passed Commercial Wharf about ten-thirty. Up one side of Fish Street and down the other after that. Waiting for the pubs, to close, I expect. Hoping for a customer. She got no takers, went back up Fish Street, remembers the clock on the Seamen's Mission striking eleven as she turned into Portugal Place. That's as far as I've got."

"Carry on," Hazel said.

Charley wished he would stand back. He felt uncomfortable with a policeman at his shoulder. He took it out on the woman. "Well," he grumbled. "What are you waiting for?"

He heard her catch her breath and was sorry he had been so rough. She began to talk as if she was doing him a favour. "I thought I might as well take a turn along the quay. Maybe catch some of the boys going back to their ships. But it just wasn't my night. The quay was deserted. I was almost at the far end when I thought I heard something behind me. It made a noise like wet fish being dumped on the quayside. I couldn't see anybody or anything. I crossed over to make for home. Then I heard it again. I tried running. Stopped for breath. Heard it a third time. I was sure I was being followed. I don't mind being followed when I can see who is behind me. But I couldn't see anything. It must having been moving flat and low on the street."

She became agitated again, forgot and forgave Charley's short-ness with her. "You don't know what it was like," she said. "Slap, slap behind me. When I walked quicker the slaps came quicker.

I ran. When I got to the corner of Coldwater Lane I was never so glad to see a phone booth. I dialled O. You answered."

Her voice and control broke. "Why doesn't somebody come?"

"They will," Charley said. "I promise they will." He wondered what had made him promise. He caught a signal from Hazel and told the woman, "Just a minute. The police inspector is here with me. He wants to talk to me. I'm not going away."

Hazel asked what she had said. Charley gave it word for word. The inspector's eyes shuttered as he pictured the district.

"The timing is right," he said to Sloane. "If I hadn't been there myself a few minutes ago I would swear she must be in the Coldwater booth. Have you checked for a crossed line?"

"Before you arrived."

"Check it again. And give me a list of all the booths in the vicinity. She was in Fish Street at eleven. Rang you at eleven-fifteen. Get all the booths within a mile of the Mission"

Sloane knew them pat. There were seven on one side of the dock, three on the north side of the water.

"Get down to the car," Hazel told his sergeant. "Radio HQ. Tell them to check those booths. Tell them to cover the north side too. She may have crossed the bridge and forgotten to tell us." He made a mental note to slap a soliciting charge on the woman when he found her. He wasn't going to have his night ruined with nothing to show for it.

Somebody brought in a cup of tea for Charley, gave him a cigarette at the same time. Charley got two deep puffs and the woman swore.

"You're smoking," she said accusingly. "It's all right for you. My cigarettes are finished."

She spoiled Charley's enjoyment of the smoke. He nipped off the glowing end of the cigarette and put the stub in his shirt pocket. It didn't seem right when she didn't have a cigarette too.

"Any sign of the thing?" he asked for the sake of making conversation.

"Not since I told you."

"Maybe it's gone, whatever it was."

"I don't think so. I would have heard. Wait—" He heard her breathing stop. Then she went on: "No, it's still there. I tried pushing the door."

Charley could not contain his admiration. "You're pretty brave," he said.

"Brave! I'm like a jelly."

"I think you've got guts. Not many people would have tried to push the door with a thing like you described outside." What Charley really meant but could not bring himself to say was that he would never have been so foolhardy. He changed the subject and asked, "Can you see any lights moving? The police are cruising all round where you are."

"The only lights I can see are the one above my head and a street lamp about fifty yards down the lane. Round the quayside corner it's pitch black. Nothing to be seen at all."

Charley's experience helped him to picture the scene. He could tell by the faint rustle when she turned to look behind her. He even knew that she changed the phone from one hand to the other. But a squeaking noise puzzled him until he realized she must have been wiping condensation off the glass. He wondered if she was sweating as much as he was. Probably worse, he decided. A phone booth is no place for fresh air.

"You," the woman said. "Operator." Her voice had taken on a new shade of fear. Hysteria was gone. Mad panic had given way to an acceptance of doom. "Operator, the thing is climbing up the side of the booth. That's why I can't see the harbour lights. Can it ... is there any opening on the roof of the box?"

Charley's skin prickled. He wished somebody else would take over. This was a job for somebody like Sloane. He was not clever with the smooth phrase. He was only an operator.

"You'll be safe enough," he said, doing the best he could. "There's a small ventilator, nothing big enough for even a mouse to creep through."

"It squeezed through the edge of the door!"

"Keep your matches handy. It was scared by the light."

"That's what your boss said but he was wrong. It may be dark outside but it's bright in the booth."

"It must be the heat then," Charley said, thinking furiously to keep her from hysteria again. "That's what it is, the heat of the match flame."

She tore up his explanation. "If it's scared by heat, why is it trying to get in here? It's a damn sight hotter inside than out."

Again Charley wished he had a glibber tongue. He was glad to catch sight of Hazel's man coming in. It gave him a chance to tell her to wait while he heard what the sergeant had to say.

The sergeant, Hazel and Sloane went into a huddle. It was Sloane who passed the information on to Charley: "She isn't in any of the dockside booths!" He did not sound happy. Charley wondered if it was possible that even Sloane wished there was somebody more competent to deal with the situation.

He amended the news before giving it to the woman. "I didn't mean to be off the line so long," he said. "But there seems to be some kind of a mix-up. Nothing for you to worry about, but—"

He frowned at the sudden suspicion that she was not listening. "Hello!" he said sharply. "Are you there? Hello!"

He turned to beckon Sloane but the woman made a slight sound and he pressed his phone to his ear. She seemed to be moving around the booth. From the absence of breathing sounds he guessed the phone was lying on the coin box. He heard three quick threshing sounds, a tinkle of glass, the deafening clatter of the phone falling off the coin box and swinging at the end of its wire, hitting the side of the booth with each swing.

The noises became difficult to identify. Occasionally he heard a fleeting breath from the woman. He decided she was trying to catch the swinging phone. He wondered why it should take her so long.

"It's me!" she shouted suddenly. "Wait a minute!" And the phone rattled again. Then there were scuffling sounds and another clatter and she was back on the line.

"I'm done for now," she moaned. "It's coming in at the ventilator. I saw it. I forgot what you said about the matches. Tried to hit it with my bag. All I did was break the lamp. I can't see at all. It must be crawling down the wall to get me. God! God! God! I wish I'd been a better woman!"

"Shut up!" Charley made a desperate attempt to steady her. "Have you got your bag again?"

"It's somewhere on the floor."

"Find it. Use your feet. When you touch it, bend down, take out your matches. Light them one at a time. Get each match as close to the thing as you can. As soon as it retreats, don't strike another match. It seems to take a while to recover from the effects of each flame. It shouldn't bother you again for at least fifteen minutes."

He waited while she found the handbag.

"The matches aren't in it!" she sobbed.

"Take it easy," Charley commanded. "They must be on the floor somewhere. Get down on your hands and knees. Sweep the floor with your hands. Do it systematically. Don't make wild swipes."

"I'm scared!"

"Do what I tell you!" Charley was surprised at his own firmness. The slender link between him and the lonely booth on the dockside passed on the sounds of her obedience.

"You were right," she said eventually, all out of breath. "Three matches did it." She began to giggle.

"Shut up!" Charley repeated. "I was trying to tell you about the police."

Then he wondered what he could tell her that had any gleam of hope in it. He fabricated a lie with a fluent ease that astonished him; it was a thing he had never been able to do successfully with any woman, especially with his wife. What surprised him even more was that he did not care what the inspector thought as he lied:

"The police are fools," he said into the phone. "I distinctly told them where you are, yet they mucked it up and went to the north side of the dock. The inspector said to tell you he's sorry. He'll see they do it right this time. Just hang on a bit longer. Try not to panic or do anything silly again."

She giggled once more but it was gentle and not so insane.

"Just imagine!" she said. "The cops actually on my side! Trying to help me. Me!"

Her voice went soft as she continued, "I don't know your name, mister, but I want to thank you. Nobody ever went to so much trouble on my behalf before. I don't suppose we'll ever meet. I don't suppose I'll ever get out of here alive. But thanks, anyhow."

"Stop thinking like that. It will be all over pretty soon. And you don't have to thank me. It's my job." He had never thought of his work objectively. It made a change.

"What time is it?"

Charley lifted his head to look at the clock. He was amazed to see a ring of faces, every one hanging on the conversation. He swallowed and tried to be nonchalant but his new importance was too much for him. His voice shook as he answered, "Just gone two."

"That's nearly three hours I've been here," she said. "I didn't think it was so late. Funny, isn't it? It seems like years since I ran in here and yet its queer to think I've been cooped up for three hours."

"Yes, it's funny," Charley agreed. He turned at a squeeze on his shoulder and added, "They want to talk to me. I'll leave the line open so you'll know I'm still here. But don't say anything unless you must."

He looked at the inspector's hand on his shoulder, and waited for the worst. However he quickly saw that the scowl on Hazel's face had nothing to do with his slander of the police. Hazel was just plain flummoxed, completely out of his depth in the face of something which could not be resolved by the book.

"You *did* go to Coldwater Lane?" he asked his sergeant. And when the younger man stiffened he said, "Yes, of course you did."

Sloane too looked helpless. "Check that line again," he told the engineer in an attempt to hide his confusion by doing something positive.

"I've checked it twice already," Rubens complained.

Sloane's mouth twitched. "Check it another twice!" he snapped.

Hazel was not to be outdone. He felt just as helpless as Sloane and was just as annoyed about it. Like Sloane, he vented his anger on his subordinate.

"Sergeant," he said, "get back to the quayside. Call the nearest patrol car, tell them to pick up every available man from the local stations. Set up a complete cordon around that phone booth. And don't move until I tell you to. Keep in touch with me here by radiophone."

"The booth is empty, Inspector." The sergeant's expression was deadpan. He was not being insolent or rebellious. He simply stated the fact in self-defence, just to let the inspector know it was no fault of his that the booth had been found empty. He turned briskly and was gone before Hazel could reply.

Charley said the worst thing possible when he asked, "What do you think is really happening? I mean, how can she be there and yet not there?"

"You pay attention to what you're doing," Sloane grunted.

Charley was not cowed. "I've got to tell her something." he said. "You'll have to give me something I can tell her. I can't just say we haven't any—"

"You concentrate on keeping that line open," Sloane ordered. "Leave the rest to us. We'll think of something."

The inspector saw Rubens come out from behind the switchboard looking grim and said, "What? Exactly what are we going to think of?"

The woman stole Charley's attention again. "Is it all right for me to talk yet?" she asked.

"What is it?" he said cautiously.

"It's been again. It was all round the booth like a wet newspaper. It tried to come in at the edge of the door down at the bottom and in at the ventilator too. I knew when it was squeezing in because it got cold all of a sudden and I remembered it got cold the other times too."

Her matter-of-fact tone affected Charley deeply. He marvelled that she had withstood the thing's latest assault without a murmur—and just because he had asked her not to speak.

"I tried not to use too many matches," she apologized. "But I'm afraid I'm down to my last two. I hope you don't think I wasted them."

Charley shivered. Sweated and shivered. He had some difficulty getting his words past the sudden constriction of his throat. "I don't think that at all," he said. He felt there must have been something better he could have said, an inspiring phrase, uplifting words to bolster her courage. He tried hard to think of something but nothing would come so he simply said, "You did fine. You did the right thing."

As he spoke, he shivered again because he knew what was shackling his mind and his tongue: it was despair. With the hands of the exchange clock advancing towards three, he realized it was too late now to save the woman. He had caught the infection of despair from the woman herself; but it would never have taken hold if it was not for the fact that he knew—knew without a shred of doubt—that she was doomed.

He revolted against the thought. His revolt made him angry and gave him courage to voice his anger. He turned to Sloane and the inspector and told them: "Somebody hasn't done his job right!"

Nobody argued with him and he went on, "The way I see it she *must* be in Coldwater Lane. She named all the streets, gave all the directions for getting there. The engineer has checked four times that I've got that booth on the line. Why haven't the police found her?"

"They'll find her this time," the inspector said. But his voice had none of the conviction of his words.

The radiophone number lit up. Sloane took it, passed it to Hazel. Just by looking at him—without hearing a word of the conversation—Charley guessed the sergeant was reporting that the booth was completely surrounded. And still empty.

It was then that Charley went cold altogether. For all the effect it made, the central heating system could have been working in reverse. Charley shivered again. His despair enveloped him like a cold shower. And overlaying the chill of despair there was an icy frosting of dread; he had a hair-bristling suspicion that the events of the night could only be explained by invoking the supernatural.

He voiced his suspicion to himself: "She might be calling from another world altogether—"

Any other time and in any other circumstances, the inspector would have snorted. But the best he could manage was a reflective nod and a concurring statement that it was adjectival uncanny.

"Isn't there anything else she can tell us?" he asked.

Charley stared at the jack in its hole. He was getting to the point where he was reluctant even to hear the woman's voice again. She had nothing more to tell them. Already her plight sat like a weight on his shoulders—why make it heavier by hearing it again? It would be better to accept the sergeant's word, pull the jack and forget all about the affair.

But still the new stature that had come to his small spirit fought. He refused to admit defeat—as yet, anyhow. He refused to take the easy way out.

"I'll try," he mumbled and put his mouth to the phone.

He apologized for making her go over the facts again. "You see—" he said, being forced at last to give her at least part of the truth, "—you see, the police have been where you said and they can't find you."

She could not recognize the truth when she heard it. "You're lying," she said.

"Why on earth should—"

She refused to have any excuses. "You're lying," she repeated. Her voice was flat, dispirited and full of cynicism. "I might have known it," she told Charley. "All that stuff you gave me about the cops wanting to help me! As if they would!"

Charley had no anger now. He was tolerance personified as he said gently, "They've done everything possible. When they couldn't find you the first time, the inspector sent them back. They're down there now. The booth is surrounded. They even got reinforcements—"

He counted the fingers that Hazel stuck in front of his nose. "There's a dozen of them," he said.

"Why don't they get me out, then?"

Charley swallowed. He saw that he must give her the whole truth. "They say the booth is empty."

He expected a thoughtful silence but her reply came quickly. "I get it," she scoffed. "You're just as bad as they are—you think I'm making it all up. You don't even believe I'm in trouble. You don't believe there's a thing outside, waiting to—"

"I believe you—"

She went on, heedless of his protestation. "You think I'm crazy or something. I bet you never even told the cops about me."

"You've got it all wrong. Everybody is doing his best to—"

She laughed—a short grim sound. "If has to happen to me. I would pick a booth that doesn't even have a vide-screen! You'd believe me all right if you could see me!"

It was Rubens, the engineer, who shone the first real light on the problem. When Charley had finished retailing the woman's complaint, Rubens was the first to speak.

"She *is* crazy!" he declared. "Or else she knows something she shouldn't know and she is using it to make us believe her story."

The inspector left Sloane to do the quizzing. The exchange supervisor took Rubens aside to do it. When he had heard what the engineer had to say, he began by reminding the inspector and Charley that everything connected with the telephone company was subject to the Official Secrets Act.

He continued, "Knowing that this will go no further, I can now tell you that Rubens' information—which, incidentally, is news to me—is disturbing. And that's putting it mildly. It appears that only last week Rubens attended a technical conference which was convened to discuss the possibility of introducing a new system employing sound *and vision* telephony!"

The inspector immediately began to think of the implications as they would affect police work. Sloane mistook his silence for incomprehension. He said, "Don't you understand? The woman is talking about something which Rubens says won't have been *started* on for at least five years!"

"I wasn't far wrong," Charley put in. "I said she must be in another world." He sounded quite awed when he added, "But

I didn't think it was a world of the future." And where trained
experienced men were hampered by their convictions it was left
to Charley to find the only explanation that ever forthcame.

"You know," he said, "maybe she forced herself into our time
because she was so desperate. I mean—well, look at ghosts and
things like that. They're always somebody who died in terror."

He fumbled for words to explain himself. "Look how ghosts are
usually murder victims. Or people who were executed. Couldn't it
be that when somebody is in agony or really terrified, their minds
are so desperate for help that they can jump out of their own time
into another?"

From the stony expressions he got, he realized that Sloane and
Hazel already considered the incident closed; the woman was
beyond help, beyond reach even and it was futile to continue going
through the motions. The question did not arise as to whether
Charley's explanation was valid or not. As far as the supervisor and
the police inspector were concerned, there was nobody in the booth
in Coldwater Lane. There was nothing further to be said or done.

Once again Charley revolted against the notion that the woman
was doomed. He said, "I think I can do something. Is it all right
if I try?"

The supervisor shrugged. "Please yourself. But don't be long
about it. I'll need your evidence for my report."

For the tenth time Charley told the woman, "You've got to do
as I say. It's your only hope."

And for the tenth time she answered, "I'm too scared. It must
be all around me. Besides, what if there is a wind and it blows out
the flame?"

"It won't. Not if you tear the directory pages out singly. Don't
have them in thick bunches. When you have enough to make a

good blaze, smash the glass with your shoe and ram the burning paper through the hole."

"No. I couldn't! It might come in before I got the flames near it."

Charley's patience was infinite. "I'll go over the drill again," he said. "You have the booth filled with paper. Right? You take a handful, light it, break the glass, stick the flames into the hole. The thing backs off a bit. You use your other match to light all the rest of the paper. All of it, understand. Keep your nerve and stay inside until it's really alight. You might get burned but better that than the other thing. When you can't stay there any longer, come out on the run. The door should open all right because the thing will have retreated. Come out running and kick out as much of the burning paper as you can. If the thing isn't killed by the fire it will at least be scared. You should get a good start. Then run like hell, run like bloody hell! Do you hear me?"

She was silent. Charley checked the time. Five-twenty, the clock said and Charley prayed the woman would do what he had ordered.

He listened intently. He tried to analyse every little sound. He thought he heard her tearing up the directory. He willed her to hurry. He heard her come near the reclining phone. He heard the scratch of match on box. The sound of breaking glass. Then the rattle of plastic on metal as she fumbled for the phone on its shelf and used one of her last precious seconds to say "Goodbye!"

He kept the line open a long time, just listening. He pulled the jack reluctantly when Sloane signalled that he was wanted at the supervisory desk.

The inquest that followed was anticlimax. The exchange had grown as cold as Charley, whose tones were distant as he answered all the questions Sloane needed for his report.

He went out of his way to pass the corner of Coldwater Lane on his route homewards after the supervisor had noticed his pallor and dismissed him at six o'clock in the morning. The police had withdrawn and he thought it was strange to see the booth standing there as if nothing had ever happened—with not even a faint smell of smoke when he pulled open the door and looked inside.

He wondered how the affair had ended. Had the woman's courage lasted out? Had she managed to strike her last match without the shake of her hands bungling it? And if her courage and the match had not failed her, had she been able to run fast enough? He wanted to believe she had.

Then he wondered what he would say to his wife when he went home two hours early. She would be worried. He felt an urgent, unaccustomed need to speak to her. He turned up his collar against the morning mist and began to hurry.

STORY SOURCES

The following gives the first publication details for each story. They are listed in alphabetical order of author.

"The Book of Worlds" by Miles J. Breuer, first published in *Amazing Stories*, July 1929.

"The Reign of the Reptiles" by Alan Connell, first published in *Wonder Stories*, August 1935.

"The Branches of Time" by David R. Daniels, first published in *Wonder Stories*, August 1935.

"Friday the Nineteenth" by Elizabeth Sanxay Holding, first published in *The Magazine of Fantasy & Science Fiction*, Summer 1950.

"Omega" by Amelia Reynolds Long, first published in *Amazing Stories*, July 1932.

"Tenth Time Around" by J. T. McIntosh, first published in *The Magazine of Fantasy & Science Fiction*, May 1959.

"The Clock That Went Backward" by Edward Page Mitchell, first published in *The New York Sun*, 18 September 1881.

"Manna" by Peter Phillips, first published in *Astounding SF*, February 1949.

"Dial 'O' for Operator" by Robert Presslie, first published in *Science Fantasy* #27, February 1958.

"Look After the Strange Girl" by J. B. Priestley, first published in *The Other Place* (London: Heinemann, 1953).

"The Shadow People" by Arthur Sellings, first published in *New Worlds*, July 1958.

"Thirty-Seven Times" by E. C. Tubb, first published in *New Worlds*,
    January 1957 under the pseudonym Alan Guthrie.

"The Queer Story of Brownlow's Newspaper" by H. G. Wells, first
    published in *Ladies' Home Journal*, February 1932.

'It's a hazardous experiment,' they all said, 'putting in new and untried machinery.'

Caution – beware the menace of the machine: a man is murdered by an automaton built for playing chess; a computer system designed to arbitrate justice develops a taste for iron-fisted, fatal rulings; an AI wreaks havoc on society after removing all censorship from an early form of the internet.

Assembled with pieces by SF giants such as Isaac Asimov and Brian W Aldiss as well as the less familiar but no less influential input of earlier science fiction pioneers, this new collection of classic tales contains telling lessons for humankind's gradual march towards life alongside the thinking machine.

The voice which came back through a clamour of noise greater than any before was that of a stranger; it was hysterical, raging futilely into the void. "The sun's blown up!"

Join humanity on the brink of destruction in fourteen doom-laden tales exploring our fixation with how and when our end will come, selected from the SF magazines and rare literary journals of the British Library collection.

Illustrating the whole gamut of apocalyptic fiction from cosmic calamities to self-inflicted nuclear annihilation, this explosive new selection also includes accounts of post-apocalyptic worlds from the speculative warnings of the 1890s to Ray Bradbury's poignant vision of a silent planet after the last echoes of humanity have died away.

In 1925 Muriel Jaeger, dissatisfied with the unrealistic utopian stories of H.G. Wells and Edward Bellamy, set out to explore 'The Question Mark' of what a future society might look like if human nature were truthfully represented.

Her hero, disgruntled office worker Guy, is pitched 200 years into a future London where each citizen is offered free education and a personal 'power-box' granting access to communication, transportation and entertainment. To Guy, the great challenges facing society seem solved, but its inhabitants tell a different story of fractured life in this supposed utopia.

Preceding the publication of Huxley's *Brave New World* by five years, *The Question Mark* is a significant cornerstone in the foundation of the dystopia genre, and an impressive work of literary science fiction.

BRITISH LIBRARY SCIENCE FICTION CLASSICS

SHORT STORY ANTHOLOGIES
EDITED BY MIKE ASHLEY

Lost Mars:
The Golden Age of the Red Planet

Moonrise:
The Golden Age of Lunar Adventures

Menace of the Machine:
The Rise of AI in Classic Science Fiction

The End of the World
and Other Catastrophes

Menace of the Monster:
Classic Tales of Creatures from Beyond

Beyond Time:
Classic Tales of Time Unwound

CLASSIC SCIENCE
FICTION NOVELS

By William F Temple
Shoot at the Moon
Four-Sided Triangle

By Charles Eric Maine
The Tide Went Out
The Darkest of Nights

By Ian Macpherson
Wild Harbour

By Muriel Jaeger
The Question Mark

We welcome any suggestions, corrections or feedback you may have, and will aim to respond to all items addressed to the following:

The Editor (Science Fiction Classics)
British Library Publishing
The British Library
96 Euston Road
London, NW1 2DB

We also welcome enquiries through our Twitter account, @BL_Publishing.